THE
HURRICANE
WARS

THE
HURRICANE
WARS

A NOVEL

THEA GUANZON

HARPER Voyager
An Imprint of HarperCollins*Publishers*

HarperCollins books may be purchased for educational, business, or sales promotional use. For information, please email the Special Markets Department at SPsales@harpercollins.com.

Harper Voyager and design are trademarks of HarperCollins Publishers LLC.

FIRST EDITION

Endpaper map illustration and part and chapter opener art © Virginia Allyn

Library of Congress Cataloging-in-Publication Data

Names: Guanzon, Thea, author.
Title: The hurricane wars : a novel / Thea Guanzon.
Description: First edition. | New York : Harper Voyager 2023.
Identifiers: LCCN 2023001586 (print) | LCCN 2023001587 (ebook) | ISBN
    9780063277274 (hardcover) | ISBN 9780063277267 (ebook)
Subjects: LCGFT: Fantasy fiction. | Novels.
Classification: LCC PR9550.9.G763 H87 2023 (print) | LCC PR9550.9.G763
    (ebook) | DDC 823/.92—dc23/eng/20230301
LC record available at https://lccn.loc.gov/2023001586
LC ebook record available at https://lccn.loc.gov/2023001587

ISBN 978-0-06-327727-4 (hardcover)
ISBN 978-0-06-334480-8 (international edition)

23 24 25 26 27 LBC 5 4 3 2 1

I did this for the rats.

Prologue

He heard the girl before he saw her, a high and golden hum that cut through the chaos of battle like the first flare of sunrise.

Sheets of floating ice seesawed and creaked under his boots as he ran across the frozen lake, making his way toward the sound. It beckoned to him amidst the other noises piercing the winter air—the screaming, the rattle of crossbows, the roar of cannons, all from the burning city that lay behind the ancient forest at the water's edge. The fanned gaps between the longleaf pines offered glimpses of destruction in veins of red-gold embers, their needle-pricked canopy silhouetted against a crown of smoke beneath the seven moons.

There was smoke out here on the ice as well, but it was the smoke of aetherspace, not inferno. Shadow bloomed over frost in shivering rings, trapping everyone trying to escape the city, everyone except him and his legionnaires. With a wave of his gauntleted hand, each dark barrier parted before him, until—finally—

There she was.

Loose strands of bedraggled chestnut hair streamed in the montane wind, escaping her braid to frame an oval face with freckled, olive-skinned features. She was coltish on the bobbing ice, light blazing in her hands against the swirling darkness, the twitching body of one of his men crumpled at her feet. He hurtled forward, a weapon of his own blocking what would have been her killing blow to his erstwhile legionnaire, and as she staggered back, her eyes met his, her magic reflected in shards of gold setting fire to brown irises, and perhaps this, too, was how a war began. In the space between heartbeats. In the room of night.

He lunged at her.

PART
I

CHAPTER ONE

Wartime weddings were all the rage in a land where every single day threatened, quite emphatically, to be one's last, but the skies could rain stones for seven nights without ever hitting an available officiant. Most clerics were at the front lines, singing to Sardovian troops of Mahagir the Saber-Heart's courage and guiding the souls of dying soldiers to the eternal twilight of Adapa the Harvester's willow groves. By some rare stroke of good fortune, however, there was *one* cleric remaining in the mountain city of Frostplum, where Talasyn's regiment was stationed and where her fellow helmsmen Khaede and Sol had decided to pledge their troth.

Not that it's any great mystery as to why they left this grandfather behind, Talasyn mused, watching from a dim corner of the thatched longhouse as the stooped, elderly cleric in pale yellow robes struggled to lift a large pewter goblet over the crackling fire that was reflecting off his marble-ball scalp. In reed-thin and quavering tones, he meandered haphazardly through the closing words of the marriage rite while the bride glared at him.

Khaede had a glare that could cut through metalglass. It was a miracle that the frail little man wasn't sliced into ribbons on the spot. He eventually managed to hold the smoke-warmed goblet to the groom's lips and then to Khaede's, so that the couple could drink of the golden lychee wine consecrated to Thonba, goddess of home and hearth.

From where she hung back at the edge of the crowd, Talasyn applauded along with the other soldiers when the cleric tremulously pronounced Khaede and Sol bonded for life. Sol flashed a shy grin, one that Khaede was quick to press her lips against, her ire at the bumbling officiant a thing of the past. The raucous cheers from their comrades echoed off the thick limestone walls.

"Think you might be next, helmsman?"

The jovial quip came from a point over Talasyn's shoulder and she rolled her eyes. "Nitwit." As Khaede's closest friend, she'd been on the receiving end of similar wisecracks all evening and it had left her feeling rather defensive. "Why would that even be on my list of priorities—" Her brain caught up to her tongue as she turned around, and she snapped to attention upon realizing who the jester was. "Respectfully speaking, sir."

"At ease," said Darius, an amused smile lurking underneath his bushy beard. When Talasyn joined up five years ago, the coxswain's hair had been salt-and-pepper; now it was mostly just salt. He lowered his voice so as not to be overheard by the people around them. "The Amirante would like a word."

Talasyn's gaze darted to where she'd spotted Ideth Vela in the crowd earlier. The woman who held supreme command over the entirety of Sardovia's armed forces was now in the process of disappearing into a side room, accompanied by a portly officer sporting a black horseshoe mustache. "General Bieshimma's back from Nenavar already?"

"Just arrived," said Darius. "As I understand it, the mission went belly-up and he had to pull out. He and the Amirante need to discuss a crucial matter with you, so—go."

Talasyn made her way through the crowd. She didn't hesitate

to use her elbows, her sights fixed on the door at the other end of the longhouse behind which Bieshimma and the Amirante had vanished. She was so curious that it *burned*. And it had only partly to do with the fact that she'd been summoned.

The embittered league of nation-states known as the Sardovian Allfold had sent General Bieshimma southeast of the Continent to the mysterious islands of the Nenavar Dominion, in an attempt to form an alliance. Perhaps even rekindle one, if the old stories were to be believed. The general was a former political adviser who'd swapped his badge of office for sword and shield, and he had been expected to utilize all his diplomatic prowess in convincing the Nenavarene queen to help Sardovia defeat the Night Empire. Things had clearly not gone according to plan, given his swift return, but still— Bieshimma had been to *Nenavar*.

Talasyn's stomach fluttered with the blend of intrigue and unease that thoughts of the Nenavar Dominion always, without fail, evoked in her. She'd never been there, had never so much as strayed from Sardovia's dwindling borders, but the slightest mention of that reclusive archipelago across the Eversea always left some part of her oddly hollow, as though she'd forgotten something very important, and she was desperate to find out what it was.

In all her twenty years, she had yet to tell a soul about the strange connection she felt to Nenavar. It was a secret, too fragile to be spoken out loud. But talking to someone who had just returned from there seemed as good a step in the right direction as any.

Despite her eagerness, Talasyn slowed down when she passed by one of the lance corporals who had escorted General Bieshimma on his diplomatic mission. The boy was pink-cheeked from the cold outside, snowflakes melting on the upright collar of his uniform as he recounted the adventure to a small circle of raptly attentive wedding guests.

Everyone else was in uniform as well, including Talasyn. Wool breeches, thick boots, and padded coats the color of orange peels. There was no time for pretty dresses or an elaborate ceremony. This wedding was a stolen moment in between skirmishes.

"It went as badly as it did when we *last* sent an envoy to the Nenavar Dominion," the lance corporal was saying. "Remember, a couple of years back? Although I'll grant that this time they let us make landfall instead of turning us away at the harbor again, it was only so we could rest and resupply. Their queen, the Zahiya-lachis, still refused to see us. Bieshimma gave the harbor guards the slip and set out for the capital on horseback, but he wasn't even allowed into the royal palace, apparently. The concerns of outsiders are not the concerns of the Dominion—that's what the harbor guards told us when we tried to state our case."

A bowman leaned forward with a conspiratorial twinkle in his eyes. "See any dragons while you were there, then?"

Talasyn stopped walking altogether and other conversations happening nearby petered out as several soldiers craned their necks in interest.

"No," said the lance corporal. "But I never left the docks, and the skies were overcast."

"I don't even think they're real," said an infantryman, sniffing. "All we have to go on are rumors. If you ask me, it's smart what the Nenavarene are doing, letting the rest of Lir believe that their dragons exist. People won't bother you if you've supposedly got an army of giant fire-breathing worms at your disposal."

"I'd kill for a giant fire-breathing worm," the bowman said wistfully. "We'd win the war with even just one."

The group started bickering over whether a dragon could bring down a stormship. Talasyn left them to it.

A surfeit of vague images rushed through her head as she

stepped away: from nowhere, so sudden, in the space of only a moment's breath. She could barely make sense of them before they darted out of reach. A coil of slick scales undulating in the sunlight, and maybe a crown as sharp as diamond, as clear as ice. Something inside her, awakened by the soldiers' conversation, tried to fight its way out.

What on *earth*—

She blinked. And the images were gone.

It was likely an effect of the pine-scented smoke from various firepits suffusing the longhouse, not to mention the sheer heat radiating from so many bodies crammed into one narrow structure. Sol was kind and charming and much loved, and it showed in how nearly a quarter of the regiment had turned up for his wedding.

They were definitely not here for his bride—rude, prickly, caustic Khaede—but Sol adored her enough for a hundred people, anyway.

As she reached the closed door of the side room, Talasyn glanced back at the newlyweds. They were surrounded by effusive well-wishers clutching mugs of hot ale while the regiment's field band struck up a lively tune on fife, bugle, and goatskin drum. A beaming Sol pressed kisses to the back of Khaede's hand and she tried to frown in annoyance but failed miserably, the two of them looking as radiant as it was possible to look in helmsmen's winter uniforms, the garlands of dried flowers around their necks serving as the only nod to their status as bride and groom. Once in a while, Khaede's free hand would come to rest on her still-flat stomach and Sol's blue-black eyes would shine like the Eversea on a summer day against his oak-brown skin.

Talasyn had no idea how these two planned on caring for a baby in the midst of a war that had spread throughout the whole Continent, but she was happy for them. And she wasn't *jealous*, exactly, but the sight of the newlyweds stirred in her the same old yearning that she'd lived with for twenty years as an orphan. A yearning for somewhere she could belong, and for someone she could belong to.

What would it be like, Talasyn wondered as Sol chuckled at something Khaede said and leaned in to hide his face in the slope of her neck, his arm looped around her waist, *to laugh like that with someone? To be touched like that?* An ache shivered through her as she let herself imagine it, just a little bit, reaching for a phantom of an embrace.

A nearby drunken soldier stumbled forward, splashing ale all over the floor by Talasyn's boots. The sour odor assailed her nostrils and she flinched, briefly overcome by childhood memories of caretakers stinking of steeped grains and curdled milk, those men of harsh words and heavy hands.

Years ago, now. Long gone. The orphanage in the slums had been destroyed along with the rest of Hornbill's Head, and all of its vicious caretakers had probably been crushed underneath the rubble. And she couldn't discuss a *crucial matter* with her superiors while in the throes of despair over some spilled ale.

Talasyn straightened her spine and steadied her breathing; then she rapped smartly on the door of the side room.

As though in response, the deep, brassy tones of warning gongs pierced through the limestone facade of the building, cutting across the merriment like knives.

All music and chatter ceased. Talasyn and her comrades looked around as the watchtowers continued their urgent hymn. They were stunned at first, disbelieving, but gradually a tidal wave of movement swept through the firelit longhouse as the wedding guests sprang to action.

The Night Empire was attacking.

Talasyn ran into the silver night, adrenaline coursing through her veins, a numbing layer against the freezing cold air that bit at her exposed face. Lights were winking out all across

Frostplum, window-squares of cheerful gold fading into blackness. It was a precaution to avoid becoming an easy target for air raids, but it wouldn't do much good. All seven of Lir's moons hung in the sky in their various phases of waxing and waning, shedding a stark brilliance over the snowy mountains.

And, if Kesathese troops had brought in a stormship, the whole city might as well be a dandelion puff in a stiff breeze. Its houses were erected from stone and mortar and covered in wooden roof trusses and multilayered thatch, built strong enough to withstand the harsh elements, but nothing could withstand the Night Empire's lightning cannons.

Due to its remote location, all the way up in the Sardovian Highlands, Frostplum had always been a peaceful settlement, drowsing in evergreen blankets of longleaf pine. Tonight, however, it was plunged into mayhem, fur-clad cityfolk stampeding to the shelters and shouting frantically for one another amidst a whirlwind of military activity. It was finally happening, what everyone had feared, why Talasyn's regiment had been sent here in the first place.

While bowmen took up their positions on the walls and infantrymen assembled barricades in the streets and helmsmen hurried to the grid, Talasyn squinted up at the starry heavens. There probably *wasn't* a stormship, she conceded—she'd have spotted its hulking silhouette by now.

She quickened her pace and joined the scramble toward the grid, dozens of army-issued boots trampling snow into mud. It seemed to take ages before they reached the outskirts of the city, where slender coracles bearing Allfold sails striped orange and red were docked atop platforms of honeycombed steel. Curved at the ends like canoes, the small airships, nicknamed wasps because of their diminutive size and lethal sting, gleamed in the copious moonlight.

In the mad dash to her coracle, Talasyn found herself running alongside Khaede, who was also heading for hers.

"You can't be serious!" Talasyn yelled over the clamor of warning gongs and officers' barked instructions. "You're two months along—"

"Not so loud," Khaede hissed. The line of her ebony jaw was resolute against the falling snow. "The bean sprout and I will be fine. Worry about yourself." She clapped Talasyn on the arm and was gone before the latter could reply, swallowed up by the throng of helmsmen.

Talasyn scanned the grid for Sol, swearing under her breath when she spotted his wasp already in the air. She doubted that he'd signed off on this. Unless Talasyn missed her guess, Khaede and Sol were due for their first fight as a married couple.

But she couldn't dwell on that now. In the distance, the Night Empire's own coracles surged over a forested ridge. These vessels were called wolves, vicious things with sharp prows that hunted in packs and were armed to the teeth, so numerous that they blocked out the horizon, their black-and-silver sails streaming in the chill breeze.

Talasyn hopped into the well of her ship, pulling on the pair of brown leather gloves that she'd tucked into her coat pocket, and she yanked at several levers in swift succession with the ease of familiarity. The wasp raised its sails and the crystalline aether hearts embedded in its wooden hull flared a bright emerald, bringing the craft to life as they crackled with the wind magic from the Squallfast dimension that Sardovian Enchanters had distilled into them. Static blared from the transceiver, a box-shaped contraption inlaid with dials and filaments of conductive metals, the aether heart within it glowing white, laden with magic from the Tempestroad, a storm-streaked dimension that produced sound, normally in the form of thunder, but it could be manipulated to carry voices across a distance through what was known as the aetherwave.

Fingers around the spoked wheel, Talasyn took off from the grid, her vessel spitting out fumes of magical green discharge, and she slipped into an arrowhead formation with the other Sardovian airships.

"What's the plan?" she asked into the mouthpiece of her transceiver, her question echoing through the aetherwave frequency used by her regiment.

From the head of the formation, Sol replied, in that calm and easygoing manner of which only he was capable during combat. His words emerged from a horn atop the transceiver, filling the well of Talasyn's coracle. "We're outnumbered ten to one, so standard defensive tactics are our best bet. Try to keep them away from the city walls until the residents are in the shelters."

"Affirmative," said Talasyn. She couldn't risk telling him about Khaede, not with so many of their comrades listening in, not when they needed him to be at his most focused. Still, she couldn't resist adding, "Congratulations on your marriage, by the way."

Sol laughed. "Thanks."

The Sardovian wasps formed a tight swarm around Frostplum's walls and the Kesathese vessels met them head-on. While a wasp coracle couldn't hold a candle to the multi-stacked repeating crossbows and iron-hurling ribaults of the Night Empire's wolves, it more than made up for that by virtue of sheer agility—an agility that Talasyn used to full advantage over the next few dizzying minutes. She careened through the night air, dodging one deadly bolt after another and firing off several of her own from the crossbows affixed to her ship's stern. The enemy coracles lacked maneuverability and her aim was true most of the time, ripping through sail-cloth, splintering wooden hulls.

But there were just so *many* wolves, and it wasn't long before they broke through the defensive perimeter, roaring closer and closer to Frostplum's moonlit sprawl of thatched rooftops.

And in the distance . . .

Talasyn's heart sank into the pit of her stomach when she spotted the monstrous double-masted silhouette of a Kesathese ironclad looming up over a snow-capped peak on whirling clouds of emerald aether. To meet it, two Sardovian frigates—full-rigged and square-sailed, and smaller but just as replete with cannons—rose from the nearby valley where they had been lying in wait for such a vessel to appear.

It was going to be a bloodbath. But at least the Night Empire hadn't brought in a stormship. As long as there was no stormship, there was still a chance.

Talasyn sailed to where the combat was thickest, hurling her wasp headlong into the fray. She fought and flew as hard as she ever had. Out of the corner of her eye, her comrades' ships burst into flames or shattered against battlements and treetops around her. Only a little while ago, they had all been safe and carefree in the longhouse, celebrating Khaede and Sol's wedding.

That had been an illusion. No warm place, no sliver of joyous time, was safe from the Hurricane Wars. Everything that Kesath's Night Empire touched, it destroyed.

The first faint embers of burning rose within her. It crawled from her core to the very tips of her fingers like white-hot needles, lurking beneath the skin.

Snap out of it, she ordered herself. *No one can know. You promised the Amirante.*

Talasyn swallowed the burning back down, quieting the inferno in her soul. Too late, she realized that several wolves had managed to outflank her while she was distracted. Their ribaults' iron projectiles pummeled her airship from all sides, and soon the world was nothing but free fall as she spiraled to the waiting ground.

CHAPTER TWO

In her dream she was fifteen years old again and the city of Hornbill's Head was all rammed earth and wooden lattice and animal skin, rising up from the straw-colored grass of the Great Steppe like a precariously layered cake nestled within soaring walls of mudbrick and salt. She was running from the watchmen, the pockets of her tattered clothes stuffed with flatbread and dried berries, cursing the shopkeeper's alertness with her every labored breath.

Hornbill's Head was—had been—taller than it was wide. Its inhabitants learned from an early age how to go vertical, higher and higher, and Talasyn was no exception. She scrambled up ladders and ledges and sped over rooftops and crossed the rickety bridges that connected one building to the next, all while the watchmen chased after her, puffing on their bird-bone whistles. She ran and ran, climbing ever higher, feeling the familiar ache the city left in her limbs and the rush of fear as the watchmen snapped at her feet. Yet on she went, up and up and air and sky, until she reached the battlements of the west wall. The frigid wind dug hard fingers into her hair and stabbed at her chapped lips as she hoisted herself onto the battlement, the whistles shrill and insistent behind her.

She had planned to skirt around the city walls and then drop back down into the lower slums, where she lived with the other bottom-dwellers, and where it was too much trouble for the watch to continue tracking an orphaned street rat who had stolen a few loaves and some fruit. However, as she straightened, balancing on the mudbrick ledge, the Great Steppe spread out miles below her feet in a vast expanse of tallgrass and rabbitbrush, she saw it.

The stormship.

It loomed on the flat horizon, arthropodous and elliptic, lightning cannons dangling from bow to stern like an array of jointed legs. In Talasyn's memory it was five hundred meters in length. In her dream, it was as big as worlds.

Fueled by scores of aether hearts that had been imbued with rain and wind and lightning magic by Emperor Gaheris's cunning Enchanters, pulsating sapphire and emerald and white through the metalglass sheets comprising the translucent hull, the stormship approached Hornbill's Head with all the grim finality of a tidal wave, dragging black thunderclouds in its wake: the endless sea of burnished grass bowed beneath it, bent by the gales from the Squallfast that its enormous turbines spun under a steadily darkening sky.

Talasyn stood frozen in terror. In her memory she'd run away, heading low, diving into the first shelter she could find, but in this dream her body refused to obey. The stormship drew nearer and nearer and the wind blew through her heart like iron bolts and suddenly—

She woke up.

Her eyes flew open, a gasp escaping her parted lips. Thick smoke rushed into her lungs and she coughed, her throat spasming as it was seared through. The world was lit red, sparkling with shattered metalglass. Her gloved hands fumbled with the buckle at her waist until the harness gave way and she fell onto a bed of snow, shards of her wasp's sidescuttle raining down all around her.

There was a moment of disorientation as the fog of unconsciousness lifted, the veil between dreams and reality disintegrating into splinters of fire and winter, her heart beating faster than she could count. She wasn't in Hornbill's Head, and she wasn't staring up at a Night Empire stormship as it eclipsed the heavens. Instead, she was somewhere outside Frostplum, glancing over her shoulder at her wasp, which had crashed on its side, its slender foils bent at odd angles, its striped sails consumed by bright flames from the cracked Firewarren-infused aether heart that powered the lamps, slowly licking their way toward the rest of the vessel.

She drew in one slow breath after another, until time returned to her. Until she was twenty years old, and all trace of civilization on Sardovia's Great Steppe was long gone. Eradicated by Kesath's forces as a punishment for refusing to bow to the Night Emperor.

If Sardovia lost tonight's battle, the same fate would befall its Highlands—to which Frostplum was the gateway.

Coughing out the last of the smoke, Talasyn crawled away from the wreckage. The wolves had sent her damaged wasp spinning over the longleaf-pine forest that bordered Frostplum and all the way to the other side of the glacial mountain lake. Over a distance marked by ice floes and dark water, through the gaps between stout trunks, she could glimpse the ruined buildings, the rushing silhouettes, the burning. There was no sign of the coracles, the Kesathese ironclad, or the Sardovian frigates, which meant that both sides had switched to ground warfare; she must have been unconscious for a *while*. Eventually her head stopped spinning and her legs remembered how they worked and she was hauling herself up, she was standing, she was scrambling over the lake, navigating a treacherous path from one large chunk of ice to the next.

By the World-Father's untrimmed beard, it was colder than the Night Emperor's heart out here. Mists of silvery vapor curled into the air with her every exhalation. Through them, she glimpsed a panicked crowd spilling from the forest on the far shore: Sardovian soldiers and cityfolk alike. Some headed for the caves while others took their chances on the ice. The light of Lir's seven moons bore down upon them all, casting the surrounding white mountains into harsh relief.

I have to make it across the lake, she thought. *I have to make it back to Frostplum. I have to rejoin the fight.*

Talasyn had almost reached the forested bank when fumes of darkness unfurled from the trees and drifted over the snow, consuming the ice floes in a creeping wash of inky black.

She skidded to a halt and the darkness encircled her, rippling with aether. It wasn't the darkness of the night or the smoke from the fighting that had already broken out on the mountain. It was deeper and heavier, more alive. It *moved*, curling over the frozen lake like tendrils.

She had encountered these shadows before, on many a battlefield. When they formed rings like this, it effectively trapped all those who were caught within. Sardovian regiments had learned the hard way that trying to pass through these barriers resulted in grievous injuries, if not outright dismemberment. It was a favorite tactic of the Shadowforged warriors that made up the Night Empire's fearsome Legion. If Emperor Gaheris had let them out to play, suddenly the chances of Frostplum fending off this siege seemed considerably slimmer.

As were her own chances of survival.

She stood statue-still, listening to the creak of footsteps on the ice and the cries from people she couldn't see through the murky black wreathing the air.

"Pick off the stragglers," a masculine voice, greasy and guttural like an oil slick, instructed from not so far away. Talasyn bit back a curse. If the Legion was sweeping the lake, that meant there was no further need for them in the city and the Sardovian regiment had scattered. Frostplum was lost. The rest of the Highlands would follow, with its most strategically located settlement now in the clutches of the Night Empire.

Horror and panic tore through her in equal measure, and then ceded ground to a boiling rage. She hadn't asked for this; the people of Frostplum hadn't asked for this. No one in Sardovia had. A few hours ago her regiment had been celebrating Khaede and Sol's future and now they were being mowed down like voles across pack ice. Snuffed out one by one. There was only herself, the night, the black water, and the lurking Shadowforged encircling her like a cage. She would *not* let it end like this.

With Talasyn's rage came the spark of an ember in her core. She felt it burn the way it had earlier, but more intensely this time. Sharp, radiant, and demanding justice.

And it hurt. It felt as though her entire being was aflame. She had to let it out before it consumed her.

Don't let anyone see, the Amirante had warned. *You're not ready yet. They can't know.*

You will be hunted.

Talasyn closed her eyes in an attempt to center herself, swallowing her emotions as if they were bile. No sooner had she succeeded in doing *that* than the ice shifted beneath her feet and she heard frost crystals crackling under heavy armor. Her nape prickled with the weight of a stare that must be surveying the Sardovian Allfold's crest—a phoenix, the same one emblazoned on the regiments' sails—stitched on the back of her coat.

"You lost, little bird?"

It was that oil-slick voice again. Measured steps drew near and the telltale growl of static could be heard as the Shadowgate was opened. The fire in Talasyn rose up as if a dam had finally given way.

There was nowhere left to run.

I'm not going to die. Not here. Not now.

Talasyn whirled around to meet her attacker head-on.

The legionnaire had to be at *least* seven feet in height, every inch of him covered in obsidian plate, and his gauntleted fists clutched an enormous greatsword crafted from pure darkness, shot through with streaks of silver aether. The edge of the blade crackled as he raised it above her head.

It was the same now as it had been the day Hornbill's Head was destroyed. It was instinct. It was the body fighting tooth and nail to survive.

The magic spread through her like wings.

Talasyn met the Shadowforged sword with a wave of radiance. The tapestry of aether that bound the dimensions and held all elements appeared in her mind's eye and she yanked at its strings, opening the way to the Lightweave. It shot out from her splayed fingertips, raw and shapeless and uncontrolled in her alarm, painting the immediate vicinity in hues of brilliant gold.

The last time this happened—when Kesathese troops crept through the ruins of Hornbill's Head after the stormship had flattened it, searching for survivors to make an example out of—the soldier aiming his crossbow at Talasyn's fifteen-year-old self had died instantly, flesh and bone devoured by the Lightweave. This giant legionnaire managed to block, his greatsword transmuting into a dark oblong shield with which the radiance collided in a fiery flash. However, Talasyn was desperate and he'd been taken by surprise, and he screeched as light consumed shadow and he was blasted to the ground in a heap of singed armor.

Sardovian forces had arrived too late to save Hornbill's Head but in just enough time to rescue those who had withstood the stormship's wrath. Coxswain Darius had been the one to witness her kill the Kesathese soldier and he'd ushered her away, taking her straight to the Amirante.

Tonight on the Highlands ice, though, no one was going to come for her. She was on her own until she made it back to her regiment in Frostplum.

And she wasn't going to let *anyone* stand in her way.

Focus, the Amirante would say over and over during their training sessions. Words to meditate on. *Aether is the prime element, the one that binds all the others together and connects each dimension to the next. Every once in a while, an aethermancer is brought into this world—someone who can traverse the aether's path in specific ways. Rainsingers. Firedancers. Shadowforged. Windcallers. Thunderstruck. Enchanters. And you.*

The Lightweave is the thread and you are the spinner. It will do as you command.

So, tell it what you want.

The giant legionnaire was flailing on the ice like a turtle on its back, his bulky armor cracked in several places, blood seeping through. Talasyn narrowed her eyes at him and stretched an arm out to the side, her spread fingers tugging back the veil between this world and others, opening the Lightweave once more. The weapon that appeared in her open palm, summoned from one of several realms of magical energy that existed within aetherspace, resembled the long, wide-bladed daggers that had saved many Sardovian infantrymen's lives in melee, except that it was fashioned solely from golden light and silver aether. Its serrated edges blazed in the gloom like wisps of sun.

The Shadowforged's panic was almost tangible, despite his mask. He scrambled backward on his elbows as Talasyn advanced. It looked as though his legs weren't working, and perhaps, in the time before, a part of her would have quailed at the thought of killing someone so obviously incapacitated and defenseless. But he was one of the Legion and the Hurricane Wars had hardened her, loss after loss whittling

21

away at the child she'd once been until there was nothing left but fury.

And sunlight.

Talasyn plunged the dagger into his chest—or she *tried* to. In that scant sliver of a second before the tip of the blade met the plate mail encasing his torso, something—

—*someone*—

—loomed up from out of the darkness—

—and her dagger slid against the crescent's edge of a war scythe conjured from the Shadowgate.

With her concentration disrupted, the light-woven dagger fizzled out of existence and Talasyn was left clutching at empty air. It was instinct, too, the thing that made her leap back, narrowly avoiding her new assailant's next sweeping strike.

The coin-bright rays of the seven moons sketched in mottled hues another legionnaire that, while not as statuesque as the giant that Talasyn had just felled, was tall and broad and imposing nonetheless. Over a long-sleeved chainmail tunic, he wore a belted cuirass of black and crimson leather, with spiked pauldrons and scaled crimson armguards connected to black gauntlets, their tips pointed like claws. The fur-trimmed hood of a winter cloak the color of midnight framed his pale face, the lower portion of which was shrouded by an obsidian half-mask embossed with a design of two rows of wickedly sharp, wolfish teeth, captured in an eternal snarl.

The effect was nightmarish. And, while Talasyn had never encountered this Shadowforged before, she knew who he was. She knew what the silver chimera on the brooch atop his collarbone meant. A lion's roaring head affixed to the serpentine body of a brocaded eel, rearing up on the hooves of the spindlehorn antelope—Kesath's imperial seal.

Fear stole the breath from her lungs, as razor-edged as the winter on this mountain.

People always said that Alaric of House Ossinast, Master

of the Shadowforged Legion and Gaheris's only son and heir, had the most piercing gray eyes. Those eyes shone a bright and chilling silver with the glow of his magic under the seven moons, looking directly into hers.

She'd been warned about him. She had known that she would one day have to face him.

That day had come too soon.

Then he was upon her with his flickering scythe of smoke and ink, and doubtless her terror was etched all over her face and across her trembling lips. Acting on pure instinct, she resummoned the Lightweave into the shape of two daggers, one in each of her shaking hands. The scythe clashed against the dagger on the right, sending vibrations all the way up her arm as she raised it overhead. She put all her strength into shoving him away, but he was quick to recover, coming at her again.

Oh, it was *on*.

Talasyn often sparred with the Sardovian regiments' Blademaster as part of her training, but no blow from a metal sword could hold a candle to the sheer pulsating magic of the Shadowgate, and practicing with a mentor was a fair wind compared to someone actively trying to kill her. *Especially* when that someone was nearly twice her size and had reportedly been trained in the ways of the Shadowforged from the moment that he'd learned how to walk.

It was all Talasyn could do to dodge and to parry as Alaric drove her across the ice floes, his injured subordinate forgotten. Each dark barrier dissipated as they passed through it, as if he were banishing them—but to what end? Perhaps he took some sadistic joy in drawing this out, in playing with her as a cat would play with a mouse. She would never know and she wasn't about to try to ask him.

Kesath's crown prince was relentless; he moved like a thunderstorm, powerful and everywhere all at once. Shadow careened into light in a conflagration of aether sparks—once, twice, a million times. The flimsier patches in the sheets of ice cracked under the soles of her snow boots, spatters of lake water splashing at her woolen breeches, painfully cold wherever they landed. His blade easily dwarfed both of hers, and on more than one occasion she tried to shape her desperate will into a shield, tried to achieve what had eluded her ever since she began aethermancing, but she still *couldn't*. More than once, she left herself wide open as she failed to conjure a shield, his scythe breaking through the flimsy weapon that she hastily cobbled together at the last minute, and she received sharp and shadow-spun cuts to her arms for all her trouble.

And then there came a moment when Talasyn teetered on the very edge of the ice floe and Alaric swung the war scythe from the side and there was no time for her to turn, to block, and she didn't know how to make a shield—

She brought her hands together. The two daggers turned into a morningstar flail and she swept the shaft in his direction. The golden chain wound around the scythe's blade and *caught*, and she hauled him toward her with all her might.

He shifted his weight and dug his boots into the ice, foiling her attempt to outbalance him. They stood mere inches from each other, both of them one ill-advised movement away from falling into the lake, their weapons tangled together at their sides. Alaric's hood had slipped off at some point, revealing a tousled halo of wavy black hair. The eyes that Talasyn could see above the fanged snarl of his half-mask were sharp and unnervingly intent. He was tall enough that she had to lift her chin to meet his gaze.

She was breathing heavily from the exertion and he seemed a bit winded as well, his broad chest rising and falling in unsteady beats. But when he spoke, it was in smooth, low tones, so deep that it seemed as though the night grew darker around them.

"I was not aware that Sardovia had a new Lightweaver at their disposal."

Talasyn's jaw clenched.

Nineteen years ago, in what was now known as the Cataclysm, two neighboring states in the Sardovian Allfold had gone to war with each other—Sunstead, which had been home to every Lightweaver on the Continent, and the Shadow-ruled kingdom of Kesath. After Lightweavers slew Ozalus Ossinast, his son Gaheris ascended to the throne and led Kesath to victory, forcibly annexing Sunstead; in the same breath, Kesath tore away from the Sardovian Allfold and began styling itself the Night Empire. Gaheris had taken on the mantle of Night Emperor, and he and his Shadowforged Legion had killed all the Lightweavers and destroyed their shrines, leaving no trace of them on the Continent. Except . . .

"Your murderous tyrant of a father missed one," Talasyn spat at Alaric, and she surged up on her toes and—

—*slammed* her forehead into his.

Splinters of white-hot pain exploded across her vision. Amidst them, she saw the Kesathese prince recoil, the inky scythe vanishing from his grasp, his gauntleted hand coming up to nurse what she dearly hoped was a crack in his skull.

But she didn't stay to find out. She reshaped the morning-star flail back into a dagger and plunged it clean through his shoulder and he let out a grunt. She whirled around, the radiant blade disappearing, and she *ran*—through her splitting headache, over the ice floes, through the moonlight, toward the trees.

Not once did she look back, afraid of what she might find.

CHAPTER THREE

The mournful wail of a horn rang throughout the mountain just as Talasyn plunged into a thicket of longleaf pine and bramble. It was the signal to retreat, and she changed course, heading not for the city proper but the docks. With a bruised and blood-streaked face and cuts on her arms, a padded coat soaked through with sweat, and ears ringing from echoes of adrenaline and injury, she broke past the treeline.

The evening sky was tinted arterial red by the smoldering inferno of Frostplum's remains. The great wooden carracks of the Sardovian Allfold unfurled their sails in the smoke-ridden breeze before her, their bilges already several feet above the ground while long rope ladders spilled from the sides of the decks. Fleeing soldiers and cityfolk were swarming up them like ants. Talasyn quickened her pace in the direction of the largest of the carracks, the *Summerwind*, and she clambered up the first rope ladder that she came to, engulfed by a mixture of relief and foreboding.

Her comrades hadn't left her behind yet, but they *were* leaving, effectively ceding more ground to the Night Empire. Ground that they couldn't afford to lose.

Talasyn landed on the deck on her hands and knees. It was

chaos. People were rushing about; healers were tending to grisly wounds. Talasyn could only tell the soldiers from everyone else by patches of uniform amid the soot, grime, and blood.

The rope ladders were retracted as the carrack set sail over the snow-laden Highlands on emerald clouds of wind magic. Talasyn gazed upon Frostplum, its burning rooftops and broken walls growing ever smaller with distance. She turned, unable to keep looking at what was left of the place where they'd found a moment of peace and happiness, and she stopped dead as her gaze fell on a couple several feet away. And what was left of her world was pulled out from under her.

Huddled against the bulkhead, Khaede held Sol's limp form in her arms, his head pillowed on her lap. Both their clothes were spattered with his blood, pouring out of a gaping hole in his chest. A crimson-drenched crossbow bolt lay across the wooden planks.

Talasyn knew, even before she walked over on unsteady legs, that Sol was gone. His blue-black eyes stared up at the heavens, unblinking. Tears streamed down Khaede's cheeks as she stroked his dark hair, the wedding band that he'd slipped onto her finger only a few hours ago gleaming in a tangle of moonbeams and lamplight.

"He almost made it," Khaede whispered once she realized that Talasyn had sat beside her. "Our wasps crash-landed and we fought our way to the docks. We went up the ladder—he made me go first—and when I turned around to help him climb over onto the deck, there was that"—she nodded jerkily at the crossbow bolt—"that *thing* sticking out of his chest. It happened so fast. I didn't even see it actually happen. I . . ."

Khaede took a deep, shuddering breath. She fell silent, not so much as sniffling, although her tears continued to flow. Her hand dropped over Sol's heart and stayed there, beside where the Kesathese bowman had hit true, her fingers running all the redder from his fatal wound.

Talasyn was at a loss what to do. She knew Khaede was the type of person who despised what she considered pity, who would brutally rebuff any attempt at comfort. Talasyn couldn't even cry for Sol because her early years on the Great Steppe had dulled the part of her that wept, long before the Hurricane Wars. She had considered this a good thing in its own way— if she cried for everyone who fell in battle, she'd never be stopping—but now, looking at Sol's lifeless body, remembering the kind smiles and good-natured jokes, remembering how happy he'd made her friend, her numbness sickened her. Surely he deserved the tears that she was too exhausted to give?

Her gaze strayed to Khaede's midsection, and bile surged up her throat. "You have to tell Vela that you're pregnant. So she can pull you off active duty."

"I'm fighting until I can't," Khaede interrupted in a low growl. "Don't you *dare* tell her, either. I'm the best helmsman in the Allfold. You need me." The hand that wasn't on Sol's unmoving chest touched her stomach. "The baby will be all right." Her bottom lip quivered before she pressed her mouth into a taut, resolute line. "They're strong like their father."

The mixture of sorrow and defiance on the other woman's face made Talasyn decide to let it go. Now wasn't the time. Instead, she looked around the busy decks for any sign of the cleric who had officiated at the wedding—only to see pale yellow robes peeking out from a makeshift shroud draped over a still, supine form.

She would have to do it, then. As she'd done for others on battlefields all across the Continent, when they'd been too far from god-shrines and healing houses.

Talasyn leaned over Sol and gently closed his sightless eyes, his skin devoid of life's warmth beneath her fingertips. "May your soul find shelter in the willows," she murmured, "until all lands sink beneath the Eversea and we meet again."

Beside her, Khaede drew another harsh breath, one that was

almost a sob. The carrack flew on, over the mountains and the valleys, on the oars of winter and of starlight.

"Why didn't Kesath bring in a stormship?"

Talasyn's question broke the tense silence that had settled over the Amirante's office after her debriefing. She'd helped wrap Sol in a shroud and gotten Khaede settled in a spare berth half an hour ago. Now she was seated across from Vela, her damp and singed outerwear traded for a blanket draped over her cotton-clad shoulders.

"Given the terrain and the existing conditions, adding more weather would have been disastrous for all parties involved. Avalanches tend to put quite the damper on morale." Vela spoke with calm authority from behind her desk. "Not to mention that, with Frostplum's small size relative to cities on the plains or the coasts, the rate of civilian and allied casualties would have been too high."

"That's why *we* didn't bring in a stormship," Talasyn pointed out.

"Quite so." A hint of a sardonic smile darted across the Amirante's weathered bronze features. One of the Legion had gouged out her left eye the year before, and in its place was an intricately carved patch of copper and steel that only added to the redoubtable figure she cut among her troops. "In Kesath's case, I suspect that they believed they didn't need one to win. I *also* suspect that they were content to merely run us off instead of giving chase because they'd gotten what they came for."

"They did," Coxswain Darius said shortly. He was leaning against the wall, arms crossed, a haggard imitation of the good-humored officer that Talasyn had spoken to at the longhouse. "Now that he has Frostplum, Gaheris is in prime position to conquer the rest of the Highlands. It won't be long before he brings the King on the Mountain to heel." Vela made no response and Darius sighed, fixing her with a morose gaze.

"Ideth, the Sardovian Allfold's holdings shrink with each year that passes. Soon there will be nowhere left for us to run."

"What would you have us do, then?" countered Vela. "Surrender is not an option. You and I both knew that when we left Kesath. Gaheris made it plain: anyone who stands in the way of his empire's destiny will meet a terrible end."

It was Darius's turn to say nothing, although he kept his eyes fixed on the Amirante while she returned his stare. Not for the first time, Talasyn felt like an intruder witnessing a conversation that she couldn't hear. Vela and Darius had their own silent language; they had known each other since Vela was a new recruit to the Kesathese fleet, and ten years ago they had defected together with several other officers and some loyal soldiers, taking eight stormships with them over the border to Sardovia.

Vela and Darius were resolute in their determination to prevent the Night Emperor's cruel reign from encompassing the whole Continent. But the Hurricane Wars had dragged on and Sardovia was down to five stormships, and Talasyn was starting to see the cracks in her superiors' facades.

Darius rubbed a weary hand over his face. "If only Bieshimma had been successful," he muttered. "If only the Nenavar Dominion had agreed to help."

"It was a long shot in the first place," said Vela. "They'd already turned away our previous envoy. I'm sure that the Nenavarene are still smarting from the *last* time they sent aid to a Sardovian state."

There it was again, the quickening of Talasyn's pulse that accompanied anything and everything to do with the Dominion. "So it's true, then?" she blurted out. "Nenavar sent airships to help the Lightweavers of Sunstead during the Cataclysm?" She'd heard the old stories; they were whispered in taverns and marketplaces, bandied about in the barracks.

"Yes," Vela confirmed. "I was a quartermaster in the Kesathese fleet at the time. I saw the Nenavarene flotilla from a distance, but they never reached our shores. Emperor Gaheris sent the stormship prototype out to meet them."

"It was his father's pet project," Darius added, lip curling in distaste. "Ozalus had just been slain in battle. Gaheris was newly crowned, and angry and desperate. He ordered the first stormship to be deployed. It hadn't been tested yet, but it worked. The Nenavarene flotilla never stood a chance."

Talasyn pictured it—bursts of straight-line winds, torrents of heavy rain, waves of destructive lightning, unfurling over the dark blue Eversea and crushing the Dominion's airships as though they were matchsticks. After Kesath annexed Sunstead and became the Night Empire, they had kept on building more of these dread weapons. Huge armor-plated vessels, nearly impossible to bring down and wreaking untold devastation on the land.

Each stormship required hundreds of aether hearts to be fully operational, but Kesath's mines were on the brink of depletion, and so Gaheris had looked to his neighbors. The remaining states of the Sardovian Allfold had refused. Deciding to take Sardovia's supply of aether hearts by force, Gaheris began conquering one Allfold city after another, his Night Empire growing with each victory. Vela and Darius and their men had rebelled and brought stormship technology to the Sardovian forces and now, a decade later, here they all were. Fighting a war without end.

"Speaking of Gaheris," said Vela, her remaining eye flickering to Talasyn, "and fathers and sons—"

"That's right." Darius grew even more solemn. "So. Alaric Ossinast knows you're a Lightweaver."

Talasyn nodded.

"He will have informed Gaheris by now," said Vela. "They will stop at nothing to neutralize you. Not only can your magic cancel out theirs, but it's *personal* for them. Gaheris watched Sunstead Lightweavers kill his father, and he has instilled that same desire for vengeance in his son. You have a target on your back."

"I'm sorry," Talasyn mumbled, shame heating her cheeks. Sardovia had needed helmsmen and she'd shown an aptitude for the wasp coracles, but she'd been warned over and over again to hide the fact that she had the ability to channel aether magic, that she could tread the line between dimensions and make one in particular do her bidding.

"You did what you had to do to survive," Darius conceded. "But this *does* mean that it's time for you to start training in earnest."

"Training won't suffice," Vela said grimly. "Not for long. Fortunately, we may have found a way around that."

Before Talasyn could ask what she meant, the Amirante spoke to Darius. "Check if Bieshimma's at the door yet."

He was. It was only when Darius stepped aside to let Bieshimma into the office that Talasyn remembered they had wanted to meet with her back at the longhouse in Frostplum. Although thinking about the wedding made her heart ache, a shard of her former curiosity managed to shine through, along with a healthy dose of wariness.

The officer with the black horseshoe mustache acknowledged Talasyn's salute with only the barest of noncommittal grunts. She didn't take it personally; Bieshimma looked as though he was deep in thought as he unrolled what appeared to be a map over Vela's desk.

The Amirante beckoned Talasyn nearer and she complied, standing beside Darius. Up close, she saw that the old, fading map was that of Sardovia's southeastern coastline and of the Nenavar Dominion, the grid of the Eversea stretched between them. In stark contrast to the intricate details of the Sardovian portion of the map, Nenavar was rendered as a scattering of islands, roughly sketched and mostly unlabeled, as if the cartographer hadn't had time to study the terrain.

Which made sense, Talasyn supposed. The map had to have been drawn up from onboard an airship, and none but the foolhardiest of crews would loiter in skies rumored to be guarded by fire-breathing dragons when their vessel was made mostly of wood.

Still, there were freshly inked markings on the rust-tinged paper. Place names, landmarks, and notes. Most conspicuous of all was the black X over a frieze of mountains that was halfway between Port Samout, where Bieshimma's airship had docked, and the Dominion's capital city, Eskaya, which the general had apparently stormed all by himself, according to that lance corporal.

"As I was saying before we were so rudely interrupted by Kesathese scum," Bieshimma rumbled, "I think it's doable." He dipped a stylus into a nearby inkwell and traced a route in a series of dashes. "A lone wasp is certainly less conspicuous than a carrack, so she needn't go the roundabout way like we did. If she leaves central Sardovia via the Shipsbane and hugs forest all the way to the coast, she'll be able to make a clean exit. The Night Empire will never know as long as she steers clear of their outposts in the Salt Cays."

Talasyn raised an eyebrow. "Why do I get the feeling—*sir*," she quickly added when Bieshimma shot her a pointed look, "that this *she* we're talking about is, in fact, *me*?"

"Because it is." Vela's tone was so stern that Talasyn immediately desisted from mouthing off any further. The Amirante was fearsome when she wanted to be; a former Kesathese defector could not ascend to leadership of the Sardovian Allfold's army by being the sort of person who suffered fools.

"By now, those damnable chatterboxes that I was saddled with for escorts have most assuredly spread the news that I made a break for the Dominion's capital," Bieshimma said to Talasyn.

Put on the spot like that, she couldn't do anything else but shrug, which was as good a confirmation as any.

33

"I thought that perhaps the Nenavarene Zahiya-lachis wouldn't be able to refuse an audience if I showed up on her doorstep." Bieshimma's expression soured. "Unfortunately, the palace guards nearly ran me through with their spears. Nearly ran my horse through, too. I fled on the poor beast without catching even a glimpse of Queen Urduja. But there was something that I *did* see." He pointed at the X on the map. "On the way back to Port Samout, the sky to my left flashed as brilliantly as though the sun had come crashing down. A pillar of light shot out from a mountaintop, illuminating the heavens for miles upon miles around. I couldn't investigate further as I needed to get back to the airship as soon as possible. After the scene I made in front of her palace, I feared that Urduja would call for my head and the heads of all my crew. However, I know what I saw."

The general straightened up and steadily met Talasyn's questioning gaze. "It was a Light Sever," he stated. "Such a one as has not existed on the Continent since Gaheris invaded Sunstead and destroyed all instances of the Lightweave here."

Talasyn's eyes widened. A Light Sever. A tear that the aether had ripped into the material world, where the Lightweave existed without having to be summoned. A nexus point that she could tap into to amplify and refine her magic, in the same way that the Night Empire's Legion grew in strength and skill because of the numerous Shadow Severs that dotted Kesath. Hope and excitement lanced through her.

Then she remembered precisely *where* this Light Sever was located, and her soaring emotions shifted into something that was close to dread.

She looked at Vela. "You want me to go to Nenavar. By myself."

"I'm sorry to ask this of you," said the Amirante, "but General Bieshimma is correct in his assumption that one wasp is less likely to be noticed. The way that things have gone with the Dominion, I doubt they'll grant you free passage through their territory no matter how many envoys we send— and we don't have the time to send any more. The Night Empire is closing in."

Talasyn swallowed. "So, I need to infiltrate."

"Get in, commune with the Light Sever, get out," said Vela. "And don't let anyone catch you."

"Easier said than done," Talasyn grumbled before remembering that she was supposed to abstain from wisecracks.

Vela frowned. "I'm serious, helmsman. We cannot risk angering the Nenavarene more than a certain someone already has with his little stunt." She glanced at Bieshimma as if gauging his reaction, but his features barely rippled.

"I deserved that," he said.

Vela's lips twitched. However, when she spoke again, it was addressed to Talasyn. "Believe me, if I thought that requesting the Dominion's assistance in this one matter would do any good—"

"No, you're right, Amirante," Talasyn interrupted, shaking her head. "We don't have time."

After a decade of conflict, Sardovia had been whittled down to half of its former land area. Less than half, now that the Highlands were all but lost. There was no other option. This was their last hope.

"The girl can't just sail into Dominion territory with no preparation." Darius spoke up for the first time since Bieshimma joined them. "If she gets caught, if she can't fight her way out—"

"Good point." Vela mulled it over for a while, her gaze fixed on the map, on the miles that needed to be traversed before reaching the Light Sever. "In a fortnight, then. Talasyn, starting tomorrow, you will be training more intensively with me and with Blademaster Kasdar. We'll send you off to Nenavar fully equipped to defend yourself."

"That also gives me enough time to sketch out the overland route to the Light Sever in as much detail as possible," said Bieshimma. "I'll cross-reference with what few historical documents and intelligence reports we have as well. I'll do my best."

Rolling up the map, he tucked it under one arm and saluted Vela before leaving the office. Alone with Vela and Darius once more, Talasyn sensed that the Amirante seemed worried—an odd emotion in such a stoic, unflappable woman.

"A fortnight isn't nearly enough time, but it's all that we can afford to spare," Vela muttered. "Alaric won't forget that you bested him in combat, Talasyn. He was a haughty, tenacious boy who grew up to become a prideful, unforgiving young man. I don't even dare imagine what he'll do when you encounter each other again."

"Perhaps I killed him," Talasyn offered with a shred of optimism. "Y'know, when I stabbed him in the shoulder."

Darius let out a mirthless chuckle. "That would solve so many of our problems, wouldn't it?"

"It will take more than a light-woven dagger to the shoulder to kill Alaric," Vela said. "He is the most powerful Shadowforged to exist in centuries. There's a reason he became Master of the Legion back when he was barely eighteen. The next time you face him, Talasyn, you need to be ready."

Her heart in her throat, Talasyn thought about the dark prince she'd met out on the drifting ice. The lethal dance that he'd drawn her into. She thought about the way his gray eyes had shone silver beneath the seven moons, regarding her as if she were his prey.

She shivered.

CHAPTER FOUR

Two sennights crawled by. After her failed attempt at persuading Khaede to let the Amirante know of her condition so that she could take leave until the baby came, it was ironic that Talasyn found herself the one pulled out of active duty so that *she* could focus on training. Khaede had a good chortle at that, and Talasyn couldn't begrudge her. There were precious few reasons for Khaede to even so much as smile these days. Talasyn had to concede that, in a way, it was probably for the best that Khaede was being kept busy with airship battles.

Their regiment's new base was in the Wildermarch, a deep, fertile canyon in the Sardovian Heartland. Winter here was not as harsh as it was on the mountains, and the grounds were still tinged in a rather glorious autumn. It was a world away from the dilapidated orphanage in Hornbill's Head. That leaky-roofed, rammed-earth compound tucked into the slums of a drab brown city where no trees grew, with its mold-flecked straw pallets and overflowing latrines and apathetic caretakers who spent all the meager funds on women and dice and riesag, a potent cocktail of distilled barley and fermented musk-ox milk that was the cheapest and most effective way to stay warm on the Great Steppe. No matter where she went, it was better than that, but Talasyn had scarce opportunity to appreciate the beauty of their new barracks.

Her every waking minute was spent aethermancing under Vela's watchful instruction or sparring with Mara Kasdar.

The Lightweave could cut through physical weapons as though they were nothing, so Talasyn and the Blademaster fought with swords, daggers, spears, and flails. It was strenuous but, as the days passed, she noticed that she was getting quicker on her feet and more focused when it came to channeling her magic.

At least there was no longer any need to keep her abilities hidden from her regiment. There had been fears of espionage, or captured soldiers confessing that a Lightweaver walked among them. Since Kesath already knew, Talasyn could train in plain sight, frequently drawing crowds of amazed spectators.

Her aethermancy training had previously been limited to what few hours could be spared. There'd been no use sending her to the front in her capacity as a Lightweaver when there were hundreds of Shadowforged to reckon with. But now that Alaric Ossinast was aware of her existence, now that Gaheris would be even more determined to crush Sardovia because they harbored the last Lightweaver on the Continent—

Well. Talasyn had to start making sure that she was hard to kill.

She thought about Alaric a lot. It was never on purpose but, to her chagrin, he had the disturbing tendency to pop up in her mind when she least expected it. Alaric in all his height and armor, wielding his magic with a lethal confidence that was in such stark contrast to her own scattered, flailing attempts. Although the cuts on her arms had long since healed, she kept going over their duel. Kept pinpointing all the instances he could have easily hacked her head off but didn't. Was she lucky to have survived? Or had he been holding back? But why would he?

Maybe he wasn't as good a warrior as everyone said he was. Maybe his reputation lay mostly in his forbidding appearance. Those eyes—

Every time Talasyn thought about Alaric's eyes, about the silver sheen to them set against a pale and half-shrouded face, about the way they had focused on her and only her, she was assailed by the oddest mixture of sensations. There was fear, yes, but there was also something magnetic. Something that insisted on hauling this memory of him into her orbit, so she could . . .

Could *what*, exactly?

No matter. She would keep training and she would commune with the Light Sever, and the next time she saw Alaric she would be more than a match for him. *She* wouldn't hold back.

Meanwhile, the battle for the Highlands raged on. The bulk of reinforcements were sent from the Wildermarch a few days after they'd settled in, and so, in addition to fretting over her upcoming mission to Nenavar, Talasyn also spent her days fretting over Khaede and feeling powerless that she wasn't there to help. Fortunately, Khaede returned safely the day before Talasyn was set to leave. *Less* fortunately, she'd returned to wait for new orders, because most of the alpine cities had surrendered and the War Council had begun discussions on shifting all available resources to the Heartland and the Coast.

A strategic retreat, many called it. It seemed to Talasyn that the Hurricane Wars were one strategic retreat after another on Sardovia's end, but she kept that to herself. Morale was low enough.

"Do you even know *how* to commune with a Light Sever?" Khaede challenged. "What is the process, specifically?"

They were sitting on the burnt umber grass and crisp fallen leaves outside the barracks, beneath a shedding but still exuberant coppery cypress. The sun was setting on the

Wildermarch, its crimson light rendering the canyon ablaze at the edges as a stiff wind rolled in from the north, carrying with it the glacial bite of faraway polar tundra. This particular spot overlooked a riverbed that would flush turquoise come the spring thaw, but for now it was just a wide ribbon of cracked earth, edged with gorse and sagebrush.

The riverbed would have been wholly unremarkable if not for the fact that it was the site of a Wind Sever, where the Squallfast sometimes bled through. A white-cloaked Sardovian Enchanter stood on the bank with a chest full of empty aether hearts at his feet, patiently waiting for the Wind Sever to discharge so that he could collect its magic.

While they couldn't directly summon any of the dimensions into existence, Enchanters were the most prized of aethermancers throughout the world of Lir for their ability to manipulate the Tempestroad, the Squallfast, the Firewarren, and the Rainspring—as long as there was an existing source to draw from. Here on the Continent, they were the backbone of both sides of the Hurricane Wars, kept away from the fighting to craft the hearts that powered the airships and the stormships day in, day out. It was a thankless, taxing role, and Talasyn felt a twinge of guilt. She'd crash-landed so many wasp coracles during combat, wasting the multiple aether hearts that were built into each one.

With her gaze still trained on the Enchanter, she set about answering Khaede. "I'm not sure, but the Amirante and I have discussed in the past what would happen if I ever came across a Light Sever. She thinks that it shouldn't be much different from how the Shadowforged meditate with *their* nexus points and that my instincts will tell me what to do."

"So, you're going to sneak into a country that's notoriously unfriendly to outsiders and might possibly have dragons with the sole purpose of finding the Lightweave high up on a mountain using only a roughly sketched map, and you have no real idea what to do once you get there." Khaede placed a hand over her eyes. "The war is lost."

"Well, when you put it like *that*, of *course* it sounds impossible," Talasyn shot back. "But I'll figure it out. I have to."

They sank into a desultory silence. It blew in with the northern wind rustling the cypress leaves. Talasyn wondered if she should broach the topic of Sol. They'd buried him here in the canyon, with the other dead, and Khaede had sailed back to the Highlands shortly after. But before Talasyn could decide on what to say and whether she should say it, Khaede spoke again.

"What do you know about Nenavar?"

I know that it calls to me, Talasyn thought. *I know that it's familiar for some reason. I know that I want to find out why.*

She longed to tell Khaede—to tell *someone*—about all the emotions that Nenavar stirred in her, but she couldn't bear to do it. She was too much like her friend; she didn't want to open herself up to other people's pity. Khaede would surely think that she was just desperate for any sense of connection, indulging an orphan's foolish hopes.

Instead, Talasyn patched together everything she'd heard over the years from other Sardovians regarding their enigmatic neighbor across the sea. "It's made up of seven large islands and thousands of smaller ones. The climate is tropical. It's a matriarchy." She'd learned that word from a Hornbill's Head shopkeeper chatting about Nenavar with his patrons while she waited for an opportune moment to slip his wares into her pockets.

"Don't forget all the gold," Khaede helpfully supplied.

"Right." Talasyn cracked a smile as she echoed one of the older children at the orphanage, in the slums of her early years. "A country of islands ruled only by queens, where the skies are home to dragons and the streets are made of gold."

41

She couldn't fathom a nation so rich in the precious metal that they *paved* with it. Perhaps that was why the Dominion refused to get involved in the affairs of the outside world: they had too much to lose.

But something *had* in fact motivated them to break tradition and lend aid to the Lightweavers of Sunstead, nineteen years ago . . .

"Have you ever heard of the Fisherman's Warning?" Khaede asked.

Talasyn shook her head.

"No, I suppose that you wouldn't have. You grew up on the Great Steppe." Khaede worried her lower lip, uncharacteristically pensive. Perhaps even nostalgic. "It's a Coast thing. A legend, of sorts. Once every thousand years or so, a bright glow the color of amethyst illuminates the horizon over the Eversea, heralding months of rough waters and meager catch. The last time it supposedly happened, the Sardovian Allfold hadn't even been formed and we sure didn't have airships yet. Most inhabitants of the Coast agree that the Fisherman's Warning is simply a myth, but those who *do* believe—the older ones, and this used to include my grandfather, may his soul find shelter in the willows—they say that the glow comes from the southeast. From Nenavar."

"Guess I'll let you know if I find any strange purple lights hanging around there, then," Talasyn quipped.

Khaede offered her a fleeting smirk. "Bring back a dragon instead. That would be more useful."

We'd win the war with even just one, the bowman had said at the stone longhouse in Frostplum. The memory that was so innocuous on a surface level sent a pang through Talasyn. Everyone was tired, but they didn't want the conflict to merely end—they wanted to emerge from it victorious. Because the alternative was to spend the rest of their lives bound by the chains of shadow and empire.

She would do her part. For Khaede, for the Amirante. For Sol, and for everyone else who had died to let the dawn break over Sardovia once more.

"How are you feeling?" Talasyn finally worked up the nerve to inquire.

Khaede went tense, her dark eyes narrowing into a glare. Then something in her seemed to crack, and she slumped as one would after an exhale that had been a long time coming.

"It's hard to believe. That he's really gone," she admitted, her voice thick with grief. "I keep thinking that this is a nightmare I'll wake up from at any moment. And then there are times when it hits me that I'll never see him again, and I start missing him so much that it hurts to breathe." Khaede twisted her wedding ring around her finger; the gold band glinted in the fading light. Her shoulders stiffened with determination. "But Sol would want me to keep moving forward. He went to the willows believing in the Sardovian Allfold, believing that we would triumph. And I'll make sure that we're going to. My child will grow up in a better world."

"They will," Talasyn said softly. She meant it with every fiber of her being, even if no one could tell the future. There were just some things that *had* to be true, because, if they weren't, what was the point in fighting?

Khaede reached over and patted Talasyn's knee. "Come back in one piece. I can't lose you, too." She leaned against the cypress trunk, withdrawing her hand to rest an open palm on her stomach. The sunset cast its burnished gloss over her face in such a way that it made the sadness lingering there all the more stark. Made her look older than her twenty-three years.

It was then that Talasyn truly understood: Khaede would be haunted by Sol's death for the rest of her days. A part of her would always be missing, buried with him in the canyon, lost forever to the Hurricane Wars. And although Talasyn knew that it was selfish to take her friend's pain and contextualize it in terms of her own self—although she knew that it probably made her a terrible person—she couldn't help but be oddly grateful for the lack of belonging that had plagued her all her life, because it meant that she would never experience such a harrowing ache. She couldn't help but think, *Thank the gods that I will never love someone that much.*

Talasyn met with Vela after supper. The Amirante provided her with a more detailed map and intelligence dossier courtesy of General Bieshimma, as well as a slew of last-minute instructions. Then Vela went over to the bow windows of her office, which offered a panoramic view of the Wildermarch in its moon-silvered splendor, her hands folded behind her back.

"I think that it will be all right," she muttered. "Even if they catch you, there is no cell—no manner of restraint—that can hold a Lightweaver for long."

"They won't catch me," Talasyn declared. It wasn't that she had a *wealth* of confidence in her abilities. It was more the fact that she couldn't allow herself to get caught, and so she wouldn't be.

"You understand why you have to go, don't you?" Vela held out an upturned palm. Wisps of shadow magic curled into the space above her fingers, the strands shifting and unfurling like smoke, swallowing up what rays of starlight were there to touch them. "It was a stroke of luck for us that the Lightweave and the Shadowgate can be summoned and manipulated with the same basic methods, but they are still fundamentally different in nature. There is only so much that I can teach you."

"I'm well aware," Talasyn quietly replied. "I need to do this so that we can win the war. Of course I'll go."

For Sardovia.

For Khaede's child, who will never know a father.

44

For myself. Because I have to understand why Nenavar calls to something inside me, and because I have to give Alaric Ossinast the fight of his life the next time we meet in battle.

She just hoped it would be enough.

The Hurricane Wars were coming down to the line and the Allfold's sole Lightweaver had to start doing *something*. At the moment, however, Talasyn knew only how to shape weapons and fight with them. According to the stories, the Lightweavers of Sunstead had toppled buildings and created barriers around entire cities and called down strikes from the heavens. The last time *she* had tried to create a protective barrier, she'd lost control and nearly zapped Khaede's wasp out of the sky.

The Light Sever in Nenavar offered Talasyn a chance for her magic to reach the heights it was truly capable of. A chance for her to actually be useful.

The Amirante closed her fist around the swirling darkness and it vanished. "Get some rest, then. You'll leave at first light tomorrow."

Talasyn had one hand on the doorknob when a question occurred to her. One that she'd wanted to ask for years but hadn't had the guts to until today, when it had never before seemed so stark that there might not be a tomorrow to ask it.

"Amirante? Before you defected—when you were still with the Kesathese army, I mean—why didn't you join the Shadowforged Legion?"

The older woman didn't respond for so long that Talasyn thought she never would.

"I was very young when I enlisted as a helmsman," Vela finally said, still looking out the window. "My abilities manifested much later. But I made the decision to hide them because—well, I didn't have a clear idea of what was right and what was wrong back then. All I knew was that I didn't want to be the person that the Legion would have required me to become. Had I given in to that darkness, the Night Empire would have swallowed me whole." Her gaze met Talasyn's in the glass, in the vague shards of their star-etched reflections. "You have a chance to end this, Talasyn. To become the light that guides us out of the shadows, and to freedom."

Talasyn leaned against the wall outside Vela's office, attempting to center her emotions. The weight of the Amirante's words hung heavily on her heart, but that wasn't what preoccupied her. In a little over twenty-four hours from now, she would be in Nenavar. At last, she would learn what was pulling her there.

Come off it, she chided herself. *Here you go again, looking for connections where there aren't any.*

As she had so many times before, she recited a mantra of cold logic to herself. Her parents were most likely descendants of the Sunstead Lightweavers, which explained her magic. They had, for whatever reason, left her on the doorstep of the Hornbill's Head orphanage. And she would never know why, so it was better to make her peace with that instead of live on wishful thinking, nurturing the part of her that believed she would still be able to find them again one day. It was better to go to Nenavar focused solely on the mission that she'd been entrusted with, and nothing else. Everyone was counting on her.

Slow, shuffling footsteps resounded through the quiet hallway. Coxswain Darius was approaching Vela's office, with the ponderous steps of one who carried the world on his shoulders. He stopped when he reached Talasyn.

"You're off, then?"

She gave a cautious nod, unable to speak. The coxswain looked—*defeated*. As if he'd been running on fumes for months and now there was nothing left.

"Not sure how much good it will do now," Darius mumbled,

almost to himself. He shook his head, as though belatedly remembering that there was someone in the hallway with him. "Word has just come in from the Highlands," he told Talasyn. "It's over. The King on the Mountain bowed to the Night Empire. And the Shadowforged Legion cut off his head."

Dread swept through Talasyn's veins in an icy wash.

Following the Cataclysm between Kesath and Sunstead, the Sardovian Allfold had been composed of the Great Steppe, the Hinterland, the Highlands, the Coast, and the Heartland. Now, after a decade of ground warfare and stormship battles, Sardovia was down to those last two states. Surrounded on all sides except seaward.

"It's *not* over," Talasyn insisted to Darius, trying to convince him as well as herself. "We'll fortify our defenses. I'll commune with the Nenavarene Light Sever and then I'll come back and I'll be there on the front lines—"

"What is the *use*?" Darius burst out. His words echoed off the stone walls, and Talasyn paled, remembering the Hornbill's Head orphanage, a time when a caretaker's raised voice heralded his palm ringing against her cheek.

Darius didn't strike her, of course. Instead, he continued in a quieter tone that was raw at the edges with despair, "What good will one trained Lightweaver be against the entire Legion? And that's assuming you'll even be able to access the Dominion's Light Sever. The Amirante is grasping at straws, Talasyn. We're—" He swallowed. His next words quavered on his tongue. "We're all going to die. The Shadow will fall across the Continent and Gaheris will show us no mercy. Why would he? We've been a thorn in his side for so long."

Talasyn stared at him. She had never witnessed a Sardovian officer crack like this—least of all Coxswain Darius, who had been as steady as a rock since the day they met. Across the span of years, a child in rags screamed as a Kesathese soldier who'd spotted her through the dust and the rubble pulled his crossbow trigger, the light inside her growing until he was burned to dust. She remembered Darius calmly leading her through the wreckage of Hornbill's Head, away from the Kesathese soldier's light-ravaged bones, assuring her that everything would be all right as she trembled, afraid of what had just happened, not understanding what she had done and how she'd been able to do it. He had saved her that day.

How difficult it was to reconcile that memory with the broken man before her now.

"I have to report the Highlands' surrender to Ideth," Darius choked out before Talasyn could respond, which was just as well because she didn't have the slightest idea *how* to respond. "Safe travels, helmsman. May Vatara's breath grant you a fair wind and carry you back to us."

He pushed open the door of Vela's office and shut it behind him, leaving Talasyn alone in the hallway to wrangle with the fact that the success of her mission was now so much more critical than ever before.

Before the sun had risen the next morning, her wasp coracle glided out of its dock and shot over the deep gash of the Wildermarch, cloaked in the gloom of nautical twilight.

No one had seen her off; she'd said her goodbyes the night before. A faint tinge of guilt mixed with worry waged within her at leaving Khaede, but if she didn't, there would be nothing left for any of them.

Forty-five minutes flew by before she lowered the sails—plain ones, replacing the striped cloth with the phoenix crest that would have easily marked her vessel as Sardovian—and gradually brought down the lever that controlled the Squallfast-infused aether hearts, reducing speed as she slipped into the zigzagging ravine that was aptly called the Shipsbane.

She needed to concentrate here. Navigating the sharp and rocky turns in daytime was already a challenge for even the most veteran of helmsmen, and as this was a covert mission, the Firewarren-powered lamps affixed to her tiny airship's bow were dimmed. However, despite her concerns, the wasp wove through the treacherous ravine with minimal trouble.

Still, Talasyn didn't allow herself to relax until the narrow maze of earth and granite opened up into an expanse of sycamore forest. She flew low, as close to the treetops as possible, the aether hearts emanating their fumes of greenish light.

Some of her earliest memories involved sitting on the front stoop of the orphanage at night and looking up at the rushing sound of the Squallfast, her eyes widening in wonder at the sight of coracles streaking overhead and trailing aether in their wake like emerald shooting stars. Back then, she would never have imagined that she'd grow up to steer one of these things. There had been no space in the Hornbill's Head slums for dreams like that.

As the sky lightened into a less oppressive shade of gray, Talasyn extinguished the fire lamps and unfolded the map that Bieshimma had provided, checking it against her compass to make sure that she was on the right course.

A Shadow Sever picked that moment to discharge, its distant guttural shriek piercing the air. She looked out the sidescuttle to her right and saw an enormous pillar of dark magic erupt from the earth in whorls of thick smoke, just past the Sardovian side of the fraught southern border. It blossomed over the treetops, inky tendrils reaching for the heavens like clouds of ash spewed forth from an enraged volcano.

Zannah's Fury, older Sardovians called it whenever a Shadow Sever flared into existence, ascribing the phenomenon to the goddess of death and crossroads. Talasyn could almost believe it, viewing the harrowing display even from afar. The Shadowgate had brought nothing but horror and anguish to the world.

She tore her gaze away from the billowing column of magical

energy. There were ten more kilometers' worth of forest to go before the coastline. If she sped up, she'd be able to reach the Eversea before true sunrise and minimize the risk of being spotted by Kesathese patrols.

It would be a lie to insist that she wasn't nervous. She didn't know what lay in store for her in Nenavar or if she could even get in—or *out*, for that matter—in one piece. She knew only that she couldn't let Sardovia down.

She had to keep moving. That was the only way to survive the Hurricane Wars.

Talasyn accelerated. Her wasp roared through the stillness as it sped toward the waiting horizon.

CHAPTER FIVE

Alaric knew that he would have to kill the girl eventually. The Shadow could only fall when there was no light to banish it. As long as the girl drew breath, she was a symbol for the Sardovians to rally around. As long as Sardovia stood, Kesath would never be safe. Would never be free to achieve the greatness that it was meant for.

All around us are enemies, Alaric's father reminded him time and time again. And the Lightweaver *was* an enemy. From the moment Alaric first heard the hum of her magic, first saw her on the ice, bathed in moonlight, bringing a golden dagger down over his legionnaire's broken form, he had known that there was no way that she could be allowed to live.

Which was all well and good, but he couldn't exactly set about killing her if she was nowhere to be found. She seemed to have gone to ground after Frostplum, sitting out the rest of the battle for the Highlands.

Alaric redirected all his frustration into glowering at the Light Sever as it spilled over the side of the cliff, a waterfall of radiance that shone against the rough, dark granite.

It wasn't a true Sever but, rather, the remnants of one. The cliff's summit bore several collapsed archways and piles of rubble, which were all that was left of a Lightweaver shrine, situated in what had once been the border between Sunstead and the Hinterland, before the Night Empire conquered the two states. The legionnaires originally assigned to destroy this Light Sever hadn't been thorough and, as a result, some of it had lingered deep beneath the bones of the earth, gradually rising to the surface.

It was a good thing, Alaric reflected, that Sardovia had withdrawn from this region long ago and a Kesathese patrol had spotted the stream of blazing magic before the Lightweaver got to it. The girl's power was formidable enough without the assistance of a nexus point.

With a final outpouring of the Shadowgate from splayed, black-gauntleted fingers, a slim section of the struggling Lightweave vanished and Alaric rappelled further down the cliffside, his steps quick and steady on the granite ledges. There were three legionnaires below him, poring over a wider fracture, chipping away at it with inky masses of the Shadowgate that curled like smoke amidst the air and rock of this high altitude.

"Work faster," he instructed once he had joined them. "The Night Emperor requires our presence at the Citadel." They were planning a multipronged attack on several Sardovian cities; the Legion would join the first wave alongside Kesath's conscripted regiments.

"Easier said than done, Your Highness," Nisene replied, her throaty voice just the slightest bit petulant. "This one's stubborn. For every inch we remove, a foot comes back, it feels like."

"We should just blast this section," opined Nisene's twin sister, Ileis. She aimed a fitful kick at a nearby boulder to emphasize her point. "Expose the whole vein so we can dismantle it at the root. I've got some shells in my pack."

Alaric shook his head. "That could trigger a landslide. It

might even bring down the entire cliff—we don't know how deep this Light Sever goes."

"And so what if it brings down the entire cliff?" Nisene asked slowly.

"There's a village at the base," Alaric pointed out. "I do not consider it wise to destroy their homes for the sake of saving time."

"Your father wouldn't care about Sardovian villagers," Ileis retorted. "If the decision were left to him."

"They are no longer Sardovian. They are Kesathese, like us." Alaric frowned behind his half-mask. "And I am not my father. The decision is mine to make, not his. I'm the one leading this mission."

The twins turned to him in eerie unison, subjecting him to the weight of sly, searching gazes from two sets of brown eyes glimmering silver with magic, peering out from identical helms that crisscrossed over their bare faces in whorls of obsidian, sporting winglike projections along the sides. He gritted his teeth against what threatened to be a migraine. Ileis and Nisene could drive a man to drink, and *not* in the flattering way that such an adage was usually meant.

"Prince Alaric's right, my ladies," Sevraim called out from where he dangled a little further away on fixed ropes, pouring shadow into light. He'd removed his helm a while back and the sheer amount of concentration required to dismantle a Light Sever had caused beads of perspiration to dot his smooth brow even in the cold mountain air. "How many times do we have to tell you two that not *everything* can be solved with explosions?"

"Oh, fuck off," Nisene said blithely.

Alaric's lips pursed in disapproval at the coarse language. Sevraim merely grinned, lopsided and amused, teeth flashing white against mahogany skin. Ileis cocked her head with interest, and Alaric dearly wished, not for the first time, that he had subordinates who were capable of attending to the task at hand rather than their baser urges.

He was stuck with these three, though. He and Sevraim had grown up together, had trained together since childhood, and once they became legionnaires and met Ileis and Nisene, Sevraim had immediately roped the twins into those antics of his that Alaric bore on sufferance. There was a certain irreplaceable kind of trust that came with having spent most of their lives fighting a war side by side. Within the Legion, their combat formations were the most seamless, and Alaric supposed that he tolerated Sevraim, Ileis, and Nisene well enough during downtime.

A soft fluttering sound made the four Shadowforged look up. Alaric was expecting a skua, the standard messenger bird of the Kesathese army, or a raven, the messenger bird used exclusively by House Ossinast. To his consternation, however, what descended toward him in a swift glide was a mop of ashen feathers, binding a slender bill and beady orange eyes into a plump frame.

A pigeon.

It landed on Alaric's shoulder with a gentle coo and extended a spindly leg to which had been tied a rolled-up scrap of vellum, waiting patiently while his legionnaires looked on in bewilderment.

"Is it *lost*?" Ileis demanded.

"Can't be," muttered Sevraim. "All messenger birds are aether-touched. They always fly true to the intended recipient."

"Someone in the Sardovian regiments has finally grown a brain and decided to come on over to the winning side, then," said Nisene. "Better late than never, I suppose."

"The *audacity*," breathed Ileis, "to directly contact the crown prince—"

Alaric thought that maybe he should add *speaking only when spoken to* to his mental list of desired qualities in subordinates.

He slipped the missive loose from the knotted twine around the bird's leg and unfurled it in his hands. The pigeon flapped its dusky wings and took to the air once more, soon vanishing behind the clouds.

It turned out to be two sheets of vellum, rolled together. Alaric scanned the message that had been hastily scrawled on one sheet, then folded up the other and tucked it into his pocket. "I have to go," he announced. The Shadowgate poured forth from his fingertips, ripping the message apart until it was nothing but ashes that scattered in the breeze.

"Where?" Nisene asked in deeply suspicious tones.

"That's classified."

"Ooh, a secret mission," Sevraim gushed as Alaric began climbing back up the cliff. "Do you need a partner, Your Highness?"

Alaric rolled his eyes at Sevraim's transparent attempt to escape the current tedium. "Negative. The three of you will stay here and finish dismantling the Sever; then you will proceed to the Citadel for the meeting with Emperor Gaheris."

"Without you?" Ileis prodded. "How are we to explain your absence to His Majesty?"

"What makes you think I'm not off to do his bidding?" Alaric challenged, scrambling onto another ledge without looking back.

"You aren't," Nisene called out.

He smirked to himself as he climbed higher. "Just tell him that I have an urgent matter to take care of."

Upon reaching the summit, Alaric headed straight to where their four wolves were docked on a large, partially collapsed platform that rose up from the sea of temple ruins. So named for their pointed snouts, the coracles gleamed jet-black in the early-afternoon sun, their barrel-chested hulls bearing the Kesathese chimera in silver paint. Alaric slid into the well of his coracle, raised its black sails, and took off, the wolf's prow slicing through the air like a scimitar, its aether hearts spitting out iridescent fumes of emerald green as it soared over the cliffs. Toward the Eversea.

Here is a token of good faith, the message had begun. *Exchanged for the hope of clemency.*

It could only have been a matter of time before a Sardovian officer switched sides, Alaric supposed, but the turncoat really couldn't have picked a better moment. If they could get information on the Allfold's defenses, it would assure the success of the Night Empire's upcoming attack—one that would be launched on such a scale as had never been seen before on the Continent, and thus bore the equivalent amount of risk.

And as for the information that the turncoat had *already* shared . . .

Alaric dug into his pocket for the map that the pigeon had brought him and perused it, mentally charting the most expedient route. The Lightweaver had over half a day's lead on him but he was confident that he would be able to catch up. If not in the air, then on land, within the borders of Nenavar. He had to stop her before she reached the Dominion's Light Sever.

Alaric did his best to ignore the cynical inner voice telling him that if he had just cut her down on the frozen lake a fortnight ago, he wouldn't have had to abandon all his other responsibilities for this wild chase that already had the makings of a diplomatic crisis stamped all over it. No matter what, Gaheris would be furious once he learned that Alaric had acted on new intelligence without consulting him. After all, what if this was a trap? And if it wasn't, and the worst-case scenario happened, the Night Emperor would find out that his heir had angered the Zahiya-lachis by trespassing on her realm. Either way, the consequences were going to be severe.

It would be far kinder, Alaric thought sardonically, for the Nenavarene to execute him instead of handing him back to his father.

Still, there was no other choice. In all his twenty-six years, Alaric had never seen the Sardovian Lightweaver's ilk before. She was a slip of a thing who bulldozed her way through combat with willpower like iron, besting him and one of his deadliest legionnaires even though she had neither legitimate training nor regular access to a nexus point. With the latter, there was a very real possibility that she would be unstoppable.

He really *should* have just finished her that night on the outskirts of Frostplum. But Alaric had been . . . *fascinated*. Perhaps it was too generous a term, but that was honestly how he'd felt. They'd been surrounded by a plethora of dark barriers, each one strong enough to shred her into a million pieces despite her built-in resistance, but he hadn't let that happen. He'd followed some *impulse* and waved the barriers aside. She'd been a frightened little rabbit at first and he'd put her through her paces on the ice, under the seven moons, studying the way she moved, the way she bared her teeth at him, the way the aether gilded her olive skin as her features twisted from fearful to murderous. The way her narrowed eyes shone golden with her magic, reflecting the distant fires of the battlefield.

Then she'd cracked her skull against his and stabbed him in the shoulder, and he'd spent the next few days concussed and unable to use his right arm. Once he was more or less recovered, his father had meted out the necessary punishment for allowing the first Lightweaver to crop up in nineteen years to escape, and Alaric had been unable to get to his feet or do much of anything for another few days.

He had let his guard down and he had let the girl go, and now everything that Kesath had achieved—had toiled and risen above the fray to become—was in jeopardy.

The end of the Hurricane Wars was in sight. Sardovia was cornered, and cornered animals were the most dangerous. Affording them any sort of advantage at this point could spell disaster for the Night Empire.

All around us are enemies.

Sunstead had attacked Kesath when they learned about the stormship prototype that his grandfather King Ozalus's Enchanters were building. The Lightweavers had wanted to steal the technology for themselves. They had killed thousands of Kesathese, including Alaric's grandfather, to do it. And the rest of the Sardovian Allfold had simply stood by and watched.

If not for the Lightweavers, Ozalus might still be alive and Gaheris wouldn't have been thrust into power ill-prepared and in mourning, his country already at war.

If not for the Lightweavers, Gaheris wouldn't have become what he was today and Alaric's mother wouldn't have fled the Continent.

Alaric's jaw clenched. His mind was once again going down a treacherous path. As he steered his airship over an expanse of barren gorges and waterfalls sluggish from the cold, so too did he steer his thoughts in a direction more befitting the crown prince of the Night Empire and the Master of the Shadowforged Legion.

Gaheris had the strength and courage to do what was necessary, even if all of Lir itself were against him. Alaric was proud to be his son.

And he needed to focus on what he had to do: get into Nenavar; kill the girl.

Talasyn, Alaric thought, the name summoned from the turncoat's message as his wolf glided over the rocky south-eastern coastline. *Her name is Talasyn.*

CHAPTER SIX

On first approach, the Nenavar Dominion was exactly as the map suggested: an endless array of islands. What it hadn't shown was how verdant they were, embedded in deep blue waters, like beads of jade scattered carelessly on a bed of sapphire silk. They glowed in the fiery light of the rising sun, beckoning Talasyn closer.

The sheer beauty of it took her breath away.

Growing up on the landlocked Great Steppe, Talasyn had often dreamed of seeing the ocean and had always been hungry for tales of water in such mind-boggling amounts, and fighting for Sardovia had taken her everywhere on the Continent *but* the coasts, it seemed. When the azure waves first stretched out below her tiny airship in the daylight, completely unimpeded by any form of land whatsoever, it had been a welcome thrill. However, at some point around the ten-hour mark, she'd started to consider that perhaps there was such a thing as *too much* water.

Still, Nenavar more than made up for the wearisome journey, even just from the air. Its beaches alone were a wonder that Talasyn had never imagined possible: soft and gentle, curling along the blue-green shallows in ribbons of pearlescent sand, dotted with spiky-leaved palm trees that swayed and dropped their round brown fruits in the breeze. The water was so clear that she could see schools of fish darting amidst mossy ochre seagrass and rainbow-hued corals rippling along with the current.

This land, it—it *filled* something in her. After being both intrigued and curiously unsettled by stories of this archipelago all her life, she had finally reached it: she was soaring over these strange shorelines that glinted like a promise, that felt as though they had been waiting for her.

And then the world turned *violet*, and in her surprise Talasyn nearly sailed her wasp into the damn ocean.

It began with a shivering at the edges, as though some great hand were tugging at the fabric of reality to expose the bones of aetherspace underneath. The air *warped*. Plumes of brilliant plum-shaded magic erupted from somewhere in the heart of the archipelago, unfurling over green jungle and white sands and blue waters, setting the sky within a radius of several miles ablaze with its translucent mist that spread above the islands like flickering flames.

Once every thousand years or so, a bright glow the color of amethyst illuminates the horizon, Khaede had said. This, then, was the Fisherman's Warning that the Sardovian Coast spoke of—and it was a Sever. But for which dimension in aetherspace, Talasyn had no idea. She'd never even heard of violet-hued magic before. When distilled into aether hearts, the Squallfast was green, the Rainspring was blue, the Firewarren was red, and the Tempestroad was white. Each of their Severs were plentiful on the Continent, but there had never been any evidence of a significant presence of their corresponding aethermancers, unlike the Shadowforged and Lightweavers.

Or there *might* have been, in times past. There was quite a multitude of blank spaces between recorded eras, times from which only the barest scraps of writings or artifacts had been unearthed. Perhaps it was merely lost to history, some great migration of Windcallers and Rainsingers and Firedancers and Thunderstruck, brought about by the power struggles that had plagued the ancient Continent before the Allfold was formed. That alliance had provided only a fleeting dream of peace in the end.

Nonetheless, it was generally accepted that, aside from Enchanters, the Continent had largely only ever been home to Shadowforged, whose Severs were as black as midnight, and Lightweavers, whose Severs were said to resemble pillars of blazing sunlight.

This Sever, here in Nenavar, belonged to a type of magical energy that Talasyn doubted anyone back home knew about. Did that mean that there was a unique breed of aethermancers among the Nenavarene as well? Her curiosity heightened along with the sunrise as she watched from her little airship while the magic unfolded. The amethyst glow was nowhere big enough to be seen from Sardovia, but there were likely several Severs and perhaps they very occasionally discharged all at once, which might have been how the Coast's tale of the Fisherman's Warning came about. She wondered what the effects of this new dimension were. Rather than take the form of any particular element—wind or water or fire or storm—it seemed to be pure energy, like the Lightweave and the Shadowgate. Could its aethermancers also craft weapons?

It took a while, but Talasyn finally tore her gaze away from the strange magic and coaxed her wasp into a slow descent. The odd Sever stilled, its violet glow abating, just as she pulled up level several inches above the ocean's surface.

Talasyn was to take the circuitous route, avoiding the watchful port cities and the main inland roads. She steered clear of the central bulk of the archipelago and into a cluster of outlying islands shrouded in mist that swallowed her wasp whole. For the next several minutes, she flew low over the water, every fiber of her being tense. The rumble of aether hearts was too loud in the silence. She half expected a Nenavarene patrol to catch her or a dragon to swoop down at any moment.

But there was no sign of movement on any of the surrounding islands. None that she could make out through the veils of fog, anyway. And neither Bieshimma nor his crew had spotted any hint of the gigantic fire-breathing beasts that were rumored to prowl the Dominion.

Perhaps the dragons *were* just a myth. A story to scare off outsiders.

Once Talasyn made it to the shore of the island where the Light Sever was located, she soared higher, sails catching the breeze, avoiding the patchwork of rooftops that indicated villages and the glinting metallic towers that were obviously cities, all nestled amidst clouds of greenery as though they were part of the jungle itself. When she docked her wasp, it was inside a large cave halfway up one of the many rolling mountains—a tight fit, and she estimated that she would have to hike for several hours to reach her destination, but at least it minimized the risk of any Nenavarene coming across an airship of foreign make.

She clambered out of the well and, with the aid of her trusty compass, carefully marked the cave's location on the map that Bieshimma had provided. Even if she were to reach the Light Sever and successfully commune with it—and that was a big *if*—she would be in worse trouble if she got lost looking for her only means of escape.

She shoved a generous piece of hardtack into her mouth, chewing perfunctorily before washing it down with a swig from her waterskin. Once the meager nourishment was in her system, she began the long trek.

*

The miles between the cave and the nexus point were covered in dark green jungle, and the first problem that she ran into was the humidity.

Gods, the humidity.

Although most of Sardovia was cold year-round, Talasyn had spent fifteen years of her life on the Great Steppe, a region of extremes. She was used to the scorching, arid heat of a northern summer, not Nenavar's damp variety that lay heavy on the skin and filled the lungs even in the dense, overgrown places where sunlight was a distant dream. She'd stripped down to a thin white smock and brown breeches, and she still felt as if she was being crushed in the World-Father's unwashed armpit, drenched in perspiration and her breath emerging in harsh bursts after five hours' hiking beneath a canopy of various types of trees that she had no names for. Their branches were draped in profusions of vines that she had to hack her way through with a light-woven cutlass.

The undergrowth contained a host of vegetation that was new to her as well. There were ferns that fanned out in plaited rows along the tree trunks, creeping shrubs whose leaves folded shut when she brushed past them, and plants that dangled red-lipped sacs filled with a clear liquid in which all manner of small creatures drowned. There were black flowers shaped like bat's wings, yellow petals that looked like frothy trumpets, and enormous velvety blooms speckled white that gave off a foul stench of decaying flesh, making her gag.

The jungle also teemed with insects and birdsong, the branches overhead replete with jewel-scaled reptiles and furry brown things that could have been either rodents or primates skittering out of sight at her approach. There didn't seem to be another human around for miles.

It was worlds away from Sardovia in every sense.

Talasyn hadn't objected much to being sent on this dangerous mission because she had another goal—one that she'd kept from her superiors and even Khaede. No one knew about the disquieting sensations that hearing about Nenavar made her feel. No one knew about the uneasy familiarity that she felt for it. She'd set out for the Dominion expecting . . . *something*. What that something *was*, she couldn't rightfully say. She was searching for answers to questions that she couldn't put into words.

Thus far, however, there didn't appear to be a lot of answers here. She was tired, coated in grime, and sweating out more water than she could drink without prematurely exhausting her supply.

In the afternoon, Talasyn climbed a tree to work out where she was. The tree looked sort of like an old man, hunched in on itself and covered in wispy leaves, its gnarled branches dripping with aerial roots. The bark was twisted as well, as though made of ropes of wood braided together, and it was riddled with hollows.

With the help of a grappling hook and the juts in the rough, thick trunk that served as natural footholds, it was an easy ascent, and along the way she encountered dozens more of those furry brown creatures that she realized now were *definitely* primates, even though they were no bigger than her palm. Most fled, but some froze where they clung to the branches with elongated digits and watched her guardedly through round golden eyes that took up nearly all of the space in their tiny skulls.

"Don't mind me," Talasyn huffed as she scrambled past three of the creatures. "Just passing through."

These were the first words that she'd spoken out loud to another living thing in over a day. Far from being honored, though, the three little rat-monkey-things chittered indignantly and—*disappeared*.

There was no fanfare to it. One moment they were there and the next they were gone.

They had *probably* just scurried into the leaves too quickly for her to catch, but the overall impression was that they had willed themselves out of existence to avoid her talking to them any further.

"Story of my life," Talasyn muttered.

By her reckoning, the tree was four hundred feet tall. When she hoisted herself onto one of the uppermost branches and broke through the jungle canopy, it was to the sight of this foreign wilderness spread out all around her in ridges that were carpeted a deep, dense green. The pale blue silhouettes of even more mountains loomed in the distance, wreathed in fog. Flocks of birds soared past her perch, their plumage splashed with every bright hue imaginable, their tailfeathers streaming out behind them like sprays of aether, filling the air with the flutter of iridescent wings and the mellifluous lilt of a song like glass chimes.

The wind blew cool on Talasyn's face, a staggering relief from the humidity. It carried with it the scents of rain and sweet fruit. It carried memory on its monsoon currents, vague and fleeting but enough to make her tighten her grip on the branch for fear that she might fall from how it made her reel.

I've been here before. The notion took root in her mind and it refused to let go. *I know this place.* Images and sensations raced through her in a tumultuous stream, swiftly shifting, ever shapeless. But she thought that she could grasp—

Rough hands on her face. A city of gold. A woman's voice telling her, *I will always be with you. We will find each other again.*

Wetness spattered Talasyn's cheeks. At first, she assumed that the rains had come, but, when the liquid dripped in through the corner of her mouth, it tasted like salt. She was crying for the first time in years. She was crying for something she couldn't name, for someone she couldn't remember. The wind rustled through the swaying treetops and it whisked her tears away.

I'm sitting in a tree in the middle of the jungle and sobbing, she thought mournfully. *I am the most ridiculous person alive.*

Then there was a sound like thunder. A pillar of light rose up from one of the northern peaks. It suffused the jungle canopy with golden radiance, a firebrand so bright that it was almost solid, rippling with threads of silver aether as it shot toward the sky.

Talasyn stared at the conflagration, her heart pounding. The Light Sever beckoned to her; it called to something in her blood. She nearly cried out in protest when it vanished, the pillar swirling and crackling with renewed intensity before it finally winked out of existence and left no sign that it had ever been there at all.

She began clambering down the tree. She vowed that she would find out why Nenavar felt so familiar. The answer was *here*, somewhere. It was within her reach.

But first things first—she had to get to the Light Sever.

It rained in the late afternoon, a deluge that turned the ground to mud. Talasyn sought shelter in another old-man tree, tucking herself into one of its many hollows with her legs curled against her chest.

She dozed in that position while waiting for the downpour to subside. It could hardly have been helped; she hadn't gotten a wink of sleep since she left the Wildermarch. She dreamed of Hornbill's Head again, and of the stormship that had taken everything, although she hadn't had much to begin with. This time, at the end of the dream—when the hurricanes had shattered all the wooden bridges, when the grasslands had reclaimed the city and dust had flooded through its ruins—there was a woman, holding her close, stroking the back of her head, telling her that things would be all right and she had to be strong.

The woman in the dream called Talasyn by another name.

One that wasn't hers, one that faded from her memory as soon as she woke up, along with the woman's face.

Talasyn's eyes flew open. The rain had stopped, and the jungle was damp and drowsy in the twilight. She eased out of the hollow and resumed her trek, conscious of how much time she'd wasted. Her every step vibrated with nervous energy as she tried to recall more details from her dream.

Was the woman the same person whose voice had come rushing back to her on the crests of the Nenavarene wind? Who had touched her face with rough hands?

And what about that city of gold? She'd never been to any such place as she'd glimpsed amidst those wild monsoon currents. Why had her mind's eye afforded her that image only now? Had it been a city *here*, within the borders of the Dominion?

There was a part of her that fled from that thought the moment it surfaced. It filled her with fear, because she wasn't supposed to tell anyone . . .

Tell anyone *what*?

If they found out, she would be hunted.

No, that was what *Vela* had told her, about being a Lightweaver.

Right?

"I'm going mad in this heat," Talasyn said, because she was apparently in the habit of talking to herself now. "Absolutely stark raving."

The jungle was gradually plunged into darkness. The trees grew close together here, and not even the seven moons could penetrate their leafy roof. Talasyn's light-woven cutlass now served to illuminate her path in addition to slicing through the vines that blocked it. She had hoped to catch a break from the sweltering heat by nightfall, but no such luck. The evening was muggy, sticking to her form in moist, warm sheets.

But she pressed on, deeper into the damp jungle. She could feel the Light Sever. The nearness of it.

As the ground sloped steadily uphill, the cutlass in her hand burned ever brighter, as though the magic that she had coaxed into this shape was being amplified tenfold. A strange taste blossomed on her tongue, weighty and metallic like ozone, or blood. Thorny shrubs scratched at her arms as she quickened her pace, but she paid the shallow cuts no mind. There was power here, old and vast, overwhelming her senses until she felt drunk with it, her skin prickling with goosebumps and her heart thundering against the bones of her ribcage, until, at last—

She gave a start of confusion and disbelief when the jungle parted to reveal a shrine. Perhaps one like those that Lightweavers had built all over Sunstead. And, just like those, it was in ruins. It looked as if it had been in ruins for centuries. Moss-covered slabs of sandstone jutted out haphazardly from the riotous undergrowth, their rough edges catching the moonlight. There were no signs of life.

Had Nenavar's Lightweavers suffered the same fate as the ones on the Continent? Had they all been eradicated?

Talasyn cautiously walked beneath a vine-entangled, half-toppled entrance arch and down a cracked passageway lined by pillars etched with intricate reliefs that she would otherwise have paused to examine, but she was focused on the nearby nexus point. Its pull on her soul was magnetic. It called to her like the monsoon winds.

The shrine was vast. A complex rather than a single building: snaking halls and rubble-strewn chambers, the doors of which had collapsed long ago. She negotiated her way through the debris and stepped out into a courtyard the size of a stormship hangar. It was open to the sky but already reclaimed by the wilderness, dozens of those enormous old-man trees having anchored themselves firmly in what was left of the stone facade, their thick roots and myriad grasping arms choking out the paved floor and the surrounding walls and rooftops. The seven moons circled the heavens, raining down a light that was as bright as day.

She ventured further in. At the center of the courtyard, amidst the tangle of shrubs and tree roots and overgrown grass, stood an enormous fountain, which was the only structure that appeared untouched by the passage of time and whatever destruction had befallen the complex. It was carved from sandstone, built around a depression in the flooring as wide as several trees clumped together, its spouts fashioned to look like snakes—or maybe dragons, she realized as she peered at it more closely.

This was undoubtedly the location of the Light Sever. Talasyn's every instinct screamed that it was so. The magic sang to her veins from behind the veil of aetherspace. She just had to wait for it to break through again.

"There you are," a familiar voice rasped behind her. The unmistakable shriek of the Shadowgate flaring to life shattered the still air.

Talasyn didn't freeze even as the hair on the back of her neck stood on end. She didn't say anything. She didn't waste a single second, transmuting her cutlass into a poleaxe and spinning on her heel, leaping straight at the tall figure clad in black and crimson standing several paces away. Her wide blade caught in the prongs of a shadowy trident, light to darkness, the resulting sparks glinting off Alaric Ossinast's narrowed silver eyes and his obsidian mask carved into a wolf's fanged snarl.

They'd met like this on the ice floes a fortnight ago, and he'd been a tight coil of menace and determination while she had been scared out of her wits. But this time was different—this time, she wasn't afraid.

This time, she was *angry*.

Talasyn set upon the Kesathese prince in a barrage of short, quick strikes that drove him backward even as he deflected with masterful swiftness. She was hoping to corner him against one of the pillars, but he managed to sidestep around her, bringing the trident down over her shoulder. She slanted her own weapon at a defensive angle, and her teeth *rang* from the force of his blow.

"You've been practicing," he told her.

She blinked at him through the haze of their intersected magic.

"There is some improvement in your combat technique, I mean," he clarified.

"I know what you meant," she snapped. "Do you make it a habit to compliment everyone who's trying to kill you?"

"Not everyone." His eyes flashed with a hint of amusement. "Just you. And that was *hardly* a compliment—I'm merely relieved that you're much more interesting to duel now."

She pushed against him with a newfound burst of strength, sparked by her ire, and she managed to slip free of the blade-lock. Once more they waltzed, in flashes of gold and midnight, over the stone and the roots, through the warm moonlit evening.

Talasyn didn't want to think about how she was almost *enjoying* this. There was something to be said about letting her magic run free in this wild and ancient place. There was something to be said about testing her mettle against a man like Alaric, and making him break a sweat even as she fought for her life.

But she wasn't *supposed* to be feeling anything remotely close to enjoyment. He was in her way; he was wasting her time.

Their weapons caught and held once more.

"How are you even *here?*" she demanded. She wasn't enthused about how shrilly the words emerged from her lips, but she was so *annoyed* with him. And he was standing incredibly close to her. "How did you find me?"

"You have a traitor in your ranks." He said it matter-of-factly, and that was somehow so much worse than if he'd been smug. "Your people are switching sides because they know that the war is already lost."

"Calm down, it was only one person," she retorted even as she wondered with no small amount of alarm who it could be. Someone close to Bieshimma or the Amirante, no doubt, for them to know about her mission and to have acquired a copy of the map— but she would deal with that later. She had to finish this first. The fact that Alaric had allowed such information to slip meant that he didn't intend for her to make it back to the Continent and alert her superiors. She was going to *enjoy* foiling that particular plan of his.

Talasyn kneed Alaric in the stomach, taking advantage of his momentary falter to put some distance between them, couching her limbs into a two-handed guard with her blade held to the right side of her body.

"I must admit that I went too easy on you, back on the lake." Alaric assumed an opening stance of his own, the hilt of the trident angled to the ground, his feet closely spaced. "You have proven to be far too much trouble. Consider my misplaced compassion formally rescinded."

"You and I have very different definitions of compassion."

When they crashed into each other again, it was vicious and relentless, both of them going straight for the kill with each strike. The shrine's ancient stone foundations shook and the jungle was ablaze with sound and fury. When they skidded apart after another exchange of blows, Alaric's gauntleted hand stretched out and unleashed tendrils of the Shadowgate to constrict around Talasyn's waist, lifting her off her feet and hauling her toward the screeching edges of the trident. Summoning all of her strength, she twisted her body in midair so that she slammed into *him* instead; his weapon and the crackling tendrils vanished as he landed hard on the floor of

71

the courtyard, flat on his back with her straddling his hips, her poleaxe transmuting into a dagger that she held to his throat.

"Who is the traitor?" she growled.

Alaric's fingers twitched. With a mighty groan, the tree looming over them from one of the rooftops was ripped apart by splinters of shadow magic. What was left of the trunk came toppling down over their heads, and Talasyn instinctively made to get out of the way—but, the moment the dagger was lifted from his neck, Alaric surged upwards, rolling her over and to the side. The light-woven dagger disappeared from her grasp and the ground shook as the dislodged tree slammed into the spot where they had been a scant half-second ago.

Now the one on her back, Talasyn glared up at the impassive, half-shrouded face above her. "You could have killed us both!"

"Given our respective objectives, it would probably save a lot of time if we died together," Alaric mused.

"You talk too much." Her fingers scrabbled over the stone tiles as she readied to conjure another weapon, but he was having none of it. He pinned her wrists to the floor with heavy hands, the sharp points of his clawed gauntlets raking into her skin.

And then the Lightweave . . . *left*. It fled from Talasyn's veins. That was the only way to describe it, the sudden absence akin to the immediate ringing stillness after a door had been slammed shut. Inside her there was—*nothing*. Absolutely nothing.

"What was that?" Alaric hissed, his body tense and strained on top of hers. "Why can't I . . . ?"

The ability to open the Shadowgate had apparently left him, too. Talasyn opened her mouth to issue some form of snappy retort, to rail at him for ruining everything and for being a blight on her existence and on the world at large. At that precise moment, however, a smattering of footsteps reverberated throughout the courtyard.

"On your feet!" a stern masculine voice commanded. "*Slowly.* Hands up where we can see them."

The words were in Sailor's Common, the trade language that the Continent had made its mother tongue centuries ago, but it was in a thick accent that Talasyn had never heard before. The light of the seven moons shone down on thirty armored figures that had, unnoticed by either Talasyn or Alaric, come swarming out of the ruins to surround them, taking careful aim with long iron tubes that had triangular handles and some form of trigger apparatus. More than a few soldiers were carrying what looked like metal birdcages on their backs, strapped to their shoulders and waists.

There was a gaping hole in Talasyn's soul where the Lightweave used to be. She and Alaric extricated themselves from each other and stood up. She would have shoved him away from her in a fit of sheer pettiness if instinct hadn't warned that any sudden movements would be ill-received. "If we manage to get out of this alive, I'm going to wring your neck," she promised him.

"*If,*" he emphasized crisply.

Talasyn calculated the odds of her being able to fight her way out of this. She couldn't aethermance for some reason, but she had her bare fists, her teeth. Eventually, she had to concede that there were too many soldiers and she didn't know what those iron tubes did, what they were capable of. They reminded her of cannons, a little, but—*handheld* cannons?

The Nenavarene who'd ordered her and Alaric to their feet stepped forward, allowing Talasyn to get a closer look at his armor. It was a combination of brass plate and chainmail, the cuirass embellished with lotus blossoms wrought from what appeared to be genuine gold. Its wearer was lean, with the calm, authoritative demeanor of a distinguished officer, a graying undercut, and dark eyes that stared at Talasyn—

—at first with anger, and then with some combined shard

of recognition and disbelief, and then with a sorrow that made her skin prickle.

The officer shook his head and muttered something to himself in a language that Talasyn could not parse but was unsettlingly familiar to her ears all the same. He raised his voice and issued a clipped order to his troops.

Streams of violet magic shot out of the iron tubes. The same magic that Talasyn had witnessed flaring from a nexus point earlier that day, but paler, more subdued. At the corner of her eye, she saw Alaric crumple to the ground and she moved to dodge, to fight back, but the barrage emanated from all sides. She felt lit from within by a rush of heat and static as several beams collided with her form, and then—

—*darkness* . . .

CHAPTER SEVEN

When Talasyn regained consciousness, her first thought was that she really ought to consult a healer as soon as possible. Getting knocked out twice in the span of two sennights could *not* be good for anyone's head.

Her second thought was that she was in a cell, somewhere. She had been deposited onto a small cot that was only marginally softened by a thin mattress and a threadbare pillow, the battered frame creaking as she sat up and looked around. There was a lone window high up the far wall, outfitted with iron bars. They were too closely spaced to squeeze through, but they let in generous amounts of muggy tropical air and silvery illumination from the radiant night sky. Enough for her to see, without any problems, the hulking figure sitting on the cot opposite hers, his gauntleted fingers digging into the edge of the mattress and his booted feet planted firmly on the floor—right beside his obsidian mask. Talasyn assumed it had been removed by their captors as she couldn't imagine one of the Legion willingly parting with his armor in this situation. The mask's lupine fangs snarled up at her in the moonlight, but it was quick to fade from her awareness because the presence of its owner sucked all the air out of the room.

She swallowed nervously as she realized that she was looking at Alaric Ossinast's bare face for the first time.

He wasn't what she'd expected, although she wasn't sure *what* she'd been expecting in the first place. Someone older, perhaps, given his fearsome reputation and his prowess in battle, but he appeared to be in his twenties. Waves of disheveled black hair framed pale angular features dotted with beauty marks. He had a long nose and a sharp jawline, the overall harshness alleviated by a pair of full, soft lips.

Talasyn found her stare lingering on those lips. They were— *petulant*, almost. Or maybe *pouty* was the correct term, and that was *not* an adjective that she would have ever guessed that she'd one day use to describe the heir to the Night Empire.

It was probably just the novelty of never having seen the lower half of his face before. Her gaze flitted upward to meet his, an act that brought her back to less unusual territory; his gray eyes were as hard as flint, regarding her with caustic dislike.

"How long was I out?" Talasyn demanded, matching Alaric's glare as best as she could.

"I came to shortly before you did. However, our gracious hosts have not seen fit to grant us the luxury of a wall clock." Unmuffled by the mask, Alaric's voice was low and deep, with a hint of hoarseness around the edges. It shouldn't have shocked her, but it did. It made her think of rough silk and honey mead in an oaken barrel.

Then he added, in a snippy tone that was quite effective in dismantling all her fanciful notions, "In any case, telling time is the *least* of our problems."

"Our problems?" Talasyn bristled. "You mean this mess that *you've* gotten us into?"

"There were two people creating a ruckus in that courtyard," he reminded her.

"One of whom shouldn't have been there in the first place!"

Alaric smirked. "I missed the part where you received an

engraved invitation from the Zahiya-lachis to make use of her Light Sever."

Talasyn sprang to her feet, agitated, and crossed the distance between them. "You were the one who followed me all the way to Nenavar to pick a fight!" she yelled, looming over him. As much as she could loom, anyway. She had the advantage of barely an inch even though he was sitting down. "The shrine was abandoned. I could have easily gotten in and out with the Dominion none the wiser. But you *interfered*!"

"I had to." Alaric's reply was pure ice. "You could not be allowed to access the nexus point. That would have put me at a severe tactical disadvantage."

"And I suppose that getting captured in a foreign land by people with a documented loathing for outsiders who can somehow take away our powers and wield magic that we've never encountered before is the *height* of strategy," she sneered, jabbing a finger into his broad chest. It was . . . irritatingly solid. It had no give at all.

He grabbed her wrist before she could draw it back. "I liked you better when you were afraid of me," he drawled.

"Well, I liked you better when you were unconscious. And I should never have been afraid of you at all," she retorted, flushing at the reference to their first encounter. "You're just your father's dog. I bet you've never had an independent thought in your head—"

Alaric stood up, crowding Talasyn in the space that she refused to cede to him. She attempted to pull her hand out of his grip but he tightened it, nearly hard enough to bruise. He was so close that she could *smell* him, the sweat and smoke of battle mingling with the lingering balsamic spice of sandalwood water. It was a heady combination and, coupled with the wrath in his star-cut eyes, she felt as though she was drowning, would drown *in* him—but she held her ground, lifting her chin, baring her teeth.

"You'll pay for that, Lightweaver," he said. It was a raspy promise, rolling off his tongue on the fumes of a simmering, contained rage.

She balled her free hand into a fist and punched him square across the jaw.

Alaric reeled backward and Talasyn advanced. "Tell me who the traitor is." She had some hazy idea of beating the information out of him if he didn't cooperate. They were stuck in a cell, after all, and there was nowhere for him to run. "Be good for something, for once in your *miserable* life—"

He pounced too fast for her to react. Before she knew it, he'd swept her onto her back on his mattress and he'd pinned her down, the cot groaning under their combined weight. He clasped her shoulders loosely as she lay sprawled beneath him. The clawed tip of one gauntleted finger dragged along the side of her neck, raking a path of heat and static across her skin. "Knowing the identity of some random informant won't do you any good." His eyes caught the moonlight, blazing silver like a knife's edge. "The Sardovian Allfold is on the verge of being eradicated. Nothing you do can stop it, especially now that you're so far away from home." The corner of his lush mouth twitched in a sardonic half-smile. "It's too late."

She stared up at him. Was he hinting at an impending attack? She had to go back. She had to warn everyone.

The door to the cell creaked open, and the officer who had apprehended them at the ruins walked in. He stopped in his tracks, raising an eyebrow at the sight of Alaric frozen above Talasyn on the cot.

"It would seem that this is a habit for the two of you," he commented wryly.

The prisoners were to be interrogated separately and Talasyn had the dubious honor of going first. Her wrists cuffed behind her back with steel restraints, she was escorted by no less than

78

five Nenavarene soldiers, two of them gripping each of her arms and one nudging an iron tube—cannon—*thing* at her spine. The other two flanked the group, hemming her in, those birdcage-like contraptions strapped to their shoulders.

Talasyn snuck surreptitious glances as the officer led the way down a narrow corridor of split bamboo lashed together with rattan vine. One of these birdcages had also been hung outside her and Alaric's cell and she suspected that whatever lay within was responsible for suppressing their ability to tap into aetherspace. She had never thought that such a thing would be possible, and she itched to know what lay within the cages, but they were covered with panels of opaqued metalglass shielding the contents from view.

Eventually, she was ushered into an austere lamplit chamber and made to sit at a table over which the pack that she'd brought with her from her coracle had been emptied, her supplies and navigational equipment arranged in neat rows. There was also water, a pewter cup full of it, outfitted with a wooden drinking straw. The soldiers placed the two birdcages in opposite corners of the room and filed out, leaving Talasyn alone with the officer, who took the chair across from hers and pushed the pewter cup closer to her.

The Nenavarene were *benevolent* captors, at least. Or they just didn't want her to drop dead of thirst before they finished their questioning. In any case, she was hardly going to refuse.

With her hands still bound behind her back, Talasyn leaned forward as best as she could and sealed her lips around the straw, drinking greedily. There was nothing subtle or polite about it. She drained the cup in seconds, not stopping until she was slurping loudly on air.

The officer observed her with a trace of amusement, but he didn't say anything. In fact, the amusement soon vanished after she'd straightened up. His dark eyes raked over every inch of her face until she fidgeted from the intense scrutiny and he cleared his throat in a manner that could have been considered apologetic.

Talasyn decided that, if she had to sit with her hands bound in an interrogation chamber, she might as well let loose with some questions of her own. "Those tubes your men carry—"

"We call them muskets," said the officer.

"All right, muskets," she said flippantly, trying her very best to not stumble over the unfamiliar word. "What was that magic that they fired? That *was* from aetherspace, wasn't it?"

"I gather that the Northwest Continent has yet to discover the Voidfell dimension," said the officer. "It is a very useful type of necrotic magic. It can kill, and it can also be calibrated to merely stun," he added, casually enough, but his meaning was clear. The next time his men fired at Talasyn if she tried anything funny, their muskets would *not* be set to stun.

The muskets . . . Her brow furrowed. The crystals that both Kesath and Sardovia mined to contain energy from the dimensions that they *had* discovered were the size of supper plates. Aether magic destabilized if it was contained in anything smaller. Not anything small enough to fit into those slim iron tubes. "What kind of aether hearts—"

The officer spoke over her with the air of one who had indulged somebody else long enough. "I am Yanme Rapat, a kaptan of the patrol divisions, charged by Her Starlit Majesty Urduja of House Silim, She Who Hung the Earth Upon the Waters, to keep our borders safe," he announced in a formal tone of voice. "The remnants of the Lightweaver shrine on Mount Belian are under my jurisdiction and, as such, the judgment for your trespass falls to me. Foreigners are not permitted in the interior without a dispensation from the Zahiya-lachis."

"And yet here I am," Talasyn muttered. "Where's *here*, exactly?"

"The Huktera garrison on the Belian range."

Talasyn had gleaned from Bieshimma's dossier that Huktera

was the collective name for the Nenavarene armed forces. And it was a relief to learn that she wasn't all that far from the ruins. Once she escaped, it would be easy to lose any pursuers in the dense jungle, regain her bearings, and make her way back to the cave where she'd stashed her wasp coracle.

But perhaps there was no need to escape. Perhaps this officer, this kaptan, could be reasoned with. "Look," she said, "I'm sorry for trespassing. I truly am. I meant no harm."

Rapat leaned forward and plucked the map from the assortment of Talasyn's belongings. "This, relatively speaking, is very detailed, considering that we are not in the habit of disseminating our nation's layout to the rest of the world. Aside from marking the Light Sever's location, whoever made this also charted the entire route from our harbor to our capital city. So that you could engineer your course to avoid the busy thoroughfares, I think. The most recent outsider to have gotten that far inland—thus, the only one who could have drawn up this map—was General Bieshimma of the Sardovian Allfold, who flouted our laws by not remaining in port and attempting to infiltrate the Roof of Heaven. The royal palace," he clarified, noting the confusion on her face. "A fortnight later, here you are, wreaking havoc at one of our most important historical sites. These are not the actions of a people who *meant no harm*."

Presented like that, the facts *were* damning. Talasyn tried to recall if she'd ever heard of outsiders being executed for sneaking into the Nenavar Dominion. Then again, if that was par for the course, it wasn't as though anyone would have lived to confirm it. Perhaps she would just be detained indefinitely—but that was another set of problems in itself.

Her willingness to go on this mission, and Vela's willingness to assign it to her, had hinged on a Lightweaver's ability to fight their way out of anything. Without *that*, the options were severely limited.

Talasyn's gaze flickered to one of the opaque birdcages in

the corner. If only she could figure out how they worked—*what* they were—and how to disable them. She'd already surmised that whatever they did to suppress aethermancy was contained to a fixed radius, given that the Nenavarene made sure to keep them in her and Alaric's periphery, but she had no idea how wide the area of effect was.

Following her line of sight, Rapat flashed a tight smile. "A sariman cage," he explained. "You won't find its like anywhere else on Lir. Most garrisons have at least a couple, but my men are the only ones who carry several while on patrol, precisely to guard the Belian Sever from unauthorized Lightweavers such as yourself. The fourth Zahiya-lachis commissioned the prototype as a countermeasure against the aethermancers. Such power could not be allowed to go unchecked, you see. Enchanters were useful, but the others . . . they were a threat to the ruling house."

"You drove them all out," Talasyn guessed. She saw the collapsed, ghostly shrine in her mind, tangled in wilderness. "Or you killed them."

"The Lightweavers, the Shadowforged, the Rainsingers, the Firedancers, the Windcallers, and the Thunderstruck all left Nenavar voluntarily countless generations ago," said Rapat. "They did not wish to submit to the sariman cages and the will of the Dragon Queen, so they went elsewhere in search of other nexus points."

Dragon Queen, Talasyn noted, wondering if it was literal or simply a part of their nation's mythology. "And what of the aethermancers that could access the Voidfell?"

"The Voidfell has never had any corresponding aethermancers here in Nenavar. My point is"—Rapat waved off the tangent with a dismissive hand—"there was no genocide. The Dominion is not Kesath."

Talasyn's jaw clenched. "So you *do* know what's been happening in Sardovia."

"We do," Rapat confirmed. "It is unfortunate, but we cannot help. Nenavar has survived for so long precisely because we do not interfere with other nations' affairs and they in turn do not interfere with ours. The one and only time a portion of our fleet sailed northwest, it ran into the teeth of Kesath's stormship." For a fleeting moment, the shadow of an old pain fell across the kaptan's features. "Queen Urduja was right. They never should have gone."

Talasyn was confused. "Did they sail without her permission? Isn't she the sovereign—"

"I am not the one being interrogated here," Rapat interrupted with the alacrity of one belatedly realizing he'd given away too much. "If you cooperate, perhaps we will be more lenient. Now, what is your name?"

She answered begrudgingly. It was a name that had been given to her at the orphanage, a play on *talliyezarin*, a kind of needle grass that was ubiquitous on the Great Steppe and had no discernible purpose whatsoever. She'd never liked it even on a good day.

Rapat fired off one inquiry after another and Talasyn responded every time with a combination of the truth and as much vagueness as she felt she could get away with. When he slid the map over to her and asked where she'd docked her wasp coracle, she marked a random location on the outer edge of the coastline. She *did* tell Rapat who Alaric was and why they'd been fighting—a vindictive part of her hoped that the kaptan would be unnerved by the revelation that he had the Kesathese crown prince in his custody and, therefore, the beginnings of a diplomatic incident on his hands, but his expression didn't change in the slightest—until . . .

"There remains just one more question to be asked." Rapat took a breath, as if steeling himself for whatever was to come, looking for a moment much older than his years. "What is your relationship to Hanan Ivralis?"

Talasyn blinked. "I have no idea who that is."

Rapat frowned. "Who are your parents?"

Her heart skipped a beat. "I don't know. I was left on the doorstep of the orphanage in the city of Hornbill's Head, on Sardovia's Great Steppe, when I was about a year old."

"And how old are you now?"

"Twenty."

Rapat's composure had slipped. A visible tremor ran through his frame as he stared at her, seemingly at a loss for words. Before Talasyn could ponder this odd turn of events, the door opened and one of the soldiers poked his head into the room, speaking to Rapat in the Dominion's lyrical tongue.

"His Highness Prince Elagbi is here," Rapat translated for Talasyn's benefit, still looking at her as though she'd sprouted several extra limbs. "I requested his presence. I think it best that the two of you should meet."

This only made the situation even more perplexing. Was it their custom for royals to interrogate random trespassers? When she left Sardovia, Talasyn had been prepared for a long flight, an exhausting trek, and perhaps *some* combat. She hadn't bargained on Alaric Ossinast figuring in that last bit, and she certainly hadn't bargained on having to encounter yet *another* hoity-toity title.

A few minutes passed before the man who was obviously Elagbi swept into the room. Despite his slender build, the Nenavarene prince's regal bearing still managed to ensure that he cut an intimidating figure in his pale blue tunic and flowing cape of gold silk. His graying hair was pushed back from his high forehead by a gilded circlet crafted in the likeness of two serpentine forms intertwined, and the face beneath the intricate arrangement of precious metal was immaculately proportioned and fine-boned despite the lines of age.

That wasn't the only reason Talasyn was gawking, however. The Dominion prince was also *familiar*, in a way that she couldn't place but nagged at her like a dull toothache. It was almost as though she'd seen him before, but that was impossible.

Wasn't it?

Elagbi's jet-black eyes had been trained on Rapat from the moment he padded into the interrogation chamber. He spoke to the other man in Nenavarene, which Talasyn felt was a *bit* rude—and also dangerous, if she didn't know what they were planning to do with her.

"Excuse me," she loudly interrupted. "I don't understand what you're saying."

Without missing a beat, Elagbi switched to Sailor's Common. "I was telling the esteemed kaptan that he had better have a good reason for summoning me from the capital in the midst of the succession debate—"

Elagbi broke off abruptly as his gaze darted to Talasyn. And stayed there.

She was no stranger to haunted expressions. She'd seen it on her comrades' faces when they spoke of all that they had lost in the Hurricane Wars. This was different, though: more potent on a soul-searing level. The prince of the Nenavar Dominion was looking at her as if she were a ghost.

"Hanan," he whispered.

That name again. Before Talasyn could open her mouth to demand who that was and what was going on, Rapat spoke up. "My men and I were on a routine patrol when we found her and another intruder fighting at the temple, Your Highness. They are both from the Northwest Continent. The other intruder is Alaric Ossinast, the Night Emperor's heir. She says that she was abandoned as an infant and she has no memory of her parents. However, she is currently twenty years of age and she is a Lightweaver—"

"Of course she is," Elagbi murmured. He ignored the news of Alaric's presence in the holding cell entirely, never taking

85

his eyes off Talasyn, who was simply sitting there and weathering the scene with blank confusion. "It's passed down via the bloodline, isn't it?"

"We don't know that for sure," Rapat hastened to tell him. "I recommend—"

"Have you gone *blind*?" Elagbi snapped. "Do you not see what is in front of you, that she is the spitting image of my late wife? And she can spin the Lightweave, just like Hanan. There is no doubt about it, Rapat."

He then said the words that brought the world to a halt.

"She is my daughter."

CHAPTER EIGHT

Talasyn had dreamed about this moment for nineteen long years. As she plodded through the long grass and the bitter wind of the Great Steppe and stole and sold what she could to scrape out a meager existence in the Hornbill's Head slums, as she curled up in whatever corner of the orphanage and then of the fetid streets she had claimed for the night, as she mixed seeds into water just for something to fill her stomach—and, much later, as she huddled in deep trenches with comrades that were now long dead, as she closed her eyes while storm-ships screamed through the land—her imagination had been her refuge, conjuring a different set of circumstances every time. She'd often wondered what her family would say when they found her, if they would hold her in their arms, if the only tears shed would be happy ones at last.

In none of even the most dramatic, far-fetched scenarios had she been in restraints, and she'd never imagined that her first words to the man who was purportedly her father would be: "I'm your *what*?"

"My daughter," Elagbi repeated, his aristocratic, copper-skinned features softening as he took a step toward her. "Alunsina—"

She sprang to her feet, some latent sense of panic spurring her to retreat further into the room, shaking her head. "My name is Talasyn."

For a moment, Elagbi looked as if he was about to argue. But Talasyn could feel the blood draining from her face and her eyes growing wider and wider with each second that passed, and such a ghastly picture must have convinced him that a more delicate touch was required.

"Yes, you are Talasyn," he said slowly. "Talasyn of Sardovia, who walks between this world and the aether. But you are *also* Alunsina Ivralis, only child of Elagbi of the Dominion and Hanan of the Dawn. You are Alunsina Ivralis, granddaughter of Urduja, She Who Hung the Earth Upon the Waters, and you are the rightful heir to the Dragon Throne."

"Your Highness, I must counsel against such premature declarations." Rapat looked aggrieved. "Despite the striking resemblance to Lady Hanan, Her Starlit Majesty would never accept—"

Elagbi waved a dismissive hand. "Of *course* there will be a thorough investigation for formality's sake. However, it will only confirm what I already know to be true." His full attention swung back to Talasyn, who noticed, much to her discomfiture, that his eyes were wet with tears. "I *know* you, you see. You were such a mischievous, tiny thing, always trying to yank this"—he motioned to the circlet that he wore— "off of my head every time I carried you. But I could never stay mad for long because you'd blink up at me with your mother's eyes and smile her smile . . . I would know you anywhere. Another nineteen years could have passed before we found each other again and my heart would still tell me that you were mine. Do you not remember your *amya* at all, even if only a little bit?"

No, Talasyn thought, *I don't.*

Things were finally clicking into place, however. The connection to Nenavar that she'd always felt. The dreams and visions that it dawned on her now had been memories all along.

She had gone to the Dominion searching for answers and here they were. But it had never occurred to her that she *wouldn't* feel an instant connection to her family once she was reunited with them. The Nenavarene prince was familiar, yes, but she was bewildered by the odd situation, helpless with her hands bound and the Lightweave blocked off. This was such a far cry from the joyous meeting of her childhood fantasies that she felt cheated—and *furious*.

"You *can't* be my family," she snarled at Elagbi as a horrible aching sensation burned through her chest. "Because that means—look, people dump their children all the time because they can't provide for them or keep them safe. You're—you're *royalty*." She practically spat out the word. "So, either you left me behind in Sardovia *or* you sent me there because—because you didn't *want* me."

It was a possibility that she'd always secretly feared but couldn't bring herself to acknowledge. She'd had to live on hope as she fought over scraps in the dirt with the other bottom-dwellers. The hope that her family loved her, that *surely* there was someone out there who loved her.

"You can't be my family," she repeated. "I won't believe it."

"Alun—*Talasyn*," Elagbi corrected himself, seeing her hackles rise as he started to call her by the name that was *not* hers, "please allow me to explain. Let's sit down. Rapat, take those blasted restraints off her. It is exceedingly bad form to treat the Lachis'ka like a criminal."

Lachis'ka? Had she just been insulted in the Nenavarene tongue? Talasyn glared at Elagbi as Rapat cautiously approached, sidling around her to unfasten the restraints. She shook feeling back into her wrists and stretched arms that had been locked in one position for too long, but she stayed where she was, on her feet. She might need to make a break for it should things go downhill.

No, she needed to make a break for it *anyway*. If the Sardovian Allfold was about to come under some brutal assault, as Alaric had insinuated, then she needed to *go*.

If he was bothered by her refusal of his invitation to sit down, Elagbi didn't show it. Instead, he remained on his feet as well, casting an imperious look at Rapat and inclining his head in the direction of the door. The beleaguered kaptan opened his mouth as if to argue, but then he appeared to think better of it, shooting one last searching glance at Talasyn over his shoulder as he left the room.

"Yanme Rapat is a good man," Elagbi remarked once he and Talasyn were alone. "A fine soldier, if still smarting a bit from his demotion nineteen years ago."

Talasyn couldn't figure out why she was supposed to care about Rapat and his erstwhile career in the regiments. Was Elagbi attempting to make small talk? *Now*, of all times?

He sighed. "I want to tell you everything, Talasyn, and I very much wish for you to let me, someday. However, given your current mood and the circumstances, I think that it would be best to skip ahead and address the issue of why you were sent away. Believe me, if there had been any other option . . ."

The prince trailed off, staring into the distance at some harrowing event in the past that only he could see, before speaking again. "When you were a year old, a civil war broke out here in Nenavar. My older brother, Sintan, led a rebellion. He amassed many followers, and they believed in their cause strongly enough to kill anyone who got in the way. They attacked the capital and routed our forces, and you and Her Starlit Majesty were evacuated in separate airships. I would have given anything for us to stay together, but I had to defend our homeland and our people."

Elagbi's voice grew low and tense. "You were in so much

danger. You were the Lachis'ka, the heir. Only women may ascend to the Dragon Throne and Sintan would never have spared your life, no matter how young you were, no matter that you were his niece. His ideology had twisted him, rotted him from the inside. I killed him myself a sennight later on the Roof of Heaven and, with his death, the tide of war changed and the Huktera managed to retake the capital and crush the rebel forces. Queen Urduja returned, but you did not. We couldn't find you. Your airship had gone dark over the aetherwave."

"Who else was on board?" Talasyn asked in little more than a whisper.

"Accompanying you were your nursemaid and two members of the Lachis-dalo—the Royal Guard," said Elagbi. "They were supposed to bring you to the Dawn Isles, your mother's homeland, but you never made it there. It's halfway across the world from Sardovia. I don't know how you ended up in the latter."

"My . . . my mother"—how strange those words felt on her tongue—"she's not Nenavarene?" Elagbi shook his head, and Talasyn continued, "Where is—"

She stopped. She already knew, didn't she? She'd heard Elagbi talk to Rapat about his *late wife*. Perhaps that was one of the reasons she hadn't wanted to believe him in the first place. If he truly was her father, that meant that her mother was dead.

"Hanan passed away shortly before you were spirited out of the capital," Elagbi replied, his sorrow shining through the span of years in such a manner that one could clearly imagine how it must have blazed when the wound was still fresh. "It was an illness. A swift fever. She succumbed before the healers even knew what to make of it."

Talasyn couldn't react to that. She couldn't pick apart the tangled thread of her mixed emotions and attempt to understand what she felt—grief? nothing?—for a woman she didn't know. Not now, on top of everything else. She didn't have the space.

So, instead, she asked, "How did the civil war start? Why did Sintan rebel against Urduja?"

It had happened around the same time as the Cataclysm between Kesath and Sunstead. Were the two events connected? Did the Nenavarene civil war have something to do with the airships that the Zahiya-lachis hadn't wanted to send to the Sunstead Lightweavers' aid?

Elagbi opened his mouth to respond, but it was at precisely that moment all hell broke loose.

Five women thundered into the interrogation chamber. Talasyn assumed that they were the Lachis-dalo that Elagbi had mentioned: statuesque and clad in heavy armor plate. They surrounded the Dominion prince in a well-practiced, protective circle, speaking to him in that lyrical language rendered fast-paced and urgent.

"Alaric Ossinast has escaped," Elagbi translated for Talasyn. "He is no longer contained by the sariman cages. We have to get to safety—"

Talasyn grabbed her map and her compass off the table and shot out of the room like a crossbow bolt, stuffing the items into her pockets as she ran. She had to subdue Alaric or, failing that, she had to get back to the Continent as soon as possible. Sardovia was in danger because of the unknown traitor and whatever the Night Empire had planned. There would be time to process everything else later. She shoved past the guards, ignoring the cries that trailed in her wake, running as fast as her feet could carry her down the bamboo corridors where the air rang with warning gongs, running along with soldiers carrying muskets that she already knew wouldn't do any good, not when Alaric had recovered the Shadowgate.

The Lightweave returned to her, too, about seven meters away from the sariman cages. It crashed through her in waves, bringing with it the burning. Some of the soldiers pouring out of the barracks tried to stop her—they probably thought that *she* was the reason for the alert—but she swept them aside with raw, shapeless blasts of blazing magic, their bodies slamming against the walls, their weapons clattering to the floor. Eventually she outpaced them all, darting from the garrison's main building and into the warm night, where the overgrown landing grid was littered with the collapsed forms of badly wounded men, where a scythe made of shadow and aether shrieked beneath a net of silver constellations as it slashed at the last soldier standing.

The man fell to the dew-damp grass, chest shadow-scarred but still alive, like the rest of his injured comrades. Alaric was showing a restraint that Talasyn had never imagined the Legion capable of; then again, he probably didn't want to put the Night Empire in hotter water with the Nenavar Dominion than it already was. Across the distance between them, she met his silver eyes, their corners crinkled with the smirk that she could tell hid behind the obsidian half-mask that he'd donned once more. She spun two daggers and ran at him while he stood and waited for her, his war scythe at the ready, crackling with deadly challenge.

He was so close, he was within striking distance, when she heard a multitude of footsteps clattering to a stop behind her. Followed by the low roar of the Voidfell and a searing flash of amethyst and a cry from Prince Elagbi.

Both Alaric and Talasyn turned to the stream of violet magic hurtling in their direction. Just the one, the other Nenavarene soldiers lowering their muskets as they heeded what appeared to be orders to stand down from both Elagbi and Rapat, but it was wide and unstoppable, nonetheless.

There was no time to dodge, no time to think. There was no time to do anything but act on instinct alone. Alaric transmuted his scythe into a shield and held it in front of him, while Talasyn—who had yet to master crafting shields or anything that couldn't be used to stab or club someone—flung one dagger at the oncoming violet haze, hoping to intercept it.

Her plan didn't work.

At least, not in any manner that she'd expected it to.

The instant that her light-woven dagger grazed the edge of Alaric's shadow-smithed shield, they . . . *merged*. That was the only way that Talasyn could think to explain what happened. Shield and dagger blurred into each other and, at the point of contact, whorls of aether blossomed like the surface of a moonlit pond disturbed by a stone. The ripples grew in size as swiftly as lightning strikes, encasing Alaric and Talasyn in a translucent sphere that shimmered black and gold with a combination of Shadowgate and Lightweave. The current of void magic collided with the sphere and harmlessly washed over it, trailing to the ground in wisps of violet smoke.

And every blade of grass that the Voidfell touched turned brown and shriveled, forming withered patches amidst a carpet of green.

Necrotic, Talasyn remembered Rapat describing this new dimension, and that was as far as she got with regard to processing what had just occurred when the protective sphere surrounding her and Alaric vanished. He wasted no time in making a break for the nearest coracle on the grid and climbing into its well.

"Oh no you *don't!*" she shouted, even though he wouldn't be able to hear her over the roar of Squallfast-infused aether hearts whirring to life. She scrambled to commandeer a coracle of her own, and none of the Nenavarene tried to stop her. Indeed, when she glanced over at the soldiers, and at Elagbi and at Rapat, they were all frozen in what seemed like shock, looking as though they had just borne witness to something impossible.

But Talasyn barely spared a thought for any of the Nenavarene.

The world of Lir had narrowed to encompass only Alaric's stolen airship as he coasted over the treetops. It wasn't long before she followed, her knuckles clenched white around the wheel, the ground falling away, the aether hearts shrieking, the jungle opening up into air and sky.

CHAPTER NINE

The girl was so *mad* at him.

Alaric found it amusing at first, but soon enough he had to admit that he was quite possibly in trouble.

The ivory-hued hull of the Dominion coracle was constructed from an opalescent, lightweight material that made it a dream to maneuver. It was roughly cylindrical and tapered at both ends, with blue-and-gold sails that flared out from port and starboard like wings and another set of sails that extended from the vessel's stern in the shape of a fan. After a few seconds of fiddling with the controls, Alaric discovered the levers that operated the airship's weaponry—only, instead of ribaults or repeating crossbows, what opened fire was an array of slender, swiveling bronze cannons. And instead of iron projectiles, they shot those strange bolts of shivering violet magic that lit up the night, their glow more intense than that which the soldiers' tube-shaped devices had fired.

This coracle was a marvel of engineering. An elegant yet deadly weapon.

The problem lay in the fact that the Lightweaver was currently manning one as well.

She chased him over the woods. Aetherspace surged through

her vessel's cannons, pelting him with wave upon wave of amethyst that took all of his skill and cunning to dodge. She was out for blood and he couldn't resist goading her, and another round of fiddling granted him access to the aetherwave. "This hardly seems like the time and place to have it out," he remarked into the transceiver.

"Shut the fuck up." Talasyn's voice echoed through the well, a growl of static-tinted rage. She set her cannons to stutter-fire and clipped at Alaric's sails. For him she existed as a silhouette against the moons in their different phases, sliding along the crescent of the Second, vanishing briefly into the eclipse of the Sixth, coming at him from the shadows of the Third's waxing gibbous.

"Aren't you in the least bit curious about that barrier that we created?" he asked.

"I am," she said silkily. "Retract your cannons and stop moving around so we can talk about it."

A chuckle rose in his throat, unbidden, but he hastily swallowed it back down. "Nice try."

He let her have her fun firing at him for a while before he pulled into a sharp ascent, spiraling in the air and then dropping back down behind her. He'd hoped to have the element of surprise on his side but, unfortunately, Talasyn's reflexes were razor-sharp, bringing her coracle into an abrupt about-face that he was mildly surprised didn't snap her pretty little neck. They hurtled toward each other, the strange magic spouting from the cannons meeting in violent conflagrations that trailed sparks down onto the jungle canopy, withering every leaf and branch that they came into contact with.

They were on a collision course. His brow knitted as he realized that she wasn't going to give way any time soon. Sardovia's lone Lightweaver had no sense of self-preservation. It was a miracle that she'd survived this long into the war.

Alaric swerved to the right mere seconds before what would

have been a devastating impact. His head spun with the dizzying move, but he managed to activate the transceiver again. "See you at home," he drawled, for no purpose other than to rile her, and then he darted up into the star-strewn heavens.

Talasyn didn't give chase, which was a rare show of common sense on her part, Alaric thought. After all, they were still deep in what had become enemy territory. Unless he missed his guess, the Nenavarene were not going to take kindly to their historical ruins being vandalized, their soldiers maimed, their airships commandeered, and one of their bird *things* set loose from its cage.

Remembering the bird made Alaric shake his head at how odd this country was. Shortly after Talasyn had been led away for questioning, he had pounded on the door of the cell, demanding to use the facilities. There had only been one guard stationed outside, young and spotty-faced and far too confident in the fact that the prisoner was cut off from the Shadowgate. It had been easy to take him by surprise, to wrestle his weapon out of his grasp and fire at the cage hung outside the cell. Alaric had feared that aether-based weaponry wouldn't work, either, but the nullifying device apparently only affected aethermancers, and the cage was blasted off its hinges and sent rolling to the floor by unchecked streams of magic that he didn't know how to control. He certainly hadn't been prepared for the twisted golden beak and the blaze of red-and-yellow feathers that had come into view as the cage shattered and the bird glided away with an affronted chirp, but the Shadowgate had reopened for him by then and he'd knocked the guard unconscious and crept through the garrison in search of the exit—until the alarm was raised and he'd had to *fight* his way through.

Alaric's mission had turned out to be quite the catastrophe and he didn't even have a dead Lightweaver to show for it. He would pay dearly upon his return to Kesath.

But, now that he was well away from the garrison and its

hostile forces, he had the opportunity to reflect on what the Nenavar Dominion's unique arsenal meant for the Night Empire. In addition to their lightweight but deadly coracles, their aethermancy was highly advanced; it had to be, seeing as they had tapped into a dimension of death magic that he'd never even heard of. They'd somehow outfitted even their smaller munitions with it when the only weaponry in Kesath built large enough to hold the required number of heartstones were the lightning cannons of the stormships. As if *that* wasn't enough, the Nenavarene also had creatures that could block both the Lightweave and the Shadowgate.

Even if the Zahiya-lachis was willing to let bygones be bygones with regard to this incident, Nenavar could still pose a problem in the future.

At least the dragons seemed to be a myth. For what felt like the hundredth time since he'd made landfall on Dominion shores, Alaric furtively scanned the skies and found nothing of interest.

He had docked his wolf in a clearing near the coast. No sooner had he entertained the notion of retrieving it when he began to consider the airship that he was currently steering. How fast it was, how gracefully it moved. How its dizzying array of controls could unleash magical beams a thousand times more powerful than iron projectiles. Beams that shriveled every living thing that they touched.

This was valuable technology. It would be the height of stupidity to let it go to waste.

And he had to hurry to tell his father about how his and the Lightweaver's magic had combined. He'd never heard of *that* before, either.

Alaric set course for the Night Empire.

Talasyn landed on a riverbank, thumping the control panel once the stolen Nenavarene airship had powered down. That failed to take the edge off her frustration, so she screamed, the wordless sound ear-splitting in the coracle's dark and silent well.

Abandoning the vessel, she navigated the moonlit jungle on foot, steadily retracing her steps back to her wasp. Occasionally she would hear the drone of aether hearts overhead and duck beneath the tree cover to avoid being spotted by what were most certainly search patrols. Part of her desperately wanted to return to the garrison and demand more answers from the Dominion prince, but another part was . . .

Afraid. It took a few more minutes of stumbling through the undergrowth for her to figure out that she was afraid. What if there was a thorough investigation and it revealed that she *wasn't* of Elagbi's blood, that her resemblance to that woman—Hanan Ivralis—was pure coincidence? After all, the whole thing was too outlandish to believe. She was a bottom-dweller; she was a soldier; she was no one. She was definitely *not* a long-lost princess.

Was *princess* even the right term? Elagbi had called her something else. He had called her the Lachis'ka.

The heir to the throne.

Talasyn shivered in the humid breeze. If she *was* Alunsina Ivralis, that seemed more ominous, somehow.

If they find out, you will be hunted.

Who had told her that? Was she simply mixing up Vela's warnings about the Lightweave with this startling new revelation? Or had it been the Nenavarene who brought her to Sardovia? *Why* had they brought her to Sardovia, to *Hornbill's Head*, of all places, instead of her mother's homeland?

So many questions, and not a single answer in sight.

Talasyn found Alaric's wolf coracle first, at the edge of the jungle, black and sleek against the moss and the leaves. Aside from giving the hull a petulant kick as she passed by, she left well enough alone. Let there be proof that the Night Empire had trespassed on Dominion territory.

Another hour of hiking brought with it the faint beginnings of sunrise and led her to the cave where she'd stashed her wasp, which was now playing host to a gaggle of alarmingly large fruit bats that darted away shrieking at her approach. Once inside her own airship, Talasyn stared at nothing for a good long while as she went over the events and weighed her options. But there really was no question as to what she was supposed to do, was there?

"I have to go," she said out loud, testing the words on her tongue. She balked at the prospect of leaving without a resolution to the mystery of her past, but the Sardovian Allfold needed her. She had to tell them that there was a traitor in their midst and that the Night Empire was planning . . . *something*. There was the family she'd wanted to find and there was the family she'd found along the way, and she knew where she had to be right now. She dreaded having to admit her failure to commune with the Light Sever to Vela, but there was no point in returning to the shrine. The Nenavarene were already on high alert.

As the wasp sailed out of the cave and into the dawning skies, Talasyn thought of Elagbi and the unceremonious way that their reunion, if that was what it was, had ended. She wondered if he could see her at this very moment, if she was a comet trailing emerald fumes away from where he stood on the Belian mountain range.

I'll come back, she vowed. Someday, when the Hurricane Wars were over and she owed nothing more to the bonds that it had formed. *I promise.*

Day bled into evening and then day again as Talasyn sailed northwest over the Eversea and made landfall in Sardovia. The wintry air was a shock to her system after Nenavar's muggy tropical heat.

There was more activity in the Wildermarch than was usual for such an early hour. Shipwrights were running checks on the carracks and the large-caliber siege weapons were being oiled and restocked. The distant horizon behind a cluster of outlying buildings glowed a nebula of various colors, which meant that the Enchanters were inspecting the stormship hearts. The air swam with the rustle of feathers as messenger pigeons carried important missives to and fro.

"Tal!" Khaede strode up to her just as she was about to head into the building that housed the offices of the Sardovian War Council. "You're alive!"

"You don't have to sound *so* surprised."

"It's far too easy to get a rise out of you, you know," Khaede remarked with a smirk. It was nice to see her playful, even if it was at Talasyn's expense. "How was your little trip? See any dragons?"

"No."

"See *anyone*, then?" Khaede pressed.

Talasyn lowered her gaze.

"What's that expression? What's wrong? It's all right if you weren't able to commune with the Light Sever. Honestly, it was a fool's errand—I always thought that. What matters is that you made it back safely and now you can go on *more* fool's errands—"

"It's not that." Talasyn stopped walking and Khaede followed suit. "I mean, I *wasn't* able to commune with the Light Sever, but that's only part of it."

"Well, go on, tell me everything," Khaede ordered. "But make it quick. The whole base is in an uproar. Not long after you left, we started getting reports of significant Kesathese movement, ironclads amassing on the border and all that. To top it off, Coxswain Darius has vanished; there's no sign of him anywhere in this entire blasted canyon—"

Talasyn blanched as realization set in. "It's him," she blurted out, seeing in her mind's eye the abject defeat on Darius's weathered, bearded face. Remembering how his voice had cracked when he spoke of how they were all going to die. "He's the traitor."

She told Khaede the whole story as quickly as she could, barely pausing for breath between sentences, not particularly caring that she would have to repeat herself to the Amirante in a few minutes. She *wanted* her friend to be the first to know everything. At first, Khaede listened stone-faced, nodding in all the right places, but the more that was recounted to her, the further her jaw dropped, until she was outright gaping at Talasyn.

"You're a *princess*?"

"Not so loud!" Talasyn hissed. She glanced around to check if anyone had overheard, but the few people that were also outside the officers' building seemed to be too preoccupied with their own tasks to care about a conversation between two helmsmen. "We don't know that for sure. And this is very sensitive information, don't go around *shouting* it—"

"Well, can you blame me? That was a lot of unexpected news to get in such a short amount of time," Khaede grumbled. She set off at a brisk pace, past the entryway and down the narrow brick corridors, Talasyn falling into step beside her. "Incidentally, I hope that Darius dies a slow and painful death. May Enlal's griffins feast on his liver until the Unmaking."

"I could tell something was wrong with him," Talasyn muttered over the hollow ache in her chest. "Before I left."

"Guess that makes you smarter than Vela." Khaede rapped sharply on the door of the Amirante's office, flinging it open without waiting for permission to enter. "Darius has defected— *again*—and Talasyn's a princess," she announced as she strode into the room.

"*Khaede!*" Talasyn scurried over the threshold as Vela blinked at her. "I *told* you, keep your voice down—"

"Oh, I'm *so* sorry, Your Majesty—"

"Don't call me that!"

"I'm almost afraid to ask what's going on but, unfortunately,

I have to," Vela interrupted. "Sit down, both of you. Talasyn, please explain."

Vela listened to the entirety of Talasyn's debrief with far more composure than Khaede had shown. She showed no reaction to Darius's betrayal, which wasn't to say that she took it in her stride; a mask slammed over the Amirante's features, as inscrutable as any crafted from obsidian metal that the Shadowforged Legion would wear.

After Talasyn had finished speaking, the silence that hung over the office was so thick that it could have been cut with a knife. *Summer silence,* she thought, a little frantically. The tense, oppressive stillness of high noon, when everything went dormant in the stifling heat that baked the Great Steppe. Only, this time, she was in the canyon of the Wildermarch and it was early in the morning, faint beams of sunlight filtering in through the windows, falling on furniture and charts and Vela's lone eye, which was staring at her as she fidgeted in her seat. Khaede had reverted to her usual bored, caustic self, slouching in her own chair and crossing her arms.

"I can't even begin to guess how your and Alaric's magic combined," Vela finally said. "I'll ask our Enchanters if they've ever heard of such a thing happening before. It might also be possible for you and me to replicate the effect, so we'll work on that as well. What I *do* know, for certain, is that aetherspace holds all the dimensions—including time. Perhaps that's why, as you got closer to the nexus point, you began remembering things a one-year-old would have forgotten."

"Perhaps." Talasyn was uneasy. It was all conjecture. What specific knowledge the Sardovians had amassed pertaining to the Lightweave over the centuries had been lost when Kesath invaded Sunstead.

"But Nenavar *has* to help us now, right?" said Khaede. "Elagbi, at least—his daughter grew up here and Tal's fighting for us, so—"

"Unfortunately, the Dominion prince doesn't make the decisions. That's the Zahiya-lachis's job." Vela pursed her lips. "And, after all the havoc that Sardovia has wrought within her borders, I am not so certain that Urduja will be inclined to assist us. Even if we *are* harboring her granddaughter."

"I would just like to state, for the record, that it was all Alaric Ossinast's fault," Talasyn said with as much dignity as she could manage.

The Amirante cracked a fleeting smile. "True enough, I suppose. Maybe we can try sending envoys again, when the situation has calmed some. At the moment, though, we need to concentrate all our resources on repelling whatever the Night Empire has planned." She appeared almost conflicted for several long moments, eyeing Talasyn with something like sympathy. Eventually, though, her features hardened into the resolute practicality that had been a major factor in Sardovia surviving for as long as it had.

"It's not a coincidence that Darius broke down when you spoke to him and that he disappeared just as Kesath's forces began massing at the borders of the Allfold. Not to mention the proof of both espionage and an impending large-scale attack that you obtained while you were in Nenavar," Vela told Talasyn. "Alaric Ossinast had no reason to lie—he believed in that moment that you were at his mercy. We should deal with that first, before anything else."

Talasyn understood. Sardovia's resources were stretched thin enough as it was; they had none to spare to help her in this matter. She was their Lightweaver and it was her duty to fight with them, and so she had to put the Dominion out of her mind for now. She'd already botched the mission to access the Nenavarene Sever—she couldn't botch *this*.

But still . . .

"There are other Lightweavers. Other nexus points," she heard herself say. "Prince Elagbi told me that his late wife"—

Hanan, the woman he thinks is my mother—"is from somewhere called the Dawn Isles."

"Too far away," Vela pointed out. "Even in a wasp, the journey would take a month at the very least. With Kesath on the move, it's time that we can't afford to spare. We're on our own."

Talasyn hesitated. She was gripped by a soul-deep ache. She wanted to talk to Vela about what it would mean if what Elagbi believed were to end up being true.

But one look at the tense strain in the older woman's posture was all that was required to dissuade Talasyn from this notion. The Amirante was visibly exhausted and, while she would probably never admit as much, Darius's betrayal must have cut deep. He had been her friend for years, and now so much information about the Sardovian regiments was compromised because of him.

Ideth Vela carried the Hurricane Wars on her shoulders more than anybody else. Talasyn couldn't add to her burden.

So she nodded, and she didn't say another word as she and Khaede waited for their new orders.

CHAPTER TEN

Although Talasyn and the Amirante attempted it many times, they were never able to replicate the barrier of light and darkness that had been woven in Nenavar. They couldn't reestablish contact with the Dominion, either, because the fighting came hard and fast, from all sides.

In the end, a month was all it took.

A month to bring a decade-long war to its conclusion. A month to tear down what was left of what had once spanned an entire continent. A month to destroy the idea of a nation and its states.

This isn't happening.

Moments pulsed like heartbeats, glinting in the arterial red light that flooded the world as a Sardovian stormship fell from the sky in a deluge of metalglass shards that cratered the streets of Lasthaven, the Allfold's vast capital and its final bastion in the Heartland. The Kesathese stormship that had dealt the final blow arced up, victorious, and drew parallel with the city skyline, unleashing a fresh barrage of ammunition over it. The enormous cannons embedded in its underbelly spat out lightning strike after lightning strike, etching swathes of rooftops in white heat before setting them ablaze. The sky of early evening rained cinders and smoke, obscuring the pale silhouettes of all moons except the Seventh, which was in eclipse, burning red-gold over the war-torn land.

On the other end of Lasthaven, it was *actually* raining. A second stormship, its midnight-black hull proudly bearing the silver chimera of House Ossinast, unleashed magic from the Rainspring and the Squallfast in the form of downpours as thick as sleet and gales so strong that they uprooted trees and houses, whisking them every which way while Sardovian soldiers and cityfolk scrambled to safety amidst storm and darkness.

This isn't happening.

The stray thought flitted across the surface of Talasyn's mind every now and then, as if the hundredth time would be the charm and she'd wake up to a reality where it hadn't taken Kesath only a fortnight to overwhelm the Coast and then another fortnight to sweep through the Heartland, effectively surrounding Lasthaven.

No one had expected Gaheris to use all of his stormships and his entire army in such a devastating assault. Kesath had grown in wealth and power precisely because of its strategy of accumulating resources from conquered Sardovian states, but the Night Emperor had apparently decided that wiping out all form of resistance was a greater priority. Most of the Heartland had been completely flattened, with countless dead. The Sardovians' base in the Wildermarch was gone and the last stand that they were mounting here in the capital was in the process of being utterly crushed.

The husks of lightning-razed mills and workshops proliferating Lasthaven's industrial district sheltered Talasyn and her two companions from the worst of the wind as they made their way through the ruins. The rains hadn't reached this part of the city sprawl yet, which was the only stroke of luck in what had been a truly *rotten* day.

"How's she holding up?" Talasyn asked, glancing over to

where Vela was being supported by a cadet. The air was thick with dust, stained crimson from the myriad fires, but Talasyn was close enough to see that the Amirante was having difficulty breathing, her complexion deathly gray. Blood soaked through the cloak that had been wrapped around her torso as a makeshift bandage, seeping out in copious amounts from the wound inflicted by a shadow-smithed greatsword.

After her frigate crashed, Vela had been attacked by the same giant Shadowforged whom Talasyn had encountered and taken by surprise on the frozen lake, a month and a half ago. It had to be him: she would have recognized his stature and the style of his armor anywhere.

Talasyn had killed him with a light-woven blade of her own. If only she had done so back on the outskirts of Frostplum that night. The Amirante was in bad shape.

"She's fading fast," said the cadet. He was still a boy, several years younger than Talasyn and shaking in his too-large boots but trying valiantly to put on a brave face. "We have to get her to a healer as soon as possible."

Talasyn squinted through the gloom. "There's a rendezvous point just up the street." Or what was left of the street, anyway. The one saving grace was that this district had already been obliterated and, thus, the Night Empire had focused its attentions elsewhere. The area was deserted, heaps of debris walling it off from the ground skirmishes scattered throughout the rest of the city.

From the moment she had saved Vela and the cadet from the giant legionnaire, Talasyn had been operating on the hope that the rendezvous system was still in place. The spots had been marked before the battle; there should be healers there, as well as teams to ferry people to the carracks for evacuation.

Not that there would be anywhere left to evacuate *to* when this was over, but she tried not to dwell on that.

A tower had collapsed onto their intended path; there was

an opening between the mounds of twisted metal wide enough for their party to squeeze through one at a time. Talasyn motioned for the cadet to go first. She then gently nudged Vela forward, murmuring words of encouragement to the injured, disoriented woman, whose bones felt impossibly brittle beneath Talasyn's fingertips. No sooner had Vela disappeared through the gap when Talasyn heard the shriek of the Shadowgate, crackling with sharp malevolence.

Fuck.

"Go," she told the cadet through the gap. "I'll hold them off." He started to protest but she interrupted him brusquely. "You need to get the Amirante to the rendezvous point, and someone has to buy time. *Go.* I'll catch up."

Once Vela and the cadet were safely away, Talasyn whirled around to confront the three helmeted figures emerging from the battle's mists. She slipped into . . . not an opening stance, not exactly. Instead, she stood stock-still in an almost meditative posture, assessing the situation as the Shadowforged fanned out, the better to launch a simultaneous offensive from different directions.

The figure directly in front of her was quite possibly the legionnaire who had carved out Vela's eye with a shadow-smithed knife the year before. Talasyn couldn't be entirely sure because their mirror image was to her right, identical in build and armor from head to toe, but it had definitely been one of them. The distinctive style of their helms showed their brown eyes, which regarded her with twisted delight. She'd encountered them the previous sennight as well, in a vicious battle onboard a Kesathese ironclad that Sardovian forces had tried and failed to commandeer. In her head she called them the Thing and the Other Thing.

"Hello, little Lightweaver," purred the Thing. "Lasthaven has fallen. The remains of your fleet are scattered. It's not too late to beg. Perhaps then we'll make this quick."

"I understand that this might come as a shock, but I don't exist to make your life more convenient," Talasyn said evenly.

The figure to her left let out a chuckle. He had a lithe build and a relaxed pose that belied the dark, crackling, double-bladed staff that he was casually resting on his shoulders. "I wouldn't banter too much if I were you," he hummed. "You might be in for a world of pain. The twins are already pissed off because you killed that big lug, Brann. They were sweet on him, you know—"

"Shut up, Sevraim," growled the Thing.

It dawned on Talasyn that Brann had been the giant legionnaire's name. She shrugged, trying for flippancy. "May his shade find shelter in the willows from Zannah's all-knowing eye, but, honestly, I doubt it."

The Other Thing, the Shadowforged to Talasyn's right, spoke up then, her black cloak rustling as a barbed mace materialized in her gauntleted fists, already slanted into an attack position. "You're finished, Lightweaver. The Sardovian Allfold is no more."

Talasyn spun two curved swords, one shorter than the other. They were like molten radiance in her hands, filling the air with golden heat. "In that case, there's nothing left to do but take all of you down with me."

The three legionnaires charged and she sprang into action, her blades of light clashing against staff and knife and mace. Talasyn made liberal use of crumbled pillars and toppled ledges, springing off them and spinning and slashing at her foes as she counted the minutes in her head, trying to determine when would be the best time to retreat. It had to be once Vela and the cadet were close to the rendezvous point, but already Talasyn was at a clear disadvantage, staggeringly outnumbered. Still, she had a chance if she could move *faster*, if she could strike *harder*—

There was a new flare of shadow magic from somewhere

else. From *someone* else. Chains of darkness wrapped around a sizeable chunk of fallen stone and hurled it into the back of Sevraim's hand a split-second before his staff could find its mark on Talasyn's skull.

Sevraim swore under his breath, his weapon winking out of existence. He rotated his wrist experimentally, as though checking for broken bones. "What did I do wrong *now*, pray tell?" he complained as Alaric Ossinast placed himself between his legionnaires and Talasyn. She could only stare, dumbfounded, at the crown prince's broad back. The spikes on his pauldrons glinted, grotesquely skeletal, in the glow of nearby fires.

"Find your own plaything," Alaric instructed in his deep rasp. "I have a score to settle with this one."

Talasyn bristled. As soon as the other Shadowforged had reluctantly melted back into the smoke and rubble, she brought her two swords together and melded them into a single sharp javelin, which she hurled at him with a fierce cry. Alaric brought up one gauntleted arm, folding it in front of his chest; the javelin crashed into a shield of shadow, and both fizzled out of existence. His left flank was unguarded and she didn't give him any opportunity to correct his stance. She was upon him in an instant, back to curved swords again, one blazing in each hand.

Alaric quickly conjured a whip from the Shadowgate, wrapping it around Talasyn's ankle. He gave a sharp tug and she fell, flat on her back on the ground, the wind knocked out of her by the impact. He transmuted the whip into a falchion and brought it down over her prone form just as she sprang up, crossing her swords in front of her, timing it just right, timing it so that the blades intersected over his, trapping it between them. And, just like that, she was looking up at the Kesathese prince's half-shrouded face for the first time since Nenavar.

They strained into each other. For Talasyn, the rest of the world faded, eclipsed by Alaric in all his danger, hawklike gray eyes burning down at her above the obsidian half-mask.

"Nice to see you again." His sarcasm cut through the air as precisely as any knife, the lethal edge of the shadow-falchion almost grazing her neck.

"Why, did you miss me?" she retorted, trying her very best to angle one of her blades in such a way as to stab him in the throat.

Alaric scoffed; then he pushed her away from him. She staggered back, regained her footing to fly at her opponent once more. They fell into a frenetic sequence of blows and parries and counterattacks, their footwork carrying them all over the ruins of the industrial district. Lightning rolled on beneath the Seventh moon's blood-red eclipse.

Talasyn was eventually forced to concede that she needed a new strategy. Alaric kept her on her toes while simultaneously being a brick wall who refused to budge, and she couldn't duel him forever. Not when Sardovian troops badly needed her help to retreat elsewhere. She banished the shorter of her two swords and transmuted the other one into a bear spear, its enormous blade shaped like a bay leaf and the length of its handle quite suitable for fending off a bear of a man while waiting for the opportune moment to escape.

Alaric regarded her quietly. His gray eyes were inscrutable, but he *had* to know as well as she did that the war was over. Talasyn's fate along with that of her comrades was written in each peal of thunder, in each collapsing building, in each wasp cornered overhead, in each crossbow bolt piercing through an Allfold emblem. After this battle, there would be nothing left of Sardovia.

"Perhaps you should just yield," Alaric said. His deep voice was hoarse at the edges.

Long day of shouting commands to kill people, Talasyn thought with a scoff. She brandished her spear, poised to attack.

He came at her with shadow-smithed sword and shield, and

the next time his weapon clashed against hers it was devoid of the usual brute strength. Almost as if his heart wasn't in it, which was ridiculous—wasn't it? He dove beneath her swing and then they were putting each other through their paces, light and darkness and aether illuminating their gloomy surroundings as the sky continued to fall.

She lured him away from the direction of the Allfold's rendezvous point. Their lethal dance of spinning, slashing magic carried them from one demolished street to the next, until they stumbled into a ground skirmish between Sardovian and Kesathese infantrymen. The space sang with crossbow bolts and ceramic shells as soldiers from both sides scrambled to get out of the way of the two aethermancers cutting a path through the field of combat. Light and darkness sparked and shrieked along with the metal zipping through the air, the bodies all around them slumping to the ground. The hulking shadows of the stormships drew ever nearer with each jumbled, blood-soaked moment that passed.

It was when Talasyn had to skirt around a splinter of a newly crashed wasp coracle that Alaric leapt at her in an overhead strike. Her spine nearly bent in half as she blocked with the handle of her spear, the intersected beams shrieking at her throat.

"It's over, Talasyn." His gaze was blank but he sounded— odd. Too quiet, somehow, too lacking in the triumph that such a declaration should have warranted.

She almost fell backward in shock. It was the first time he had ever said her name. He held it carefully on his tongue, as though testing the weight of it, his tone at odds with the mask that he wore, with its carven grimace of wolf's teeth, with the way that their weapons crackled violently mere inches from each other's skin.

"It's over," he repeated. As though he was attempting to calm her down, or to come to terms with something himself.

"*And?*" she bit out sharply. "Let me guess—if I surrender, you'll let me live?"

Alaric's pale brow creased. "I can't do that."

"Of course not," she mocked. There was a well of bitterness building up inside her. "You'll kill me quickly, then? A *merciful* death? The Shadowforged Legion loves promising me *that*."

He just stared at her. She had the distinct and unsettling impression that he didn't know what to say. She split her spear into two daggers and kicked his legs out from under him and, as he fell, she lunged . . .

Only to freeze as a stray ceramic shell rolled over the ground nearby and burst, the incendiary mixture within it hitting its critical point. A mighty stone column in front of her was blasted off its plinth, falling forward with a horrible, crumbling lurch.

Talasyn hated herself for what happened next. She hated how instinctive it was, how she didn't think twice. She glanced over at Alaric and some—*understanding*—passed between them, swift and white-hot like a lightning bolt. She hurled one of her daggers at the falling column and he followed suit with a shadowy knife of his own. The two weapons dissolved into each other and there it was again, that black-gold sphere, that radiant night, unfolding in rippled currents with a sound like silver glass. The column disintegrated upon contact with the barrier, splintering into thousands of tiny shards. The sounds of battle became muffled, as though Talasyn were hearing them through water.

Alaric got to his feet, his every move slow and measured as his predatory gaze stayed fixed on her. She clenched her fists at her sides as nets of magic glimmered around their forms, casting a charged veil through which the Seventh in its blood-red eclipse still managed to burn bright.

He was far enough away from her that the column wouldn't have so much as grazed him. He had *helped* her. The epiphany brought with it such confusion that Talasyn's mind all but blanked. She once again remembered that first chase over the ice, how he'd parted each ribbon of Shadowgate so that she could pass through unscathed.

What was his game plan? She was Sardovia's Lightweaver. If he killed her, he would avenge his family and make Kesath's inevitable victory all the sweeter.

Maybe he was just savoring the moment.

A deep furrow carved its way between Alaric's sweeping dark brows. It occurred to Talasyn, distantly, that he might look conflicted behind the mask.

"You could come with me." His words tumbled out too quickly to have been thought through. "This phenomenon— this merging of our abilities—we can study it. Together."

Talasyn's jaw dropped. The man was two sails short of a full rig. And *she* was, too.

Because it was her turn to speak without thinking.

Because, instead of telling Alaric that she would rather eat dirt than go *anywhere* with him, what she said was . . .

"Your father would never allow that."

His gaze flickered. He almost, very nearly, seemed to flinch.

What a strange person, she mused, with no small amount of awe at his gall. It wasn't that she *wasn't* curious about these barriers that she could apparently only create with him, but—

"Do you honestly expect me to believe that the Night Emperor will welcome a Lightweaver into his ranks with open arms?" Talasyn demanded. It suddenly hit her that this was what said Night Emperor's son had to be up to, and she narrowed her eyes. "Did you really think that I would fall for such an obvious trap? That I'd be so grateful for the chance to save my own skin that I'd throw away all common sense?"

The more she took Alaric to task, the more color leached into his skin. She had presumed him incapable of anything as common as flushing, but his thick dark hair had been so disheveled by stormship winds and ground battles that the tips of his ears peeked out, and they were as red as the eclipse. The anger that she nursed for him and all his ilk didn't *recede*, exactly, but it was somewhat dulled by confusion.

What was *wrong* with him?

"Never mind," Alaric gritted out, abruptly vicious. "Forget I said anything."

The clanging of gongs resounded through the air, dulled as it permeated the black-gold sphere but insistent, nonetheless. It was the signal for all Sardovian forces to retreat, leaving behind the dust and the rubble and the dead. Talasyn tugged at the threads of her magic and Alaric did the same, unraveling the tapestry that they had woven together. The barrier dissipated in the next instant, revealing the chaos that beset the street. The Sardovian soldiers who weren't currently fleeing were covering their comrades' escape with rattling streams of crossbow bolts and more ceramic shells, and Talasyn braced herself for Alaric's next attack.

It never came.

"Until we meet again, Lightweaver." His gray eyes were back to being hard and impassive. "In the meantime, do try not to let more falling rocks get the best of you when I'm not around to help."

Talasyn shook with bewilderment and blinding rage. She couldn't muster any sort of comeback, phantom snatches of words weighing heavy on her tongue and refusing to budge. She couldn't re-engage him, either. She needed to help fend off the Kesathese troops while Sardovia pulled out.

Alaric was clearly well aware of it, too. The corners of his eyes lifted, as though he were sneering behind his fanged mask. And yet, something gnawed at her. There was something . . . *off* about the situation, some jarring thing that lurked beneath the veneer of this moment. Beneath his coldly regal tone and the unreadable flint of his gaze.

She didn't realize what it was until he had turned around, clearly prepared to leave her standing there.

"You're letting me go?" Talasyn blurted out.

Just like that?

Alaric froze. He didn't look back at her, but one gauntleted fist clenched at his side.

"There is no use killing someone who has already lost." His response was soft, but it sliced through her world like thunder. "It's a waste of energy on my part, as you will probably die in the retreat soon enough."

With that, he walked away, leaving her seething, leaving her to wonder why he did the things that he did. Even as Sardovia fell to pieces all around her.

CHAPTER ELEVEN

The *Summerwind* limped through the air above the Eversea, leaving the Continent behind. It had been so badly damaged that it leaned to one side, its wooden frame riddled with dents and cannonball holes and its once proud sails in tatters. Several of its Squallfast-infused hearts had imploded as well, with few empty crystals to spare, so that the airship could only crawl along in its journey south.

The other vessels accompanying it were in similar shape—and there weren't a lot of them, either. There was only one other carrack in addition to the *Summerwind*, a heavy frigate, a dozen wasp coracles, and the Sardovian stormship *Nautilus*. The *Nautilus* plodded along behind the rest, a floundering leviathan, the glow of its aether hearts dim through the soot-stained metalglass layers of a battered hull.

Talasyn stood on the quarterdeck of the *Summerwind*, her arms folded over the railing, her eyes tracking the fluffy cotton-hued clouds without truly seeing them as they drifted past. A short distance away, white-cloaked Enchanters pored over the airship's frantically whirring dashboard, scrambling identifiable aetherwave signatures and handling the transmissions that were being sent back and forth across encrypted channels as what was left of the Allfold tried to keep track of their comrades. The *Summerwind* and its convoy weren't the only vessels that had made it out, but the evacuation had been hopelessly disorganized and, after several long days, the Sardovians were scattered throughout these reaches of the Eversea.

Every once in a while, an aetherwave signature would go dark, and Talasyn would determinedly suppress thoughts of what might have happened to the airship on the other end. That way lay madness. She had to focus on the present moment, on keeping everyone in her convoy alive.

But she was so worried about Khaede.

Khaede had been recalled from the front lines a sennight ago, when a particularly nasty bout of morning sickness finally forced her to reveal her condition. Talasyn had glimpsed her in the crowd shortly before the battle for Lasthaven started, manning an evacuation route for the cityfolk—and then never again.

In situations like this, the simplest explanation was often the correct one, but Talasyn refused to accept it. Any minute now, Khaede's voice would crackle to life over the aetherwave, from an airship that she'd managed to escape Lasthaven on . . .

Bieshimma went over to Talasyn, resting the arm that wasn't in a sling on the quarterdeck's railing. He looked as though he'd aged a decade since the retreat.

He was in command while Vela recovered from her injuries, so Talasyn asked quietly, "What now, General?"

"Now?" Bieshimma peered at the shimmering ocean miles below their feet, as though searching for answers in its blue currents. "We need a place to hide. Somewhere to take stock of the situation and regroup with the others."

"Where, though?" Talasyn asked, even though she already knew that Bieshimma didn't have answers any more than she did. All of the Continent had been ripped out from under their feet, and the world was vast, but it was full of realms who had ignored Sardovia's pleas for help for years, either disinterested or unwilling to risk the Night Empire's wrath. There was nowhere left to run, but they couldn't drift above the Eversea forever.

Her head spun with the weight of everything, the surreal cutting through the present like shards of glass. It felt as if it had only been hours ago when she was telling Khaede about the Nenavar mission, with the other woman torn between shock and amusement at the revelation of Talasyn's heritage. And now Khaede was nowhere to be found and—

Talasyn went still as an idea began to take shape.

There *was* somewhere that they could go. It hadn't been an option before, but things were different now.

Maybe—just maybe—it would work.

The convoy headed southeast. It was another two days of slow and arduous travel before they stopped, time that Talasyn spent helping tend to the injured and discussing the plan with General Bieshimma and a bedridden Vela, as well as monitoring the aetherwave for any sign of Khaede. Initially she didn't have the stomach to assist with disposing of those who died from their wounds, but she eventually pitched in with that, too; the *Summerwind* was woefully shorthanded. She wrapped bodies in shrouds cobbled together from rags and spare scraps of canvas and she closed their sightless eyes before they were tossed overboard, disappearing into the Eversea in ripples of wave and foam.

So many died. If Kesath was giving chase, all the Night Empire would have to do was follow the trail of corpses in the water. The air was heavy with salt and grief.

The sun had just begun to set on the second day along their new course when Talasyn clambered up the mainmast of the *Summerwind*. It was 120 feet tall, which was nothing to her, nothing to someone who had grown up in Hornbill's Head, where buildings sprouted on top of one another and everyone knew how to go higher. She had just helped wrap Mara Kasdar's body in a makeshift shroud and drop it into the Eversea and she needed to be alone, away from the crowded cabins and the decks full of people wandering around in a shell-shocked haze.

The mast was as far as she could go. Talasyn squeezed into the barrel-shaped crow's nest and just—*stayed* there, her heart heavy and her mind blank. Blademaster Kasdar had been an institution. She'd been there almost from the very beginning, and she had personally trained all of the recruits. Her death seemed symbolic of the demise of the Sardovian army itself. She was the one who had taught Talasyn how to fight with swords and spears and daggers and all kinds of other weapons that the latter initially hadn't even known which end of to hold. Kasdar had been a demanding instructor and they rarely got along, but it was starting to sink in for Talasyn that she would never see the burly, stone-faced veteran ever again. That realization brought with it a dull ache that experience had shown her would soon scab over on top of layers upon layers of all the other old scars.

When will it end? Talasyn asked herself at this great height, her vision afire at the edges with the crimson sunset that gilded the empty horizon and the shifting waves. The Hurricane Wars took and took, but there was still so much left to lose.

She turned around, the wooden planks that made up the bottom of the crow's nest creaking beneath her boots. Her gaze fell on the *Nautilus*. It lumbered after the two carracks, nearly seven times their size combined.

Khaede had lived in a fishing village before the hurricanes thundered through it and she fled to the arms of the Heartland. She had once told Talasyn that the stormships reminded her of the otherworldly creatures that sometimes got tangled in the nets along with the day's catch. These were beings from the darkest depths of the Eversea—bottom-dwellers as Talasyn had been, in the lowermost slum levels of Hornbill's Head—and they looked more like insects than like fish, their bodies segmented and oval, the softer parts protected by shells as hard as armor plates.

What protected the *Nautilus* and all its ilk, though, was an external steel frame binding together panels of extremely durable metalglass and iron ore. Because of its immense size, it took the work of entire flotillas to bring down even just one stormship—and, more often than not, the stormship had already caused massive amounts of damage by then. When Kesath's first such vessel took to the skies, it had completely altered the nature of warfare. And now, nineteen years later, an entire fleet of them had helped Gaheris realize his ambition of total control over the Continent.

Talasyn hated the stormships. So many would still be alive if not for them. Even the ones that Vela had stolen when she defected hadn't been of much use in the long run. The Sardovian army had rarely unleashed them on areas where there would have been high numbers of innocent casualties and, in any case, what were eight stormships compared to the Night Empire's fifty?

Three now, she reminded herself with bitterness. *Maybe even fewer.*

It was a terrible situation. Talasyn's plan gave what was left of the Sardovian Allfold only the barest glimmer of a fighting chance. The odds of it panning out were *not* in their favor.

Once the sun was a molten half-sphere jutting from the horizon and the pale silhouettes of the seven moons hung in the heavens, a flurry of activity swept through the decks, a cry spreading among the *Summerwind*'s passengers. *Land, ho.* Talasyn tore her gaze from the gargantuan form of the *Nautilus* and angled her body toward the bow of the carrack—and there they were, in the distance: the countless green isles of the Nenavar Dominion, rising up from a darkening ocean in towers of rainforest and earth. Something in her chest trembled at the sight before her. She had an unsettling sensation that she was about to pass the point of no return.

The convoy paused in its flight, hovering over the ocean, the wasp coracles sliding into their hangars on the *Nautilus*, and Talasyn climbed back down to the *Summerwind*'s quarterdeck. Enchanters had found several nearby frequencies on the aether-wave, but their attempts to patch through were being rebuffed, eliciting a deep scowl from Bieshimma.

"Bunch of airships clearly in distress show up on their doorstep and they won't even deign to make contact," the general muttered under his breath.

"The Nenavarene know about the war," Talasyn pointed out. "Maybe they don't want to invite trouble."

"Let's hope that changes when we tell them we have their long-lost princess."

Talasyn bit down on her lower lip to stop herself from shushing a superior officer, but she cast a furtive glance at the crew milling about. As far as everyone else was concerned, they'd flown to Nenavar simply because it was the nearest realm and they were hoping to appeal to the Dragon Queen's charity.

They eventually decided to send one of their few remaining pigeons to Port Samout. Bieshimma scribbled a message in Sailor's Common and tied the roll of vellum to the cooing bird's leg, then set it loose in the direction of the shining harbor.

"Do you think they'll respond?" Bieshimma asked Talasyn as they watched the pigeon flutter away.

"I'll honestly be surprised if they don't just shoot it down," Talasyn replied.

"Don't even *joke* about that, helmsman," he warned her. "This is the only chance we have."

Khaede would have butted in with something to the effect of, *That's Your Worship to* you, *General,* and once again Talasyn felt the pang of loss. Felt that familiar fear crawl its way up her throat.

Their little winged messenger soon returned, with neither the original message nor a response. They waited and they waited. Hours passed and night slowly descended in starry black velvet curtains over the Eversea. Talasyn could barely taste the boiled salt beef that she had for supper, so anxious was she that the Nenavarene really would ignore them, after all. Maybe they had concluded that she *wasn't* Elagbi's daughter, that she had no connection to them. Maybe what she'd done the last time she was here was too great an insult to let slide. Maybe they were preparing to attack the convoy with those fatally elegant winged coracles.

Granted, it wasn't as though supper would have been laden with flavor even if she'd eaten it while in the best of moods, and there was far too little of it as well. Supplies had dwindled considerably after a sennight in the air. The *Summerwind* had simply not been equipped to take on this many passengers for a long haul. Food was being strictly rationed but, still, it wouldn't be long before they ran out.

Perhaps a month. More likely less.

Talasyn slept out on the quarterdeck, not willing to risk missing a transmission from Nenavar—or from Khaede. As the night crew puttered around her, she fell asleep on the wooden floorboards, under a net of constellations. She dreamed of her city of gold.

A strong wind rustled across her face and she woke with a start, her mind screaming *stormship attack.* But it was a false alarm. The carrack's moonlit decks were quiet and the gust of wind that fluttered the edges of its furled sails smelled of seagrass and dried fish, with the underlying tang of sweet fruit.

"Anything yet?" she called out to the white-cloaked figure stationed at the aetherwave transceiver.

The Enchanter shook her head drowsily, and Talasyn swallowed a lump in her throat. Still no word from Khaede or from Port Samout.

Going back to sleep was impossible with so much anxiety eating away at her. She cast her bleary gaze around the *Summerwind* and it landed on Ideth Vela, a solitary figure at the prow, shoulders squared as though she were holding up the sky.

A small team of healers had stitched up the Amirante's wound, and her body's innate shadow magic had fought off the worst effects of the legionnaire's blade. However, blood loss and minor organ damage had taken their toll, and Vela's remaining eye was clouded over with suppressed pain and her lips were pale when Talasyn went up to her.

"You should be resting, Amirante."

"I've been laid up in my cabin all this sennight. Besides, fresh air does wonders," Vela said with a trace of her usual dismissiveness. "So—it looks like you'll be seeing your family again, after all."

Talasyn blanched. "I didn't want *this*."

Vela's features softened. "I know you didn't. Just some dark humor on my part. But I do wonder what will be in store for you, should the Dominion respond."

"What do you mean?"

Vela countered Talasyn's question with her own. "You said that Prince Elagbi called you the heir to the throne. I take it that Urduja Silim has no daughters?"

"I don't—" Talasyn broke off as a memory from that fateful night came back to her. "Elagbi mentioned that Rapat had called him away from the capital in the midst of the succession debate."

"No man may rule the Nenavar Dominion," said Vela. "Accounts have been sparse over the millennia, naturally, but it is generally accepted that the title of Lachis'ka always passes

126

on to the eldest daughter. If the queen has only sons, the firstborn's wife is expected to take the throne."

"I guess that the Nenavarene are a bit confused about what to do, seeing as Hanan passed away, and if the other son . . ." Talasyn faltered as the connection lanced through her: her *uncle*, the uncle who had wanted her dead. "If the other son"—she tried again—"was married to someone who survived the civil war, she would be a traitor's wife, wouldn't she?"

"Yes," Vela said thoughtfully. "A most untenable set of circumstances. Perhaps we are delivering the solution right into their hands. But I suppose we'll deal with that storm when it makes landfall."

"I suppose," Talasyn echoed.

In truth, it was a relief that they were letting it go for now. She was exhausted; she felt defeated even while clinging tightly to that one last shred of hope that she had led Sardovia to sanctuary instead of doom.

Then Vela surprised her by asking, "We haven't heard from Khaede yet, I take it?"

"No, Amirante."

In the past, Vela had rarely, if ever, discussed personal matters with her troops, always focused on the next battlefield, the next tactical maneuver. Perhaps she wasn't herself due to her injury, or perhaps there was time now that they were waiting for the Nenavarene response. Whatever the case, she sighed, sneaking a glance at Talasyn before transferring her gaze to the moonlit ocean.

"The last thing I said to her was that she couldn't fly on account of her pregnancy. I ordered her to help get the cityfolk to safety instead. She put up less of a fight than I expected."

"Which is how we know that she was *really* sick," Talasyn muttered.

Vela cracked a wan smile. One that was quick to fade. "I never told her how sorry I was about Sol. There was never enough time for that. There was never a correct moment. I hope—" She paused abruptly, as though seizing a chance to regain composure. "I hope that she and the baby are all right."

"They are," Talasyn said, willing herself to believe it as well. "Khaede is fast and she's smart and she's strong. If anyone can survive this, it's her."

Vela gave a slight nod, and the conversation ebbed along with the tide, a heavy silence settling over the airship's bow, which no one else occupied. It seemed to Talasyn that it was just her and the Amirante, alone together, at the end of the world.

A crewman shook Talasyn awake shortly before dawn. The bulb on the aetherwave transceiver was blinking yellow. She crowded around it with several crewmembers while a runner was dispatched to the officers' berths.

The feminine voice on the other end of the line spoke in crisply accented Sailor's Common. "You have been cleared for an audience with the Zahiya-lachis on her flagship," it announced without preamble. "To get there, you may take only one carrack with no escort. The rest of your convoy will stay where they are, *especially* your stormship. Only a small party of unarmed individuals will be allowed to board the *W'taida*. Failure to comply with these instructions in the presence of the Zahiya-lachis will result in the Dominion opening fire on your ranks."

The voice then reeled off a detailed slew of coordinates and the transmission came to an abrupt end, with no one on the *Summerwind* allowed to get a word in edgewise.

By now, Talasyn was no stranger to déjà vu where Nenavar was concerned. This time, however, she understood where the feeling came from. She *had* been here before—and not that long ago, in fact. Little more than a month had passed since the sun rose through the mists as she wove her way through the same numerous craggy islands that the carrack was coasting over now.

The elevated quarterdeck was serene compared to the other sections, where people jostled one another and the swell of the throng pressed against the railings as the war-weary and forlorn angled for a better view of mangroves and rainforests and white-sand beaches. The fog was thick and cool, swirling all around, encasing faces and exposed limbs in fine dew. The *Summerwind* laboriously plowed through it, the fire lamps that adorned the stern and the masts burning bright as Vela and the rest of the officers gradually made their way to the quarterdeck.

The coordinates they'd been given took them further south along Nenavar's disjointed stretches of coastline than Talasyn had previously ventured. The outlying islands grew thinner and taller and steeper, until they were pillars of sheer rock scattered through with the occasional streak of greenery here and there. The sun had almost fully risen when the *Summerwind* arrived at its destination, carefully navigating around a tightly packed cluster of stony peaks.

An awed hush fell over the pitiful band of refugees.

A mile away, hovering in the mist-laced air above blue waves and endless islands, was what could be none other than the *W'taida*. It was unlike any airship that Talasyn had seen before. It actually took her a while to come to terms with the fact that she was looking at one.

Mounted on a roughly circular bed of glossy, midnight-black volcanic rock that was nearly as wide as a stormship, wreathed in the emerald veils of what must have been *hundreds* of aether hearts, was a massive assemblage of steel towers and ornate copper-sculpted battlements, speckled with a plethora of large metalglass windows tinted pink by the dawn's rosy light, threaded through with huge, whirring clockwork gears, and capped with golden spires.

129

This, then, was the flagship of the Nenavarene queen, and it was—

"A castle," General Bieshimma said blankly. "A *floating* castle."

"These people certainly do well for themselves," Talasyn groused.

A deafening roar shattered the early-morning stillness.

It was a sound that only some monstrous wild animal could make. It seemed to come from everywhere all at once, echoing off the steepled islands, surging forth from the Eversea.

Acting on instinct, Sardovian soldiers scrambled for their weapons and took defensive positions all along the decks. Talasyn splayed her fingers, ready to spin whatever she would need out of light and aether. But it wasn't long before it became obvious that no crossbow or blade—perhaps not even the Lightweave—would do much good.

A winding shape unfurled in the mists to the north. It easily dwarfed the *Summerwind*, was longer even than the *Nautilus*. It was a serpentine creature covered in barnacle-encrusted sapphire-blue scales, with two forelimbs that bore wickedly curved claws the color of steel. The swift roll of its slithering caused its massive spine to form mountains that collapsed into themselves and took new shape in the next breath. Propelled on a pair of leathery wings that spread out to cast vast shadows over the world, it flew closer with alarming speed, and the sunrise washed over it as it sliced through the fog and circled overhead.

The beast's head was crocodilian, its snout draped in slender whisker-like barbels that twitched as though trawling the wind currents. Narrowing its rust-colored and star-pocked eyes at the gawking Sardovians, it unhinged its great jaw wide, revealing two rows of sharp, sharp teeth, and it emitted another roar. Talasyn's flesh broke out in a million goosebumps—and then a *second* such creature erupted from the surface of the Eversea.

This one had blood-red scales instead of blue, glistening wet and dripping with seaweed tendrils. It shot into the air, sending up an eruption of salt water so immense that it drenched the passengers closest to the *Summerwind*'s railings. It joined its fellow in sweeping wide arcs across the sky in a dance of lethal grace. The dawn air swelled with the scents of plankton and overturned seabed, of the rotten wood of shipwrecks and the soft things that lived and died in them, there in the black depths where sunlight couldn't reach.

Bieshimma's disbelieving tone cut through the stunned stillness suffusing the quarterdeck. "I guess that Nenavar *does* have dragons, after all."

CHAPTER TWELVE

Talasyn stared at the dragons. They were too big for her senses to encompass but she drank in the sight of them, anyway.

It *had* struck her as odd that the Zahiya-lachis's flagship didn't have an armed escort. Even if the *W'taida* possessed weaponry hidden somewhere in its black-and-gold facade, amidst its copper struts, surely a handful of coracles wouldn't have gone amiss, given that the head of state was about to deal with an unpredictable element in the form of desperate, battle-hardened outsiders.

But who needed coracles, who needed cannons, when they had *these*? The two dragons positioned themselves on either side of the floating castle and hung aloft on the wind, flapping their mighty wings. They eyed the carrack warily, ready to spring to action at a moment's notice, at the first sign of threat.

They probably breathed fire as well. There was no reason to presume otherwise, now that the age-old rumors of their existence had ended up being true. Those who'd posited that a dragon could bring down a stormship had been correct. Those gargantuan claws alone looked perfectly capable of tearing through metalglass in one swipe.

Talasyn was struck by the overwhelming urge to—to cry.

To scream. To rage at the heavens. The creatures were terrible and beautiful, and what was left of the Sardovian Allfold beheld them far too late. She thought about how many lives would have been spared if the Dominion had agreed to help in the fight against the Night Empire. The stormship fleet wouldn't have been Gaheris's trump card for long. The Hurricane Wars would have ended before the cities in the Heartland were razed to the ground. Darius would never have become a traitor, Sol and Blademaster Kasdar would still be alive, and Khaede wouldn't be missing in action.

But all it took was one glance at Vela's expression for Talasyn to pull herself together. The Amirante looked *stricken*, as though her thoughts were running in a similar vein. Not wanting to add to the burden, Talasyn schooled her features into something blanker and more restrained and, after a while, so did Vela.

The aetherwave crackled to life. The brisk voice on the other end ordered the *Summerwind* to halt and informed them that they could now send a small boarding party "at their earliest convenience," whatever *that* meant.

"I think they're implying that they'll have those big damn worms eat us if we don't get a move on," Bieshimma grumped.

Bieshimma could not, of course, join the boarding party, given what he'd done the *last* time he'd been in Nenavar. After some discussion, Vela decided that a group of two people was as small and as non-threatening as it could get, and she and Talasyn headed for the grid that contained the carrack's skiffs—tiny flat-bottomed vessels that were frequently used as shuttles or escape pods.

The crowd of soldiers and refugees parted for them deferentially, but Talasyn was all too aware of their mutterings of unease and their lost, questioning gazes. She couldn't blame them; they were within range of the dragons, and one good blow from those scaled tails could probably break the

Summerwind in half. All eyes were on her as she helped the Amirante into the skiff, fired up the aether hearts, and steered away from the carrack's decks, toward the shimmering castle in the sky.

The dragons were huge from a distance. Up close, the sheer breadth of them made Talasyn feel about as significant as an ant. Their jewel-toned eyes tracked every movement of the skiff and its passengers, missing nothing. She didn't breathe until she and the Amirante made it to the landing grid carved into the rock at the base of the castle—and, even then, she didn't, *couldn't* relax.

Elagbi was waiting for them at the threshold of the main entrance, accompanied by the same Lachis-dalo who'd been guarding him on the Belian range. Stock-still at first—nudged forward only by Vela—Talasyn approached the regal figure nervously, having no idea what the standard procedure was for greeting your estranged father on your second meeting. Should she hug him? Gods, she hoped not. Perhaps she was expected to curtsy, since he was a prince, but *she* was the heir to the throne, wasn't she? Did she rank above him? Maybe *he* was the one supposed to curtsy—no, that was wrong, men didn't—

Elagbi solved her dilemma by clasping her hands in his. "Talasyn," he said warmly, the gentleness in his dark eyes somewhat at odds with his aristocratic demeanor. "Everything pales before the joy of seeing you once more. I regret that it has to be under such grievous circumstances."

"I—I'm sorry about—about last time," Talasyn stammered, inwardly cringing at how very undignified she sounded compared to him. "I had to get back right away—"

"No harm done," said Elagbi. "We recovered the *alindari* that you commandeered without any trouble. And you were not the one who left a trail of injured Nenavarene soldiers in your wake." His expression soured as he uttered this last part,

134

and in that moment Talasyn felt a crystal-clear kinship with him. She was all too familiar with what it was like to have one's day ruined by Alaric Ossinast.

Talasyn labored through the introductions. Vela inclined her head at the Dominion prince, and Talasyn belatedly noticed that she was standing tall even though the newly stitched wound that raked her from sternum to hip was surely still aching.

"Your Highness." Vela's usual flinty tone was somewhat more restrained. "We thank you for granting us an audience."

Elagbi smiled and bowed, one leg drawn back across the ground, right hand pressed to his abdomen while the left swept out in an elegant flourish. "Amirante. It is my honor. I in turn thank you for taking my daughter in and treating her kindly all these years. Now, if you'll please follow me . . ."

The Lachis-dalo swarmed around them as they filed into the castle. The winding hallways of the *W'taida* were every inch as opulent as its exterior suggested. The walls and floors were lined with gold-flecked marble in a muted bronze hue. The metalglass windows were paneled with dark ivory and offered panoramic views of the islands in their bed of turquoise waves, the dragons hovering watchfully above. Talasyn would have been hard-pressed to believe that she was on an airship, if not for the hum of aether hearts beneath her feet.

Elagbi and Vela engaged in quiet, somber conversation as they discussed what had happened, how Sardovia's last bastions had fallen and why the survivors had set course for Nenavar. Talasyn was grateful that Vela had taken the reins. It felt as if there was no end to the castle and she didn't think that she was ready to traverse its many long corridors while making small talk with the man she had only recently learned might be her father.

They came to a halt at a set of golden doors covered with intricate carvings. There were two guards stationed on either side and, while Elagbi spoke to them, Vela fell back to murmur to Talasyn, "If I may offer some counsel for our upcoming meeting with the Dragon Queen: it would be best if I do the talking. By which I mean to say—do *not* let your temper get the best of you. And don't cuss."

"I don't cuss *that* much," Talasyn retorted with no small amount of belligerence. "Why do we have to walk on eggshells, anyway?"

"Because, if the old stories are to be believed, it takes a certain kind of woman to hold on to power in the cutthroat nest of political intrigue that is Nenavarene society," Vela replied. "Queen Urduja would be very much that kind of woman, given how long her house has reigned. We must proceed with care."

The guards pushed open the doors, and Elagbi summarily ushered Vela and Talasyn into the presence of the Zahiya-lachis.

In contrast to the rest of the *W'taida*, where the dawn streamed in like rivers, the throne room's floor-to-ceiling windows were shrouded by opaque drapes of rough navy silk—for privacy, Talasyn supposed. This would have made the large chamber impossibly dark if not for the presence of fire lamps, different from the ones of the Continent in that they gave off a pale and radiant light with a tinge of silver-blue, casting an ethereal gloss over the marble pillars and the celestial-patterned tapestries, over the unmoving silhouettes of the queen's Lachis-dalo stationed at various ingress points, and over the dais at the end of the hall, upon which perched a stately white throne. The woman sitting on it was too far away for Talasyn to make out her features, but something about her posture called to mind the highly venomous adders that lurked in the grass of the Great Steppe. They would watch from atop gleaming coils when another life-form encroached on their territory and took their time deciding whether the intruder was worth the effort needed to strike.

"This place is normally bustling with courtiers," Elagbi said as he led Vela and Talasyn deeper into the throne room. "However, due to the sensitive nature of this meeting, my mother and I thought it best to be discreet."

"Seems to me they could've taken a smaller airship, then," Talasyn mumbled to Vela.

"It's a show of power," Vela replied calmly, also keeping her voice low. "Of strength and grandeur. An intimidated opponent is much easier to negotiate with."

Talasyn wondered at the Amirante's use of the word *opponent*, but she couldn't help agreeing that it was difficult not to feel cowed as they approached the dais and she got a closer look at the Dragon Queen.

Urduja of House Silim was old in the way that mountains were old—imposing and awe-inspiring, having transcended the ravages of time while other lesser entities had been destroyed. Her snow-white hair was gathered into a tight bun by chains of star-shaped crystals that trailed down to decorate her high forehead, underneath a crown that looked as if it had been carved from ice, twisting gracefully up toward the star-studded ceiling like many-pronged antlers. The tips of her long lashes were spiked with tiny fragments of diamonds that glittered over eyes the color of jet, and her lips were painted a shade of blue that was almost black, striking against her olive skin. She wore a long-sleeved dress of currant-red silk shot through with silver thread, its wide shoulders and the flared hem of its hourglass skirt embellished with a multitude of iridescent dragon scales and fiery agate beads. The column of her throat was encased in layers of fine silver bands flecked with rubies, and the fingernails of one hand, adorned with gem-encrusted silver cones as sharp as daggers, tapped idly on the armrest of the throne as she waited for the group to break their silence.

Elagbi cleared his throat. "Most Revered Zahiya—"

"Let us dispense with the formalities. My sycophants are

not around to appreciate them." Urduja spoke in flawless Sailor's Common, her voice as cold as her crown. "Amirante Vela, after all these failed attempts on your part to rally the Dominion to your cause, I *had* hoped that you would get the message. Instead, you bring the Hurricane Wars to my borders."

"It is a war that we can still win, Your Majesty," Vela declared. "With your help." At first glance she seemed every bit as confident as Urduja, holding her head up just as high, but Talasyn was close enough to notice the Amirante's pallor and her clenched fists—no doubt from the strain of soldiering on through her injury.

The Zahiya-lachis arched one elegantly sculpted brow. "You are asking me to send my fleet into battle against the Night Empire on your behalf?"

"No," said Vela, "I am asking you for sanctuary. I am asking you to open your borders to *my* fleet and allow us to shelter here while we regroup our forces once more."

"Then I would be harboring Kesath's most despised enemies," Urduja drawled. "Gaheris has not yet turned his eye to Nenavar, but I highly doubt that he would be willing to let *this* lie."

"He doesn't have to find out—and, even if he does, what can he do?" Vela argued. "This archipelago cannot be breached by warships en masse, not with your dragons."

"I wouldn't be too sure of that. Outsiders are very unpredictable." A trace of anger finally leached into Urduja's frigid tone. "That general of yours—Bieshimma, if I recall—did a perfectly good job of trespassing not too long ago."

"So did I," Talasyn blurted out.

Everyone turned to look at her, but she only had eyes for Urduja, who stared down from the dais with a carefully blank expression. Talasyn's common sense was screaming at her to be quiet and let Vela handle things, but she was tense and anxious from recent events, desperate to help her comrades who were scattered throughout Lir trying to evade Kesath's wide nets. She had to do *something*.

"I trespassed, too," she continued, willing her voice not to crack. "That's how your son found me." Was she talking too loudly? She couldn't accurately gauge her volume over the adrenaline pounding in her ears. "If Prince Elagbi is right, that means that I'm your granddaughter. That means I can ask you to *at least* hear us out."

Urduja studied her for several long moments. There was something in the Dragon Queen's eyes that Talasyn didn't like—a certain shrewdness, a certain glint of triumph that made her feel as though she'd walked into some sort of trap. Vela reached out and gripped her arm, a gesture that elicited a lump in Talasyn's throat from how protective it was, even though she didn't understand the reason behind it.

"You're right, she *does* look like your dead wife," Urduja said to Elagbi after a while. "More than that, I recognize the backbone. Perhaps it is Hanan's, perhaps it is even mine. I believe that she is Alunsina Ivralis. But, tell me"—she cocked her head—"why should I listen to the daughter of the woman who instigated the Nenavarene civil war?"

The blood froze in Talasyn's veins. Her stomach hollowed out. At first, she thought that she'd misheard, but the seconds continued to tick by and the Zahiya-lachis continued to wait for her answer. Silent and deadly. The serpent about to strike.

Talasyn remembered asking Elagbi how the civil war had started, how he hadn't been able to respond before the alarm for Alaric's escape went up. She looked at the man who was her father, and he had turned pale; she looked at Vela, and the Amirante had retracted her hand from Talasyn's arm, clenching it into a fist even though she remained stone-faced upon being confronted with this unexpected information.

"Well." Urduja's cold drawl was initially addressed to Elagbi.

"I see that you haven't told her *everything*." To Talasyn she said, "Not only did your mother, Hanan, cause turmoil by refusing to be proclaimed my Lachis'ka after this son of mine brought her here and married her, but she *also* went behind my back to send a flotilla to the Northwest Continent, to help Sunstead in their conflict with Kesath. The sole reason being that the people of Sunstead were Lightweavers like her. Not a single outrigger from that flotilla made it back home, thanks to Kesath's stormship. My *other* son"—and here her nostrils flared with a trace of anger—"used that catastrophe to further his own ends. He blamed me for it, he said that I was weak, and he led hundreds of islands in a bid to oust me from the throne so that he could take it for himself. Half a year of bloodshed that pushed a millennia-old civilization to the brink of ruin, and it can all be traced back to the outsider, Hanan Ivralis. You are of my blood, true, but you are of *her* blood as well. How can I trust you, *Lightweaver*?"

Urduja spat the name as though it was a curse. Talasyn was stunned, unable to come up with a way to salvage the situation, her thoughts somehow racing while at the same time contained in sluggish patterns.

"Harlikaan." Elagbi squared his shoulders, his dark gaze entreating as it fixed on the Zahiya-lachis. "You know as well as I do that my wife was manipulated by your enemies. It wasn't her fault. Even if it were, Talasyn wouldn't be similarly responsible. She grew up in an orphanage, far away from the bones of her ancestors. She is a victim of these circumstances, not the one who should be blamed for them."

Urduja still didn't look convinced. Granted, she didn't look much of anything at all, her pristine features giving very little away, but Talasyn was at her wits' end. If Nenavar didn't agree to harbor the Sardovians, it was over. They didn't have enough supplies to continue sailing the skies above the Eversea until they reached other nations that might not even welcome

The Hurricane Wars

them at all. Not to mention the fact that every minute spent over open water was another minute that they risked discovery by Kesathese patrols.

A decade of sacrifice—of blood and sweat and heroes and loss—couldn't come to such a floundering end. Talasyn would do anything.

"I'll do whatever you want," she blurted out. "I can't apologize for something that happened when I was only a year old, but if you agree to grant us sanctuary you won't be getting any trouble from me. I swear."

She held her breath. And waited.

Urduja's dark lips curved into a smirk. "Fine. I've made my decision. There is a cluster of uninhabited islands in the westernmost reaches of my territory. We call it Sigwad, the Storm God's Eye. It is located in the middle of a narrow strait that none may enter without my permission, as the waters are turbulent and the winds are always rough—and it is the site of Nenavar's Tempest Sever, which activates frequently. Those islands will provide sufficient refuge for the Sardovian fleet, I believe." For a brief moment, she seemed amused by the bewildered silence that followed her announcement. Then she addressed her next words to Vela. "To clarify, the Tempestroad steers clear of the island group, but it *does* wrap around it, filling the rest of the strait. The way to the Storm God's Eye is dangerous, yes, but it's very remote while still under my jurisdiction, and no one will bother you there. That makes it the best option for your purposes. Therefore, Nenavar's borders will be open to Sardovia for a fortnight, during which you may evacuate your troops into the strait. My patrols will be instructed to look the other way, but I do not guarantee my protection should you give them any cause for complaint. Any airship or *stormship*—" she sneered around the word—"that attempts to enter the Dominion after the allotted time will be shot down on sight. But the Allfold may shelter here until they are ready to take back the Northwest Continent."

Talasyn could not feel relief. Not yet. There was a frenetic current in the air—as well as a stiffening in Vela's posture—that told her that there was a catch.

And, indeed, it wasn't long before the Dragon Queen added, "In exchange, Alunsina will, of course, stay in the capital. Where she will assume her role as Lachis'ka of the Nenavar Dominion."

In the privacy of his suite on board the *Deliverance*, the largest of Kesath's stormships and his father's primary mode of conveyance in both war and affairs of state, Alaric removed the obsidian wolf's-snarl mask that covered the lower half of his face, placing it on a nearby table.

He'd just come back from scouting to the west of the Eversea, having found no trace of the Sardovian remnant. Not even wreckage. Gaheris was in a relatively pleasant mood, still exulting in his decisive victory, but that wasn't going to last when he once again remembered that his son had let the Lightweaver escape.

Alaric *was* to blame, honestly. He'd allowed her to slip from his grasp, for reasons that were still unclear to him after long hours of combing through his memories of their encounter during the siege of Lasthaven. Something had made him walk away, something that he had no name for—and, shortly before that, something had made him propose that she come with him.

He cringed every time he recalled *that* part in his mind.

Gaheris had professed some curiosity about the Lightweave and the Shadowgate combining, but in the end he had decreed that Shadowforged needed nothing from Lightweavers. So *why*, in the name of the gods, had Alaric put forward such a suggestion to the girl who was his greatest enemy?

And why couldn't he stop thinking about her now?

Perhaps he felt sorry for her. Everything she'd ever known was dust.

Alaric strode over to the windows and peered out, through layers of metalglass, at the twisted remains of several Heartland cities several miles below. The death toll for the capital alone numbered in the hundreds of thousands. It was a scale of destruction the like of which had not been seen since Kesath annexed the Hinterland, the same event that had led to Ideth Vela's defection and begun the Hurricane Wars.

But it was well and truly over. The Night Empire had triumphed. The Shadow had fallen over the Continent, as it had always been meant to.

Alaric gazed down upon the wasteland, with its leveled buildings and its sea of corpses, and he wondered if it had been worth the cost. A stray thought and nothing more, but it lingered, right up until the aetherwave transceiver in his suite crackled to life and he was informed by one of the Legion that his father wished to see him.

While Ideth Vela's sternness was a thing of legend, Talasyn had rarely seen her truly vexed. The woman who had received news of Coxswain Darius's betrayal practically without batting an eye was now pacing the length of the small anteroom where Urduja had agreed to let her and Talasyn have a few minutes alone to discuss the proposal.

"Did you see how quickly she came up with those terms?" Vela demanded. "She planned this from the very beginning, before we even set foot on this ship."

"It *was* rather fast, Amirante," Talasyn cautiously agreed.

"This means that her reign is in jeopardy," Vela muttered. "She needs to secure the line of succession. The other noble houses are surely vying to replace a queen with no heir. Urduja's willing to do whatever it takes to keep her throne."

You'd better have a good reason for summoning me from the capital in the midst of the succession debate, Talasyn once again remembered Elagbi saying to Rapat. Had the Zahiya-lachis been besieged even then? Perhaps even since Sintan's rebellion was vanquished and the ship bearing Alunsina Ivralis never returned . . .

Vela rounded on Elagbi with startling alacrity as soon as the Nenavarene prince joined them in the anteroom. "*You,*" she thundered, seeming not in the least bit cowed by his royal rank. "Did you know about this? Did you know what the Dragon Queen had in store for us?"

Elagbi held up his hands in pleading, in promise, his eyes fixed on Talasyn. "I swear to you, I did not."

The Amirante's rage would not be quelled. "We came here in good faith," she retorted bitterly. "Not so that your daughter could be coerced into your nest of vipers."

"No one is coercing her," said Elagbi, pale-faced and looking as miserable as it was possible for a prince to look. "You have the Zahiya-lachis's word that you will be free to go should you decide not to take the deal."

"And *then* what, Your Highness?" Vela snapped. "Let the Night Empire weed us out like rats as the months pass? Let Talasyn be burdened by the knowledge that she could have prevented it? This *is* coercion, whether or not you dress it up with pretty words."

A slow, anxious horror was dawning on Talasyn at the prospect of being separated from her comrades and thrust into some bizarre new world. She wanted nothing more than to rage at the unfairness of it all and at the uncertainty of the time to come, and maybe even burst into tears at the fierceness with which Vela was fighting for her. But she'd decided back in the throne room that she needed to do something and this *was* something. This was the *only* thing. She had to be strong.

"I've made my choice," she announced. She stared only at

Elagbi, because the sight of Vela's face might shatter her resolve. "I'll do it. I will be the Lachis'ka."

Gaheris kept a utilitarian office on the *Deliverance*. It was not a large room, as most space on the stormship had been allotted to its vast array of aether hearts. It was constantly plunged in shadow, the only sources of illumination a few weak slivers of afternoon sun filtering in through the gaps in the window drapes, well out of reach of the seated figure in the middle of the room—until a withered, skeletal hand was extended into the grayish light, beckoning Alaric closer.

Alaric had long suspected that light hurt his father's eyes and the perennial gloom that he draped himself in was to hide his current state. Though Gaheris was only fifty years of age, he looked easily twice that number. He had accomplished great feats of shadow magic during the Cataclysm and he had, in the years that followed, spent most of his time experimenting with aetherspace, pushing his body to the limit. It had taken a physical toll, although his magical prowess was now beyond measure.

Alaric had been seven when the war between Kesath and Sunstead broke out. He'd witnessed his father's gradual deterioration, often wondering if it was a glimpse into his own future. For all of Gaheris's assurances that knowledge was worth the cost, he had yet to teach Alaric his more taxing secrets—the Master of the Shadowforged Legion was needed on the front lines.

"You have not yet found the Sardovian remnant." It was a statement rather than a question. The voice was a hoarse rattle, burbling icily from a wizened throat. "You let the Lightweaver get away and now you cannot find her and the others. She could be on the other side of the world by now—and, with her, Ideth Vela. The realm is not secure as long as Vela draws breath and as long as there is a Lightweaver for people to rally around. A *match* to strike against the darkness."

Alaric bowed his head. "I apologize, Father. We have searched extensively, but if you will clear us to sail southeast—"

"No. Not yet. We are not yet prepared to tangle with the Nenavar Dominion. They might be on high alert, as they have every right to be after what *you* did."

Alaric held his peace. Silence was a pitiful defense, but it was the best recourse available to him at the moment.

"It is not yet the time. I have plans for the southeast," Gaheris continued. "Plans that I shudder to leave in your less-than-capable hands, but who knows—perhaps the added responsibility will do you good."

Alaric stilled.

"Now the real work begins. I pray that you will not disappoint me," his father intoned. "Are you ready, *Emperor*?"

Alaric nodded. He felt strangely hollow. "Yes."

PART
II

CHAPTER THIRTEEN

Four months later

The rope stretched taut as Talasyn scaled the Roof of Heaven's tallest tower, the grappling hook's steel barbs straining against the sides of the crenel a dozen meters above her head. It was late morning in the Nenavar Dominion and she squinted in the brilliant sunlight, the humid breeze fanning her sweat-dotted brow. Higher and higher she went, heart pumping and adrenaline rising as the capital city of Eskaya grew smaller and smaller, until the rooftops were nothing more than a carpet of multicolored jewels on a field of green. Clenching her teeth, she pushed up on her knees and straightened her spine so that she was practically *walking* along the side of the building's alabaster facade, her body slanted against horizon and blue sky.

Over the months of making the climb a daily ritual, Talasyn had grown to treasure these moments when it was just her and the tower and gravity. It was a form of moving meditation that kept her reflexes sharp, kept the vertical ramshackle slums of Hornbill's Head alive in her heart. It was good to remember where she'd come from. It ensured that the upgrade in her living situation didn't turn her head.

She hauled herself up over the battlement and onto a balcony, her feet on flat, solid flooring once more. The royal palace was perched atop steep limestone cliffs that overlooked the sweeping city of gold that she had once seen in a vision. From this tower, she had an excellent view of lush gardens, gleaming waterways, and busy streets dotted with landing grids where constant streams of airships—coracles and freighters and pleasure yachts and consular barges alike— came to dock. The skyline was dominated by curvilinear buildings fashioned from stone and gold and metalglass, although none stood as tall as the Roof of Heaven itself, and tucked among them were pockets of residential areas, where houses atop wooden stilts sported brightly colored facades and ornate stucco pillars, capped by upturned eaves and multi-inclined roofs that were home to bronze weathervanes depicting roosters and pigs and dragons and goats, swiveling with each breath of wind.

Surrounding the urban sprawl—sprouting up immediately right along its borders, in fact—was a rainforest that went on for miles upon miles in every direction, interrupted only by patches of the odd small town here and there. The horizon was ringed with the blue-gray silhouettes of distant mountains.

Aside from the thousands of skerries, atolls, cays, sea stacks, and smaller inhabited clusters jutting out from their bed of turquoise waves, there were seven main islands in the Nenavar Dominion. One for each moon of Lir, as chroniclers enjoyed pointing out. Eskaya—and Port Samout, and the Belian range— were located on Sedek-We, largest of the seven and Nenavar's hub of governance and commercial activity. Talasyn had spent most of her time here, under close watch, becoming more acquainted with her father and her grandmother when she wasn't being taught Nenavar's language, history, culture, and social graces by a never-ending slew of tutors. She had been formally presented only two months ago, but the Zahiya-lachis remained tireless in ensuring that her heir was up to snuff. It was a monumental task, getting the aristocracy and the masses to accept an outsider to someday rule over them. Talasyn needed to look, sound, and act as Nenavarene as possible. *Always.*

"Alunsina Ivralis." She said the name out loud, testing the shape of the name on her tongue. The passage of time had done nothing to take away from its unwieldiness. She frowned to herself. "Bit of a mouthful."

There was a melodious laugh from somewhere behind her. "You'll get used to it, Your Grace."

Talasyn turned around. Jie, her lady-in-waiting, was leaning a slim shoulder clad in shell beads and silk against the doorway leading out to the balcony, arms folded and ankles crossed in a jaunty pose.

This was another aspect of Talasyn's strange new life that was taking some getting used to—the fact that she *had* a lady-in-waiting. Jie was from a noble house and would one day inherit a title of her own. Her family had sent her to court so that she could gain political experience and make promising alliances. She was the one who made Talasyn look presentable and accompanied her during meals and the stretches of idle hours between lessons.

"You and the guards don't have to watch me *all* the time, you know," Talasyn told Jie in Nenavarene, the words coming easily to her thanks to a combination of intensive study and some innate adeptness that she could only ascribe to her magic. Since being here and in the proximity of a Light Sever, the aether within her had responded like a seedling to sunshine. "The Roof of Heaven is a fortress. I hardly think that random kidnappers or assassins would be able to infiltrate so easily."

"Most dangers come from inside the palace walls, Lachis'ka," Jie replied. "But, as it is, Her Starlit Majesty has sent for you."

Talasyn struggled not to groan. She had quickly learned

that even the tiniest sign of disrespect for Urduja made most people uncomfortable, if not alienated them completely. "Lead the way, then."

"Actually . . ." Jie giggled, tucking a windblown strand of wavy brown hair behind her ear, coffee-colored eyes flickering over Talasyn's sweat-stained tunic and ratty breeches. "Let's get you freshened up first, Your Grace. It's a tea."

The Dragon Queen's salon was an airy complex in the eastern wing, decorated with frescoes and geometric carpets dyed bright shades of purple, orange, and red. Like most other rooms in the royal palace, it boasted white marble walls and accents of ivory and gold, shining in the sunlight that filtered in through stained-glass windows.

The gauze-woven hibiscus blossoms adorning the champagne skirt of Talasyn's chiffon dress rustled as she crossed her legs—or, well, as she *tried* to cross her legs, anyway. If she shifted her thigh up any further, she'd rip a seam. There was no doubt in her mind that Khaede would be cackling her head off if she could see Talasyn right now.

Not like you *would look any better,* Talasyn imagined snapping at her absent friend.

Khaede was still missing. Talasyn had fallen into the habit of having pretend conversations with her as though she weren't. It was childish, perhaps, but better than torturing herself with all the worst-case scenarios.

She placed one pointy-shoed foot back on the floor as Urduja observed her from across a rosewood table laden with delicate pastries and porcelain cups. The Zahiya-lachis had yet to apply the elaborate cosmetics that she donned for public appearances, but her bare face was every bit as intimidating with its granite-carved features and its penetrating stare.

"I want to ascertain that there is no bad blood between us after my last command," Urduja said in a tone that implied

Talasyn didn't have much choice in the matter. "You must have come to your senses by now."

"I have, Harlikaan," Talasyn assured her, mustering a reasonable facsimile of a contrite expression as she addressed Urduja with the Nenavarene equivalent of *Your Majesty* and lied through her teeth. They'd had a screaming match a few days ago because Urduja had declared it too risky for Talasyn to continue frequenting the Sardovian hideout in the Storm God's Eye. Talasyn had decided that *no one* was going to tell her where she could and could not go, but her grandmother didn't need to know that. It would be all too easy to liberate a moth coracle from one of the many hangars in the dead of night and be back in Eskaya by dawn. For that plan to work, however, Urduja had to believe that Talasyn was compliant.

The Zahiya-lachis dropped the subject. She never discussed the Sardovians, if it could be helped. Her closest allies had been taken into her confidence but, generally, as far as the Dominion was concerned, no deal had been brokered and Ideth Vela's fleet did not exist in any capacity within the boundaries of the archipelago.

Instead, Urduja moved on to the next point of contention that had featured in her and Talasyn's blazing argument a few days prior. "I understand that you wish to know more about these abilities of yours, which is why you have incessantly lobbied to be granted access to the Belian Sever. However, such access was not part of the terms. You are my heir and it is high time that you focused on your royal duties and on learning how to rule. I am not long for this world and I would rather like to head to the next one secure in the knowledge that I have left my realm in capable hands."

Talasyn bit back a multitude of retorts. Sneaking into the ruins of the Lightweaver temple would be difficult, given the soldiers that regularly patrolled the area, but she would just have to try. "I bow to your judgment as always, Harlikaan," she placidly stated.

She'd laid it on a little too thick—Urduja shot her a glare of deepest suspicion. Talasyn blinked with as much innocence as she could manage. Overall, though, her demeanor toward the older woman was softened by no small measure of surprise. This was the first instance of Urduja mentioning her own mortality in her granddaughter's presence and, while four months was scarcely enough time to establish any sort of familial love on Talasyn's end, her stomach still flipped uneasily at the thought of this powerful, seemingly unassailable woman dying.

"Already my courtiers scramble to sink their claws into you," Urduja warned. "You must become adept at discerning who is trustworthy and who is not. Most of them fall into the latter category, but play your cards right and none will dare question your reign. The Zahiya-lachis is She Who Hung the Earth Upon the Waters, as good as a goddess."

From there the audience proceeded in a brisk, purposeful manner, with Urduja lecturing Talasyn on various topics pertaining to the Dominion as they nibbled on pastries and sipped tea. Every once in a while, Urduja would ask a question and Talasyn would answer as best as she could, building on previous lessons and her own personal observations. It was all routine, and yet these discussions had become more and more technical in nature as the months passed, and it was all in a language that she had begun learning only recently. By the time a servant entered the room to announce the arrival of Prince Elagbi, Talasyn was mentally exhausted and grateful for the reprieve.

She stood up to greet her father. She didn't have to—officially, she outranked him—but he was the closest thing to a true ally that she had at court. Aside from Jie and the Lachis-dalo, who shadowed her every step, Elagbi was the one she spent the most time with, day in, day out, except for when his duties took him away from the capital. She couldn't stop herself from smiling when he kissed her cheek: exactly the sort of thing she used to imagine her parents doing every morning or as they bade her goodnight.

"Had I known that you were joining us, I would have had the servants prepare the orange loose-leaf instead of the Etlingera green," Urduja chided her son once he and Talasyn were seated.

"Orange loose-leaf was the only tea that I didn't passionately abhor as a child," Elagbi explained to Talasyn. "I never cared for the beverage in general."

"The two of you have that in common," Urduja remarked.

Damn, Talasyn swore to herself. She thought that she'd mastered the art of looking neutral while choking down what was essentially bitter leaf water, but she needed more practice, apparently.

Elagbi turned to address Urduja. "I apologize for dropping in like this, Harlikaan, but I have urgent news." He paused, glancing hesitantly at Talasyn. The Zahiya-lachis gestured for him to continue, making good on her resolve that it was time for the Dominion's heir to learn more about ruling and, consequently, to have access to the kind of confidential information that came along with it. "One of our fishing boats on the far edge of its northern route sent an aetherwave transmission to Port Samout a few hours ago. They've spotted a flotilla of at least thirty Kesathese warships heading our way, with a stormship bringing up the rear. The Grand Magindam is worried that an offensive might be imminent. Nenavar is the only realm in this direction for thousands of miles."

"Ridiculous." Talasyn set her teacup down with a clatter. "Not even that wretched boil on the World-Father's behind is stupid enough to think that he can attack the Dominion with so small a force."

155

The two other people in the salon blinked at her.

"That wretched boil on the World-Father's behind?" Urduja queried in a witheringly dry tone.

Elagbi cleared his throat. "I believe that the Lachis'ka is referring to the new Night Emperor, Harlikaan."

"I am." Talasyn glowered. The Dominion had an extensive spy network that kept tabs on the affairs of other realms and, a few sennights after Talasyn had settled in Nenavar, she'd been informed that Alaric Ossinast had ascended to the throne of Kesath. She had no idea if that meant that he was in charge of all the decisions now—especially since his father was reportedly still alive—but *surely* he wouldn't attack an entire archipelago with only thirty warships and one stormship.

"Alaric was captured on the Belian range with me," Talasyn continued. "He knows what the Dominion is capable of. He's been on the receiving end of void magic and he's flown a moth coracle. He could also have seen a dragon while he was here but, even if he didn't, that's not the sort of thing that any commander in their right mind would leave to chance."

"Indeed," said Urduja. "Recklessness isn't a quality that one might expect to find in a person who would infiltrate a foreign land hostile to outsiders with not a single reinforcement in sight."

Talasyn flushed. It seemed that her grandmother wasn't in any hurry to let her *or* Alaric live that down.

"Well, I, for one, am very happy that you infiltrated us, my dear." Elagbi reached out to pat Talasyn's hand. "Her Starlit Majesty is very happy, too, even if she doesn't deign to show it."

"Sentimentality will get us nowhere at the moment," Urduja huffed. "Returning to the *situation*: whatever this may be, it doesn't feel like an invasion attempt. Not yet, at least."

"Could Kesath have learned the whereabouts of the Sardovians?" Elagbi asked, his brow furrowed, and Talasyn went cold. "Perhaps they seek to intimidate us into surrendering our refugees."

If there was one thing that Talasyn had figured out about the reigning monarch of the Nenavar Dominion, it was that she always kept her cards close to her chest, never letting on what was truly on her mind. This time was no different; Urduja rose to her feet, an abrupt dismissal. "I shall speak with the Grand Magindam to determine the best way to handle this development. In the meantime, I expect utmost discretion from the two of you regarding this matter."

Elagbi led Talasyn to another wing of the palace. "Your grandmother is rattled," he told her as they walked.

"I find that difficult to believe, to be honest," Talasyn remarked.

"You learn how to tell after a while." Although the hallway was deserted save for the Lachis-dalo trailing the two royals at a courteous distance, Elagbi lowered his voice. "This could easily turn into a crisis. If the Night Empire manages to enter Dominion territory and catch wind of a Sardovian presence, their wrath will know no bounds. You have not revealed the bargain to anyone else at court, have you?"

Talasyn shook her head. Since there had been too many witnesses on the Belian range, Urduja had had to disclose to the other nobles that Talasyn had grown up on the Northwest Continent and that she was a Lightweaver. However, no one knew that she hadn't returned to claim her title of her own free will—no one except for House Silim's closest allies and the Lachis-dalo who had been present at the *W'taida* meeting, who were bound by sacred oaths to keep the secrets of the royal family.

"I suppose that there is no use worrying about it until Alaric Ossinast makes his intentions clear," said Elagbi. "For now, let us speak of happier things."

Talasyn was actually *quite* worried about it, but their relatively brief time together had enabled her to form a comprehensive picture of this man who was her father. As the younger son, Elagbi was the despair of Urduja's eye, a laidback sort of fellow who possessed no grand ambitions and absolutely none of the cunning that the Nenavarene aristocracy was infamous for. He was, in Talasyn's very affectionate opinion, *flighty*, and it was endearing.

"What sort of happier things should we talk about, then?" she gamely asked.

Elagbi looked proud of himself. "I found some more old aetherlogs."

In the Nenavarene prince's study, a beautiful woman cajoled the squirming infant in her arms to look at some unseen nearby lens, a moment immortalized in grainy black-and-white flickers on a field of canvas.

Talasyn would never cease to be amazed by the Dominion's ingenuity. Back in Sardovia, aethergraphs were not unheard of, although rare. These were contraptions mounted on wooden tripods that used the light of a Firewarren-imbued aether heart to transmit an image onto a sheet of silver-plated copper. Here in Nenavar, the aethergraph had been modified to be capable of imprinting a *series* of images in strips of cotton film that could then be projected in rapid succession on a flat surface. The result was that the subject of the images looked as if it was moving.

This, then, was the sort of thing that could be created in a nation whose inventors and Enchanters weren't devoting all their time and energy to the war effort. These days, Talasyn often found herself feeling a twinge of melancholy for what Sardovia could have become without the shackles of a ten-year conflict.

But, on this particular morning, she focused on nothing else beyond the woman and the child on the canvas.

No matter how many times Talasyn beheld her mother's likeness, the eerie resemblance always caught her off-guard. It was as if she were peering not at the past but at the future, at an older version of herself. In all the oil portraits and aethergraphy, though, Hanan Ivralis's smile tended to be brittle at the edges. She had not been very happy at court, preferring instead the jungles that reminded her of her homeland and the ruins of the Lightweaver temple on Mount Belian, where she could commune with the only Light Sever to be found in the country.

In the aetherlog, Talasyn was only a few months old, yanking at strands of her mother's hair with chubby fingers and her features scrunched up, her mouth open in a soundless wail. It was so close to being *familiar*, like a word on the tip of her tongue. If she strained harder, if she dug deeper, surely she could discover this half-minute in the depths of her memories. Surely she would be able to recall what it had felt like to be held in her mother's arms.

Prince Elagbi cranked a lever on the aethergraph, rewinding the film without having to be asked. Talasyn could have watched it forever. Just this moment, just this sliver of love, on a loop. Somewhere out on the Eversea the Night Empire fleet was amassing, but it took no great effort on her part to push that concern aside for now. For just a little while longer. The Hurricane Wars had taught her that these moments of grace were few and far between and she had to take what she could get. *When* she could get it.

"Tell me again how you and Hanan met," Talasyn requested, not taking her eyes off the canvas.

Even though Elagbi had repeated this story quite a few times over the months, he was glad to indulge her once more. "I traveled often in my younger days, exploring Lir and learning about other cultures. I was still the second son then, with no major responsibilities to my name." A shadow fell over his features, the way it always did when he thought of Sintan, the brother he had killed in battle, but it passed quickly, with an acceptance that time had taught. "On one such sojourn, I stumbled upon a group of islands west of Nenavar, where the sky constantly blazed with Light Severs."

"The Dawn Isles," Talasyn breathed.

"How did you guess?" Elagbi teased gently. "My airship was caught up in one of the discharges and we crashed. The crew and I survived the impact, but we were stranded in the middle of the jungle for days. I thought that it was rather miserable luck at first, but then I bumped into your mother beneath the trees. I startled her, to be more accurate—she nearly ran me through with a light-woven spear."

"She had a temper," Talasyn said with a grin.

"A formidable one," Elagbi confirmed, chuckling. "We couldn't understand each other initially. Sailor's Common is not widely spoken in the Dawn Isles. Through an inspired combination of pantomime and drawing in the dirt with a stick, I was able to convince her to bring me and my crew back to her village. Her mother was the clan matriarch, and we were begrudgingly offered shelter and assistance. It took almost a month to repair the airship, during which time Hanan and I got to know each other better."

"And fell in love," Talasyn supplied, her smile widening.

Elagbi smiled back. "It was a whirlwind romance. When I finally left the Dawn Isles, she went with me. We were married within days of our arrival in Nenavar. The Zahiya-lachis as well as the whole court didn't take too kindly to an outsider joining the royal family, especially since Hanan refused to be proclaimed the Lachis'ka and it jeopardized the succession because Sintan had yet to take a wife. But mine and Hanan's marriage remained steadfast. After a year, we had you."

In the aetherlog, Hanan Ivralis's slim shoulders shook with silent laughter as she tried to extricate strands of her hair from where they'd wrapped around a three-month-old Talasyn's curious fingers. This time, the twenty-year-old Talasyn, who was watching the scene, registered the vague scent of wild berries and knew, without a doubt, that this was what her mother had smelled like.

It was a start. It was enough for now.

She and her father never talked about the role that Hanan had played, however inadvertently, in the civil war. For Urduja, Hanan would probably always be the naive, easily manipulated woman who had nearly destroyed the Dominion. Elagbi, on the other hand, held his wife's memory sacred, and even though the Nenavarene civil war had consigned Talasyn to a life of hardship for several long years, she chose to believe in the recollections that were borne of love.

"I want that for you, too, you know." At Elagbi's cryptic statement, Talasyn turned to him, not understanding what he meant. He cupped her face between both hands. "Whirlwind or not, be it a lightning bolt or a slow fall, I want you to someday have what your mother and I had."

"I don't think there's time for that," Talasyn said dismissively. Romance was a foreign concept to her. And, from what she'd learned about them, the majority of the Nenavarene lords and ladies didn't seem to set much store by it either, focused as they were on power plays and financial gain. Urduja's marriage to Talasyn's grandfather, who had died before Elagbi was born, had been a purely strategic choice, a consolidation of territories between two noble houses to resolve a centuries-old border dispute.

Elagbi was the outlier, and perhaps there was no greater proof that Talasyn was his daughter because there was a small part of her that was *curious* about it. About how it felt to love somebody so much that you could defy tradition or leave behind everything you had ever known.

And then she remembered what had happened between

Khaede and Sol, the grief that she knew Khaede was carrying wherever she was and would carry until the end of her days, and she thought about how bittersweetly her father spoke of his long-gone wife.

Talasyn revised her opinion. Surely no romance was worth all that.

"Someday, dearest one," Elagbi repeated. "Of course, whoever it is will have to go through me first, and I shall have no qualms about telling them that they aren't good enough for you."

CHAPTER FOURTEEN

At noon the following day, with the sun of perpetual summer high in the sky, Talasyn grabbed her climbing gear and snuck out of the royal palace, testing her recently devised escape route. Over the balcony of her bedchamber, down the white marble walls, down the limestone bluffs. She timed her descent to coincide with the roving patrols' brief periods of shift changes and blind spots that she'd spent several sennights taking note of. Upon reaching the base of the cliff, she drew up her nondescript gray hood to cover her face, which had dominated Dominion newssheets these past few months, and forged onward into the bustling city.

She had to hand it to the Nenavarene living in Eskaya. Although an alert had been issued and commonfolk throughout the islands had been advised to prepare to take shelter from the Kesathese warships at a moment's notice, for the most part life in the capital was proceeding as usual. Taverns and wet markets were still doing business at a brisk pace; the blue skies were littered with trade ships; and carts gently rattled down the streets, pulled by amiable sun buffaloes, bearing milk jugs and sacks of rice. The only thing separating today from any other was the fact that news of the approaching Kesathese flotilla was on everyone's lips.

Or *almost* everyone's, Talasyn mentally corrected herself as she skirted around two children on the sidewalk. They were playing a hand-clapping game without a single worry on their nut-brown faces.

"*The west wind sighs, all moons die,*" they sang, palms slapping together in time to the melody. "*Bakun, dreaming of his lost love, rises to eat the world above.*"

Talasyn slipped through the drifting crowds, careful to stick to Eskaya's gloomy alleys and the quieter residential avenues whenever possible, but she took the extra precaution of keeping her head bowed all the way to the docks, where she rented an airship from the most apathetic-looking proprietor she could find. Her gamble paid off and the man spared her only the most fleeting of glances as he pocketed the handful of silver coins she gave him. He motioned her toward the vessel that was now hers for the day.

It was . . . Well, Talasyn supposed that it *could* be called an airship, in the sense that it possessed aether hearts, an aetherwave transceiver, and a sail. However, unlike the imposing outrigger warships or the graceful moth coracles or the ostentatious pleasure yachts, this particular Nenavarene design was what was called a *dugout*. It was little more than a hollowed tree trunk, with a yellow sail that had clearly seen better days.

Talasyn knew that the dugouts were sturdier than they appeared. They were a common enough sight in Dominion skies, being a cheap and convenient mode of travel between islands. But that did little to allay her fears that her tiny airship would fall apart in a stiff breeze.

Still, beggars couldn't be choosers, and a few minutes later she was soaring away from the docks and over the city rooftops and the expanse of wild rainforest that hemmed them in.

Wind and sunbeams whipped at her face as she set sail for Port Samout.

Ever a reliable source of court gossip, Jie had confided to Talasyn over breakfast that the Kesathese flotilla was now within sight of Nenavar's shores. No one would tell her anything more, so Talasyn had decided to see for herself. She didn't have any afternoon lessons scheduled today; all that she'd needed to do was endure another frustrating, bewildering morning session with the dance instructor before she retired to her chambers with a pretend headache, leaving strict orders not to be disturbed.

Even if she *was* being provided with a detailed report every few minutes—as her grandmother most assuredly was, judging from the constant parade of officers filtering in and out of the Roof of Heaven's throne room—Talasyn still wasn't going to sit idly in her luxurious prison while the Night Empire made their move, whatever said move entailed. An age-old fury built up inside her the moment she glimpsed the unmistakable outlines of Kesathese ironclads massing on the horizon, silhouetted against a clear blue sky that had, by the time she docked atop a sandy cliff near the port, turned overcast and gloomy with the promise of rain.

It was mere coincidence. Nenavar could shift from sun-drenched to waterlogged in the blink of an eye. Despite knowing this, Talasyn couldn't help the shudder of both fear and revulsion that lanced through her being. She couldn't help feeling as though the Night Empire stormship had brought the clouds with it.

We'll be all right. She chanted it to herself over and over again. *We have the dragons.*

And we have the Huktera fleet.

She exited the dugout and scrambled to the edge of the cliff on her hands and knees, sand scraping at her spread palms and her brown breeches until she found a decent vantage point where she could lie flat on her stomach. She retrieved a golden spyglass from her pack and put it to her right eye, squeezing the left one shut as she homed in on what was happening north of Port Samout.

Forming a defensive arrowhead a few miles off Sedek-We's coast were the outriggers of the Dominion—triple-decked warships bristling with rows upon rows of bronze cannons, with their keels curved like crescents, bows fashioned into snarling dragons' heads and the sterns into lashing tails. Their crab-claw sails bore the dragon emblem of Nenavar, wings spread, the lower half of its serpentine body coiled, blazing gold against a field of blue. The outriggers hovered in the air on fumes of wind magic, amidst clouds of moth coracles, above an Eversea that had begun churning along with the darkening of the sky, its frothing currents the color of old machine oil, mirroring the tense atmosphere.

At the tip of the formation was the *Parsua*, the flagship of Elaryen Siuk, Nenavar's Grand Magindam, a rank that Talasyn had deduced was similar to that of the Sardovian Amirante. Siuk seemed as unfazed as Ideth Vela would be in this situation, standing on the command deck and drinking coffee as she surveyed the Kesathese vessels that had come to a stop just slightly beyond firing range, cannons already swung outward.

Talasyn shifted her spyglass further north. Her brow furrowed. There was something different about the Night Empire's ironclads and their wolf coracle escorts. Their hulls seemed to be made of thicker plate, the cannons slimmer. Or maybe she just hadn't seen them in so long. Behind them lurked the stormship, a nightmare assembled from aether and fog, and it was . . .

Her fingers shook around the spyglass as her fury spiked to a magnitude far greater than her body could contain. It was the *Deliverance*. The Night Emperor's flagship.

No longer Gaheris's, but Alaric's.

Talasyn's magic stirred within its banks, raring and restless, itching to reach out across the turbulent waves to sink light's fiery claws into her nemesis. She pictured Alaric on the enclosed bridge of the stormship, his silver gaze dispassionately regarding the white shores of another land that his empire had come to wreak havoc on. And because she couldn't do anything from this distance, because she felt as though her hatred would eat her alive, she swung her spyglass back to the Nenavarene side of the standoff in a bid to distract herself by waiting for Siuk's next move.

A shadow fell over the *Parsua*'s many decks. A dragon had wandered down from beyond the mountains—one of the green-eyed ones, its great length covered in salt-crusted copper scales. It was either curious or protective. No one would be able to tell for sure, save for the dragon itself. While none of its kind ever harmed those with Nenavarene blood, and they were known to protect the Dominion in dangerous times, they could not be commanded. The dragons were creatures of the aether, even more so than the spectrals that could vanish at will and the sarimans that could nullify magic.

This particular dragon emitted a roar of challenge as it swooped toward the Kesathese ships. Talasyn wondered what Alaric's reaction was to witnessing such a creature bear down upon him. She wished she could see his face.

She gave a start, accidentally knocking her head against the spyglass. Why was she thinking about Alaric Ossinast's *face*?

Mentally castigating herself, Talasyn resumed tracking the dragon's slithering flight, watching intently as it closed in on the Night Empire's ranks.

Flares of brilliant amethyst lit up the horizon. The ironclad spearheading Kesath's formation fired off dozens of huge bolts of void magic, several of which hit the oncoming dragon squarely in its left wing. Talasyn's cry of disbelief was swallowed up by the leviathan creature's scream of pain as the rot

167

set in, patches of black decay blossoming over copper scales. Its survival instinct kicked in as it dove into the Eversea with uncharacteristic clumsiness, badly wounded, confused to find itself on the receiving end of the only aether magic in the world that could penetrate its hide.

How—

Alaric, Talasyn realized. He'd taken the stolen moth coracle back to the Continent, and Kesath's Enchanters must have been put to work extracting the new magic from its aether hearts.

As the dragon disappeared beneath the tide, Talasyn rushed back to the dugout. She no longer cared about secrecy. She had to warn the Roof of Heaven that the Night Empire had developed their own void cannons, and then she had to join Grand Magindam Siuk's fleet, to help them in the battle that was sure to follow. But no sooner had she activated the dugout's transceiver when a message rolled in on the aetherwave. It was from the lead Kesathese ironclad, and it overrode all nearby Dominion frequencies.

"Greetings," a woman's clipped tones said in Sailor's Common. "I am Commodore Mathire of the Night Empire. Bringing up the rear is His Majesty Alaric Ossinast. More warships are on their way. I regret that we had to harm your dragon, but it was in the interest of preventing further losses. We wanted to show you that we are in possession of this magic as well, and it would be wise to take the path of least resistance. Before the sun has set, you will send an envoy to discuss the terms of the Nenavar Dominion's surrender. Or we invade."

On the bridge of the *Deliverance*, Alaric stalked over to the aetherwave transceiver and yanked at the lever that put him through to the *Glorious*, Mathire's ironclad.

"Commodore." He kept his tone level, much too aware of the many crew members within earshot. "I gave orders to fire only if it was a matter of life and death."

"With all due respect, Your Majesty," Mathire replied, her civility matching his, "the beast was flying right at us. Any leader worth their salt would have made the same call. At least now the Dominion knows that we're serious."

Or they'll declare all-out war because we injured one of their dragons, Alaric retorted, but only in the silence of his own head. He couldn't argue with one of his officers in public; he was so very *newly* emperor, after all, and Mathire was one of the old guard. A hero of the Cataclysm. It wouldn't do to run afoul of High Command's panel of veterans and their loyalists just yet.

Alaric settled for instructing Mathire to remain on the alert before he signed off. And then there was nothing left to do but wait for Nenavar's response—and think about the dragon.

It had been truly monstrous. A snakelike hellbeast that blocked out the sky. Many in Alaric's crew had screamed and gasped to see a myth come to life in the distance, coiling through the heavens, approaching their formation with inscrutable intent. A myth whose claws and fangs suddenly made their dread stormship seem nothing more than a fragile construct, built by mortal hands.

Alaric grudgingly admitted to himself that it was in many ways a relief to have proof of the new cannons working against such a creature. Gaheris had been instantly enamored with the Nenavarene magic and he'd had his Enchanters toil day and night to master it, to spin out enough of it to arm a good portion of the ironclads and the wolf coracles. But the supply was limited, and the former Night Emperor, who was now styled Regent, was eager to gain access to the amethyst dimension's nexus point. Hence, this expedition southeast, mounted as soon as the cannons were ready to go.

And it wasn't just that.

With their technology and vast wealth, the Nenavar Dominion would be a fine addition to any empire. Even if it weren't, this nation had tried to help the Sunstead Lightweavers nineteen years ago, and Alaric knew that they could never be a trustworthy neighbor if he left them to their own devices. *All around us are enemies. Remember this, my son.*

Nenavar's response came much more swiftly than expected. Within the hour, in fact. As though they had anticipated Kesath's maneuver and had planned for it accordingly.

Alaric regarded their envoy with no small amount of wariness as she swept into the meeting room of the *Deliverance* as if she owned it.

As indicated in the Dominion's tersely worded missive, which had been delivered to the stormship via a crested brown-and-white eagle the size of a canoe, the envoy was Niamha Langsoune, the Daya of Catanduc. Her cross-collared peach-and-apricot robes swished gently with every step, celestial patterns embroidered in copper thread bringing out the burnished tones of her smooth skin. Elaborately stylized paints and powders adorned her graceful features underneath a jewel-encrusted scarf that had been wrapped around her jet-black hair like a halo. Alaric did his best not to gawk, acknowledging her flawless curtsy with a nod before gesturing for her to take the seat across from him at the long table. It was a private audience, with both side's guards waiting outside the closed doors.

"Daya Langsoune," Alaric began, "I trust that your journey was a pleasant one." From Port Samout, it had taken all of fifteen minutes for her skerry to reach the Night Empire airships, but he figured that it didn't hurt to be polite.

"As pleasant as can be expected, with the threat of war looming over our heads." Niamha's voice was disarmingly bright and clear, like a glass bell. In truth, she seemed far too young to have been designated envoy for such a delicate matter. Alaric estimated her to be around the same age as Talasyn was, and then he steadfastly banished his treacherous thoughts about the missing Lightweaver from his mind.

"It doesn't have to be a war," he told Niamha. "Should the Zahiya-lachis deign to swear fealty to the Night Empire, not a single drop of Nenavarene blood need be shed."

"I would not be so certain, Your Majesty. Let me tell you something about my people." Niamha leaned forward, as if about to impart a great secret. "*We will not be ruled by outsiders.* If Queen Urduja bows, our islands *will* revolt."

"And what are your islands compared to Kesath's ordnance?" Alaric drawled. "I have the advantage. I have the stormships *and* your magic. I could decimate the Nenavar Dominion's army in a fortnight using only half of the imperial fleet."

"You *could*, but then you will be king of ashes," Niamha shot back. "We would sooner salt our fields and poison our waters, burn our castles and bury our mines, and kill every last one of our dragons before we let any of it fall into the Night Empire's hands."

"While that would certainly be tragic, it's still a preferable outcome to Kesath having to share this corner of the Eversea with an independent, uncooperative monarchy. One that sought to destroy us nineteen years ago," he retorted. "We are wasting time, Daya Langsoune. I expected us to either discuss surrender or to declare hostilities, not to posture and play word games."

"I did not come here to surrender, Your Majesty. And only a fool would declare hostilities while behind enemy ranks." Niamha's ink-black eyes gleamed. "Queen Urduja wishes to avoid bloodshed, same as you. Luckily enough for all of us, Nenavar has a time-honored tradition of settling differences between rival factions via one very efficient method."

Alaric's jaw clenched. "Which is?"

"I bring you an offer from She Who Hung the Earth Upon the Waters," said the envoy. "An offer of marriage to the heir of her throne."

At first, Alaric was absolutely certain that he'd misheard. After several moments passed with Niamha watching him patiently, he found his voice, his brows knitting together. "Over the years, we have been gathering what intelligence we can on the Nenavar Dominion, as I am sure that the Dominion has done with Kesath." She smirked, giving away nothing and everything all at once, and he continued, "According to these reports, you have no Lachis'ka. Elagbi's daughter disappeared during a failed uprising and is presumed dead."

"Your reports are outdated," Niamha declared with relish. "Alunsina Ivralis was returned to us some time ago. A union between our two realms would be beneficial for all, don't you think? The Dominion retains its autonomy and the Night Empire gains access to Nenavar and the riches within." She stood up. "I'll take my leave before I outstay my welcome, Your Majesty. We shall await your response to either begin marriage negotiations or exchange broadsides, and rest assured that we are prepared to do either. But *do* take your time—you *have the advantage*, after all."

Niamha swept out of the room in a rustle of silk, leaving Alaric alone and stunned, wrestling with the enormity of the choice set before him.

"They want something."

His father's voice echoed low like distant thunder through a place that was not a place. A room that did not exist in the material world.

Gaheris called it the In-Between, this pocket dimension accessible via the Shadowgate. He had found it when he began delving deeper, past the known boundaries of magic. It was a space that could be occupied by more than one aethermancer at the same time, facilitating a method of instantaneous communication across even the vastest distance. The In-Between required tremendous focus and effort to maintain, and thus far

Alaric was the only one among the Legion who had mastered such an art.

As a child, he'd clung to the fanciful notion that the In-Between was special, something that belonged to him and his father alone. Perhaps there was a small part of him that still believed so now.

Amidst flickering walls of shadow energy and aetherspace, Gaheris was deep in thought, head bowed, long fingers curled under his chin, unmoving. By contrast, Alaric was restless even as he stood respectfully still, his gauntleted fist clenching and opening at his side in slow, tentative spasms.

"The Dominion wants something from us," Gaheris repeated. "Given how quickly they responded, they had their offer ready well before we made contact. I must admit that I'm curious." He looked up, his gray eyes holding Alaric prisoner in their murky depths. "But, in any case, Daya Langsoune is right. A conjugal union between the Night Emperor and the Lachis'ka of the Nenavar Dominion would be most pragmatic."

"Father." The protest was ripped loose from Alaric's throat before he could stop it. "I cannot marry a woman I do not know." He couldn't marry at all. A wife had never figured in his plans, and he had no wish to be shackled by the same sort of arrangement that had hung his parents out to dry.

"We must all make sacrifices for our cause. It would not do to falter now." Gaheris's tone took on a sinuous cajolery, sinking its thorns into Alaric's soul. "It is your destiny to rule. With the wealth of Nenavar at your disposal, with the Huktera at your back, you will build an empire on a grander scale than even I could have ever dreamed."

"It won't be my wealth, it won't be my fleet," Alaric muttered. "It will still belong to—"

"Your bride. Who will one day be the Zahiya-lachis. Who will be all too eager to share her earthly possessions with her husband if she is properly wooed."

Alaric grimaced. Pride kept him from saying it out loud, but Gaheris seemed entirely too confident in his son's abilities to woo anyone. "I don't know if it would be advisable to wager the future on a woman's heart," he remarked instead.

"What about a woman's duty to her people? A woman's sense of self-preservation?" Gaheris asked, changing tactics with the usual abrupt sharpness that always threatened to draw blood. "Once we have established a foothold in their archipelago, the Dominion will not dare test us. After your marriage, we shall be in a position to hold the sword over their head."

"Romantic indeed." Alaric flinched the moment that the words rolled off his tongue, caustic even to his own ears. His stomach dropped once he realized what he had just done, and he immediately sank to the shivering ground, prostrating himself at the regent's feet. "I apologize, Father."

"It would appear that you have gotten quite drunk on the power that I deigned to bestow upon you, my little lordling," Gaheris said coldly. "While you may be the face of this new empire, *I* am its architect. Your word is law but it is *I* who speaks through you. Have you forgotten?"

"No." Alaric squeezed his eyes shut. "It won't happen again."

"I should hope so. For your sake," Gaheris rumbled from his throne, thousands of miles away yet inescapable. "If you insist on acting like a petulant child, then I shall order you around as if you *are* one. You will marry this Alunsina Ivralis and form an alliance to herald the dawn of a new age, or you will suffer the *consequences*." Alaric lifted his head to nod, and Gaheris's next words were softer, the line of his mouth twisting into a smile laden with dark humor. "Do not fret, my son. You spoke of romance and I would be the first to tell you that such feelings have no place in this, but I've heard it said that Nenavarene women are the most beautiful and well-mannered in all the world. It might not be as unpleasant as you fear."

*

174

"*I won't do it!*"

Talasyn shook with fury, aiming a virulent glare at the Zahiya-lachis, who, in turn, regarded her with an impassive expression from the scroll-wing chair in her private salon.

"I won't agree to this." There was a beast trying to claw its way out of Talasyn's chest, some vile, ugly thing birthed from anger and disbelief, but she might as well have been the sea, crashing desperately against the insurmountable rock that was her grandmother's iron will. She turned to Elagbi, who had also gotten to his feet at Urduja's declaration but was otherwise not saying a word. "You can't make me do this!" Talasyn snapped at him. "All your talk about wanting me to be happy, to have what you and Hanan had. I won't find it with that—that *monster*—" Her voice broke. "Please—"

After Mathire's aetherwave transmission, Talasyn had returned the dugout to its proprietor and then rushed back to the palace on foot. Common sense had kicked in long enough for her to pretend that she'd still been laid up in bed when Jie came knocking to say that the Zahiya-lachis had summoned her. She hadn't been all that confident in her ability to act surprised as she sat in her grandmother's salon and was told about the Kesathese flotilla and their weaponry, but then the *offer* had come up and there was no longer any need to feign shock and horror.

"Talasyn is correct, Harlikaan," Elagbi told Urduja quietly. "She has already assumed her role at court under duress, and now you are offering her up like a sacrificial lamb to the Night Emperor."

"The alternative is to fight a war that we cannot win," said Urduja. "This is what is best for our people."

"Then *you* marry him!" Talasyn spat.

The Dragon Queen raised an eyebrow. "I am not the one he chased over the Eversea, the one he crossed blades with and met his match in. Who better to keep a Shadowforged husband in line than a Lightweaver wife?"

"With what training?" Talasyn let out a harsh, humorless laugh. "I haven't fought in months and I can't even commune with the Belian Sever. Your *terms* made sure of that!"

"And you accepted those terms, did you not? To save your friends. Tell me, what do you think will happen to them if the Night Empire attacks us and finds out that they're here?" Urduja asked pointedly. "With Alaric Ossinast as your consort, you will have greater control over where his forces may go. We will retain sovereignty of the archipelago and we will be able to keep the Night Empire away from Sigwad, where your comrades are hiding. If you won't do this for Nenavar, then do this for Sardovia."

"You have all the answers, don't you?" Talasyn narrowed her eyes at the woman whom she just couldn't bring herself to like, even as she'd come to grudgingly respect her power and political acumen. It was a sad thing to realize that the family she'd been searching for was a far cry from perfect— sadder still that one of them was actually capable of making her vision go *dim* with rage. "Did you know that this would happen? Were you plotting to use me as a bargaining chip right from the start? Did you *anticipate* that the Night Empire would come calling?"

"I suspected that it would be a possibility," Urduja said with maddening calm. "New empires are always so eager to make their mark, and who could resist the siren song of the Dominion? A strategic halfway mark between Kesath and both the southern and eastern hemispheres, oozing with precious metals and fertile land and advanced technology . . . Yes, I suspected. And I planned accordingly, because *that is what a leader does*."

"Leaders fight for their people!" Talasyn yelled. "They don't unlock the gates and welcome the enemy with open arms!"

"You *foolish* child," Urduja hissed. "Don't you understand yet? This *is* how we fight. We give them the foothold that they're after, but we dictate how they move."

"You're using *we* an awful lot, considering that I'm the only one who's going to be a tyrant's wife!" Talasyn's gaze shot to Elagbi once more but he remained silent, the look on his face conflicted. Her shoulders slumped. Her father might profess to love her but, in the end, he would never go against his own mother, his queen. The Zahiya-lachis was as good as a goddess, her word law.

"You promised, Alunsina," Urduja reminded her quietly. "You swore that you wouldn't give me any trouble if I agreed to shelter you and your comrades. I am holding you to that now."

In spite of her defiance, Talasyn knew that she again had no choice. This time, it wasn't just the continued survival of the Sardovian remnant that was at stake, but all of Nenavar as well. Even if by some miracle she and her comrades managed to escape from the Dominion unscathed, she would be leaving an entire country at the mercy of the regime that had thought nothing of wiping entire cities from the map. She was well and truly ensnared.

"Take heart, my dear." Urduja must have sensed Talasyn's belligerent acceptance, because she now sounded marginally more sympathetic. "Many empires have come and gone since the first Zahiya-lachis took the throne. Nenavar has watched them rise and she has watched them fall, and she will outlast this one, too. The Night Empire will not destroy us, and neither will they destroy you, for you are of our blood. Now—save us all."

CHAPTER FIFTEEN

Emerging from the depths of the *Deliverance* the next day, the Kesathese shallop drifted past the Nenavarene harbor, lugsails on its twin masts rippling black and silver in a breeze too warm for Alaric's liking. It was surrounded by a formation of ghostly Dominion coracles steered by helmsmen who were not only guiding the outsiders to the capital city but also watching their every move like hawks.

Alaric entertained the possibility that this was a trap, that he and his retinue would be slaughtered upon landing at the Roof of Heaven. It was an unlikely prospect, but he found himself *almost* wishing for it. A swift, violent death seemed preferable to marrying a stranger, some coldly beautiful, viperous Nenavarene woman.

As he stood at the bow of the shallop while it cruised further inland, a lush paradise unfolded miles below his feet, a maze of winding roads and rivers embedded in an expanse of green jungle. He scarcely had eyes for any of it, however, because for some reason his thoughts had strayed to Talasyn.

As the months had worn on without any sign of her, the notion that she might be dead had begun to creep up on him. It bothered him more than he cared to admit that their paths might never cross again, that he might never again see her teeth clenched in a snarl and the wiry muscles of her arms straining with every pulse of the radiance that she spun from her fingers. Granted, if she were still alive, that would only be prolonging the inevitable, but . . .

But the last that Alaric had glimpsed of Talasyn was her unkempt braid tossing in the wind as he turned and walked away from her amidst a tangle of smoke and ruins. And that felt wrong, somehow. Unceremonious, and far too abrupt.

He wondered, without really meaning to, what she would think if she ever heard about his impending marriage. He wondered this while feeling a vague, dull ache that he didn't understand.

Talasyn looked up as the door to her chambers swung open, puzzled that it was Elagbi who entered instead of Jie, who was supposed to prepare her for the initial meeting with the Kesathese delegation.

"What are you doing here?" Her tone was a little too sharp, but she couldn't bring herself to care.

"I wanted to apologize." There were bags under her father's eyes. "I know that you are resentful because I didn't speak up as emphatically as I should have."

"The Dragon Queen's word is law," Talasyn muttered. "No one in the Dominion defies her."

"That's no excuse. You are my daughter and I should have fought for you, right then and there," Elagbi said gravely. "I have since attempted to sway her from this course. Her mind is set, but I was able to persuade her to let you attend the marriage negotiations."

Talasyn cocked her head. "How did you manage that?"

Elagbi flashed her a tired, solemn smile. "A great deal of appealing to Her Starlit Majesty's compassionate nature . . ." At this, Talasyn snorted. ". . . as well as reminding her that the Night Empire needs to be made aware that the Lachis'ka has power of her own. And, also, by promising her that I'll stop you from punching Ossinast the moment you see him. I'm not as young as I once was, though, so I might move a touch too slowly."

The corner of Talasyn's lips twitched in a reluctant smirk. She was far from mollified, but at least her anger had been redirected to those more deserving. The negotiations were supposed to be conducted between the two heads of state and their trusted advisers. This concession that Elagbi had managed to wrangle had been hard-won.

"One more thing," said the Dominion prince. "The mood at court is currently divided. There are those who see this union as a lucrative deal, and there are those who see it as a betrayal of everything that the Dominion stands for. Kai Gitab, the Rajan of Katau, belongs firmly in the latter group, but your grandmother has assigned him to the negotiation panel."

Talasyn blinked. "*Why?*"

"To mollify the opposition. Queen Urduja felt that it would be wise to ensure that *all* interests are represented, especially since she has assigned Lueve Rasmey of Cenderwas the role of chief negotiator. Daya Rasmey is one of Urduja's closest allies, so the addition of Gitab balances things out. He has earned a name for himself as incorruptible and devoted to his ideals. With him on the panel, no one can accuse the Zahiya-lachis of selling out Nenavar. And with *you* reining in your distaste for the situation, more of the court will follow your lead."

"I wouldn't be so sure of that," Talasyn muttered. "They've known me only a few months."

"That is immaterial," said Elagbi. "You are She Who Will Come After. There is no shortage of nobles striving to prove themselves indispensable to your future reign. However, since Gitab is on the negotiation panel, I advise you to tread with care." He sighed. "At least Surakwel is off gallivanting elsewhere, or we'd have an even bigger problem on our hands."

"Who's Surakwel?" Talasyn asked.

"A damnable headache," Elagbi replied with a trace of humor. "His young lordship Surakwel Mantes is Daya Rasmey's nephew. He is one of the main critics of Nenavarene isolationism, believing that the way forward is for us to integrate with the rest of Lir. Around three years ago, he and a few other nobles began lobbying the Dominion to join forces with Sardovia against the Night Empire. If anyone is going to be vigorous in their objection to this betrothal, more so than Gitab, it's Surakwel."

"I like him already," Talasyn said. "What did you mean by *off gallivanting*? Where is he?"

"No one knows. Bit of a wanderer, that boy. He spends most of his time away from Nenavar, getting all sorts of foolish outsider notions into his head."

"You were a wanderer in your younger years, too, Amya," Talasyn chided. "And you *married* an outsider."

Her father flushed with pleasure as he always did when she called him the Nenavarene word for *father*. It was the joy of lost time found again. "That I was, and that I did."

Elagbi left when Jie arrived, gingerly carrying the Lachis'ka's crown perched atop its velvet cushion. Talasyn stared at the object as she felt Jie's apprehensive gaze dart over her form. She'd never made an effort to conceal how much she hated being prissied up, and it always took a lot of gentle cajoling to get her to cooperate. Today, however, was a different story.

An intimidated opponent is much easier to negotiate with, Vela had said four months ago on Queen Urduja's flagship. While Alaric was in possession of superior ordnance, it was Talasyn who had the element of surprise on her side. He didn't know that *she* was Alunsina Ivralis. And Elagbi was right—the

181

Lachis'ka *did* have power of her own, and she could submit to this farce of a marriage on *her* terms.

But she needed to look the part.

Taking a deep breath, Talasyn undid the frayed band that was holding her hair in the simple braid that she preferred, letting the whole chestnut-colored mess tumble down her shoulders. "All right," she said to Jie, "do your worst."

A congregation of Dominion nobles received Alaric at the front steps of the Roof of Heaven. They were led by a tall copper-skinned man who regarded him with stern jet-black eyes.

"Emperor Alaric."

This appeared to be the signal for the other nobles to sink, as one, into the briefest and most perfunctory of curtsies and stiff bows.

Alaric nodded, surmising the man's identity from his dragon-shaped circlet. "Prince Elagbi. Well met."

"It is good of you to think so," Elagbi replied with dripping sarcasm, and Alaric bit his tongue to avoid snapping, *I don't want to marry your daughter, either.* Fine diplomacy it would be if he and the Dominion prince came to blows.

As Elagbi led the way, his guards immediately closed in, covering all avenues of escape with martial precision—all women, whose imposing frames and alarmingly heavy-looking armor made Alaric wish that he'd brought more soldiers of his own. He had his legionnaire Sevraim and the shallop's crew for protection, and the latter group wouldn't even be accompanying him inside. Kesathese High Command had clamored for a display of strength, but Alaric had pointed out that an overabundance of warriors at what was ostensibly a peacemaking overture would have made the other side more defensive than they already were. Besides, Nenavar was well aware that the wolf at the door had fangs—or dragonslaying magic, to be more accurate.

Alaric had brought Mathire with him, too. She wasn't the most politically adept of his officers, but he'd banked on a woman in a position of authority making the matriarchal Dominion more well disposed toward them. Of course, that was *before* Mathire had given the order for her ship to fire on the dragon. Gods, he hoped the thing wasn't dead.

Nevertheless, the small retinue was a show of good faith, as was Alaric's agreeing to the negotiations being held on Nenavarene soil and the lack of the mask that he normally donned in situations wherein there was a high chance of a battle breaking out before he'd even stepped foot in the palace.

And it was a magnificent palace. Of that, there could be no doubt. Shining in the morning light, its facade of pristine white marble gave the illusion that the limestone cliffs on which it rested were laden with fresh snow in the heart of a verdant rainforest. It possessed an array of stained-glass windows, slender towers, and golden domes. The ornate arch over the main entrance was gold as well, and as they passed beneath it, Alaric heard Sevraim curse under his breath, a sound that was in sync with the disquieting sensation of the Shadowgate being cut off. The cages that Alaric now knew contained living creatures within were hung up along the hallway at regular intervals, the bulky, opaque cylinders incongruous with the paintings, carvings, and tapestries that adorned the shimmering white walls.

"Kindly excuse us for taking such precautions, Your Majesty," Elagbi said in much the same tone as the one with which he'd greeted Alaric while nodding to the cages. "Our people do not trust the Shadowgate, especially when it is wielded in the proximity of the Zahiya-lachis."

"I don't mind at all, Prince Elagbi," said Alaric, affecting nonchalance. "I am only sorry that these cages clash with your lovely decor."

"I pray that you won't attempt to rectify the situation by smashing any of them and letting the sariman loose."

Alaric was probably not going to hear the end of *that* for a while, but at least he'd now learned that the jewel-toned birds that possessed the ability to nullify magic were called sarimans. "As long as your hospitality is not revoked, there will be no need for me to cause any trouble," he told Elagbi curtly.

Walking quietly beside him, Commodore Mathire shot Alaric a look of thinly veiled amusement. She had known him ever since he was young, and he'd always gotten the impression that she found him entertaining. That annoyed him a little. He was the Night Emperor, not some silly child.

The Dragon Queen's throne hall was *deeply* ostentatious. Alaric was used to Kesath's streamlined architecture and the practical interiors of the stormships, which emphasized functionality over aesthetic. He nearly stopped in his tracks upon crossing the threshold into a vast chamber, its walls paneled with gold leaf and draperies of crimson silk, its polished marble floors strewn with cream-and-burgundy carpets that sported intricate constellations of seed pearls and sapphires. The high-vaulted ceiling was adorned with bas-relief carvings of birds and lilies and dragons chasing one another through rollicking ocean waves. It would have emptied out the Night Empire's treasury to decorate and maintain this space. And the people—

The people fell deathly silent when Alaric's group entered. He'd never seen such a gathering in all his life, every single individual bedecked in luxurious fabrics and riotously colorful feathers, dripping with glittering gems from head to toe.

Neither had he ever been the recipient of such a concentrated mass of wary glares.

"We're not welcome here, Your Majesty," Sevraim murmured from behind his helm. "They still see us as invaders. I would advise you to tread with caution."

"Don't I always?" Alaric retorted out of the corner of his mouth. "Despite *your* attempts to influence me to the contrary?"

Sevraim chuckled. He was *strolling*, utterly relaxed, the dark eyes behind his obsidian visor alighting on the Nenavarene ladies on the sidelines with interest. If he hadn't been wearing his helm, he would have been winking at them and raking a hand through his hair, Alaric was fairly certain of that.

He should have brought the twins instead.

At the end of the hall was an enormous platform consisting of bands of white, red, and gray marble that loomed over the courtiers in the same manner that the limestone cliffs of the Roof of Heaven loomed over the capital. There were three thrones perched atop the steps; the one on the left was empty, obviously Elagbi's, while the one on the right was occupied by a feminine figure draped in blue and gold but otherwise obscured by a translucent wood-framed screen held by two attendants. Alaric wasn't ready to scrutinize his future bride too closely just yet, so he focused all of his attention on the woman seated in the middle.

Urduja Silim. The Zahiya-lachis of the Nenavar Dominion, with a twisted crown and white-powdered face and jet-black gaze like winter steel. Her throne eclipsed the two others in both opulence and breadth, a construct of pure gold with clawed feet and stylized wings sprouting from the backrest that spread halfway up to the ceiling, unfurled like a dragon's in midflight and sprinkled all over with jade, opals, rubies, diamonds, and gems that Alaric couldn't even name.

"That chair alone could commission a fleet of ironclads," he heard Sevraim remark to Mathire as they approached the platform, which also had a sariman cage mounted at each end.

Elagbi ascended the steps and took his place at his mother's side while the rest of the welcoming committee melted into the watchful crowd. Alaric straightened his spine, taking care not to let his shoulders droop into their instinctive slight hunch, and Mathire clicked her heels and saluted Queen Urduja. Alaric felt Sevraim come to a sharp halt beside him as Urduja's royal guards fanned out to both circle the Kesathese delegation and barricade the platform.

"Emperor Alaric." Urduja's imperious tones rang throughout the hall. "I bid you welcome to my court. Before we commence with the negotiations, allow me to state for the record that I would like for us to listen to each other with open minds and strive to work together in ensuring a prosperous future for our two realms. It is my sincerest wish that your journey here will not be in vain, whether by your own doing or others."

The pretty speech ended on a firm note, as if it had been a warning all along. A warning that seemed to very pointedly include their audience of nobles, who were watching the scene as if they had collectively stepped on something malodorous. Alaric could only imagine the uproar that must have taken place when Urduja announced her granddaughter's betrothal to him.

There was movement at the corner of his eye, a flash of white-streaked reddish-brown hair—Mathire had broken her rigid stance to dart him an urgent look. Right. It was *his* turn to say something.

"I thank you for your hospitality, Queen Urduja, as well as for your wisdom in facilitating a mutually beneficial solution to this territorial dispute," said Alaric. The Nenavarene needed to be reminded that this arrangement was *their* sovereign's idea. "My people are tired of war and yours would rather not start one. We are therefore united by a common purpose, and I have every faith that we will manage to broker an enduring, fruitful peace."

These weren't empty words. Not for him. He had been on the front lines ever since he was sixteen years old. This alliance was his chance, too, to know what it was like to live without the hurricanes.

Urduja graciously inclined her head. "Then, if it pleases His Majesty, you may approach the throne and meet our Lachis'ka."

Alaric felt as though his legs were made of lead as he ascended the marble steps that seemed to go on forever, an entire hall fixated on his every movement. When he reached the top of the platform, he noticed that there was a cunning gleam in the Dragon Queen's eyes that he didn't like, a gleam that made his gut curl with foreboding. Before he could dwell on it, however, the figure on the rightmost throne stood up and emerged from behind the screen and swept toward him. His train of thought screeched to a halt.

Nenavarene women are the most beautiful in all the world, Gaheris had said, but *beautiful* couldn't even *begin* to describe Alunsina Ivralis. She wore a dress of rich oceanic blue, the bodice gold-flecked and skintight, hanging from her bare left shoulder in an artful slash while her right shoulder was capped by an eagle-wing pauldron made entirely of gold, attached to a sleeve of what looked like golden chainmail encasing her slim arm. Her skirt was a voluminous, ballooning thing, studded with crystalline beadwork, the silk hem bunched up into swirling rosettes to reveal the yards of sheerer gold fabric that lay beneath, every inch painstakingly embroidered with the coiled dragon that was the insignia of the Nenavarene Royal House. Her crown of stars and saltires was made of gold, set with sapphires, and her eyes were dramatically rimmed with kohl, a smattering of gold dust at the edges—and there was something familiar about their tawny depths that Alaric couldn't parse. In fact, there was something about *her*, in general, that tugged at him. He was too flustered by his physical reaction to immediately decipher what it was, but when he finally did, the breath caught in his throat.

She reminded him of Talasyn. Her stature, the color of her swept-back hair, even the way she moved. It was a cruel joke that he would now have to wed someone so similar to the girl who plagued his thoughts.

"Lachis'ka." Alaric bowed his head, retreating into prescribed formalities the same way that he fell into combat forms by rote. "May this signal the beginning of an amicable relationship between our two realms and . . ."

He trailed off mid-sentence as he lifted his gaze back to her features. His brain was starting to catch up, starting to realize that—

—underneath the opulent silk and the lavish jewels—

—underneath the cosmetics that hid her freckles and sharpened her cheekbones and softened the strong line of her jaw—

—underneath all of that—she was—

"*Amicable relationship?*" Talasyn hissed, with narrowed eyes and a feral flash of teeth, and Alaric's heart all but stopped beating in his chest. "Not fucking *likely.*"

CHAPTER SIXTEEN

Talasyn did not hold much truck with the finery of her father's people. That wasn't to say that she detested looking at the Nenavarene lords and ladies in their resplendent attire, but actually *wearing* these things herself was a different story. Perhaps concluding that her granddaughter would be a more amicable hostage if provided some measure of freedom, Queen Urduja usually allowed Talasyn to scurry around in simple tunics and breeches when her presence was not required at a meeting. Talasyn was little used to the scratch of embroidered silk and the constraints of heavy jewelry and layered skirts.

As such, while she was aware that she currently looked very glamorous indeed, she was also, not to put too fine a point on it, *dying* inside. Jie had laced up the bodice a bit too securely in an effort to imbue curves where there were none, and the pins holding Talasyn's crown in place dug into her scalp like talons. Her face was pancaked with layers of powder and metallic pigments, her lips sticky with the peach lacquer that had been brushed over them to offset her bold eyes. She felt too stiff and too warm, and also rather like a fraud, but she gladly acquiesced to these discomforts because the look on Alaric Ossinast's face made it all worthwhile.

Her hackles had started rising practically from the moment he walked into the throne hall with his companions, one of whom she recognized as the staff-wielding legionnaire from the battle of Lasthaven. *Sevraim,* one of the twins had called him. Talasyn had been expecting Alaric to arrive in his usual armor or perhaps the grand robes of his new office, but instead he wore a starkly tailored, belted black tunic over black trousers, and in place of the clawed gauntlets of his battle regalia were plain leather ones. The only nod to embellishment was the silver brooch in the shape of his house's chimera crest, affixing a cape that flowed with his every step like a raven's wing. She would never admit it out loud, even with a knife to her throat, but the simple attire flattered his lean figure, emphasizing his broad shoulders and his formidable height. With his mane of thick dark hair framing his pale face as he'd purposefully stridden toward the platform, seemingly oblivious to the court's stares and whispers, he'd looked every inch a prince. And not a charming, gallant one like Elagbi, but a sinister prince who brought blood and battle and ill omens.

Therefore, it was all the more satisfying when his jaw dropped once he realized that *she* was Alunsina Ivralis.

Talasyn was standing right in front of him. She had the privilege of watching all trace of urbane courtesy vanish from his features as it morphed into complete and utter *shock*. His gray eyes went wide and his complexion drained of color so that he was now as white as a sheet. Even after her hostile declaration, which she had pitched low so the courtiers would not overhear, he remained silent for several more seconds, gaping at her like a fish plucked from water.

It was a petty sort of triumph that swelled in Talasyn's chest, but it quickly faded into bewilderment when something like relief spasmed across Alaric's features. The expression lasted only for a second, just long enough for her to register its similarity to the look on many a soldier's face when the

190

all clear was sounded—*we live to fight another day*—and then it was gone.

"A fine trap you've set," he said coldly, glancing around the hall as though expecting Sardovian soldiers to pop out from the shadows at any moment. There was a stir below the platform as Sevraim recognized Talasyn and tried to rush up the steps, but was blocked by the Lachis-dalo closing ranks around him, the scrape of blades being drawn piercing the silence.

"It is no trap, Your Majesty," Urduja declared. "The kaptan of the Belian garrison noticed Alunsina's resemblance to her late mother and summoned the prince. After Kesath won your Hurricane Wars, Alunsina returned to us to seek sanctuary and to claim her birthright."

"If the patrol hadn't apprehended us at the shrine, I would never have been reunited with my family," Talasyn told Alaric with venomous sweetness. "So, really, I have *you* to thank for that."

"And who else sought sanctuary with you?" he retorted. "Am I to find Ideth Vela among your retinue? Is Bieshimma long-lost royalty as well?"

"I have no idea where the others are." The lie rolled off her tongue with ease, as it should; she'd rehearsed it frequently enough. "I was separated from them during the retreat. If you think that this is some sort of ruse, you can search the Dominion yourself."

But demanding to search the archipelago would be an unforgivable breach of jurisdiction, as well as tantamount to calling the Nenavarene head of state a liar—which would hardly endear the Night Empire to an already wary populace. Alaric was in a difficult position and he knew it, and he obviously knew that *Talasyn* knew it, judging from the way that he was glowering at her. She arched a brow at him in challenge as he continued to frown down at her and she could almost see the vein throbbing in his forehead and, *oh*, she was enjoying this far too much.

"Are the two of you quite done making a scene?"

The question dripped like icicles from Urduja's lips, shattering the world that was Alaric and Talasyn alone. Talasyn wanted to argue that it wasn't as though they'd been shouting at each other but, on second thought, their tense standoff was already eliciting speculative murmurs from the gathered nobles. Not to mention the minor chaos that was erupting below the platform.

I'm always so shortsighted when it comes to you. Talasyn seethed at the sullen emperor looming over her. Alaric had the habit of eclipsing everything else, making her throw caution to the wind for the sake of crossing blades and wits with him on the battlefields they'd fought over. This magnificent hall was a kind of battlefield as well. She had to be smarter, had to start using the same weapons that Queen Urduja wielded with such skill.

"I believe His Majesty and I have finished being reacquainted." Talasyn tried to say this with an air of sophisticated loftiness, but it only sounded bitingly sarcastic. Oh, well. Practice would make perfect—she hoped. "Shall we proceed with the negotiations?"

"What the *hell* is going on?" Sevraim demanded as Alaric stalked down the platform. The legionnaire's usual nonchalance was conspicuously absent. "Why is the Lightweaver dressed up as the Nenavarene Lachis'ka? Is the Dominion in cahoots with the Sardovian Allfold? Is—"

"Be quiet, Sevraim," Alaric grunted, aware they had an audience. In a low tone, he proceeded to explain the situation to his flabbergasted companions while the gathering of Dominion nobles looked on with varying degrees of amusement and ire.

"I for one don't believe that Vela doesn't have anything to do with this," Mathire hissed when he was finished. "It's too much of a coincidence. They can't possibly think that we'll go along with it."

"We can either storm out of here and brace ourselves for another war—or we can play their game for now," said Alaric. "I will need you to be at your best during the discussion of terms, Commodore. They've already managed to blindside us with this reveal. See that it does not happen again."

The proceedings were moved to the council room adjacent to the throne hall. Studying Talasyn as she sat across from him at the mahogany table, Alaric had a hard time reconciling this vision clad in the blue and gold of Nenavar with the ragged soldier he'd come to know. In fact, despite the barbs traded a few minutes ago, he could almost believe that there had been some mistake, that she was a different person entirely. But she was currently staring at him as though he was a particularly stubborn speck of dirt on her shoe, and *that* was a very Talasyn look. One that Alaric had no problem raising an eyebrow at, which clearly served to incense her further.

If he was being truthful with himself, he'd felt relief at seeing her, once the initial shock wore off—relief to know that she was alive, after all—but this was the kind of weakness that needed to be examined in private. Right now, he would do well to govern his emotions by clinging to the more familiar territory of their mutual dislike for each other.

She was sitting between Prince Elagbi and a middle-aged brunette clad in opals and sunset-hued, loom-woven fabric, who'd introduced herself as Lueve Rasmey, Urduja's right hand and the daya whose family controlled the Cenderwas Veins, where all manner of gems and precious metals were mined. To Elagbi's left was Niamha Langsoune, who flashed Alaric a pretty little smile that he didn't trust at *all*, and further down the table was a thin, scholarly-looking sort of fellow named Kai Gitab, the Rajan of Katau.

In lieu of aristocracy, Alaric had Commodore Mathire beside him while Sevraim guarded his back, positioned between him and the wide windows that occupied the entire length of one wall to expose the sweeping vista of rainforest. Queen Urduja was similarly protected by her royal guard as she presided at the head of the table, her icy crown glittering in the light of day.

"Before anything else, let us dispose of the elephant in the room," said Urduja. "Nineteen years ago, Nenavarene warships sailed to the Northwest Continent unprovoked, with the intention of providing reinforcements to the Lightweavers of Sunstead in their war with the Shadowforged. This flotilla left Dominion shores without my knowledge or my consent. I was *vehemently* against interfering in the affairs of outsiders when such was proposed to me. The people responsible—the ones who went behind my back after I expressly forbade sending aid to Sunstead—were rogue elements of my court, who, I assure His Majesty, are no longer a factor."

Alaric's eyes shifted again to Talasyn, who had gone pale, biting her lip as she looked toward Elagbi. The prince had suddenly found the surface of the table to be of great interest.

"The present-day Dominion," Urduja concluded, "will approach these talks with the best of intentions and we will keep our end of whatever bargains are made."

Alaric was surprised by the Zahiya-lachis's bluntness, but he inclined his head graciously. She *could* just be covering her tracks but, in the grand scheme of things, her speech was harmless enough to let slide for now. This marriage alliance made it all too clear that Nenavar had already learned its lesson when the first stormship destroyed its flotilla in one fell swoop.

"We shall treat it as ancient history, Queen Urduja," said

Alaric. "There can be no moving forward while the past hangs over our heads."

Despite his words, he glanced over at Talasyn and Elagbi again, puzzled by their strange reactions to Urduja's mention of *rogue elements*. There was something curious there.

Urduja nodded at Lueve Rasmey, who spoke up in pleasant tones that were at odds with the atmosphere of the room. "As chief negotiator for the Nenavar Dominion and on behalf of Her Starlit Majesty Urduja Silim, She Who Hung the Earth Upon the Waters, allow me to formally call this meeting to order. I have been instructed to proceed as if these were traditional marriage negotiations—"

"With all due respect, they are not," said Mathire. "This is a political union between two governments, with entire armies and economies at stake. It would be a disservice to both sides—and certainly the cause of many misunderstandings—if we were to treat this as an ordinary marriage."

"The esteemed commodore can surely be forgiven," said Lueve without missing a beat, chipper smile intact, "for her ignorance of Nenavarene customs. Among the upper echelons of our society, marriage *is* a political union. With it we form alliances, broker peace between rival houses, and seal trade partnerships. This is the mindset with which we are approaching these nuptials."

The direction that the conversation had taken drove home one very important point that Alaric had somewhat been refusing to process, but was now finally starting to sink in.

Talasyn.

His would-be bride was Talasyn.

He was going to marry Talasyn.

It was surreal and it was ridiculous. Across from him, the girl in question was beginning to look alarmed, as though it was also dawning on her that it was their shared future being discussed in this room.

Alaric was suddenly gripped by the chill certainty that if Talasyn started outright panicking, *he* would, too. Seizing an opportunity to get this over with as soon as possible *and* focus on practical matters rather than his impending breakdown, he addressed Daya Rasmey. "Kesath looks forward to all the diplomatic and trade benefits that will spring forth from this union. In return, there is much that we can offer the Lachis'ka."

"Aside from the continued safety and survival of her people, of course," Mathire supplied.

"I did not realize that we were here to exchange threats," said Niamha. "Nor did I think that anyone would issue threats this deep inside territory not their own."

Alaric resisted the urge to pinch the bridge of his nose to ward off an oncoming headache. "The Lachis'ka will gain the title of Night Empress, and all the power and prestige that comes with it. Naturally, we will expect Nenavar's full cooperation as we endeavor to maintain prosperity and stability in this corner of the Eversea."

"Cooperation that we will be only too glad to provide," said Prince Elagbi, "as long as it does not infringe on our sovereignty. That is one of our two non-negotiables—that Dominion law prevails in Dominion space."

Alaric nodded. "And what is the other non-negotiable?"

"That my daughter be treated with the utmost kindness and respect." Elagbi's dark eyes were as hard as flint as he met Alaric's gaze. "That never will a hand be raised to her in anger, that never will she be made to feel any less than who she is."

Talasyn turned to Elagbi, the look on her face a mix of gratitude and disbelief. This gave Alaric pause. Her expression made him think of certain things that he'd wished for during his own childhood. How he had longed for someone to give a damn about his welfare. For a parent, for *anyone*, to stand up for him—

No. Those were a child's insecurities, the chips on a foolish boy's shoulders. They had no place in an emperor's head.

"Her Grace Alunsina Ivralis will be treated in accordance with how she behaves herself," Alaric said curtly, brushing aside how odd it felt to refer to Talasyn by another name.

"Am I to be your *obedient* wife, then?" Talasyn spoke for the first time since taking her seat, hurling each word at him like a spear. "Shall I simper while millions suffer under your tyranny?"

Gods, he really *was* going to get a headache. "Nothing that happened in Sardovia will happen in Nenavar as long as the Dominion upholds its end of this bargain."

"*I* am their end of this bargain!" While some traitorous part of Alaric had always found the Lightweaver magnificent in her defiance, gold and gemstones gave her a sharper edge, made her burn as if she were a vengeful goddess. Her eyes flashed like bronzed agates afire with the dawn. "You come here all high and mighty to seek my hand in marriage and you bring with you the commodore who razed the Great Steppe and the legionnaire who participated in the siege of Lasthaven, not to mention that you yourself have killed countless of my fellow soldiers. So—forgive me if I am not too enthused by all of this, you cruel, pompous *ass*!"

Alaric could feel a vein in the hollow beneath his left eye start to twitch, as it always did when he was about to lose his temper. Trying not to appear too obvious about it, he inhaled slowly, and when next he spoke, it was in steady tones. "Your fellow soldiers?" he repeated. "If you still consider yourself Sardovian, my lady, then these negotiations are a waste of time and effort."

He watched her lips press into a taut line. She looked so angry that it wouldn't have been a surprise if she'd started levitating. When she didn't say anything, he continued, "Even if I were spineless enough to apologize for military actions undertaken during a time of war, I would hardly do so at the behest of a temperamental *child*. We made the crossing in the hopes of coming to terms and avoiding yet another blood-soaked conflict, but if the notion offends your sensibilities so much, Lachis'ka, all you have to do is say the word and I will see you again on the battlefield."

In the stony silence that ensued, Queen Urduja leaned forward in her seat, immediately drawing everyone's attention. "I believe that tensions are too high to facilitate any sort of agreement presently. May I suggest that we put this meeting on hold?" Based on her demeanor, this was more of a command. "We can resume negotiations tomorrow, when we have all gotten suitably used to one another. In line with this, the Kesathese delegation is more than welcome to stay here in the palace, where they will be treated as honored guests."

Lueve's pleasant composure had faltered during Alaric and Talasyn's verbal duel—in fact, it had appeared as if she were having a heart attack when Talasyn called the Night Emperor an ass—but, now that her sovereign had stepped in, the chief negotiator was quick to gather her bearings. "Yes, Harlikaan, I believe that would be ideal," she said smoothly. "We shall adjourn for now."

Kai Gitab had held his peace all throughout the meeting. In Talasyn's experience, the rajan was a shrewd and extremely calculating man who dispensed words as reluctantly as a miser parted with their coins. Once the Kesathese delegation had left the room, however, he turned to Urduja. "Begging your pardon, Harlikaan, but I am not sure that it is prudent to let the Night Empire have the run of the Roof of Heaven while a formal treaty has yet to be drafted."

"I am quite certain that Ossinast won't slaughter us in our beds," Urduja said dryly, "although *some* people appear to be rather set on persuading him to do that."

Talasyn bristled as her grandmother shot her a pointed glare. Before she could defend her actions, however, Niamha piped up, drawing everyone's attention, "More of that sort of thing might prove beneficial to our side. The Night Emperor strikes me as the type of man who is very difficult to rattle. Somehow, though, the Lachis'ka rattles him. I was watching him closely earlier. It seems that he can do a remarkable job of keeping a level head until prolonged interaction with Her Grace."

"We just really hate each other, that's all," Talasyn mumbled, embarrassed.

"Hate is a kind of passion, is it not?" Niamha countered.

"I'm— *Passion?*" Talasyn echoed in a squawk, a hot blush suffusing her cheeks. "There's no— What are you *talking* about—I can't stand the sight of him and the feeling is mutual!"

Niamha and Lueve observed her with varying degrees of amusement. "It would seem," Niamha remarked with a faint grin, "that Her Grace still has much to learn about the ways of men."

Elagbi clapped his hands over his ears, which made Lueve Rasmey burst into peals of melodious laughter. "Perhaps we should stop teasing the Lachis'ka," she quipped. "I doubt that Prince Elagbi's tender paternal heart can take much more."

"Yes, well, before he starts weeping all over the place"— Urduja narrowed her eyes at Talasyn, who stiffened upon realizing that she wasn't off the hook just yet—"I cannot stress this enough, Alunsina. If Kesath hadn't gotten their hands on void magic, we might have stood a chance. As it is, however, they've already wounded one of our dragons. The Night Empire is only willing to negotiate because they don't want to expend resources any more than we do, and it is your duty to ensure that they *remain* willing. If you fail, the consequences will be dire for all of us. Govern your pride, Your Grace—or, at the very least, be smarter about how you cling to it."

*

The Kesathese delegation had an entire wing of the palace to itself. A large bronze door in Alaric's chambers opened out into an orchid garden with a miniature waterfall, bisected by two stone paths. One led from his door to a westward hallway, while the other met the first path at its terminus and linked up with what appeared to be someone else's suite of rooms in the opposite wing, judging from the canopy bed that he glimpsed through a gap in the curtains on the other side of the garden.

Such luxury was not without its price. There were sariman cages affixed to the walls and pillars at seven-meter intervals, shutting off the Shadowgate, making it impossible to speak to his father in the In-Between. And there was also the fact that the pleasant garden view was ruined by Commodore Mathire, who was trampling all over the neatly trimmed grass with pacing footsteps.

"I don't care what the Lightweaver *or* that old hag said, this *has* to be a trick." Mathire was obviously still smarting from her gaffe in the council room. Her face was pale with fury.

"First of all, Urduja Silim is *hardly* a hag," Sevraim pointed out from where he sat beside Alaric on a stone bench, "and, secondly, that's the Night Emperor's grandmother-in-law you're talking about."

"*Prospective* grandmother-in-law," Alaric corrected. "A prospect that seems to be diminishing with each passing second."

"To your very great sorrow, I'm sure, Your Majesty." Sevraim uttered this with enough sarcasm to make it sound like a joke, but not *quite* enough to disguise the shred of curiosity that lay within. He was studying Alaric with a look that verged on *knowing*, although Alaric didn't have the slightest idea what Sevraim thought he knew. "I cannot believe that the Lightweaver and the Lachis'ka have turned out to be the same person. All those months spent looking for Talasyn and she was here all along. It's—"

"A trick!" Mathire repeated hotly. "A ploy orchestrated by Ideth Vela!" She stopped pacing in front of Alaric, squaring her shoulders in determination. "Your Majesty, we are well within our rights to demand proof that there is no collusion going on. We cannot gamble the security of our empire, especially when the Nenavarene have a reputation for being less than forthright. All we have is the Lightweaver's word that she fled here after the war, but that begs the question as to who *else* could have fled here with her. If I may be so bold as to insist—Kesath *must* be allowed to search Dominion territory, to determine for ourselves that they don't have the Sardovian fleet tucked away somewhere within their shores."

"We can make that request *after* we've hammered out the terms of the marriage contract," Alaric conceded. "That way, the negotiations will be over and done with and it will be less critical to abstain from offending Nenavar."

"And if we turn up no evidence of Sardovia, Your Majesty, do you mean to go through with it?" Sevraim asked. "Will you marry a sworn foe?"

Alaric would rather eat glass shards, but his father's words were at the forefront of his mind. Of course, there was every chance that Gaheris would sing a different tune upon learning the identity of the Lachis'ka. As of now, though . . .

"I will do what I must," was Alaric's stoic reply, "for the sake of the Night Empire."

CHAPTER SEVENTEEN

Talasyn was in a terrible mood. She'd tried to sneak out of the palace, only to discover much to her chagrin that security measures had been tightened due to the Kesathese presence. Before any of the increased number of guards could notice the Lachis'ka skulking around, she crept back to her chambers and then into the garden beyond, frustration curling low in her gut. The Sardovians needed to be informed of this new development as soon as possible. She needed Vela's advice on how best to proceed.

This particular garden section of the Roof of Heaven lay open to the sky, allowing copious amounts of moonlight to come spilling down over the grass and the orchids and the artificial waterfall that tumbled into a dark, rippling pool. The combined illumination of the stars and the seven moons was almost a soft, shadowed daytime.

Standing in the middle of the garden, Talasyn tipped her face up to the pulsating celestial mazes and took slow, deep breaths. Perhaps the perfumed scent of the flowers and the gentle burble of water and the cool evening air would help her regain inner peace.

As she watched, the night sky shimmered with a haze of

deep amethyst light. The Voidfell's lone nexus point, located in the crater of a dead volcano on the Dominion's centermost island, was discharging.

Talasyn remained as curious about void magic as she'd been when she first encountered it. While she'd been briefed on most aspects of life here in Nenavar, she'd been told very little about this amethyst dimension of aetherspace. She knew only that it was more malleable than other dimensions, that it could be folded into small aether hearts and still retain its properties as a weapon. Hence, the muskets—and she could only be glad that Kesath didn't appear to be producing *those* yet.

There were times when the Voidfell flared so intensely that the whole sky was set aflame, and it filled her with apprehension. It wasn't *normal* for a nexus point to blaze that brightly from so far off. People at court assured her that there was no need to worry, that it was simply the way of the Voidfell. A part of her remained unconvinced, but she chalked it up to the general sense of not having yet found her footing in this wild land.

She wondered just how big the Void Sever was, to be visible not only from Eskaya but sometimes from the Sardovian Coast as well. *The Fisherman's Warning,* Khaede had called it. Once every thousand years.

Thinking about Khaede made Talasyn's chest hurt. Khaede hadn't snuck into Nenavar with any of the convoys, and no one could remember seeing her during the Allfold's retreat from Lasthaven.

It had been months. Khaede was either dead or languishing in a Night Empire prison. And Talasyn was about to marry the man responsible for either scenario.

"It *is* you, after all."

Like clockwork, Talasyn thought sourly. As though she'd summoned him, because her luck was clearly just *that* abysmal as of late.

The distant Void Sever quieted as she turned to the source of those deep tones, rich like wine and oak. Only moonbeams and stardust illuminated Alaric's sharp, pale features. The austerely cut black garb that he favored didn't seem so out of place in Nenavar now that it was evening. He was spun from the shadows, a very extension of the night. His gloomy presence contrasted with his surroundings, a backdrop of orchids in all shapes and colors—some as frothy and white as seafoam, some as red and riotous as forest fire, some with speckled flute-shaped petals, and some iridescent like butterfly wings. Every flower released sighs of cool fragrance into the tropical night.

It would have been an idyllic scene if they were any other two people in the world. As it was, however, Talasyn felt all that old familiar anger rising up while Alaric took in the sight of the smock and breeches she had dearly cherished changing into after a long day at court, her face scrubbed clean and her hair tugged into its usual braid.

"And here I was harboring the faint suspicion that the Nenavarene were foisting some other girl off on me," he continued. "You clean up very well, Your Grace."

"What the hell are you doing in my garden?" Talasyn demanded.

"Ask whoever thought it would be a good idea to put me in the suite directly across from yours." A smirk danced across Alaric's full lips. "Also, it would technically be *our* garden after the wedding, wouldn't it?"

He stepped forward, a man made of moonlight, bearing the undereye circles of someone unable to sleep. She'd been this close to him before, and even closer still, but always in the heat of battle, where there was no space to notice such things. He wasn't wearing his usual leather gauntlets, and for some reason that thought leapt out at her—that she was seeing his hands for the first time. They were neatly kept, and so much larger than hers.

"Tell me," he said, "how does the Lachis'ka of the Nenavar Dominion wind up a helmsman in the Sardovian regiments?"

"Wouldn't you like to know," Talasyn scoffed.

The barest hint of annoyance flickered over his face. "Perhaps you are unaware, but it is inadvisable for husbands and wives to keep secrets from each other. Quite a few marriages have come to grief because of such a thing."

She nearly took the bait. Nearly screeched at him, *I don't want to marry you, you absolute dolt!* However, she remembered what her tutors had said and her grandmother always exemplified, that losing one's composure was as good as losing an argument. "The betrothal hasn't even been finalized," she managed to serenely point out. "But with all this talk of being husband and wife and *our* garden, I'm glad that you're excited. That makes one of us, at least."

"I wouldn't go as far as to profess myself *excited*, but I *am* looking forward to peacefully welcoming the Nenavar Dominion into the Night Empire's fold."

"What would the Master of the Shadowforged Legion know of peace?" Talasyn challenged.

"Certainly more than the girl who looks like she would happily strangle me for asking a simple question," Alaric retorted.

"I don't—" She stopped, taking another deep, calming breath. At this rate, they would end up coming to blows and the treaty would be as good as null. She decided to change the topic by answering his question. "Civil war broke out when I was a year old," she said, unable to keep the ice from her tone. "I was supposed to be evacuated to my mother's homeland—she was the Lightweaver—but something happened. I don't remember what. I ended up in Sardovia, instead." She tossed back her head, deciding that it was high time *she* was the one asking questions. "And how does the heir to the Night Empire ascend to the throne when his father is still alive?"

Alaric didn't hesitate; his answer clearly practiced. "Regent Gaheris is getting on in years. He elected to take on a less involved approach while he is still capable of enjoying the fruits of his labor."

Talasyn didn't believe *that* for a second—or, rather, she didn't believe that there wasn't anything more to it. Before she could quiz him further, though, Alaric suddenly turned himself directly toward her, capturing her in another one of his penetrating stares. His eyes were enigmatic, and as he bent his chin lower, his wavy black hair caught the moons' glow, a shadow rimmed in silver.

"I was seven when the Nenavarene civil war took place," he said at last, as mildly as though he were commenting on the state of the weather.

"What does that have to do with anything?" she snapped.

"You're very young." The corner of his lip ticked upward, as if he was enjoying a private joke at her expense.

"Perhaps that's why I keep besting you in combat," she huffed. "Because you're old and slow."

One moment she was standing a couple of feet across from him; the next, she was backed up against the very edge of the pool, one wrong move away from falling into it, and Alaric was all that she could see, the expanse of his broad shoulders, the dark of his pupils wide in the radiant night, the constellation of beauty marks on his pale skin. One of his large hands circled around her to press into the small of her back, holding her upright in a mockery of an embrace, and her own fingers flew to grasp at his shirtfront—a bid for either self-preservation or vengeance, she wasn't quite sure yet. If she ended up going for a midnight swim, then she was taking him with her.

"Haven't you learned to respect your elders, my lady?" It was obviously meant as a caustic quip, but his voice was too low. He said it too close to her ear.

"Do you mean to push me into the water, then?" she inquired

with as much dignity as she could muster, tightening her grip on his shirt.

"Who said anything about pushing? All I have to do is let you go." His bare fingers stirred at the base of her spine, the pressure burning and sparking through the fabric of her thin smock that separated her skin from his.

Talasyn couldn't think, couldn't *breathe*. It wasn't that she feared drowning—she doubted that the pool even went up to her neck. No, it was the adrenaline rush, that knife's edge between staying upright and falling into the cold water, the imposing heat of Alaric's body against hers. It was the predatory glint in his silver eyes, his husky drawl, the seven moons and the countless stars that she saw over his head when she lifted her chin to glare at him in defiance, despite her precarious position.

"I respect my elders," she gritted out, "when they *act their age*—"

Her sentence cut off into a blistering expletive when he abruptly clamped *both* hands around her waist, hauling her off her feet and then swinging her around to deposit her further away from the pool. The instant she was on solid ground once more, she automatically widened the distance between them, her heart racing at how effortlessly he'd lifted her, as if she weighed nothing more than a feather.

"What are we doing?" Talasyn demanded. "This whole—*thing*. Surely you're aware that this is a horrible idea."

"It is," Alaric conceded, "but it prevents a war."

"You know what else would prevent a war? If you left Nenavar alone!"

His jaw hardened. "I cannot do that."

"The Night Empire already controls all of Sardovia," she argued. "You have the entire Continent at your disposal—"

"And who on the Continent will respect the might of Kesath once word spreads that we took one look at Nenavar's forces and turned around?" He was so calm that it was infuriating. "We did not crush the Sardovian Allfold by doing things in half-measure. You should know. You were there."

I'm going to kill him. She wasn't so enraged by his flippant remark that some part of her couldn't marvel at this epiphany. *One of these days, I am actually going to kill him.* "So you're saying that it's all worth marrying me for. *Me*, Ossinast. Think about it." Perhaps she could prevail upon their mutual loathing to sway him from this course of action—and if that meant that she sounded as if she was disparaging herself, so be it. "You can't tell me that I'm anywhere *near* the kind of person you'd take for a spouse."

Alaric's gaze dropped to the pool that he'd almost dunked her in. "I came here to marry the Nenavarene Lachis'ka," he said with hollow resolution. "That she happens to be *you* is . . . immaterial. I suggest that you resign yourself to that fact."

It was honestly a kind of talent, how he knew exactly what to say and how to say it in order to get a rise out of her. "On second thought, your lack of objection to this marriage makes sense," she jeered. "We'll finally have the opportunity to *study together*, as you seemed so keen on."

Talasyn didn't know what to expect when she threw Alaric's words from their last battle in his face. She'd puzzled over that absurd and uncharacteristic offer all these months. She braced for his anger, or his annoyance. Perhaps even his embarrassment.

Instead, he flinched. Then a blank expression slammed over his features, as inscrutable as any mask. Talasyn recognized the reaction; it was the same prideful rigidity that she had once adopted whenever the orphanage keepers struck her, because she refused to give them the satisfaction of seeing how much it had hurt, how much her ears were ringing, even as the bruises blossomed across her skin.

Back in Lasthaven, hadn't Alaric asked her to come with

him as part of some greater ploy? Why was he acting, now, almost as if—as if he'd *meant* it? And why did she feel as though she'd crushed something fragile with a clumsy misstep, something that never stood a chance to begin with?

An uneasy silence descended. Her eyes tracked the jut in the elegant column of his throat as it bobbed.

"I was curious about how our magic fused together. Nothing more," Alaric finally said, every word laced with a careful, steely precision that Talasyn could never hope to match. "You getting yourself killed before I got to the bottom of it—that was my sole concern. However, if you insist on continuing to be this difficult, then it's not worth it. Moving forward, let us focus only on this"—his mouth twisted—"*political alliance.*"

It was a knife between her ribs, this reminder that she was about to wed someone who truly despised her. It wasn't that she craved Alaric's approval—no, his was the last in the world that she wanted—but a cavernous space had been hollowed out in her heart over the years, and his words echoed there beside older ones: that she wasn't worth it; that she was too difficult for anyone to bother with. An orphan who was too mouthy. A soldier with only one friend. A Lightweaver who could barely master the basics. A Lachis'ka who was too coarse-mannered. And now a bride who would never be loved.

Talasyn once again sought refuge in the welcome and familiar surge of her fury, which was never far away when Alaric was concerned. "All right," she snapped. "Keep this in mind, then, *moving forward.*" This time she was the one who stepped into his personal space, glaring daggers up at him. She couldn't tell him to his face but she promised him silently, without him knowing it, with venom rising up her throat, that the Hurricane Wars weren't over. That someday the Night Empire would fall.

"I was Sardovia's Lightweaver," Talasyn growled. "I have held my own against you and your Legion. I am *also* Alunsina

Ivralis of the Nenavar Dominion, Elagbi's daughter and the Dragon Queen's heir. I am She Who Will Come After, and *I have power here*. The next time that you manhandle me, you will regret it. Do you understand?"

Alaric's fingers twitched and then curled back into his palms. He was regarding her as if she were some wild creature, but also a cypher that he was trying to decode. The seven moons shone down upon them, and, as the silence stretched, the trickling of the water and the heady scent of orchids reached her awareness once more.

Finally, he offered her a stiff nod. "I understand." The words should have been a surrender, but he delivered them more like a tactical retreat. "Until the morning, then, Your Grace."

Talasyn did not give him the opportunity to leave first. She turned on her heel and stomped off to her chambers, fuming, struggling against the urge to turn her head even as she felt Alaric's gaze on her back.

So much for regaining inner peace.

CHAPTER EIGHTEEN

The days that followed were a whirl of bargains and compromises and concessions, interspersed with impasses and threats, all thinly veiled by a veneer of steel-laden courtesy. Queen Urduja preferred to play the role of observer as her advisers haggled in her name, but Alaric could afford no such luxury. Every lesson imparted by his father and the tutors of his boyhood, lessons in diplomacy and governance and economics, was now put to the test.

Talasyn had a habit of livening up these meetings whenever she interjected with a pointed remark, her tone laced with suspicion and contempt, and the Nenavarene negotiators scrambled to cover up her gaffe. Every morning, she arrived in another stunning dress and headpiece, her face an exquisite painting, but Alaric's mind kept wandering to that night in the garden, when she had been in her smock and breeches and he had been able to see the smattering of freckles across her nose and cheeks. How her dark eyes had blazed like a lit match when she cut him down to size. Something had seized within his chest that night, at the sight of the Talasyn that he remembered, except this time not on a battlefield, but standing amidst orchid blooms beneath a starry, amethyst-tinted sky.

He tried not to look at her from across the council room, because every time he did a ghostly echo of sensation followed— the dip of her waist and the curve of her slender spine pressing against his bare hands, the heat of her skin seeping through the thin fabric that had bunched up beneath the pressure of his fingertips. Before that night, it had been years since he'd touched another person without his leather gauntlets. His father always insisted that armor was crucial to realizing one's full potential as a warrior; only by shutting out unnecessary external stimuli could he most effectively wield shadow magic.

But just one brush of bare skin had awakened some long-forgotten hunger. Now it was as if Alaric's hands burned with need, even though they were safely encased in black leather once more.

When it almost became too much, when he began to fear that this odd yearning might actually drive him to act, Alaric was fortunate to have another memory to distract himself with. Namely, Talasyn jeering at his ill-advised slip of tongue, back when the Hurricane Wars were drawing to an end all around them. Her jibe had felt like a blade slipped between his ribs, swift and precise.

He had no desire to examine *why* it had hurt, and he didn't begrudge her for what she said, as he certainly hadn't been on *his* best behavior, either—but it was good to have a reminder that his reactions to Talasyn weren't the reactions he had to other women, and he needed to be more careful.

By the fifth day of negotiations, Kesath and Nenavar had hammered out a mutual defense pact and were polishing the final details for a trade agreement. It was not without its casualties; Lueve Rasmey's polite smile was a little worn at the edges, and Commodore Mathire and Niamha Langsoune seemed one comment away from wringing each other's necks. Even the unflappable Urduja had begun to get snappish with her own advisers. Meanwhile, Prince Elagbi, who Alaric had determined was present for moral support more than anything else, looked bored out of his skull, as did Sevraim, who was there in his capacity as Alaric's protection and thus was expected to contribute nothing to the proceedings.

Alaric still had not figured out what it was that the Dominion actually wanted. According to Gaheris, they had to be after something more than a peace treaty to offer up their Lachis'ka so willingly. But he could no longer put off making it clear what *his* people wanted above all else.

He cleared his throat in the tense silence that had ensued after the two sides begrudgingly agreed on a price point for Kesathese long-grain rice and peppercorns. "In addition to everything that has already been discussed, we would also be interested in purchasing aether hearts from Nenavarene mines."

Talasyn snorted under her breath, but Alaric heard it, and against his better judgment his attention shifted to focus solely on her. When she caught him looking, he hid his burst of ill-advised interest behind a taunt. "Her Grace wishes to comment?"

She turned her nose up at him. "I find it amusing that Kesath embarked on its campaign of terror against the rest of the Continent for the sake of aether hearts, and now you're going around begging for more, is all."

"An empire's work is never done," Alaric said curtly. "Particularly when the defeated enemy blows up their own mines as they retreat. I sincerely hope that wasn't *your* idea, by the way. I would hate to see you castigate yourself for further motivating Kesath to sail southeast."

It was a petty remark, and not all that accurate considering that Kesath would have needed to neutralize the Dominion anyway, aether hearts or not, but Alaric had no regrets. Talasyn looked as though she was seconds from launching herself across the table at him. It was the most entertained he'd ever been inside this council room.

"In any event," he continued, "Kesath is not *begging*. We

213

will be happy to pay a fair price for Nenavarene crystals, should Her Starlit Majesty allow it."

All eyes darted to Urduja, who gracefully inclined her silver-crowned head. "As with all other goods, we shall discuss a price, Emperor Alaric. Is that the extent of your trade interests, then?"

It was a perfect segue, too freely given. Vague suspicions tugged yet again at the back of Alaric's mind, but he pressed on. There wouldn't be a more opportune moment than this. "Just one more thing, Harlikaan. We formally request that Kesathese Enchanters be granted access to what you call the Void Sever, in the interest of expanding aethermancy knowledge and in exchange, of course, for trade concessions that we will be happy to grant—"

"Absolutely not!" Talasyn interrupted him. *Again.* This time, though, one of the Dominion advisers, the Rajan Gitab, nodded in agreement with her, so fervently that his spectacles were in danger of slipping down his nose. "The Night Empire *cannot* be allowed anywhere near the Voidfell's nexus point!" Talasyn continued. "They created the stormships with the Tempestroad— who knows what fresh hell they'll come up with if provided with a reservoir of death magic? If we *willingly* hand it over to them?"

Alaric had been anticipating such a reaction, but Mathire waded into the fray before he could get a word in. "We created the stormships to keep our nation safe. We unleashed them only when a Nenavarene flotilla made to attack us unprovoked," she pointed out. The Dominion nobles all collectively stiffened. "But Emperor Alaric has already promised that Nenavar won't suffer Sardovia's fate if no terms are violated. You have nothing to worry about, *unless* you're thinking of making such an unwise move again."

"Well, forgive me, Commodore," Talasyn snarled at Mathire, and Alaric could only sit there and marvel at how his bride-to-be was ready and willing to fight with anyone, at any time, "if I don't set much store by the word of invaders—"

Urduja held up a hand, her fingers glittering with long jewel-studded nail cones and a multitude of rings. Talasyn's lips clamped together and her whole demeanor changed, slinking into a mutinous silence. It put Alaric rather in mind of a cat who'd been told to go away.

"While it would be an honor to contribute to the advancement of aethermancy throughout the Northwest Continent," Urduja said in such a way that there was only the implication of sarcasm, not the presence of it, "the Voidfell is currently . . . volatile. We ceased our own extractions the previous month, and as such we cannot in good conscience let Kesath destabilize the nexus point any further."

"What do you mean by *volatile*?" Talasyn demanded just as Alaric was about to ask the same thing.

Urduja exchanged glances with the other Dominion nobles. Glances that spoke volumes, that made it clear Talasyn had been left out of the loop regarding a critical piece of information.

"You were not told, Alunsina, because it is among other things a delicate matter pertaining to national security," said the Zahiya-lachis. "However, we are telling you now. So please listen." She then addressed the Kesathese delegation. "The Voidfell is indispensable to Nenavar. Legend has it that it was the first nexus point to break through the veil of aetherspace on our shores. Over the centuries it has provided us with a means to defend ourselves. However, there is a price—one that the Dominion pays every thousand years." Urduja looked at Talasyn. "You have wondered why the Void Sever flares so brightly. Your instincts were correct; this is not normal. Usually, it behaves like any other nexus point. However, as the sevenfold lunar eclipse draws near, the Void Sever has begun to rage within its banks. On the night all seven moons vanish, it will break free and wash over Nenavar. It will wither the fields and jungles that are in its path, killing all life. Not even fish and coral will be safe. Since they can manipulate void magic in its extracted form, our Enchanters have experimented with pushing back the Voidfell whenever it discharges in its usual manner. But for years, all attempts have been unsuccessful."

Alaric fought to maintain a blank expression. He had never before heard of any type of Sever being capable of destroying an entire country when left to its own devices. In his life so far, all the chaos that magic could wreak had been when it was shaped by human hands.

"The Fisherman's Warning," Talasyn abruptly supplied. "That's what the people of the Sardovian Coast called it—the amethyst light on the horizon."

"Here, it is known as Dead Season," said Urduja. "It takes the work of generations to rebuild in the aftermath of the Voidfell's fury. By conducting mass evacuations and storing all the seeds and livestock that we can, Nenavar gets better at mitigating the effects of the disaster each time. But it is only now that we may have found a solution to avoid it altogether." She gestured first to a stunned Talasyn, then to Alaric, who tensed in his seat as it finally dawned on him that this was what the Zahiya-lachis had been after all along, what she'd so easily traded her granddaughter's hand for. "At the Belian garrison, the two of you created a kind of shield that disrupted a void blast. Such magic has never been observed before in our history. We believe that this combination of the Lightweave and the Shadowgate could be the key to preventing the catastrophe. If Kesath wishes to be granted access to the Voidfell and to benefit from everything else that this treaty with Nenavar offers, then Your Majesty must work together with Her Grace and learn to replicate and refine the barrier until our Enchanters can determine how to magnify its effects and encompass the whole Void Sever on the night of reckoning."

Urduja stared at Alaric impassively, waiting for his response, but his thoughts were moving at a glacial pace as he processed all that had been said. At the corner of his eye, on the other side of the table, Talasyn was slack-jawed and trembling faintly with that anger of hers, which always seemed too big for her slight frame to contain. The Nenavarene had lied to her; that much was clear. She'd asked about the Void Sever's behavior and she had either been brushed off or promised that there was no cause for concern.

Why hadn't her grandmother wanted her to know until today?

"If memory serves," said Commodore Mathire, "the next sevenfold lunar eclipse, which we on the Continent refer to as the Moonless Dark, isn't for another five months. Emperor Alaric cannot be expected to neglect his duties in Kesath for so long. What if we refuse?"

"Then we will have wasted our time with these negotiations." Alaric took it upon himself to respond, because he would *not* give Urduja the satisfaction of being the one to say it. "And five months from now we will have lost all the resources that this alliance has only just made us privy to."

The resources that we badly need, he thought. Crops and livestock and aether hearts and other raw materials, to offset the infrastructural damage and agricultural losses that the Continent had sustained after a decade of warfare.

The Dragon Queen smiled as though she'd read his mind. The trap was sprung. "Full marks, Your Majesty."

"There are other nations," Mathire argued. "Friendlier ones and just as wealthy that we can form alliances with. Ones whose heirs presumptive are *not* former enemies of Kesath." Her voice rose as she warmed to her topic. "If Nenavar is going to be taken out of the equation in five months' time anyway, why should His Imperial Majesty even lift a finger to help?"

The aforementioned Imperial Majesty unleashed a slew of curses in the privacy of his own head. Alaric had known that Mathire was an aggressive negotiator, as all of his father's old guard were, but he had never expected her to be so rash. With him and Sevraim cut off from the Shadowgate, they were going to be slaughtered in this very council room.

But Urduja didn't immediately start calling for Kesathese heads. She leaned back, her jewel-coned fingers steepled together. "You *could* let us fend for ourselves," she said contemplatively, "but any treaties you'll draft with other nations won't be much good in the long run, I fear. We have exhaustively detailed records from all other Dead Seasons in the past. A pattern has emerged. Every time the Void Sever erupts on the night of the sevenfold eclipse, it has a wider and wider area of effect. Last time, the magic crossed the Eversea—into the far waters of the Northwest Continent."

"That's why the Sardovian Coast called the amethyst light a warning." Talasyn's tone was one of horrified revelation. "It heralded rough seas and months of meager catch. The Voidfell killed most marine life in the fishing holds."

"Precisely," said Urduja. "This year promises to be the worst one yet. We've calculated that the Voidfell's flare will wash over the Northwest Continent."

Mathire sucked in a shocked breath. At the periphery of Alaric's vision, Sevraim fidgeted; in contrast, he himself had gone still and tense.

"I *could* be lying, of course." Urduja leveled an inscrutable gaze at Alaric. "Would you rather find out for yourself? Nenavar knows how to survive such a catastrophe, as we have been doing this for a very long time. The same cannot be said of Kesath."

We won't *survive it.* The realization sank deep into Alaric's being, turning him cold all over. There was no choice. The Night Empire was doomed if they didn't cooperate with the Dominion.

Everything that he had fought for nearly all his life was in danger of being wiped away. Swept into oblivion by a tide of amethyst, of rot.

"Wait." Talasyn's brow wrinkled beneath her golden crown. "The nursery rhyme—the one about Bakun—this is what it's referencing, isn't it? *All moons die, Bakun rises to eat the world above.* It's about the Moonless Dark and the Voidfell."

Urduja pursed her darkly painted lips and nodded, but didn't say anything else. It was Prince Elagbi who elaborated, leaning toward Talasyn to speak in a gentle tone. "The myth of Bakun is commonly accepted to be the ancient Nenavarene's explanation for the sevenfold eclipse and the void storm, yes. What the Northwest Continent calls the Moonless Dark, we call *his* time. The Night of the World-Eater."

Alaric wanted to cut in and ask Talasyn for the specifics of the Bakun myth. But he suddenly felt like an intruder as father and daughter fixed their gazes upon each other. Talasyn looked bewildered and betrayed, and Elagbi contrite.

"Why didn't you *tell* me?" she asked him, speaking more softly now. "This was clearly the plan from the start—the very reason for this marriage alliance. How could you keep this from me?"

Elagbi's features crumpled with obvious shame at having disappointed her.

Urduja sighed. "Do not be too hard on your father, Lachis'ka. I *ordered* that he not tell you. You've fought us every step of the way regarding this betrothal, and I feared that you would have been even more unwilling if you prematurely learned that I wished for you to train together with the Night Emperor. But you must understand the gravity of the situation by now, and it is my hope that you will cooperate, as time is of the essence."

Talasyn's eyes flitted from one solemn Dominion noble to another, as if daring them to speak up. One after another, they avoided her gaze. By the time she finished, Alaric watched as her shoulders slumped in defeat, all the fight gone out of her. The Talasyn he had come to know never backed down, would never let herself be beaten in this way, and suddenly he *loathed* everything about this scene. To his left, Mathire was struggling to repress a smirk at the Lightweaver's discomfiture, and Alaric felt a wave of revulsion. He shot his officer a glare and she quickly worked her features back into a semblance of neutrality.

And what was it about this moment, Alaric wondered as he studied his betrothed from across the table, that made him understand? Talasyn was hanging her head and he couldn't see her face clearly, but he somehow knew that she was close to breaking. Had he been here before? Yes, perhaps—all those times when he reached for his father but was bitterly rebuffed. All those times when Gaheris had taken him to task for his failings in front of the entire court. The innocent hopes for a better father soon giving way to self-reproach for not being a better son.

The only way to avoid falling victim to such pain was to become stronger than it. Apparently, Talasyn had yet to master that crucial lesson.

"It's settled, then," Alaric announced, commanding the attention of everyone in the room. No one, not even the Lightweaver, should have to endure an audience for this. "Her Grace and I will endeavor to develop this new magic over the next five months. I must insist, however, that the two of us be provided with *all* necessary information going forward. Surely there is no more need for secrets between our two realms."

"Of course," Urduja replied smoothly. "I shall be the paradigm of transparency from now on."

There was a limit to how far one's rage could carry them. Talasyn had spent the past sennight fueled by anger at her impossible situation, but now it had reached its tipping point and drained away. Talasyn was beyond anger. She was beyond sadness or humiliation, even. She had agreed to this marriage not just to save her comrades, but for the Nenavarene—her people, her *family*. Not only had they allowed her to be left in ignorance, her grandmother had chosen to expose this in front of Alaric and the other Kesathese.

She laid numbly in her bed as evening crept in. There was a knock on her door—perhaps Jie, or even Elagbi, but she ignored it. All of the emotions that she should have been feeling—it was as though she viewed them through a sheet of glass, and there was nobody that she wanted to talk to.

Except . . .

What should I do? she asked Khaede.

Kill everyone, the Khaede who lived in her head promptly responded.

Talasyn almost cracked a smile at imagining that. Usually, whenever she thought of Khaede, it would be with a near-physical ache, but she couldn't even summon the strength for that now.

Only once the morning's light crept in through the window did she rise and prepare herself to meet Alaric in the Roof of Heaven's atrium. She changed into garb that suited aethermancing—a tunic, breeches, boots—silently daring anyone to challenge her on it.

Urduja had informed Alaric and Talasyn that Nenavarene Enchanters would be summoned to the capital to observe firsthand the creation of their light-and-shadow shield. When Talasyn walked into the atrium, Alaric was already present, standing beside a small group of men and women garbed in lengths of vibrant checkered fabric arranged in various ways, a mode of dress characteristic to Ahimsa, one of the seven main islands—a bustling metropolis that served as Nenavar's center for aethermanced technology.

In his severe black attire Alaric looked practically comical next to the Enchanters, like a dour, overly large thundercloud.

But, for some reason, Talasyn was fixated only on his gray eyes. They regarded her with a hint of softness as she approached. Curiosity, maybe, or concern, after yesterday's events lingered in the air between them. Her face flamed and she determinedly ignored him, turning instead to the woman who led the group of Enchanters.

Ishan Vaikar, the stout and curly-haired Daya of Ahimsa, curtseyed to Talasyn with a slight limp. Talasyn knew that hidden underneath Ishan's checkered skirt was a golden prosthetic in lieu of the right leg that she had lost fighting in the Dominion's civil war.

"Your Grace. If you and His Majesty would be so kind as to position yourselves in the middle of the atrium?"

As Talasyn complied, she searched the surrounding windows and balconies for any sign of Urduja or Elagbi, though she knew it was in vain. Security precautions dictated that they be far away when the sariman cages were removed from the Night Emperor's vicinity, and the atrium had been selected for its distance from the royal family's wing of the palace.

Talasyn *did* spot dozens of servants peeking out from behind curtains or pillars, or crouched down low looking through glass. They were technically not supposed to be watching, but mere technicalities were no match for Nenavarene curiosity.

Alaric noticed the spectators as well. "Is it always like that here?" he asked.

For once, she wasn't in the mood to order him to stop talking to her. She was tired. And, yesterday in the council room, he had to his credit taken no apparent pleasure in the hurt that she'd failed to disguise, and he'd even insisted that the Dominion be more forthcoming in the future. Granted, that last part was probably more for his own benefit—but, still, Talasyn had felt a little less alone when he said that.

Grasping at straws again, she mused, her eyes flickering over his sullen profile in the early-morning sun.

222

"Gossip is a way of life here," she told him. "You'll get used to it."

The corner of Alaric's mouth lifted slightly. An odd thought struck her then: *What would he look like if he smiled?*

No sooner had the question crossed her mind than a sliver of mortification pierced through it. Why was she thinking about Alaric Ossinast *smiling*? She was clearly more emotionally overwrought than she'd assumed.

A few meters away, Ishan stepped forward. This was the signal for the palace guards at the periphery of the atrium to take the sariman cages down from the walls and move them further away. The Lightweave came rushing back just as Ishan raised the barrel of a slender void musket, the same model that Talasyn had first encountered on the Belian range.

"I am ready when you are, Your Grace, Your Majesty," the daya sang out, entirely too gleeful for someone holding a lethal weapon, and Talasyn swallowed a nervous lump in her throat. She looked toward Alaric, and he met her gaze, searching for confirmation. They both nodded.

Ishan pulled the trigger. The violet bolt of the Voidfell streamed toward Alaric and Talasyn. They each conjured their daggers and hurled them forth, just as they'd done when that pillar in Lasthaven was bearing down upon her.

Only, this time, the result was far different.

In that there was no result at all.

Light and shadow slammed into each other, sparking, and the void bolt roared as it devoured them. Suddenly there was nothing but amethyst barreling toward Alaric and Talasyn, no shield to stop it, and the Enchanters were screaming—

Talasyn's world tilted abruptly as Alaric tackled her to the ground. She would have landed face-first, but his arms clamped around her, cushioning her from the worst of the impact. There was a guttural hiss as the void bolt swept past the space where they had just been standing. She was on her stomach, staring at the marbled pattern of the stone tiles as Alaric curled around her, over her. He expelled a quick breath, and as he did so, his soft lips grazed the shell of her ear. She could feel his heart pounding against her spine.

She didn't know how long they lay there, adrenaline pulsing through their bodies, fit to burst. She felt small tucked beneath Alaric's broad frame, surrounded by the warmth of him. As the sunlight grew hot against her head, she noted—as she had in that cell at the bamboo garrison, so long ago—that he smelled of sandalwood. There was a hint of cedar as well, and the peppery bite of juniper berry, warmed by a touch of sweet, resinous myrrh. He smelled like the alpine forests back on the Continent. What an odd thing for her to notice. What an odd thing for him to hold her like this.

Ishan and her Enchanters were running toward them, but their footsteps sounded muffled. The Kesathese crown prince blocked out everything else, as he always did.

Not the prince, Talasyn corrected herself in her daze. *He's the Night Emperor now.*

"Are you all right?" he asked, low and hesitant. The words ghosted across her cheek, causing a shiver to shoot down the nape of her neck.

"Get *off*." She elbowed him in the ribs, defensive for reasons she couldn't explain.

By the time they had both scrambled to their feet, the Nenavarene Enchanters had formed a concerned huddle around them. Ishan was wringing her hands in dismay. "Lachis'ka!" she cried, pushing past Alaric in order to inspect Talasyn from head to toe. "I *do* apologize! From the way that it was described, I assumed that the shield could be replicated like—like *that*—" She snapped her fingers. "And I solemnly swear on the wind-swept bones of my foremothers that, had I suspected there was a chance of your magic not taking effect, I would *never* have fired—oh, Your Grace, can you ever *forgive* me?"

"I'm none the worse for wear, Daya Vaikar," Talasyn hastened to reassure her. "But I don't know why it didn't work, either." She frowned, looking down to examine her hands. "The circumstances aren't much different from the two previous times."

"The eclipse," Alaric said quietly. He absentmindedly scratched at his jaw as he appeared to think it over. It was a boyish gesture, one that Talasyn couldn't help but marvel at; but, when everyone's attention snapped to him, his hand dropped back to his side and his demeanor immediately shifted, became colder, more imperious. His next words were more self-assured. "On both occasions when the Lachis'ka and myself successfully created a barrier, the moons were out and one of them was in eclipse."

Ishan's dark eyes went as round as the celestial bodies in question. Talasyn had come to know her as an inquisitive woman by nature, and now she saw Ishan's mind churning with this new revelation. "Yes. That *does* make sense. Countless feats of aethermancy are tied to the natural world. Rainsingers in lands to the south can reportedly communicate with one another across great distances by looking into fresh puddles, while Firedancers to the east can do so in the flames of wildfire. I've certainly never heard of light and shadow magic forming a greater whole before, but a lunar eclipse strikes me as the prime moment for such a phenomenon to occur." She rounded on her gaggle of Enchanters with alacrity, demanding, "When is the next one?"

"In a fortnight, my lady," one ventured.

"Then, if Her Grace and His Majesty are willing, we will reconvene at the time of the eclipse and try again." Ishan turned back to Alaric and Talasyn. "If I may also suggest—I noticed that the two of you conjured daggers earlier, which is offense magic. For our purposes, I believe that the barrier may be stronger if you were to craft shields and combine those."

Alaric nodded readily enough, but Talasyn hung her head.

"I can't make shields," she muttered. "Or anything that doesn't have a pointy end. I was taught the basics of aethermancy by a Shadowforged who defected to the Allfold. She didn't have any formal training, so both of us were at a loss on some things."

Alaric frowned, his eyes darting toward her and then away quickly. It was unclear if he was reacting to the mention of Vela or to the revelation that Talasyn had been lucky to survive the Hurricane Wars for as long as she did.

"I can teach you," he said stiffly, still looking ahead.

And, before Talasyn could even *process* that, Ishan was stepping between them, clapping her hands in delight. "Wonderful! I've no doubt that Her Grace will prove as excellent a student in this as she has been in everything else."

Talasyn shot a skeptical look over the top of Ishan's head at Alaric. "Surely the skill of the instructor has a lot to do with it."

He lifted one massive shoulder in a shrug, the ends of his thick black hair brushing against his high collar. "*I* have had formal training. That alone makes me more qualified than Ideth Vela, regardless of any complaints you might care to lodge against my character."

"Your *character*," Talasyn retorted, "is just one of the *many* complaints that I have about you, Ossinast."

They glared at each other as an uncomfortable Ishan edged away. Perhaps her anger had not run dry after all, Talasyn thought darkly. Count on her hatred for His Royal Ninnyhammer to cut through the numbness. It was a mixed blessing, but she would take it.

CHAPTER NINETEEN

A schedule was begrudgingly agreed upon. For the next fortnight, Alaric and Talasyn would attend marriage negotiations
in the morning and practice aethermancy in the afternoon. If
the negotiations wrapped up with plenty of time to spare
before the eclipse, they'd then spend whole days training.

Because Talasyn was certainly in no mood to talk to her
grandmother, it was Ishan Vaikar who prevailed upon Queen
Urduja to have the sariman cages moved further away from
the orchid garden that connected the Lachis'ka and the Night
Emperor's respective bedchambers. The atrium was too accessible to everyone, and Talasyn had no wish to be gawked at
on a daily basis.

That first afternoon, the day following the monumental
failure in front of the Ahimsan Enchanters, Talasyn arrived at
the orchid garden before Alaric.

Why was she nervous? What was the reason for these
butterflies rippling in the pit of her stomach? She thought
about yesterday, his strong arms around her, his lush mouth
at her cheek, his scent of spice and forest. She thought about
how he'd scratched at his jaw in a rare, unguarded moment.
It jarred her that the Night Emperor, the dark warrior she'd

met on the ice, could be capable of such a human gesture. It set her to questioning whether he had more of that in him, beneath the trappings of office and his lethal precision in combat.

Talasyn thought of these things without knowing why she thought of them, why they gnawed at her so. If Khaede were here—

No. Khaede would castigate her for these odd reactions that she was having to Alaric Ossinast, as would Vela and all her other comrades. Still, Talasyn yearned to meet with the Sardovian remnant, not just to discuss her impeding marriage with Vela, but to check for herself that everyone was doing all right, there in the Storm God's Eye.

And also to check if—and to hope against hope that—Khaede had made contact and reached them, and was safe along with her child.

Talasyn resolved to sail to the isles of Sigwad as soon as she could. From Eskaya, the journey took about six hours by airship, and crossing that windblown strait was perilous, especially with the ever-present threat of the Tempest Sever, but she had managed a handful of times in the past and she would again. She just had to seize the opportunity once it came.

In a bid to take her mind off things, even if only for a little while, Talasyn began feeding the fish that lived in the pool. The bright rays of early afternoon streamed into the orchid garden as Talasyn reached into the pouch that she'd brought with her when she'd changed out of her court attire and scrubbed her face bare. Retrieving a handful of pellets that she scattered across the surface of the water, which immediately clouded with flashing scales and fins that rippled like wisps of colored smoke, she smiled to herself. She could always count on the *ikan'pla* to cheer her up. They were pretty fish, with distinct individual personalities and quirks, and they knew her only as the one who fed them, not the one who would save them or who would one day rule. The lack of layers to her simple interaction with them was a balm to her soul.

There was a rustle of black at the corner of her eye as Alaric entered the garden. Talasyn paid him no mind at first, mulishly keeping her gaze fixed on the *ikan'pla* in the water. His steps were hesitant, almost as though he were being compelled to approach her even though he knew that it was a bad idea, and he sat down on the stone bench beside where she was kneeling on the grass with all the wariness of a man straying deep into enemy territory. Which wasn't too far off base—she'd made it clear to him in no uncertain terms that this was *her* turf, after all.

"Your grandmother should have told you about the Voidfell right from the start," he said after a long silence. "You deserved to know."

Hearing that from someone was like finally being able to take a breath after days in an airless room. But to hear it from *him*—of all people—

"It's nothing," Talasyn muttered.

"It *isn't* nothing. She didn't trust you and she underestimated your capacity to deal with the new knowledge. That's an untenable state of affairs, considering that you're her heir."

Talasyn hated that he had a point. But he had no idea, he could *never* have any idea, about the position that she was really in, this precarious balancing act that was contingent on remaining in Urduja Silim's good graces.

She sniffed. "I'll thank you to keep your opinions to yourself. This way of life is all still new to me and I'm only having to adapt to it because of Kesath's actions. A Kesathese is the *last* person in the world who should be passing judgment on me and my family right now."

"I was not passing judgment," Alaric said with maddening calm, "merely trying to offer some advice."

"I don't need it."

He gave a sigh that was frustrated and weary all at once, and she remembered how he'd called her difficult in this very same garden.

Good, she thought. She wasn't here to make things easy for him.

"Shall we begin?" he said abruptly. It was a command rather than a question, and he joined her down on the grass without waiting for her response.

Irked, Talasyn swung to face him. Alaric had adopted a meditation pose, legs crossed and feet upturned and back ramrod-straight, gauntleted hands resting on bent knees. She followed suit with some reluctance. Beside them, the waterfall burbled and the pool splashed merrily against its banks.

"Lachis'ka." Alaric's tone was formal. "Tell me about your training."

Talasyn didn't want to share that part of her life with someone who had helped bring about its destruction. She most especially didn't want to talk about the Sardovians when they were *here,* unbeknownst to him. But she had to cooperate if they were ever going to get anywhere. "It wasn't rigorous. The Amirante was the only one who could teach me, and she already had her hands full. I picked up on how to aethermance weapons right away, but as for shields or anything else . . ." She shrugged.

"Weaponry is the first and most instinctive skill for the Shadowforged. I suppose that it must be the same for Lightweavers." Alaric scratched at his jaw again, the sign that he was deep in thought. "According to Darius, your magic awakened when you were fifteen?"

Talasyn's fists clenched at the mention of Darius. "Yes. In Hornbill's Head—or what was left of it." Her ears rang with echoes of the dying Kesathese soldier's screams as the shapeless light that roared forth from her fingertips consumed him.

Alaric's expression grew even blanker, as though he was covering something up. She dearly hoped it was guilt. "Aethermancers usually come into their magic at a younger age," he continued. "I was three, myself."

He was matter-of-fact rather than smug, but it infuriated her nonetheless. "Well, *I* didn't grow up around other aethermancers of my kind and *my* magic didn't have nexus points everywhere I turned. I was also much more concerned with how to get my next meal and where to sleep for the night."

Alaric frowned. "I thought that you were raised in an orphanage."

"I left when I was ten. The streets were better—*any* place was better." She lifted her chin, proud, defiant. "They were cruel."

She wouldn't go as far as to presume that his features softened, but he was silent for a while. Then he looked at her as though a new facet of hers had been held up to the light and he understood it for what it was.

But how *could* he understand? The man had been born a *prince*.

"I hadn't considered that," he eventually said. "I apologize."

She nearly fell over. Never in a million Moonless Darks would she have expected to hear those words from his lips. Her first instinct was to be sharp, to be as ungracious as he deserved, to goad him about how he should also apologize for everything that his empire had done.

But what would be the point? He was never going to be sorry, and working with him was the only hope she had of saving Nenavar and its secret trove of Sardovian refugees. And this was also her chance to talk to someone who understood combat magic more than Vela did.

"I think that my aethermancy was also protecting me in its own way," Talasyn heard herself confess. "I think it hid because

231

it knew that the architects of the Nenavarene civil war wanted me dead, even if I didn't. Even if I was too young to remember."

"It's not impossible," said Alaric. "There's a lot that has yet to be learned regarding aetherspace, but we *are* aware that it holds connections to time and memory. When the Shadowforged commune with our Severs, it's also like unlocking events from our pasts, in addition to refining our magic. Enchanters seem to be immune from this effect, as they have no Sever to call their own, but myself and the other legionnaires, for example— our childhood recollections are far more vivid than those non-Shadowforged can manage, going back to an earlier age than most."

"I can't imagine you as a child," Talasyn couldn't resist quipping.

"It *was* several years ago."

"Right." She couldn't tell where her next question came from. She couldn't tell why it suddenly mattered. "And what do you remember, from several years ago?"

An icy look slammed over Alaric's face. Whatever friendliness had overlain this moment, or at least lack of antagonism—maybe the very same thing that had inspired her to ask about his childhood in the first place—fizzled out, just like that. "Perhaps if you can commune with the Light Sever on Belian, you'll be able to regain more memories of your own instead of asking for mine."

She bit the tongue that she was tempted to stick out at him. "Daya Vaikar has already proposed to the Zahiya-lachis that you and I train at the shrine, so that I can access the Light Sever when it discharges. Queen Urduja won't allow it, as she prefers to keep an eye on you and your contingent." *And on me.*

"Hasn't she allowed *you*, though?" Alaric shot back. "You have been here four months. If you'd had regular access to the Light Sever, you would probably be able to craft something as simple as a shield by now."

Talasyn looked away. "I have lessons. And duties, as her heir."

He made an impatient noise under his breath; then he changed the subject. "Let us try to get you to weave a shield, then. If you can."

Talasyn was experiencing a fair bit of whiplash from the abrupt shifts in the cantankerous Night Emperor's mood, but she decided that it wasn't her problem. She settled for rolling her eyes at him as she waited for what his idea of a lesson had in store.

What do you remember, from several years ago?

It was a loaded question. Alaric remembered a lot of things.

The Lightweavers' attack on the Citadel in the middle of the night. How there had been nothing but a bolted door and his mother's embrace between him and the screaming and all the awful, blazing magic of Sunstead, until the Shadowforged Legion rallied and was able to repel the assault.

In the aftermath, he remembered the weeping that swept through the fortress as news spread that his grandfather had been slain at the gates. He remembered his father being crowned in the middle of the battlefield, in armor drenched with the old king's blood, the promise of vengeance burning in his gray eyes, reflecting the myriad fires around him.

Alaric remembered how that night had marked a change in Gaheris, manifesting in little cruelties and obsessions that piled up over the years until Sancia Ossinast finally fled under cover of darkness . . .

Come with me. Please.

In the midst of the perfumed orchids, under the hot sunlight and blue sky of the here and now, Alaric sucked in a hiss of breath, letting it fan over the fresh ache of an old wound in his chest. He chastised himself for letting his thoughts stray into the musings of a weak fool once more. His father had done what needed to be done. His mother had not been strong enough to face it.

And he had allowed an offhand question from his inquisitive little betrothed to rattle him.

At least *she* hadn't noticed.

Talasyn's eyes were squeezed shut, her brow furrowed as she pictured a shield as Alaric had instructed her to. She had been at it for a good few minutes, which was about as long as he'd spent staring off into the distance while the past dragged him down into its mire.

"Can you see it?" he pressed. "Is it solid in your mind?" She gave a slow nod. "Now, summon it into existence just as you would a dagger or a spear." She held up one hand in front of her. "Open the Lightweave and let it flow through you—"

A shapeless flare of golden radiance burst from Talasyn's fingertips. Alaric leaned to the side as it rushed past him, its haze warm against his cheek. It collided with a pillar at the opposite end of the garden and knocked off a good-sized chunk of marble, eliciting a tremor in the air and clouds of pale dust.

Talasyn went as red as a beet. She ducked her head, her chestnut braid spilling over one slim shoulder as she hunched in on herself as though bracing for his derision.

It was a familiar posture. It brought him back to the early stages of his own training.

What do you remember? she had asked.

If you stay, his mother had whispered, *there will be nothing left of you.*

"It's all right, Lachis'ka." The gentleness that he heard in his voice surprised him. It was a gentleness that had no place in this situation, but it was too late to take it back. "We'll try again. Close your eyes."

"What was the first weapon you ever made?"

In the darkness behind Talasyn's shut lids, the hoarse richness of Alaric's voice was amplified. She fidgeted, trying not to be distracted by it.

"A knife," she said. "It took me only a few hours to perfect one that looked like the knife I stole from the kitchens when I left the orphanage. I knew that I'd need something to defend myself with, living on the streets."

There was no response for such a long time that she would have assumed he'd gotten up and left, if not for the familiar scent of sandalwood water lingering in the air. *He must splash that on after shaving in the mornings,* she thought idly.

And then it hit her—the only possible explanation as to why he was so quiet—and her natural defensiveness reared its head. "Are you pitying me?"

"No."

Alaric paused, as though weighing his next words, and Talasyn's hands curled into loose fists as she waited for the inevitable. She'd hardly gone around flaunting her past among the Sardovian regiments, but whenever people had asked and she told them, the first reaction had unfailingly been pity, followed by a pretty speech exalting her resilience.

"Going to talk about how *strong* I must have been, to bear all that?" she muttered, eyes still shut, that old bitterness rising. It fed on her defensiveness, and her defensiveness fed on it. An endless loop of the scars left by a small, ground-down life. "If so, don't bother. I've heard it all before. It's absurd, to be cold and half starved for fifteen years and then be praised for that suffering. As though—as though it's *admirable* that I fought other bottom-dwellers for space at the watering troughs where the horses drank."

Her tone had warped at the edges, becoming raw and ugly with all the things that she had never managed to outgrow. She labored to get her breathing back under control, to *meditate*, as she was supposed to be doing—why was he distracting her with this, anyway?

235

"You shouldn't have had to live like that," Alaric said quietly, and it was as though time itself stood still. "It's not pity for you that I feel; rather, anger on your behalf. The city leaders failed you. The Allfold failed you. It's reprehensible to expect people to endure their suffering when you have the means to put an end to it."

It was just like when she'd been reeling from her family's subterfuge regarding the Voidfell and he'd told her that she had deserved to know. It was the second time that he had said words that she needed to hear. She nearly opened her eyes, the desire to look upon his face as bright as burning, but at the last possible minute she kept them squeezed shut, her chest tight with some vague fear at what she might see.

She agreed with him. That was the horrific, maddening truth. She had recognized what he was pointing out long ago, but she'd buried it deep. She never would have made it through the war otherwise.

How could she fight for something she didn't believe in? How could she *not* fight, when the alternative was bowing to the Night Empire?

"The Allfold wasn't perfect, but it's not like Kesath is any better," Talasyn said stiffly. Before he could argue, she added, "Let's just get on with things. We're supposed to have declared a truce."

Alaric said something under his breath that sounded suspiciously like *Could have fooled me*. But then he was clearing his throat and they were back to training, the time constraint hanging over their heads.

CHAPTER TWENTY

No progress was made that first afternoon, no matter how hard Talasyn concentrated and coaxed her magic forth. She then had to spend the night listening, racked with guilt, to the sounds of builders fixing the pillar that she'd accidentally broken.

Unlike aethermancy training, marriage negotiations the next day proceeded for the most part at a brisk pace. Not only did Talasyn hold her tongue for practically the entire morning, not wanting to interact with her grandmother and her father any more than was absolutely necessary, but the Dominion nobles—Lueve Rasmey, Niamha Langsoune, and Kai Gitab— were marginally friendlier toward the Kesathese contingent now that, thanks to Alaric, there was a chance that their archipelago *wouldn't* be decimated by death magic before the year was out.

Shortly before the gongs throughout the Roof of Heaven tolled the noon hour, though, there was a minor crisis.

Commodore Mathire currently had the floor. "The wedding *must* be held in the Citadel," she was railing. "It is the Night Empire's seat of power and, as Alunsina Ivralis will be the Night Empress, she needs to be *there* to assume her role."

"So conduct an official coronation in the Citadel," Niamha retorted, "*after* the wedding, which needs to be held *here* in Eskaya. Her Grace may be Kesath's future empress, but His Majesty will also be *her* consort. If you want the Nenavarene to accept him as such, then the nuptials simply *must* take place on Nenavarene soil."

As the negotiators argued, Talasyn stiffened in her chair, hands fisting into her beaded skirt under the table, out of sight. She couldn't get married in Kesath. She could never again set foot on the Northwest Continent, not until the Sardovians took it back.

It would hurt too much.

"It's settled, then," Alaric interrupted just when Mathire looked as if she was about to blow a gasket. "We will *celebrate*"—he couldn't quite seem to contain his sarcasm—"the nuptials here in Nenavar, and then there will be a coronation in Kesath."

Mathire scowled but dutifully made a note on one of her meticulously organized sheaves of parchment. Talasyn's jaw throbbed from the strain of clenching it, and it wasn't long before the dam broke and her words spilled out in a rush. "I don't want to go to Kesath."

Alaric's gray eyes flickered to her from across the table. "As my wife, you will have to hold court at the Night Empire's capital every once in a while," he coolly informed her, and he didn't know, he would *never* know, the way her heart skipped a beat as he referred to her as *his wife.* "We can discuss a schedule later. It doesn't even have to be more than once every few months, if that's what you prefer. What *isn't* negotiable is your coronation."

He was so remote, so different from the sullen yet patient man who had sat with her yesterday throughout all her fumbled attempts at shield-making. It occurred to her that this was another kind of mask he wore. Not wolf, but politician.

Or maybe—maybe the patient tutor was the mask. Talasyn had no idea. She couldn't make sense out of this stranger who was to be her husband, and now the future was looming before her, a future where she would have to go into enemy territory as his bride, the spoils of war—

Her breathing shallowed. Alaric studied her warily, the beginnings of a frown tugging at his lips.

Urduja broke the regal silence with which she'd been presiding over the negotiations. "Emperor Alaric is correct, Alunsina. Your father and I will, of course, accompany you to Kesath for your coronation. As for your subsequent visits, I am sure that His Majesty will allow you to take whoever you wish to make your stays more . . . bearable."

Alaric nodded. "Each and every one of Her Grace's courtiers will always be welcome at the Citadel."

I don't want to go anywhere with you, Talasyn wished she could snap at her grandmother and her father, still smarting from their subterfuge. *Nor with you,* she wished she could hurl at her betrothed, still frustrated with his existence in general.

You have to do this, she reminded herself. She brought the faces of Vela and the other Sardovians to the forefront of her thoughts. She grasped for strength in her memories of Khaede and Sol and Blademaster Kasdar. She envisioned death's amethyst light washing over the darkened shores of this land and its people who had welcomed her back and called her their own.

You have to do this.

Talasyn subsided, leaning back in her seat, features composed in front of the Dominion nobles and the Kesathese. Her claws retracted.

This way, everyone gets to live.

She was dawdling, surely.

That was the only explanation. No one would take over

an hour to eat lunch and change into training clothes unless they were doing it on purpose.

Alaric forced himself not to fidget where he sat on the grass. In truth, it came as no great shock that Talasyn was making him wait. Earlier in the council room, she'd turned quite pale when her return to the Continent became the subject of discussion. It made sense, he supposed, that she was in no hurry to see him again.

Or to go to Kesath, for that matter.

A distant roar like the sound of a stormship being torn apart pierced the afternoon stillness. Alaric looked up, and awe blossomed within him. A dragon was flying miles and miles above the Roof of Heaven, its mighty wings silhouetted against the hot sun. The green-scaled length of it snaked through the clear blue sky in an undulating ribbon, forming loops and whorls as it soared ever on.

When it disappeared from view, Alaric's gaze fell back to earth—and landed squarely on Talasyn.

She had paused in her approach to track the movements of the great beast, but now that it had gone, her eyes met his, golden sunlight lancing through their depths to bring out the same wonder he felt. Scrubbed free of powders and pigments, her freckled features and the line of her pink mouth had gone soft. And for a brief moment, there amidst the orchids, by the waterfall, he forgot that they were anything other than two people who had just shared a marvelous sight.

Then she lifted her chin and stalked over to him in a huff, and the illusion dissipated. But perhaps a part of him was in it, still, because, once she had closed the distance between them and gracelessly settled into a meditation pose that mirrored his, he asked, "Do they truly exude flames?"

Talasyn subjected him to a penetrating stare, as though searching for the trick up his sleeve. Alaric had none, and she must have eventually realized it because she gave a stiff nod.

"The orange seaweed that I'm sure you've been served here on more than one occasion, it's called breath-of-fire. It grows only in Nenavarene waters, near where the dragons like to lair. The fire in their bodies heats up the current, making that particular variety of seaweed thrive."

"The dish *is* rather good," Alaric ventured. Breath-of-fire was silky with a hint of crunch, and had a briny flavor that the palace cooks enhanced with a piquant sauce of rice vinegar and chilies. "The same can be said for Dominion cuisine in general, I find."

"Agreed. So much better than the food back home—"

Talasyn broke off abruptly, but it was too late. The word hung in the space between them, as ominous as a thundercloud. *Home.*

"We were fighting a war." In his haste to cover up the silence before it could turn awkward, Alaric blurted out what first came to mind. "Everything was rationed. It stands to reason that our food can't compare to . . ."

He trailed off, realizing that he, too, had made a mistake.

The Continent that they both called home, the war that they'd both fought—on opposite sides. It all came rushing back, bringing with it echoes of the sore point in the negotiations earlier.

I don't want to go to Kesath.

Alaric's common sense screamed at him to direct the conversation to safer waters. To begin today's training, which was what they were here for in the first place. But Talasyn had gone stiff with combativeness, a stubborn set to her olive-toned jaw, and she was going to be his empress and he needed to make her understand—

The glimpse into her early life had filled him with cold fury, as overwhelming as it was impotent. It was long in the past. Hornbill's Head was gone, and, with it, all the squalor that had marked her early years.

Still, he was seized by the fanciful urge to resurrect Hornbill's Head just for the pleasure of having his stormships flatten it again.

He had never before felt so wounded for someone else. The girl was bewitching him.

"I know that you had a hard childhood," he told her. "But we are rebuilding. The Great Steppe, and the entirety of the land formerly known as Sardovia—it will all become better than it ever was."

"At what cost?" she snarled.

Unbidden, the aftermath of Kesath's final triumphant push into the Sardovian Heartland rose to the surface of the darkness behind Alaric's eyes. The sea of debris, of corpses. He blinked those images away. "The Night Empire was forced to destroy the Allfold before they could destroy us," he tersely explained, "but, under Kesathese stewardship, the Continent will improve. When you go back, you'll see. You might disagree with Kesath's methods, but in the end this conflict turned out to all be for a cause greater than any of our individual selves."

To Alaric's disbelief, his attempt to reason with Talasyn only made her angrier. "You and Commodore Mathire say that a lot, that you had to destroy the Allfold before they destroyed you. But since *when* did the Allfold ever give any indication—"

"When Sunstead attacked," Alaric interrupted, his grasp on his own temper slipping as past pain was excavated, laid bare beneath the tropical sun. "When Lightweavers killed my grandfather, the king. When the other Sardovian states did nothing to stop them."

Talasyn's brow furrowed at the reminder that her breed of aethermancer was responsible for his grandfather's death. However, her unease didn't last long, her shoulders soon squaring as she let loose with another retort. "The Lightweavers of Sunstead wanted to stop Ozalus from building the stormships. They knew, as well as everyone outside Kesath knows, that a weapon like that has no place in this world. But Ozalus wouldn't listen to reason, and that's why Sunstead did what they did. They had no choice!"

Rage erupted from within the depths of Alaric's soul. It was startling how swiftly it built up, rising like the tide along with his magic. The air in the immediate vicinity darkened and Talasyn scooted back, planting her hands in the grass as though prepared to spring to her feet at any moment, and Alaric knew that his eyes were blazing silver, the Shadowgate wrapping around his heart.

But he didn't care.

"Is *that* what you were taught on your side of the Continent?" he sneered. "I suppose it's to be expected that a self-serving government like the Allfold would revise history for their own ends. Shall I tell you the truth, Lachis'ka?" Talasyn watched him as one would a wounded, starving bear. As she would watch the monster that she'd grown up believing him and all the other Kesathese to be. He continued, in a low growl, "For all that you and your comrades professed to despise the stormships, you certainly had no problems using them when it benefited you. Nineteen years ago, before the Hurricane Wars, it was no different. From the moment the Lightweavers learned of the plans for the stormship, they spared no effort to take the technology for themselves. The prototype was being constructed in a valley under territorial dispute; Sunstead used this as a pretext to seize the shipyard. Kesath took it back, and we fought to make sure that nothing could be taken from us ever again."

And, two months later, his grandfather was dead and his father had ascended, in blood, in battle, in the dark of night.

All around us are enemies.

They shall tremble in the Shadow that we cast.

"That's *not* what happened!"

243

It was the strangest thing, how Talasyn, irate as she was, uncouth as she so often could be, managed to jolt Alaric back to the present, to pull him out of his clamoring head. The air lightened again and his magic fell back, as though the reminder of her presence was a sunbeam piercing through his storm of rage and grief.

"Before they did anything else, Sunstead sent emissaries to Kesath," she said, "to sway Ozalus from his course."

"They did not. They attacked without warning." Alaric was calmer now, but not by much. Speaking through gritted teeth. "It's Kesath's word against Sardovia's. It's what I know versus what you know. If it's all the same to you, I would rather believe that my family wasn't keeping the truth from me. Unlike yours, who didn't even see fit to tell you about something as important as the Night of the World-Eater."

Talasyn stood up, her small frame trembling. She placed her hands on her hips and glared down at him. "Even if what you say is true, even if I've been told lies my whole life, that still doesn't excuse what the Night Empire did to the rest of the Continent for ten years!" she shouted. "Vengeance is *not* justice. The Lightweavers of Sunstead were eradicated long before the Hurricane Wars began. Destroying the homes and killing the loved ones of innocent people didn't make Sunstead any *more* gone, did it?"

She spun on her heel and stalked away.

"Where are you going?" Alaric demanded.

"My chambers!" Talasyn yelled without looking back. "I don't want to train anymore today. Stay away from me!"

The side door leading into her room slammed shut behind her.

"*Train* anymore *today*?" Alaric scoffed under his breath. "We never even got started."

But he was speaking to empty air.

*

Fifteen minutes later, Alaric was still in the orchid garden. He had moved from the grass by the pool to one of the stone benches next to the waterfall, seeking shade from the relentless mid-afternoon sun underneath a hanging profusion of butterfly-shaped sapphire-and-cream blossoms.

He stared unseeing at his verdant surroundings, turning every second of his and Talasyn's heated quarrel over in his head. Finally, he called out, "Sevraim."

The unmasked legionnaire emerged from where he had been lurking behind a marble wall along the adjacent open hallway. He sauntered into the garden, flashing Alaric a cheerful grin. "How did you know that I was here?"

"You're my only protection on Nenavarene soil. I would be quite displeased if you *weren't* here."

"And allow your feisty wife to beat you to death with her bare hands? Never," Sevraim vowed with a chuckle. "Granted, she sounded moments away from doing just that. I was about to intervene."

"She's not my wife yet," Alaric grunted. "I assume you overheard everything, then."

"I did." Sevraim dropped down onto the stone bench, a carelessness to his movements that no one else would have dared show around Gaheris Ossinast's son. "There are two sides to each story, I suppose. But we know that *we* are in the right, so what does it matter what anyone else thinks?"

Alaric shrugged.

For the next several minutes, the splashing of the miniature waterfall was the only sound in the garden. And then Sevraim asked, "Is there something that His Majesty wishes to discuss with this humble servant?"

The words were teasing but the sentiment behind them was genuine, as only a lifelong companionship could engender. Alaric rolled his eyes and glanced at the languidly confident legionnaire who had charmed his way into almost every bed in the Kesathese court, and he scraped out, "How do I . . . talk to her?"

Sevraim's lips quirked, as though he were suppressing a guffaw. Alaric felt the tips of his ears turning scarlet. He regretted his impulsive question, but it was too late to turn back.

"It's understandable that she detests me," he said. "I don't believe that can ever be fixed. There's too much bad blood. But I would like to make the situation more . . ." He gestured limply at Talasyn's closed door across the garden. "Peaceful. Relatively speaking. However, no matter what I say or do, it sets her off."

Sevraim propped his chin up on one curled fist. "Your father trained you to be a warrior and to one day be emperor—*not* to be the Nenavarene Lachis'ka's consort. Least of all a Lachis'ka who wouldn't throw water on you if you were on fire."

"Indeed. She would be the one to set me ablaze," Alaric muttered. "With a dragon."

Sevraim snickered but didn't deny it. He nodded. "There is so much more to life than war and politics, Your Majesty. Ask her about her interests."

"Her interests," Alaric repeated blankly.

"What she likes," Sevraim clarified. "See if the two of you, maybe, like some of the same things, and go from there."

Alaric was sure Talasyn's interests consisted of his grisly demise, but Sevraim's suggestion seemed doable enough. "Very well. What else?"

"Compliment her," said Sevraim.

Alaric stared at him. "Compliment her on *what*?"

"Well, *I* don't know. I've spoken approximately ten words to her, and that was to say we were going to kill her." Sevraim scratched his head, deep in thought. "You could stand to look a little less forbidding, at least. You could perhaps even attempt to smile at her every once in a while."

Alaric didn't bother to dignify *that* with a response.

"All right, smiling might be too much," Sevraim conceded. "Just . . . You have to understand that the Lightweaver is doing this to save herself and her newfound people, just as you are doing it to prevent Kesath from becoming embroiled in another war while we recover from the previous one. She lashes out because she's anxious, as anyone in her situation would be. Don't rise to the bait she sets all the time. Mark my words, Your Majesty, you'll thank me for it."

CHAPTER TWENTY-ONE

It was rare for Talasyn to regret losing her temper, least of all when Alaric was involved, but by the next morning she had to admit that she'd messed up. There were only eleven days left until the eclipse, and she was nowhere close to weaving a decent shield.

As she marched into the council room after breakfast, Talasyn resolved to be on her best behavior. Not only during the negotiations, but also during the training in the afternoon. As far as promises went, she deemed it rather noble of her. However, it was a promise that took a severe beating when Urduja announced that there would be a banquet later that night with all the noble houses in attendance, to celebrate the Lachis'ka's engagement to the Night Emperor.

Still, Talasyn managed to give a stiff nod of acquiescence and do nothing more impolite than avoiding Alaric's eyes, which were regarding her dispassionately from across the table, with no trace of his own outburst yesterday.

Remembering that outburst elicited a most peculiar feeling in the pit of her stomach. Alaric usually had supreme control over his emotions, unlike her. The only times he'd appeared truly furious with her were yesterday and that night in the bamboo cell at the Belian garrison. In those instances, she'd needled him about Ozalus and Gaheris, respectively. His family was clearly a touchy subject.

And, yet, no matter how furious he was, he had never shouted at her. In fact, the angrier he got, the lower his voice became. Now that she thought about it, it was the one trait of Alaric's that recommended him to her. Yelling meant the orphanage, the caretakers. Talasyn yelled when she was angry because yelling for her was what anger was, how she understood it. There was something fascinating about Alaric's quiet rage, about how easily he could restrain himself.

It made her feel—

Safe?

All around her, the negotiators were talking. Bartering, compromising, laying out the road for the future. Talasyn was barely listening. Her new epiphany pounded in her ears like blood.

Yesterday, when the Shadowgate had roared forth from Alaric, she'd moved away slightly, but only so that she'd have enough ground to fight back if it came to that. But those had been a soldier's instincts. She hadn't flinched. She hadn't, even just for a moment, been afraid of him.

Talasyn darted a furtive glance at Alaric, hating that she was physically incapable of stopping herself from doing so. All of his attention was on Lueve Rasmey as the daya talked the Kesathese contingent through each step of the wedding ceremony and its corresponding cultural significance in Nenavar, fielding questions and objections from Commodore Mathire all the while. Alaric's black-gauntleted fingers drummed idly on the table, the motion a focal point with the rest of him being so still. For Talasyn, nonsensical observations and memories began to creep in—the sheer size of his hand, the way it had felt clamped around her waist the time he lifted her away from the edge of the pool—and she hurriedly shifted her focus to Lueve before these could consume her.

Lueve's multitude of opal rings glinted in the sunlight as she held up a piece of parchment covered in gold-flecked, wavelike script. It was her marriage contract, which she'd retrieved from the Dominion's archives high up in the mountains for the panel's edification; Alaric and Talasyn would sign a similar document at the dragon altar on their wedding day.

"The contract is in Nenavarene, so allow me to translate," said Daya Rasmey. *"Lueve, daughter of Akara from the Veins of Cenderwas, daughter of Viel from the Fastness of Mandayar, daughter of Thinza'khin from the Sundered Plains, is joining hands with Idrees, son of Esah from the Banks of the Infinite, daughter of Nayru from the Serpent's Trace—"*

"I think that Kesath has gotten the idea," Urduja interrupted. "Anyway, the gist is that it goes back three generations along the matrilineal line."

Alaric was already shaking his head, even before she'd finished speaking. "My mother was a traitor to the Crown. Her house was expunged from the Kesathese peerage and both my father and I have renounced all affiliation with her. It would be dishonest to enter into a marriage on those terms."

Talasyn was bewildered. As infuriated as she was with Urduja and Elagbi at present, she couldn't imagine reaching a point where she would actually renounce them, not when she'd been looking for her family all her life. The only thing that she knew about Sancia Ossinast, Gaheris's wife and the former Night Empress, was that she had disappeared a few years before the Hurricane Wars began. There were even rumors that Gaheris had killed her. And now Talasyn wondered what Sancia had done to make her son so clearly repulsed by the mere mention of her name.

Alaric's family really *was* a touchy subject for him.

"I believe that it would be for the best if we skipped the contract." Prince Elagbi broke the uneasy silence. "Hanan and I didn't sign one, either, because it isn't the custom on the Dawn Isles—"

"And because you were married in a witch's hut, with only one member of court to bear witness," Urduja groused, narrowing her eyes at her son.

"Perhaps a simpler version of the contract?" Commodore Mathire suggested—to the room at large, but her gaze lingered on Alaric and it seemed all too knowing, and Talasyn was so, *so* curious, but she'd vowed to behave and that involved keeping her mouth shut rather than demanding answers. "Just the names of the imperial couple and their titles?"

The Nenavarene side of the panel begrudgingly accepted Mathire's proposal. From there, the talks dragged on well past noon. Once they were adjourned, Talasyn left the council room, both glad that today's negotiations were over and uneasy about once again having to spend the next few hours alone with her confusing betrothed and all the secrets that lurked in his gray eyes.

Talasyn was about to head into the orchid garden for the afternoon's training session—truly, she was—when one of her guards came knocking on her bedroom door with an announcement, in compliance with the only direct order Talasyn had ever given since she settled in at the Roof of Heaven. The order to let her know when—

"The pudding merchant is here, Your Grace."

Even though she'd made a vow to behave, it took Talasyn exactly the length of a heartbeat to decide to let Alaric wait a bit longer. With the contingent of Lachis-dalo trailing after her, she scurried out of her wing of the palace, through the marble hallways, and down the front steps of the Roof of Heaven, where a small crowd of servants had gathered to greet the merchant who sailed up the limestone cliffs on his dugout twice a month.

He was a skinny man who wore a perennial betel-nut-stained smile beneath his wide-brimmed straw hat. On his spry shoulders he balanced a bamboo pole with large aluminum buckets dangling from each end. One bucket contained fresh soybean curds kept warm by a Firewarren-infused aether heart; the other, tiny pearls of palm starch suspended in brown sugar syrup.

Most of the nobles within the palace were too stuffy for street fare, but Talasyn had no such qualms. Servants bowed and curtsied to her, but they had long since learned that she preferred to wait her turn like everyone else. They *did* become a little quieter, though, a little less rowdy as they chatted among themselves and with the merchant. Talasyn rather suspected that they'd been bringing him up to speed about news from the palace and the upcoming wedding before she arrived.

She stood awkwardly in the middle of the throng. It was as though she were an island, surrounded by waves of camaraderie that steered clear of her shores. It was a sensation that she was all too familiar with from her time at Hornbill's Head and in the Sardovian regiments.

No matter her status, it seemed that it would always be her lot in life to feel alone.

Suddenly, the various streams of lyrical chatter cut off. Talasyn looked around, a nervous little flutter running through her at the sight of Alaric making his way down the palace steps.

Sevraim was never far behind his liege, but today he hung back, with Talasyn's own guards. The hushed servants scattered before the Night Emperor as he strode toward her. Some appeared afraid, others resentful—but it couldn't be denied that typical Nenavarene inquisitiveness overrode all other emotions. They stared and they stared, whispering behind their hands.

Alaric's pale features grew stonier at being on the receiving end of such unabashed scrutiny. "We have an appointment," he reminded Talasyn.

"We do," she said in even tones. "Beforehand, however, I would like some pudding."

"Pudding?" he repeated blankly. His gray eyes flitted to the merchant, whose sunny smile had faded, replaced with an expression that suggested he was tempted to dive behind his buckets for cover.

The wall of people that had previously stood between the merchant and Talasyn had melted away. "Two, please," she said kindly in Nenavarene, handing him a silver coin that she fished out from her pocket. A cupful of pudding was worth only three brass pieces, but she figured that the man deserved extra for having to put up with her betrothed.

"Y-yes, Your Grace," the merchant stammered. He retrieved two wooden cups from his dugout and ladled generous amounts of snow-white soybean curd and dark sugar syrup into them, sticking a wooden spoon into each mixture before passing both cups to Talasyn.

She held one cup out to Alaric with an air of challenge. The spectators leaned forward eagerly, waiting to see if the fearsome Night Emperor from the land across the Eversea would partake of such a humble repast.

Alaric took the cup from Talasyn as gingerly as though it were a venomous snake. The sun-warmed leather of his gauntlet brushed against her bare fingers as he did so, and that nervous little flutter coursed through her again. Where was *that* coming from?

Shrugging it off, she brought her cup closer to her lips and scarfed down a spoonful of pudding. The starch pearls burst between her teeth and the silky soybean curd melted on her tongue in a warm wash of sweet syrup. She nearly closed her eyes at how delicious it was. This had definitely been worth being late for training.

Alaric tentatively spooned pudding into his mouth, skepticism radiating from his form. One of the serving-girls giggled and was promptly shushed by another, who was desperately trying to muffle her *own* giggles.

"Well?" Talasyn demanded as Alaric chewed thoughtfully.

He was a proper little lord, she would give him that. He waited until he'd swallowed to respond. "It's interesting."

Offended on behalf of her beloved pudding, she turned her nose up at him before moving away so that everyone else could get to the merchant. Alaric followed her and they finished their cups in silence, facing each other beside the docked dugout ship. In spite of his bland assessment of the pudding's qualities, Alaric ate every last bit of soybean curd and drank the remaining syrup.

Talasyn found it surreal that the Master of the Shadowforged Legion had a sweet tooth. Then again, it must have been a novelty to him, as it had been to her when she reclaimed her birthright. Back on the Northwest Continent, sugar and soybeans had been strictly rationed due to the war effort.

They returned their spoons and empty cups to the pudding merchant. The high sun of early afternoon beat down on the limestone cliffs, alleviated by a fresh, brisk breeze blowing in from the distant Eversea. And it was some impulse—some abrupt yearning to not spend the afternoon cooped up inside the palace walls—that made Talasyn ask Alaric, "Do you want to aethermance out here today?"

He shrugged. The plush swell of his bottom lip glistened with a hint of syrup, and her gaze lingered for far too long. "Wherever you like, Lachis'ka."

Alaric could still taste brown sugar on his tongue as Talasyn led him to a grove of plumeria trees that carpeted the space between the southernmost wall of the palace and the edge of the limestone cliffs. There were plumerias in Kesath, too, but their flowers were typically fuchsia in color. The blooms speckling the green leaves of the Nenavarene variety were as pristine white as the Roof of Heaven's facade, with star-shaped splashes of yellow at their center.

Sevraim and the Lachis-dalo remained at the edge of the grove while Alaric and Talasyn wandered further in. The trees grew closely together, enough that their rounded crowns would shield the two aethermancers from view of the windows or the patrolling guards.

Alaric was glad to be free of curious stares from nosy Nenavarene, but something had been weighing on his mind all day thus far. Once he and Talasyn assumed meditation poses on the grass, beneath the plumerias, he could no longer stop himself.

"Is there something troubling you?" he asked, which marked the second instance in as many days wherein he regretted asking someone a question as soon as it left his lips.

From where she sat, framed against bark and leaves and white flowers, Talasyn blinked at him as though he'd lost his mind.

Perhaps he had, at that.

"I don't think we heard a peep out of you all morning, during the negotiations," he explained. "And you usually have quite a *lot* to say when you're around me."

Talasyn sneered and opened her mouth, then stilled as though remembering something. Finally, she said, "Let's focus on training."

Her manner was that of someone who had been told to stand down—or perhaps told *herself*, as the way she treated everyone on the Nenavarene panel these days made it clear that she wasn't on speaking terms with them. In any case, she was being cooperative, and Alaric wasn't about to scorn a miracle when it was right in front of him.

"Very well," he said. "We're going back to the basics today. I'll teach you some Shadowforged breathing meditations. The principle should be roughly the same." He had no wish to admit to anything in common with Lightweavers, but there were some truths that couldn't be denied. "Aethermancy comes from the center, the place in one's soul that is similar to a nexus point, where the wall between the material realm and aetherspace is thin. The hidden, more stubborn aspects of one's magic can be coaxed forth by mastering how to let it flow through your body in the correct way."

For the next hour, Alaric took Talasyn through the seated meditations. He taught her how to hold air in her lungs and expel it slowly, rhythmically. How to gather it behind the navel, push it out through the nose, and tuck it into the tongue. How to let the Lightweave build up and swell on the crests of it, seeping into the spaces between blood and the soul.

She was a quick study in terms of mimicking his postures and the expansions and contractions of chest, abdomen, and spine—but it was as plain as day that she had trouble clearing her mind long enough for the practice to take full effect. She was a restless thing, her coltish frame thrumming with nervous energy, and he had half a mind to leave her alone for a bit, because maybe she would be able to focus better without him.

But he didn't leave her alone. He stayed where he was. For once the blue-skied afternoon wasn't beastly hot due to a pleasant breeze that stirred the plumeria blossoms. The gaps between the trees offered glimpses of the sweeping city of Eskaya miles below, with its golden towers and its bronze weathervanes. He could almost call it *relaxing*, sitting here in this place of leaves and earth, secluded from the rest of the palace at such a great height. There was no political maneuvering to worry about, no specter of wars past or future. It was just them, and breath and magic.

Could I have lived like this? Alaric found himself idly wondering. Without a throne to someday inherit, with the stormships remaining his grandfather's impossible dream, would he have been content with this kind of life, his days passing slow and easy in some mundane pastoral setting?

Would he have been all right with never meeting *her*?

A strange thought, that. It stood to all reason that his life, whatever iteration of it, would be so much simpler without her in it. Talasyn—in all her prickliness, with that face that his gaze somehow always lingered on—was a ceramic shell hurled into his carefully laid plans.

She was currently squeezing her eyes shut, her freckled nose all scrunched up. Sunshine illuminated the golden undertones of her olive skin and her unkempt chestnut braid spilled over one shoulder. She looked *fetching*, and Alaric grimaced. What was it about her that reduced him to such nonsensical adjectives?

And then, because the gods had a twisted sense of humor, he was suddenly falling into the depths of Talasyn's honeyed eyes as they flew open, too quickly for him to abolish the grimace on his face.

"What?" she muttered with deepest suspicion. "Am I doing it wrong?"

"No." Alaric seized the first excuse that he could come up with. "I was just thinking."

"About?"

Well, he certainly wasn't going to reveal that he'd been *ogling* her. He grasped around wildly for a suitable evasion, and stumbled upon something that he had in fact been ruminating on earlier in the day. Something that had been revealed during the talks. "Your mother was from the Dawn."

Talasyn blew out a measured breath that had nothing to do with the meditations he'd taught her. "Her name was Hanan Ivralis. My father met her on his travels and brought her with him when he went back to the Dominion. She died during the civil war."

Alaric's brow creased. "The people of the Dawn Isles are

powerful warriors, by all accounts. What could kill a Lightweaver hailing from there?"

"It was a mysterious illness. And it was fast. She slipped away in only a sennight, before anyone could figure out what was wrong. I don't—" Talasyn broke off sharply, her gaze flicking from him to the waterfall. "I don't really like talking about it."

"I apologize for bringing it up," Alaric said, soft and solemn and far too sincere. Dangerously so. The defiant tilt of her chin and the way her fists clenched in her lap elicited a pang of guilt that he'd inadvertently forced her to relive her sorrow. It was a sorrow that had no root, for she would have been too young to have any clear memories of her mother. Communing with the Light Sever might be able to change that, but the Zahiya-lachis had declared Belian off-limits for now.

Talasyn's pink lips quirked. "Never thought I'd live to see the day you apologized to me."

"I know when I've overstepped," Alaric stiffly replied. "While I'm at it, I would also like to apologize for losing my temper yesterday. I hope that you weren't too—perturbed."

"I wasn't." She was still avoiding his eyes, but some of the tension had drained from her form. "I was wrong, too. For yelling and storming off. We have a common goal now. We should be working together. So let's just . . . do that."

For several long moments, Alaric was so stunned that it defied all speech. Could it be that being *nicer* to the Lightweaver made her nicer to him as well? Could Sevraim, in fact, be a genius? He could never tell him he was right.

It was only when Talasyn turned to him with a slight frown that Alaric realized he'd been silent for too long. "Yes," he said quickly. "Focusing on working together. I am amenable."

Her frown transmuted into another upward twitch at the corner of her mouth. He had the distinct and unsettling impression that she found him amusing.

Alaric stood up, motioning for Talasyn to follow suit. He

demonstrated the simplest of the moving meditations—feet apart, inhaling deeply as one palm was placed in front of the stomach and the other over the head, exhaling as the right knee was bent as far as it could go without the body toppling over. Slow and gradual movements, like a gentle ocean wave.

At first, Talasyn gave the exercise her utmost attention, with the furrowed brow and the wrinkled nose that he was starting to find so alarmingly endearing, but it soon became obvious that she was preoccupied, a distant look in her eyes. Her expression flitted to uncertainty, and then to solemn determination, and Alaric could only marvel at how unguarded she was, at how she let various emotions play across her face without thinking, the way that clouds shifted through the heavens, at turns hiding and revealing the sun. She was so different from everyone else he'd ever met in both the Night Empire and the Dominion courts.

"What happened to *your* mother?" she blurted out in the middle of another attempt at the pose.

Alaric would normally never have any desire to talk about it but, to his own surprise, he found he wanted to with her. Parting with each word more willingly than he ought to have, because fair was fair and Talasyn had shared such a dark shard of her past with him, too.

"My mother abandoned Kesath when I was thirteen." *Abandoned me* was what some part of him longed to say. *She abandoned me.* "I haven't heard from her since. I assume that she sought refuge in Valisa, where her ancestors originated." He ran a critical eye over Talasyn's stance. "Don't put all your weight on one knee. Balance it out and keep your back straight."

"Valisa," she mused. "That's all the way west, on the edge of the world." She aligned herself to Alaric's specifications and he walked around her, saying nothing, searching her form for what needed improvement.

"Do you miss her?" Talasyn asked, in a much quieter tone.

Alaric was caught off-guard. He stopped in his tracks behind her, glad that she couldn't see his features as he struggled to compose them. "No. She was weak. She faltered in the face of what it meant to be the Night Empress. I am better off without her."

Come with me.

My son. My baby.

Please.

"Sometimes I wonder . . ."

Alaric trailed off, embarrassed. He had been so cautious all his life, always weighing his words before he spoke them. Why could he never seem to do the same around Talasyn?

"If she ever thinks of you," she finished for him in a soft voice. "I wondered that every day, back in Sardovia, before I knew who I was, before I knew that my mother was dead. I wondered if she ever regretted leaving me."

There was a tightness in his throat, a certain rising lightness in his chest. Someone finally understood. Someone could give voice to all the things that he could never put into words. Talasyn was still in meditation stance, still facing away from him, and he was seized by the urge to sweep her into his arms. To embrace her in reassurance, in solidarity.

To no longer be alone.

"Keep your back straight," he said instead. "And your elbows out."

"I am!" she protested. Her shoulders visibly bunched underneath her thin white smock, as they always did when she was about to pick a fight.

"No—" Alaric stepped forward, impatient all of a sudden, eager to shake free of the chains of memory, to distract himself with something that wasn't the terrible night Sancia Ossinast left Kesath. "Like this—"

He reached out to correct Talasyn's posture at the same

time that she straightened up with an exasperated huff, moving backward as she brought her feet together. His gauntleted hands closed on the tops of her shoulders and her spine pressed flush against his chest.

The world went still.

Mangoes was Alaric's first coherent thought. That slick, succulent, golden fruit that graced every meal he had here in the Dominion, with its lush perfume of summer-warmed nectar. Talasyn smelled as if she'd been eating them, dusted in flaky sea salt. And that wasn't all. Orange blossoms and the creamy floral note of promise jasmines wafted from her hair, tempered by cool green attar of lotus and the barest hint of cinnamon bark.

Alaric's mouth watered. He wanted to *bite down*.

It didn't help matters that Talasyn fit perfectly against him, that he could tuck her head under his chin, that her bottom was slotted between his hips and shapely enough to make the pit of his stomach clench. In a daze, he watched his leather-clad fingers spread over her shoulders. Watched his thumbs graze the sides of her neck.

He had never despised his gauntlets more. He longed to peel them off, to touch her sun-kissed skin. His thumbs moved in circular strokes, caressing the elegant slopes they rested against. She shivered, every tremor passing through him, touching off inner chords within him, and what was he hoping to achieve, why wasn't he moving away, how had he never known that holding someone could feel like this?

The breeze picked up, shaking a rain of white petals loose from the plumeria trees. Amidst all those swirling snow-drop pieces of flowers that drifted on currents of faint perfume, she turned her head to look at him.

Her brown eyes were so wide in the sunlight, her breathing shallow, her pink lips slightly parted.

It overwhelmed him, then—a dark curiosity, a yearning to find out if those lips would taste like the pudding they'd just eaten.

Alaric leaned in. He lifted his fingers from Talasyn's neck and curled them along the line of her jaw, gently nudging upward. She went willingly, relaxing against his chest, tilting her chin so that her mouth was suddenly so much closer to his than ever before. Petals whirling all around them, his heartbeat tremulous, he bowed his head further to bridge the scant distance. Her eyes slid to half-mast. She waited.

"Excuse me."

Alaric and Talasyn sprang apart. Neither of them had even noticed Sevraim's approach.

"What do you want?" Alaric growled at his legionnaire.

"I hate to interrupt—" And, the thing was, Sevraim really *did* seem abashed, conscientiously looking everywhere but at the two royals. "—but the Lachis'ka's lady-in-waiting has just come to inform me that it's time for His Majesty and Her Grace to prepare for the banquet."

CHAPTER TWENTY-TWO

The mirror in Talasyn's dressing room was a polished glass oval framed by carved hummingbirds and squash vines, inlaid with lustrous chips of mother-of-pearl. She sat in front of it, once again laced into a spectacle of a garment, this one sewn from banana-stem fiber that gave it a multichromatic sheen, her neck stiff from bearing the weight of yet another gaudy crown. Jie pored over her with a plethora of long-handled willow brushes, dipped into small golden pots of various powders in order to paint on a face that would befit the Nenavarene Lachis'ka at a formal event.

Like any other day, Talasyn suffered in silence while her lady-in-waiting worked a different kind of magic. *Unlike* any other day, the inside of her head was all fuzzy with thoughts of Alaric. Of his stupidly large body so close to hers, warm and unyielding. Of his palms engulfing her shoulders, of the ridged leather of his gauntlets gliding along her neck.

By the World-Father's yellow fingernails, she'd shivered. She'd *actually* shivered at Alaric's touch, goosebumps prickling her skin. He'd taken such liberties with her, and she—

She hadn't hated it.

It had made the oddest sort of yearning bloom within her.

Never mind that he was the cruel Night Emperor, the brutal Master of the Shadowforged Legion. She had, for a few horrifying moments, stared at his mouth, her traitorous body singing as that mouth drew closer. She had leaned back against him and tipped up her chin. She had wanted to be warmed all over. To see where it led.

Sol had liked to hold Khaede that way, Talasyn remembered. He would sneak up behind Khaede and put his hands on her shoulders or around her waist, rasping out a greeting before pressing a mischievous kiss to her neck, in plain sight of everyone.

Whenever Talasyn had seen that—whenever she saw how grumpy old Khaede melted into Sol's arms—she had always wondered what it would feel like, if it was her and someone who loved her.

And now Sol was dead and Khaede was gone and Talasyn was grasping at straws again, likening the affection the two had shared to that pale parody of it in the plumeria grove which had been nothing more than an unfortunate, inexplicable accident between her and the man she hated, and who hated her.

She felt sick to her stomach.

Alaric *had* been about to kiss her, hadn't he? Granted, she could claim no personal experience regarding such things, but it had been heading there, hadn't it? *Why?*

Why would he even attempt to kiss her? And why, despite knowing what he was and all that he had done, had she even wanted him to?

Hate is another kind of passion, Niamha Langsoune had said the day the Kesathese arrived. Perhaps it was that. An aberration, like accidentally tapping into a different frequency because aetherwave wires had crossed. It could never be anything more than that, and Talasyn resolved to put it out of her mind—maybe even stab Alaric if he attempted to bring it up.

"You know, Your Grace," Jie chirped as she deftly ran a willow-stick, the tip coated in ground-up brown pigment, through Talasyn's brows, "I was just thinking the other day that Emperor Alaric isn't so terrible-looking for an outsider. In my opinion, as far as physical appearances go, you could have done far worse. I'm serious!" she exclaimed with a slight laugh as Talasyn sputtered. "He's a bit on the broody side and somewhat frightening, dressed all in black like that, but he's tall and he has beautiful hair. And his mouth, it's very—"

"Y-you stop right there!" Talasyn nearly shrieked, her reflection scarlet in the hummingbird mirror.

She couldn't tell whether Jie's lack of resentment toward Alaric was simply the girl making the best of a bad situation or genuine disinterest in the threat that Kesath posed to her homeland. Talasyn suspected that it might be the latter. Jie had grown up in a castle with a host of servants attending to her every whim, secure in the knowledge that she would one day inherit the title of daya from her doting mother. She was sixteen years old, incredibly chatty, and seemed not to have a single care in the world.

Still, a command from the Lachis'ka was a command, and so Jie didn't pursue the topic. However, her eyes sparkled with amusement as she dusted a pale shimmery powder over the bridge of Talasyn's nose. "Is there courtship on the Northwest Continent, Your Grace? Here we give small tokens of our affection, send letters, hold hands under the promise jasmines when they're in bloom, steal a kiss or two. The boys serenade us outside our windows as well. Is it similar elsewhere?"

"I wouldn't know. I never had time for any of that." It occurred to Talasyn that what Jie had said didn't quite adhere to her own observations of Nenavarene culture. "I thought that most marriages among the Dominion aristocracy were arranged."

"Yes, but there *are* those who wed for love," said Jie. "Such

as my cousin, Harjanti, the Daya of Sabtang. I hope to someday
be as fortunate." Her smile was soft and dreamy and unjaded,
so far removed from Talasyn's own experiences at that age,
fighting a war an ocean away. "And for you, Lachis'ka, I hope
that Emperor Alaric will romance you properly. Stolen kisses
and all."

Jie tittered, highly pleased with herself. Talasyn was spared
from having to respond by the musical notes of wind chimes,
as light and airy as birdsong. Jie excused herself to see who
had sounded them.

When she returned to Talasyn, she announced. "Lachis'ka,
Queen Urduja and Prince Elagbi are here to see you."

Wonderful.

Talasyn struggled not to roll her eyes. She didn't particularly
want to talk to her grandmother and her father, but—she
could. *I am amenable,* as Alaric had said in that prissy tone
of his, and remembering *that* ensured that Talasyn was biting
back a smile and shaking her head at his insufferable antics
as she followed Jie into the solar.

It was *her* solar but, just like her bedchamber, it had been
designed with the comfort of a refined aristocrat in mind.
Lustrous rosewood had been fashioned into delicate chairs
and scroll-legged tables. The white marble walls were covered
in pastel-hued paintings of cherry blossoms and egrets and
dancing figures with stars in their flowing hair, all accentuated
with generous splashes of gold leaf. Artfully scattered
throughout the airy space were bronze sculptures and elaborate woven baskets. In one corner, perched atop a dragon-shaped
pedestal, was an enormous arched harp, gathering dust; the
young Urduja Silim had reportedly played like a dream before
assuming the mantle of leadership, but Talasyn had thought
that the instrument was some kind of weapon when she first
laid eyes on it.

Queen Urduja had made herself comfortable in one of the

chairs, but Elagbi bounded up to Talasyn, beaming. "My dear, you look lovely—"

"Thank you," Talasyn replied in a flat tone of voice. She didn't return her father's embrace, and his arms awkwardly fell away from her.

Urduja shot Jie an imperious look, waiting until the girl had scampered out of the solar before telling Talasyn, "Your father and I would like to clear the air regarding certain matters."

Talasyn sat down. Elagbi did as well, his dark eyes bearing the wounded look of a pup that had been kicked one too many times, and Talasyn willed her resolve not to crumble. He had done her wrong and she wasn't willing to let him forget it anytime soon.

Urduja cleared her throat lightly. "I understand that you are angry at us for withholding the information about the Voidfell. I would like to explain why—"

"I already *know* why," Talasyn interrupted. She'd had plenty of opportunity to agonize over it. "You were afraid that the Amirante would change her mind about sheltering in Nenavar and I would have no impetus to stay and your reign would destabilize further because you had no heir."

Urduja didn't deny it. Incensed, Talasyn continued, "You said that you suspected the Night Empire would try to invade. But that wasn't exactly true, was it? You *knew* that they would, because you've been around long enough to realize that it was inevitable. And you even *welcomed* it, because an alliance with the Shadowforged while you had a Lightweaver granddaughter was Nenavar's way out of another Dead Season. You had that marriage offer ready to go—perhaps ever since it was reported to you that Ossinast and I had created a barrier that could cancel out the Belian garrison's void bolts. When I suggested to Vela that we come here, I was playing right into your hands, wasn't I?"

Urduja's dark-tinted lips stretched into a smile. And the horrifying thing was that it was *genuine*. There was no warmth in it, that was true, but there was a certain pride. "*Almost* perfect, Lachis'ka. You fail to see the entirety of the bigger picture. In the future, consider *every* angle. That skill will serve you well when you are queen."

"Harlikaan," Elagbi pleaded, "Talasyn is hurting right now. We owe it to her to explain."

"That's precisely what I'm doing," Urduja huffed. "Alunsina, I decided to leave it as late as possible—to let you and the Night Emperor find out together—for a very simple reason. Ossinast does not trust you. He probably never truly will, given your shared past. Had you known about the Night of the World-Eater before he did, had you been in on it when I sprung the new information on him, that would have made things even worse. But now he has reason to believe that you are guileless, to a certain extent. That I have not fully taken you into my confidence. That you are nothing at all like my conniving court."

He does more than believe that, Talasyn thought numbly. Alaric had *sympathized* with her. He had given her his sincere perspective on the situation. "Why—" Her voice cracked. She tried again. "Why tell me at all, then?"

"I almost wasn't going to. I deemed the risk too great," said Urduja. "But your father"—she shot a long-suffering glance at Elagbi—"felt that, if we let this go on, it would cause damage to our relationship as a family that would prove impossible to repair."

"And because it would be another lesson for me, right?" Talasyn muttered.

"You *are* learning," said Urduja.

"I'm tired of being a pawn." Where did it come from, this bluntness? Perhaps the memory of Alaric saying that her grandmother underestimated her. Perhaps even just that she was *fed up*. "I don't want this to happen again. If I am to play my part in saving Nenavar and the Sardovian remnant, we have to work together."

"You are dictating to me, Your Grace?" Urduja challenged.

"Not at all, Harlikaan," Talasyn said evenly, holding the older woman's gaze with a steel that she had never expected herself capable of. "I'm simply advising you on the best way forward. On how, as I see it, we can get out of this mess unscathed."

When Urduja finally nodded, Talasyn was left with the impression of having just *barely* dodged what would have been a killing blow. She made a valiant attempt to prevent her relief from being *too* evident, although she was certain that the Zahiya-lachis's jet-black eyes missed nothing. In the same vein, she fought back the wave of guilt that assailed her. She was doing what she needed to do. If Alaric took issue, he should have made different choices in life.

But it all came creeping up on her, like splinters of a dream just upon waking. The shadows swirling around Alaric in pain and fury as he spoke of his grandfather's death, misguided as his version of events was. His distant tone when he told her about his mother—so carefully blank, like armor drawn over a vulnerable spot.

Why should she think about these things now? Why should she care?

Elagbi clapped his hands together. "Now that *that's* been sorted out," he said, with a cheer slightly strained at the edges, "shall we head down to supper?"

A purple carpet of stars fell over the Roof of Heaven and the seven moons in their various phases emerged from behind wisps of cloud. Standing beside an open window in the corridor outside the banquet hall, Alaric peered down at the Dominion's capital city, which was so brightly lit and bustling that it could almost have been the middle of the day.

Talasyn would arrive at any moment. He was nervous, still thinking about what had happened in the plumeria grove—or what had *almost* happened. Earlier, he'd wanted to kill Sevraim, but now he was grateful for the interruption.

He was Shadowforged. He couldn't go around kissing Lightweavers, no matter how pretty and betrothed to him they were. And it would only be a marriage of political convenience, anyway. She would never feel the same—

The same as *what*? What did *he* feel?

The heat was getting to him, he decided. A humid breeze seeped in through the window, and Alaric tried not to be too obvious in the way he angled his body to catch as much of it as possible. The majority of his wardrobe was ill suited to Nenavar's tropical climate. He was far too warm in his black high-collared cutaway tailcoat layered over a shirt of ribbed ivory silk.

He knew that Sevraim and Mathire were similarly suffering in their black-and-silver dress uniforms. The two of them had been scowling when the steward ushered them into the banquet hall after informing Alaric that he and Talasyn—as it was in their honor that the event was being held—would be the last to enter, that he was expected to escort her inside, where all the other diners were waiting. The palace guards posted by the closed doors were clearly struggling to disguise their looks of suspicion and contempt as they stood within striking distance of a would-be invader, but, fortunately, Alaric didn't have to endure it for long.

Because suddenly *she* was there, appearing from around the corner.

His breath caught at the sight of her. Talasyn wore a dress spun from iridescent teal fabric, textured and crisp, with silver dragons lavishly embroidered along the square neckline, the high waist, the hem of the flowing skirt, and the cuffs of the wide sleeves that trailed almost to the floor, revealing glimpses of a blood-red lining. Her hair was loose, cascading from beneath a silver crown that resembled a multi-spired temple rising up from glimmering oceanic waves, a ruby-eyed dragon's head perched at the center.

She didn't hesitate when she caught sight of him, closing the distance between them with her chin held high. As she came to a stop a few inches away, Alaric saw her usual death stare had been replaced with uncertainty. Her eyes, which usually blazed with fury, were rendered a lighter shade of brown by the glow of the torches and somehow seemed gentler because of that, yet no less potent in their scrutiny.

The moment in the plumeria grove hung uneasily between them. He stiffly offered his arm out to her, and Talasyn turned just the slightest bit pink. It was *fetching*. Alaric briefly considered punching himself in the face.

Compliment her, he remembered Sevraim's advice from the other day. Now seemed like a good time for it, but Alaric couldn't force the words past his throat. What if *she* punched him in the face?

Talasyn took his arm while he stood frozen in indecision, tucking her hand into the crook of his elbow. "Ready?" was all that Alaric could say rather hoarsely in the end, as the guards pushed the doors open.

She nodded, and he led her forward. Into a swell of light and music and glittering people.

Alaric didn't think it was an exaggeration to presume that he'd seen city streets shorter than the table, which ran down the middle of the banquet hall. It was draped with woven cloths in a dizzying patchwork of different patterns and colors and set with an array of crystal centerpieces and jewel-encrusted plates and goblets. The red-lacquered chairs blazed bright with gilded lotus scrollwork beside it, and the people occupying them rose to their feet as one at the Night Emperor and the Lachis'ka's entrance—with the exception of Queen

271

Urduja. She watched cannily from the head of the table as the obsequious steward led him and Talasyn to two empty chairs, which he noted with some mild alarm were right next to each other and smack-dab in the middle of the table. He would be surrounded by Nenavarene all throughout supper, effectively cut off from Sevraim and Mathire.

Attending this feast already felt like a mistake.

Talasyn's slim fingers dug into Alaric's arm as they followed the steward. *She's nervous,* he realized, glancing down to see her bottom lip trembling. Whoever applied her cosmetics had done an expert job in rendering dewy skin and rosy cheeks, but no amount of soot and beeswax on the lashes or champagne-hued pigments on the lids could disguise the apprehension in her brown eyes. Not when she was this close to him.

"It's not too late to make a run for it," he quipped.

"I'm in pointy shoes," she shot back. "With heels."

"So *that's* why you seem taller. Not by much, though."

"We can't *all* be overgrown trees, my lord," she retorted, and she was so oddly adorable in that moment, in her defiance layered over the nerves that she was trying to hide, that the line of his mouth softened with the beginnings of a genuine smile.

"*My lord,*" Alaric repeated. His tone was not as mocking as he would have liked. "I certainly prefer that to all the other names that you've called me throughout our fractured acquaintance."

"Shut up," Talasyn hissed. "It's all those etiquette lessons. It won't happen again."

Her hand dropped back to her side as she took her appointed seat. The other diners followed suit, along with Alaric, whose arm, he firmly told himself, did not—*did not*—suddenly feel bereft of her touch.

*

272

Cuisine was the one aspect of Dominion culture that Talasyn had had no problem wholeheartedly embracing thus far. To someone who'd subsisted on scraps until she was fifteen and then on bland rations served in Sardovian mess halls for five more years, Nenavarene dishes were a rainbow of delights with their complex spices, enticing aromas, and scrumptious textures.

Sadly, tonight's peculiar circumstances ensured that she was unable to pay as much attention to the food as she usually did. A selection of small plates was paraded out first: slices of fermented pork and chili peppers wrapped in banana leaves; tiny, chargrilled squid served whole on the skewer brushed with garlic and lime juice; pickled greens resting on beds of glass noodles. It all tasted like dust in her mouth.

She was too conscious of Alaric's presence beside her. She felt as though she couldn't breathe properly. Her every nerve ending sparked at his nearness, sandalwood-and-juniper-scented and imposing.

Earlier, out in the corridor, she'd nearly been brought up short by the sight of him in formal attire. His high-collared black coat, embellished with the Kesathese chimera in dusky gold brocade, clung to his broad shoulders and added a lean elegance to his silhouette. The slim fit of his black trousers flattered his rangy hips, his muscular thighs, and the athletic length of his legs. With his naturally haughty expression only slightly softened by the thick black hair that fell about his face in casual waves, he looked every inch the young emperor, radiating power and self-assurance.

It did—*something*—to her. It made her heartbeat stutter over some peculiar cliff's edge between her midsection and her throat. And, to make matters worse, Jie had called attention to Alaric's lips earlier and now Talasyn couldn't stop glancing at them. The sensual fullness of them. The wickedness. How they had come so close to touching hers hours ago. She was sure she'd even caught the beginnings of a smile earlier, but she was likely mistaken. She wholeheartedly blamed her lady-in-waiting for this dire state of affairs.

It *also* didn't help that it fell upon Talasyn to make the necessary introductions between Alaric and the people seated near them, and those lords and ladies eventually began lobbing pointed conversational volleys designed to *not quite* hide their displeasure with the betrothal.

"I believe, Your Majesty, that you and Her Grace knew each other prior to her return to Nenavar," purred Ralya Musal, the feather-clad Daya of Tepi Resok, a smattering of hilly islands that comprised almost half of the Dominion's southernmost border. "Would you care to enlighten us as to the nature of that acquaintance?"

Talasyn held her breath. Everyone at the table already knew what had transpired—if not the nitty-gritty details, then the vague and overarching shape of it. They just wanted to trip Alaric up.

There was a brief silence as he picked at his plate, obviously buying time while he formulated a diplomatic answer. "Several months ago I was made aware of the existence of a Lightweaver among the ranks of the Sardovian Allfold. As Master of the Shadowforged Legion, I attempted to neutralize her, but I was ultimately unsuccessful. Now that the aforementioned Sardovian Allfold has been dealt with, I look forward to working with Her Grace to ensure an era of peace."

Talasyn would have snorted at Alaric's wry summary of their shared war-torn past, but something else drew her focus; at his mention of the Lightweave and the Shadowgate, several gazes subtly flickered to the sariman cages hung on the walls before swiveling back to him. *They fear it,* she thought, remembering her early days in the palace when Urduja had advised her to refrain from using her abilities so as not to attract undue attention. *They fear us.*

She caught herself with a frown. There was no *us* when it came to her and Alaric Ossinast. She might be marrying him, but she was *not* on his side.

By the holes on the World-Father's shirt, I'm marrying *him.*

There it was again, the throb of panic that coursed through her system like the first pulse of a straight-line wind from a stormship sent slamming through city streets, made all the more charged because Alaric was beside her and he looked like . . . like that.

"Is *that* what you were doing in the Belian garrison, Your Majesty?" asked Ito Wempuq, a portly rajan from the lotus-strewn Silklands. "You were ensuring an era of peace?"

"Call it unfinished business between myself and your Lachis'ka," Alaric replied. "However, judging by the fact that you *have* a Lachis'ka, I'd venture to say that it all worked out in the end."

He was reminding the nobles that Alunsina Ivralis had only reconnected with her heritage because of him. Which in a way was true, but that didn't make it any less infuriating. Talasyn could hardly blame the elderly Daya Odish of Irrawad when she thundered, "You committed trespass and destruction of property, injured several of our soldiers, and stole one of our airships, Emperor Alaric! How are we supposed to trust Kesath after all that?"

Alaric's grip tightened around his fork. "I do not regret my actions, as I did what had to be done at the time. The *point* of this new treaty is to prevent further discord between our realms. Upon ratification, I assure you, Daya Odish, that *I* won't be the first to renege on the terms."

More than a few pairs of eyes darted to Talasyn. The nobles were waiting for her to either defend the betrothal or join in cutting the enemy down to size, and the next words to issue from her lips would dictate the flow of the conversation.

But Talasyn's mind had gone blank. Common sense

demanded that she present a united front with the Night Emperor, yet how could she appear to submit so meekly to this marriage?

She glanced down at the new course that had arrived just a few minutes ago, that she had been in the middle of, and, in a moment of panic—

"This soup is sublime, don't you think?" Talasyn all but choked out. She had never before described anything as *sublime* in all her twenty years of existence, but the Dominion nobles seemed to swear by this adjective.

Rajan Wempuq's brow wrinkled in utter confusion. "Your Grace?"

"The soup," Talasyn repeated doggedly. "The cooks have outdone themselves tonight."

Ralya was the first to move in the abrupt stillness, bringing her spoon to her lips and tasting the dish in question, which consisted of tender chunks of pheasant stewed in a broth of ginger and coconut milk. "Yes," she said slowly, "it's exquisite."

"A marvel," Jie's cousin, Harjanti, hastened to opine. The deep-set, coffee-colored eyes that were so much like Jie's were almost beseeching as she turned to Daya Odish. "Would I be wrong to presume that such fine pheasant can only have come from Irrawad, my lady?"

Daya Odish appeared startled for a moment—and more than a little piqued that the discussion had taken a completely different turn—but social norms dictated that she respond to Harjanti's question. "Not at all. The island of Irrawad prides itself on being Eskaya's sole supplier of this particular game bird. It is one of our primary exports, second only to moon-stone."

Harjanti's curly-haired husband, whom she'd married for love, as Jie had put it, gave a jolt—almost as though his wife had kicked him under the table, Talasyn thought wryly. His name was Praset and he spoke up in a tone that was pleasant enough, aching shin notwithstanding. "I've been thinking of breaking into the moonstone-mining industry myself. Perhaps the Daya Odish could give me some tips?"

Talasyn made a mental note to thank Harjanti and Praset as the conversation shifted to mining. Beside her, Alaric raised the soup spoon to his lips, but not before she glimpsed their upward curl. Was he *smirking*? The faintly amused glance that he sent her way served to prove her suspicions. He was smirking at her for idiotically blathering on about the soup. The nerve!

She fumed all the way to the main course, but she made it a point to engage in courteous small talk with the other nobles. Alaric found his footing as well, conversing mutedly with Lueve Rasmey, who was seated to his right and who gradually looped him into her own circle of high-society matrons. Everyone was speaking in Sailor's Common for Alaric's benefit and everything was going well, for the most part. No one seemed inclined to start flinging laurel-bark wine in anybody else's face. Talasyn could relax . . .

Alaric leaned closer. "Would my lady care to share her expert culinary opinion on the roast pig?" he murmured in her ear.

"Very funny," she grumped.

"I take it that means it is less than *sublime*?"

Talasyn stabbed a chunk of bitter melon with her fork, fantasizing that it was Alaric's head. "I should have left you to Daya Odish's mercy. Or lack thereof."

She could swear that he nearly grinned.

At least they were back to their normal bickering. At least the incident in the plumeria grove hadn't changed anything between them.

In truth, it left her feeling a little out of sorts. Some indication that he, too, had been affected by their almost-kiss wouldn't have gone amiss.

"Will Her Grace remain with us after the nuptials?" queried Ralya, causing Talasyn to immediately straighten up in her seat and look away from Alaric. "Or will the Lachis'ka's court relocate to the Night Empire's capital?"

"I'm staying here, Daya Musal," Talasyn answered, and a wave of visible relief passed through all the Nenavarene who were listening.

"I remember when you were born," Wempuq told Talasyn with gruff fondness. "They rang the gongs in the Starlight Tower all morning, all afternoon. Gave me a damnable headache, but no one would have *dreamed* of leaving Eskaya at that point. There was celebration and there was feasting throughout the streets."

"The birth of the next Zahiya-lachis is always a joyous occasion," Lueve chimed in. "Of course, His Royal Highness probably remembers it differently."

The older nobles chuckled. Talasyn glanced further up the table at Prince Elagbi, who was blissfully unaware that he was now the subject of discussion. "What did my father do?"

"He was running around like one of our pheasants after its head has been cut off," said Odish with a snort. "The labor lasted all through the night, you see. Prince Elagbi was so worried that he threatened to throw the attending healer into the dungeons."

"I told him, 'Your Highness, please calm down, would you care for a drink?'" boomed Wempuq. "He then threatened to throw *me* into the dungeons as well!"

Their part of the table erupted into laughter. It wasn't long before Talasyn joined in, merriment bubbling its way up her throat at the image of her mild-mannered father ordering the Lachis-dalo to arrest random people. She threw her head back, laughed hard and long, and, when it was over—when she had settled down—Alaric sat frozen, staring at her as though he'd never seen her before.

"What?" Talasyn hissed after furtively checking to make sure that everyone else was too caught up in mirth and in

278

reminiscing to notice. "Why are you looking at me like that?"

"Nothing." Alaric shook his head as if to clear it. And then he—

He did something *odd* just then. He reached out so that his fingers brushed against the teal sleeve that covered her upper arm. It seemed too deliberate to be an accident, but he retracted his hand as swiftly as though it had been burned. As Talasyn continued to narrow her eyes at him, perplexed, he returned all of his attention to his food, and he did not glance her way again for a long, long while.

Alaric had never been one for big events. He'd suffered through a surfeit of galas that his parents had dragged him to back when they'd still been maintaining the illusion that all was well between them. This banquet was by far grander than any of those affairs, funded as it was by the Nenavar Dominion's bottomless coffers, but the feeling of revulsion that it elicited was very much the same.

It was the sheer *artifice* of it all. With the exception of his own retinue, no one at this table would hesitate to order his assassination if they thought that they could get away with it. Yet here they were, eating and chatting as if nothing was wrong, and he had to play along because that was what politics entailed.

Alaric's thoughts drifted to Talasyn and how heartily she had laughed at Rajan Wempuq's anecdote. For some reason, he had been expecting a sound lighter than air to complement her elegant gown and the stately surroundings, but her laughter had been vibrant and dulcet and unrefined. It had been a moment devoid of falsehood, her sparkling eyes warm like brandy. So he'd reached over to try to touch her, for whatever reason, like some brainless oaf, but at least he'd held himself back just in time.

He revised his previous conclusion. There was one other

person at this feast who wouldn't give any order to assassinate him. *Talasyn would kill me herself,* he thought, and it was with something that was dangerously close to affection, because that made her the most genuine person in the room.

A hush fell over the end of the table nearest the entrance, gradually spreading to the rest of the guests. Lueve trailed off in the middle of recounting an amusing story from her years as Urduja's lady-in-waiting, her mouth hanging open in mid-sentence at the sight of something to Alaric's left.

He turned to where the daya—and everyone else—was looking. A lanky figure stood in the open doorway, in an ensemble that was markedly out of place at a formal event, consisting only of an embroidered long-sleeved vest and trousers gathered at the ankles. There was an ornate band of leather and bronze slung around his hips, to which a hand crossbow was holstered. The new arrival's tousled hair fell across his forehead and his walnut-brown eyes blazed as they swept the banquet hall. The expressions of the people that gazed back at him ranged from confusion on Talasyn and the Kesathese delegation's part to full-blown alarm on that of the Dominion nobles.

"Who is that?" Talasyn inquired, sounding curious but careful to keep her voice low.

"Trouble." It was Harjanti who answered, agitated. "Lady Lueve's nephew, Surakwel Mantes."

"He *loathes* the Night Empire," added Ralya, shooting a look in Alaric's direction that could have passed for nervousness. "This isn't good at all."

CHAPTER TWENTY-THREE

Niamha Langsoune, Daya of Catanduc, ruthless and unflappable negotiator, was the same age as Talasyn but more poised than Talasyn could ever hope to be even if she reached a hundred. The young woman broke the frozen tableau that the banquet hall had become, springing to her feet with an enviable litheness.

"Surakwel!" she merrily called out as she swept toward the newcomer, a dazzling smile on her face. Her pleated overskirt had been woven to resemble the scales of a carp, and it swirled with her every step in glimmers of white and orange and yellow. "How good of you to join us—"

"Save it, Nim," the young lord snarled in the Nenavarene tongue. He brushed past her and made his way to the head of the table, his gaze meeting Talasyn's and darkening in recognition for a fraction of a second as he passed across from where she sat.

So this was Surakwel Mantes. The vagabond and pot-stirrer that Prince Elagbi had told her about. Her father's exact words had been, *At least Surakwel is off gallivanting elsewhere, or we'd have an even bigger problem on our hands.*

Now Surakwel was *here*, and Talasyn had a feeling that

she was about to find out just how big the problem could get.

He drew to a halt before Queen Urduja and dropped to one knee, head bowed, the gesture more perfunctory than respectful. Urduja regarded him warily for several long moments, as if he were a mongoose that had infiltrated her viper's nest, in the silence of a hall where even the orchestra had stopped playing.

"Welcome home, Lord Surakwel." She spoke for everyone's benefit, her icy tones ringing throughout the vast chamber in Sailor's Common. Probably so that the Kesathese delegation would have no cause to believe that they were about to be murdered in cold blood. "I trust that your journeys have been pleasant."

"The last time I saw that one was a year ago," Daya Odish told the other guests, drawing Talasyn's attention. "He showed up at court and pressed upon Her Starlit Majesty the need for us to intervene in the Hurricane Wars—rather loudly, I might add. Surakwel was convinced that the Night Empire would soon pose a grave threat to the Dominion."

Rajan Wempuq let out a gusty snort. "Well, he was right, wasn't he?" He glanced at Alaric from beneath bushy brows, as though only just remembering that the younger man was there, within earshot. "No offense."

"None taken," Alaric replied curtly.

Surakwel was now rising to his feet before the Zahiya-lachis. "My journeys were pleasant enough, Harlikaan." Unlike most of the other nobles, he spoke Sailor's Common with the ease of one who used it frequently. "My homecoming, not so much, as I have just learned that you are in the process of brokering an alliance with a murderous despot."

Like every other personage in Alaric's immediate vicinity, Talasyn stiffened in her lacquered chair, her eyes darting to him. But her betrothed showed no reaction whatsoever.

At least, at first glance.

Alaric had peeled off his black kidskin dress gloves at the start of the feast. He reached for his wine and it occurred to Talasyn that he held the goblet tighter than was strictly necessary, his bare knuckles clenched to white.

Still, his expression remained neutral as he drank. When Niamha fluttered past, clearly on her way to Surakwel's side, Alaric called out, "Your friend doesn't like me very much, Daya Langsoune."

"I *do* apologize, Your Majesty," Niamha hurried to say. "I've known him since we were children. He's rather impulsive and opinionated. I shall set him straight at once."

Niamha had barely taken another step when Urduja spoke again, freezing the Daya of Catanduc behind Talasyn's seat and effectively putting an end to the ripples of scandalized murmuring that had blossomed among the diners. "First of all, my lord, you will remove your weapons in the presence of your sovereign. Secondly, there is a proper time and place to air your grievances with my decision, and this banquet is not one of them."

"On the contrary, Harlikaan, there is no better time and place," Surakwel retorted even as he unholstered his crossbow and tossed it onto the floor. "Everyone is here to bear witness as I formally protest this union."

"The boy has a death wish!" Praset exclaimed, aghast.

"I'll say," Talasyn muttered under her breath. "Throwing a loaded weapon around like that, he's going to impale his own foot."

Alaric gave a nigh silent chuckle, the soft sound short-lived but tinged with dark amusement. It was the first display of emotion he'd shown since Surakwel stormed in.

"I've been to the Northwest Continent," Surakwel was telling the Zahiya-lachis. "I've seen for myself the devastation that the Night Empire has wrought. This is *not* what Nenavar should stand for."

"I won't sit here and be lectured by a boy who spends eight months of each year elsewhere in the world," Urduja stonily declared. "Given such a busy *schedule*, how could you even *presume* to know what Nenavar stands for?"

"I know that we don't coddle war criminals!" Surakwel shot back heatedly. "I know that we value our independence! I know that I told you *years* ago that we should help the Sardovian Allfold before the situation worsened—*and I was right!*"

"Yes, he's dead, the fool," sighed Daya Odish. "What a pity. I will miss him."

But Talasyn could see for herself that the mood at the table was slowly shifting. Some of the lords and ladies were exchanging disgruntled looks, as if they agreed with Surakwel. He was giving voice to their own resentments, their own fears.

"The Night Empire will not last, Harlikaan." He sounded earnest, impassioned, almost as though he was now begging Queen Urduja. "Justice and liberty will win out in the end. This is an opportunity for us to be on the right side of history for once."

There was some part of Talasyn that could appreciate how neatly Surakwel had cornered the Zahiya-lachis. By confronting her out in the open, he'd ensured that she couldn't fall back on the same reasons she'd given Talasyn about how it would be better to let the Night Empire think that the Dominion was willing to cooperate. Still, Talasyn was shocked that Urduja would let anyone defy her so brazenly—in full view of her entire court *and* a fellow head of state—without having him clapped in chains or banished from her sight.

Talasyn's confusion must have been apparent, because Niamha leaned in to whisper, "Lord Surakwel is popular with the younger set, and his family commands one of the largest private armies in the archipelago. Their matriarch is bedridden; Surakwel is her only child, and thus he is her heir. Not to mention that he is *also* related to House Rasmey, one of Queen

Urduja's staunchest allies. She can't afford to step on Lady Lueve's toes."

Urduja's next words substantiated Niamha's explanation. "We will discuss this some other time, Lord Surakwel," she said with an air of ringing finality, and that was how Talasyn realized that her grandmother had been caught off-guard and was now feeling around for a chance to regroup.

But Surakwel was having none of it. "*When* will we discuss it?" he pressed. "When the deal is final and Nenavar is at Kesath's beck and call? When Her Grace Alunsina Ivralis has been sent into the jaws of the wolf? You say that you won't sit here and be lectured by myself, Harlikaan, but neither can I just stand quietly by and let our Lachis'ka marry the Night Emperor!" He whirled around to glare at Alaric. "Well? What do you have to say for yourself, *Your Majesty*?"

Talasyn could hear her own heartbeat in the deathly stillness, but Alaric's pale features were still carefully blank, even though the attention of an entire hall was now on him. He slouched back in his seat and crossed his arms. "Unfortunately, there is nothing left to say," he drawled. "His lordship seems to have done all the talking for me."

Talasyn hadn't thought it possible for Surakwel to look more furious than he already did, but he was swift to prove her wrong. She could almost *taste* it, the rage of someone who believed in something. That was the most dangerous kind. It *burned*.

"Then you leave me no choice, Ossinast." Surakwel drew himself up to his full height, his demeanor taking on a certain ceremonious bent. "By my right as an aggrieved citizen of the Nenavar Dominion—"

"*Lord Surakwel!*" Prince Elagbi thundered from his seat on Urduja's left, an emphatic warning that was summarily ignored.

"—in accordance with the ancient laws of the Dragon Throne—"

Lueve Rasmey was halfway out of her chair, hand pressed to her heart. "Surakwel," she murmured, her bottom lip quivering.

"—I, Surakwel Mantes of Viyayin, Lord of the Serpent's Trace, hereby challenge Alaric Ossinast of Kesath to a duel without bounds!"

To their credit, Alaric's entourage reacted with admirable celerity; before Talasyn could even finish processing what Surakwel had just said, Mathire stood up and bolted to Alaric's side, accompanied by a man who had to be Sevraim. Devoid of helm and armor, Sevraim was lankily built, with curly dark hair and mahogany skin. He flashed Talasyn a lazy salute before speaking to Alaric.

"Your Majesty, I must strongly advise against taking Mantes up on his challenge," Mathire said in urgent tones, but she was drowned out by Sevraim excitedly sharing his individual assessments of the Nenavarene lord's strengths and weaknesses and what method of combat would be most effective against him. Still, Mathire made a valiant effort, continuing, "We are guests of the Zahiya-lachis; it will be a diplomatic headache if you end up killing him. You are cut off from the Shadowgate, which means that he might end up killing *you*—"

Alaric held up one hand in an unmistakable signal for silence. He made a show of glancing around the banquet hall, at the crystal carvings, the flowers, the sparkling cutlery, the finely dressed guests. "Here?" he asked Surakwel with a trace of bemusement.

"On your feet," snapped the younger man, "you evil, geno-cidal, autocratic *bastard*!"

The smirk on Alaric's face widened. "Here, it is." He pulled on his gloves and got to his feet, making his way to the head of the table.

Talasyn rose as well, scrambling to keep up with his long-legged strides. "You don't have to do this," she said sharply, blocking his path. A Nenavarene duel without bounds didn't end until one of the participants surrendered or died. Alaric was not the type to surrender. She didn't want him to get hurt. She—

She would have happily pushed him off the nearest cliff months ago. But that was before . . . everything else.

Before they wove the black-gold barriers that saved each other from void bolts and falling debris. Before he said, *You could come with me,* looking so young and slightly lost beneath the blood-red eclipse. Before he took her side when her family didn't tell her about the Night of the World-Eater. Before he told her about his mother and had been so patient in teaching her how to make a shield. Before he ate the pudding and teased her about the roast pig.

Something had changed.

She didn't want him to get hurt.

Talasyn let out an undignified sort of squeak as Alaric picked her up by the waist and deposited her to the side, clearing his way forward. "Stand down, Lachis'ka," was all he said, not looking directly at her.

Duel without bounds was the sole arena of Dominion jurisprudence where physical prowess mattered more than political skill. As such, it was considered a last resort. Barbaric to the point of taboo. But the rules were clear: whatever conditions were agreed upon by the participants *had* to be honored. It was therefore on tenterhooks that Talasyn and the rest of the diners watched from the sidelines as Surakwel and Alaric faced each other, about two meters apart.

"Terms?" Urduja demanded brusquely. She looked rather as if she was having a migraine, but not even the Zahiya-lachis herself could stop a duel without bounds once it had been declared.

"Should I win, Ossinast will forfeit Her Grace Alunsina Ivralis's hand in marriage," said Surakwel, "and he and his lackeys will leave the Nenavar Dominion posthaste."

"Should *I* win," said Alaric, "his young lordship will accord the Night Empire the respect that is our due and shut his mouth on matters that he knows very little of."

"What does he think he's doing?" Talasyn heard Mathire grumble to Sevraim. "He should ask for some strategic concession."

No, Talasyn thought. *He's being smart.*

Her mind raced, drawing on old lessons, on old conversations that Urduja had liberally sprinkled with advice. She saw the bigger picture. She considered every angle.

If Alaric pressed for a Nenavarene aristocrat's execution or banishment, or anything that would give the Night Empire a clear advantage, that would hardly endear him to the Dominion. It might even turn Surakwel into a martyr in the people's eyes. By being lenient in his stipulations and treating this duel as a minor nuisance, Alaric was positioning himself as a level-headed and tolerant ruler, and Surakwel as the hot-blooded troublemaker who was causing a scene at an important event.

She couldn't take her gaze off Alaric. From across the gilded space between them, he gave every appearance of being utterly composed—perhaps even slightly bored, his gray eyes hooded in disdain. And yet there was a quality about him that was so *alone*, somehow, standing tall, dressed in black, encircled by the avid stares of the Dominion court and the sariman cages that lined the walls.

Talasyn wondered if her assessment of his motives was correct. And, if it was, she wondered where he had learned all of this, if it had come to him easily or if he had struggled at first, the way that she was struggling these days.

She wondered why, even after all this time, she still couldn't figure him out.

Nearly everyone was standing up to get a better view, the feast forgotten. Queen Urduja dispatched a couple of attendants to fetch the customary weapons and, by the time they returned, the atmosphere in the banquet hall was crackling with tension.

The swords were of traditional Nenavarene make, with tapered steel blades that were narrowest at the base and had a spike protruding from the flat side of the tip. The hardwood hilts sported quillons carved with wavelike patterns and pommels that depicted crocodiles' heads, jaws split apart in soundless and eternal bellows.

Alaric initially held his sword as though testing the heft of it in his palm, an expression akin to distaste shading his pale features. It was far heavier than a shadow-sword, less maneuverable, completely immutable. He sank into the same opening stance that Surakwel had adopted, feet apart at a perpendicular angle, knees slightly bent.

There was no ceremonial beginning to the fight. All chatter ground to a halt when Surakwel lunged and Alaric met him in the middle, a metallic clash of interlocking blades. The Nenavarene lord spun away and struck again, a blow that Alaric parried by sweeping to the side.

The two men regarded each other for a while, circling like apex predators whose paths had crossed in the wilderness. It looked as though they were catching their breath, but Talasyn knew better. They had finished sizing each other up, had each gotten a feel for their opponent's reach and reaction time, and now the duel was about to begin in earnest.

It was odd to watch from the sidelines, her whole body thrumming with nervous energy but unable to do anything. It was odd to just stand there and compare the two men as they went at it in a frenetic series of attacks and ripostes. They were evenly matched, slashing and stabbing and crossing blades up and down the length of the gilded hall. Surakwel wielded his sword with the fluid proficiency of one who had been using this specific make since he was a child, but Alaric had more muscle, as well as a precision that broke through his opponent's guard time and time again. He was the one who drew first blood, the spiked tip gliding across Surakwel's bicep in one smooth slice.

Talasyn heard Lueve cry out, while, at the periphery of her vision, Niamha shuddered as though she herself had been struck. Blood dripped from Surakwel's wound onto the marble floor, but he ignored it in favor of launching a new offensive, this one speedier and more reckless than the last.

Fall back, Talasyn urged Alaric silently without knowing why she did, without knowing why her innermost self was taking his side.

Alaric gave up ground, retreating, retreating, all the way to the far wall. Surakwel's blade swept forward in the light of the torches and more blood spattered the tiles, this time from a cut on Alaric's thigh. Talasyn's heart all but leapt out of her chest. His eyes flashed with menace and she remembered the ice floes on the lake outside Frostplum. Remembered that lost winter night, the fires burning in the distance, the moonlight and the gold and the black of it all.

Alaric surged forward, driving Surakwel back until they were once more level with the banquet table. His next blow vibrated with so much raw power that Surakwel's weapon was torn from his grasp. It skidded away, far from reach, and time seemed to slow as Alaric advanced, pulling his elbow back for another strike—

Surakwel dodged the other man's wide-angle swing and retrieved his discarded crossbow. He raised his arm and fired, and Talasyn heard someone gasp—only to realize that it was she. *She* had made that sound.

Alaric automatically deflected the bolt. He wasn't wielding a shadow-forged sword that could ward off projectiles, but the blade was Nenavarene steel nonetheless, and the bolt careened off it and into the wall and dislodged one of the sariman cages, which fell to the floor and rolled away with a thud.

Talasyn was too near another cage to benefit from the break in the nullification field, but she saw the exact moment that the Shadowgate came crashing over Alaric. She saw the triumph in his gray eyes before they turned a cold, glowing silver, the wildest and highest kind of exhilaration coursing through his broad frame. There was no more room for politics, no more room for diplomacy. He was a creature of instinct, ensnared in the nets of his magic.

He tossed the Nenavarene sword aside. A black spear took its place in his hand, the guttural shriek of the Shadowgate being opened rending the air. He hurled it at his foe as the spectators cried out, and Talasyn—

—Talasyn knew that, if Surakwel Mantes died tonight, the Dominion would be up in arms. Even though the alliance had been Queen Urduja's idea, her people were more than capable of rebelling against her. They'd done it before.

With no thought for her own safety, Talasyn launched herself forward, into the field of combat. Her heels slipped and slid against the floor, but she managed to stay upright, darting between the two duelists. The Lightweave coursed back into her veins, golden and rich, as if some long-dormant pulse had been restarted. The crackling midnight haze of the oncoming shadow-spear filled her vision. She was panicking, she couldn't think of a single weapon to spin that would block it, she didn't know how to defend—

Talasyn held up a hand, unleashing a shapeless mass of radiant magic that flowed from her fingertips and collided with the spear. But Alaric had crafted his weapon with the intent to kill while *she* had no idea what she was doing, and shadow broke through light's flimsy veil like a hunting knife through butter, continuing its lethal trajectory.

Beyond the darkness and the aether, she saw his silver eyes widen. She saw his arm shoot out to the side in a slashing motion, diverting the spear right before it could pierce her

291

chest. It flew up, toward the ceiling, and there was a burst of burning pain when the edge of its blade grazed her right arm as it whizzed past her.

She sucked in a hiss of breath, but it was drowned out by the screams of the crowd and the crash of magic against marble as the shadow-spear chipped the ceiling and vanished, raining down a fine white dust.

An earth-shattering stillness fell over the hall. Talasyn lifted her chin, meeting Alaric's gaze with a defiance that she didn't quite feel, rattled as she was by what had just occurred. He was breathing hard and rough. His emotionless facade had cracked. Even though he was no longer channeling the Shadowgate, his eyes were bright with fury, and he had gone even paler. As he stalked over to her, she braced herself. This dress was *not* made for combat, but she could handle him as long as she steered clear of the other sariman cages.

Is this it? she wanted to ask. *Do we fight, here and now?* She tried to read his intent in the stiff set of his shoulders, in the heaving of his chest, in his every prowling step. *Can I take you when you're the angry one?*

When he came to a halt right in front of her, she realized that his gaze was fixed on her injured arm. The spear had torn the sleeve a few inches above her elbow, revealing a wound that leaked crimson onto the iridescent teal fabric surrounding it.

"Get a healer to see to that at once," he said through gritted teeth.

"It's little more than a scratch," she protested. "There's no need—"

He interrupted her in an *awful* voice. "Don't argue with me, Talasyn."

The next time he moved, it was to turn to the stunned, deathly quiet nobles.

"Ever since my delegation and I arrived in Eskaya, we have made every effort to treat peaceably with the Dominion."

Alaric's tone was cool, but Talasyn was close enough to glimpse the embers blazing in his gray irises. "Unfortunately, you have not seen fit to extend the same courtesy to us. All of you seem to be laboring under the delusion that we are pushovers. That ends now." He turned a withering glare in Urduja's direction. "Harlikaan, I have spent the last three afternoons training your heir, so that we can save *your* realm, and tonight she was injured because she still can't make a shield. The Lachis'ka's aethermancy will never improve as long as you keep denying her access to her nexus point. You are wasting my time and hers, and damning all of your subjects in the process—all because you are unwilling to cede control in this one matter. I will take her to Belian myself. You may no longer dictate where I can and cannot go."

It was Talasyn's first and most instinctive reaction to ask Alaric who he thought he was, interfering in this matter. However, just as she was about to open her mouth, he shot her a look of dark reproach. As though he knew that she was raring to pick a fight, and he was warning her to leave it.

Normally, this wouldn't have stopped her—but, at the same time, Alaric's choice of words leapt out at her like lightning.

He had called it *her* nexus point. Not Urduja's, not the Dominion's.

The Sever on the Belian range was made up of the same magic that flowed in her veins. It would answer to her and her alone.

"Additionally, you will no longer keep me and my Legion from the Shadowgate." His tone had taken on a sinister bent. "Remove your precious cages—I never want to see them again. Tomorrow will be the last day of negotiations. If we have not finalized the agreement by then, consider our sides officially at war. And consider yourselves on your own in five months' time, when the Voidfell rises."

Talasyn braced herself, expecting the Zahiya-lachis to put

up a fight. Instead, Urduja simply nodded, as if she, too, realized the peril that her entire realm was in.

Alaric returned the nod, although there was something vaguely mocking behind his gesture. Without another word, he strode out the doors, followed by Sevraim and Mathire. He was limping slightly from the cut in his thigh as Talasyn watched him go.

CHAPTER TWENTY-FOUR

Once the Kesathese delegation had vanished from sight, it didn't take long for the banquet hall to dissolve into chaos. While the healer summoned by Urduja tended to Talasyn's wound, the Dominion nobles started talking all at once, some shouting, others gesticulating, all arguing with one another over whether Surakwel Mantes had been in the right to challenge the Night Emperor during a royal feast.

Meanwhile, the object of contention picked himself up off the floor and sidled closer to Talasyn. "Welcome home, Your Grace. It would appear that I owe you my life," Surakwel remarked. "A debt of the self, as it were."

"Debt of the self is based on the Nenavarene code of honor," Talasyn pointed out, sucking in a sharp breath at the sting as the healer washed her wound with a tea of guava leaves boiled in palm liquor. "*You* reached for a crossbow during a sword fight. That doesn't strike me as particularly honorable."

Surakwel shrugged, unrepentant. "I saw a chance to save Nenavar and rescue you from your impending marriage in one fell swoop. My only regret is that it didn't pay off."

He had only just returned to the Dominion. He didn't know yet that hopes were being staked on the combined magic of light and shadow overpowering the Voidfell. Talasyn decided to let Niamha be the one to fill him in; the daya was rushing over to her and Surakwel with a thunderous expression on her face.

As Niamha tore into Surakwel for being a rash buffoon who had put the Lachis'ka's life in danger, the healer finished applying a poultice of garlic, honey, and camphor bark to the cut on Talasyn's arm and took his leave. She turned the events over in her mind, a chill creeping down her spine as it finally sank in how close Alaric had been to getting shot with a crossbow.

That would have meant all-out war. That would have meant the World-Eater devouring Nenavar with nothing to stand in its way.

That would have meant Alaric dying, if the bolt had hit true.

It was that last part, more than anything, that elicited in her a most peculiar kind of ache. She needed to see him. She needed to make sure that he was all right.

But first—

Talasyn let her attention drift to the squabbling nobles. Queen Urduja's close allies were angry that the future of Nenavar had been placed in jeopardy due to Surakwel's actions, but quite a few lords and ladies were now taking the opportunity to air their grievances with the betrothal. This was not something that the Zahiya-lachis could talk her way out of, and it was becoming more and more apparent that she was losing control of the gathering.

Talasyn studied the sea of proud, belligerent faces, and a staggering epiphany hit her. She could have prevented this, or mitigated it somewhat. Every time she'd treated Alaric like dirt, every time she'd let the Nenavarene cast aspersions on his character, she'd been solidifying in their minds that she was some hapless martyr. This went against the very grain of their matriarchal culture. Prince Elagbi had been right when he said that the court would follow Talasyn's lead, and her blatant aversion to her circumstances had spread through them.

She had let her emotions get the best of her, and in doing so had not only pushed the Dominion one step closer to a war they could not win, but also placed the Sardovian remnant at greater risk of discovery. And she was dooming *everyone* to the Voidfell.

Five months to the Moonless Dark.

Five months and it would all be over, if she didn't rectify the situation.

"It's not a forced marriage." Talasyn's words cut through the hubbub, and every eye in the room immediately swung to her. "I stand with the Zahiya-lachis. I accept the Night Emperor's hand of my own free will." Her voice felt as though it would crack at any moment, but she held fast, to her duty, to the part of herself that had always kept on moving, outrunning the storms and the shadow of death and whatever else the Hurricane Wars had thrown her way. "Have I not proven myself his equal in strength?" she asked, some instinct telling her that she should not let these nobles forget what they had witnessed tonight. Alaric was powerful but so was she. "There is no subjugation here. Tomorrow, when we've finalized the agreement, he will be my betrothed. And you *will* afford him all the respect that is his due as my future consort."

How it grated at her to say that. But this, like so many other things, had to be done.

Once she was alone in her chambers, Talasyn darted out the side door leading to the orchid garden. Her silver heels clacked on the stone pathway leading to Alaric's chambers. All the lights in the guest wing were out, but she took a chance and squared her shoulders and knocked. The determined rap of her knuckles elicited a flare of gold from one window as a lamp was ignited. The door swung open.

A large, strong hand clamped long fingers around her uninjured arm and yanked her into the room, releasing her immediately once she was inside. Her squawk of outrage mingled with the slamming of the door.

"What did I *say* about manhandling me—how *dare* you—" Talasyn sputtered, only for the rest of the sentence to die on her tongue when Alaric finished sliding the bolt into place and whirled around to face her.

"You will forgive me for not granting your snipers the luxury of an easy target." His tone could have frozen the waterfall in the garden. He had taken off his gloves and his coat. The ivory shirt clung loosely to his powerful frame, incapable of disguising how the lines of his upper body were utterly rigid with agitation. His gray eyes were so dark that they were almost black, glittering with barely contained menace against the paleness of his face as he glared down at her.

"Don't be ridiculous," Talasyn made an attempt at scoffing, but the effect was ruined by the fact that she knew she would likely be just as paranoid if she were in his place. "I'm here to apologize on behalf of the Dominion."

"You," Alaric said, "are a beautiful little idiot." His gaze strayed to the treated wound on her arm and lingered a little too long before flicking back up to her face. "What possessed you to throw yourself in the Shadowgate's path like that?"

Anger razed through her, a dark red pulse. "Who are you calling an idiot?"

He stalked closer. She automatically shuffled backward until her spine hit the wardrobe and there was nowhere left to go. He caged her in, planting a heavy hand beside each of her shoulders. There was but a sliver of space between their bodies, and the scent of him overwhelmed her senses, hot skin overlain with forest and juniper berry and myrrh. His hair was disheveled, as though he'd raked his fingers through the midnight waves in frustration before she came knocking. Those same fingers slid down the wardrobe until his palms drew level with her waist.

Talasyn's hands moved as well. They slid across Alaric's shirtfront to push him away but, for some reason, they *didn't*. They just stayed there. She felt the warmth and hardness of his chest beneath a layer of ribbed silk, felt his heart racing in erratic beats against her fingertips. She was pinned in place by his scorching eyes, by the formidable *maleness* of him that surrounded her, by the static charges that skittered and sighed through this moment of lightning and glass.

"Answer me, Talasyn," Alaric commanded in a harsh rasp. The syllables of her name rolled off his tongue, dripping in that deep, gravelly voice, the lush lips that had shaped them so dangerously near.

"What . . . what was your question?" she breathed out. *Gods.*

Talasyn wanted nothing more than the ground to open up and swallow her whole. But she truly could not call to mind what he'd asked—all logic, all situational awareness had disappeared.

No one had ever stood this close to her before. Even in battle, no one else had ever gotten this close. It had always only been him. His lips were a breath away from hers, as they'd been in the plumeria grove. Would they be as soft as they looked? She longed to find out, so badly. To learn what it was like to touch, to *feel*.

Alaric blinked at her. A disbelieving look came over his face, slow to be replaced by the inscrutable mask he usually wore. He wrenched himself from her and sat down heavily on the edge of his mattress, all the while studying her the way a wolf studied a hunter's trap.

"What," he finally repeated in quieter but more guarded

tones, "possessed you to throw yourself in the Shadowgate's path? How could you have done something so utterly asinine?"

Now that they were apart, Talasyn could breathe easily again. Could summon the answer from the strange inertia that her brain had been trapped in scant seconds ago. "I was preventing a diplomatic incident. I don't know what possessed *you*, continuing to advance on Surakwel after he lost his sword."

"*Surakwel*," Alaric jeered softly. "I'm glad that you and his seditious young lordship appear to have become such fast friends."

Talasyn flushed with a renewed burst of temper. Over the months she'd improved at referring to people by their courtly address, but it wasn't ingrained in her just yet. She tended to slip up when she was flustered. "Now is *not* the time to lecture me on etiquette."

"I wasn't—" Alaric broke off with an exasperated sigh. He looked away, his sharp jaw clenching, and Talasyn had the unsettling sensation that she'd missed something. That she'd misinterpreted what he'd been trying to imply.

"Anyway," she hastened to continue, belatedly recalling why she'd come here in the first place, "as I said, I want to apologize on behalf of the Dominion for what happened tonight. I know that the court hasn't exactly been welcoming, but that changes now. I'm reaffirming Nenavar's willingness to cooperate—"

"I'm familiar with how all of this goes, Lachis'ka," Alaric interrupted, his gaze snapping back to meet hers. Somehow, he seemed more incensed than ever before. "If they sent you here to do nothing but parrot your grandmother's words at me, then I believe that we can skip that part. Feel free to remove yourself from my disagreeable presence at any time." He inclined his head toward the door. "The sooner the better for both of us, I think."

Talasyn stayed rooted to the spot, hopelessly confused. She wanted to tell him that he'd gotten it wrong, that she was here of her own accord, that she'd slipped out of the banquet hall before Urduja had the chance to talk to her. But it was likely that he would never believe that, and her insistence would only make the situation worse.

Something nagged at her, forcing her to retrace the events leading up to this moment. The way that Alaric's eyes had widened through the shadowy haze in the banquet hall, the way that he'd insisted she summon a healer.

Were you worried about me? Talasyn nearly asked Alaric point-blank, but she stopped herself in the nick of time. Any concern that he might have for her welfare hinged solely on the political alliance pushing through.

She was grasping at straws as usual, thinking she deserved better than she actually did.

Perhaps it was her pride that balked at scurrying from his room like a frightened mouse. Whatever the case, her mind was frantically casting around for a reason to stay, and it wasn't long before her gaze fell to the slash in the fabric at his thigh.

"I thought that I'd help you with your wound," she said. "If you need it bandaged, I can call for a healer."

"It's taken care of," Alaric replied. "I patched myself up. Are you quite done playing the part of concerned nursemaid? You have my assurance that the Night Empire's displeasure with how this evening turned out will not interfere with tomorrow's negotiations, as long as they are concluded within the allotted time. *That* is why you came to my chambers, is it not?"

Talasyn bit down on the dozens of choice retorts that threatened to burst from her lips. Instead, she floundered, searching for something, anything, that could let her stay in this room. And in the process of letting her thoughts run rampant, she stumbled upon a realization that cut her to the quick.

It went beyond the imperative to mollify him. It went beyond her mission to ensure the continued safety of the Nenavarene and the Sardovians.

She didn't *want* to leave.

She had no desire to go back to her chambers and spend what she already knew would be a sleepless night agonizing over everything in deafening and lonesome silence. She wanted to remain here, with Alaric—to let him annoy her and distract her from the complicated tangle that her life had become, even if he himself was the knot at the center of it. She wanted to bicker with him in a language she'd grown up speaking, free to use turns of phrase that only the people of the Northwest Continent would understand. She wanted to check the wound on his thigh that the old metal blade had wrought, to make sure that it didn't fester. She wanted to tease another vague almost-smile out of him.

She wanted him to not be angry at her anymore.

Talasyn surveyed the imperious figure on the bed, with his messy black hair and his clenched jaw and the hunch of his shoulders, with his narrowed charcoal eyes and all his injured pride and simmering restraint, with that habit he had of drowning out the rest of her world. And she thought, *I want so many things.*

Impossible things.

Things that she couldn't even begin to understand.

"And what, pray tell, are you still doing here?" Alaric inquired, like the complete and utter twat that he was.

Inspiration struck, and she countered his question with one of her own. "When are we going to Belian?"

"We'll discuss that in council tomorrow. Get out." When she continued to hesitate, he added, in the frayed tone of someone on the verge of losing all patience, "*Now*, Your Grace. If you please."

While it would rankle that he'd gotten the last word, she

really had to cut her losses. She couldn't antagonize him any further.

She marched out of his quarters with her head held high, taking refuge in a dignity that no one else needed to know rang false within her. She forced herself not to look back even as she felt his eyes following her before she slammed his bedroom door between them, and she was halfway across the orchid garden when she realized something *else*. Something that had been lost in the heat of the moment but now made her stop in her tracks as she replayed their encounter.

Alaric Ossinast had called her beautiful.

Granted, he'd also called her an idiot in the same breath, but . . .

Talasyn turned around too late. Alaric's wing of the palace was already silent and still in the moonlight, his chambers once more plunged in darkness.

CHAPTER TWENTY-FIVE

Alaric found sleep difficult to come by that night. Whenever he closed his eyes, he saw Talasyn jumping in front of the shadow-spear and he saw himself veering it away almost too late, missing her heart by a hair's breadth. He saw the spear grazing her upper arm as a shout caught in his throat. He saw her blood welling up, an accusation leaking through the sheen of her sleeve.

By the gods, he had cut her, he had nearly killed her, and his knees had buckled at the sledgehammer's blow of horrified guilt, before he managed to compose himself and walk over to her to check that she was all right, while all those so-called lords and ladies gawked.

Why did it bother him so? It had been an accident. And he and Talasyn had certainly inflicted similar nicks on each other during their duels in time past. Hell, she'd *concussed* him the night they met.

Something had changed. Alaric didn't like it.

And he especially didn't like the fact that, whenever he closed his eyes, he could still see her pinned against the wardrobe, her slender frame too small for his hands, asking him to repeat his question in an uncharacteristically breathless, distracted voice, her brown eyes wide. He winced inwardly every time it came crashing back to him that he had slipped and called her beautiful to her face.

No doubt it was the blood loss that had led to such a grave error in judgment. Not to mention that the Nenavarene court in general was playing havoc with his senses, this gaudy world where it was growing increasingly difficult to separate pretense from reality. A world where the grubby, hot-headed soldier who had been his nemesis waltzed into his room in an elegant gown, spouting apologies, promising cooperation.

Talasyn had clearly been following her wily grandmother's orders. It seemed that Urduja was training his little Lightweaver to become quite the politician.

His?

Alaric bolted upright in bed, a frustrated snarl escaping from his lips as the covers slid down to his bare waist. He didn't know how long he sat there in the gloom of his quarters, its curtains drawn against the radiance of the seven moons, but eventually he felt it. Now that the sariman cages had been removed, a stern demand for entrance tugged and scratched at the corners of his magic like clawed fingers, a call that he was powerless to ignore.

You are the Night Emperor, a part of him mulishly insisted. *You shouldn't have to answer to anyone.*

He shuddered. He took a deep, meditative breath, adopting a blank, calm facade right before he opened the Shadowgate. Right before he dove into the aether, where Gaheris was waiting.

The world shivered at the edges as Alaric walked into the In-Between. "Father." He was already speaking as he approached the throne. Gaheris was no doubt displeased by the lengthy communications blackout, and he would be even *more* displeased by the identity of the Nenavarene Lachis'ka. Alaric was anxious to get it over with, so he explained the situation as quickly and as succinctly as possible. Gaheris's eyes flickered, but his expression remained impassive for the most part. The only time it showed anything resembling genuine interest was when Alaric mentioned the upcoming Night of the World-Eater.

"I must admit to some . . . *bewilderment*," Gaheris finally said, "regarding your failure to insist that you be able to contact me. Did you forget that we've had the upper hand all this time? When it turned out that your magic was *crucial* to saving them, did you not use this to your advantage?"

"The Nenavarene see me as the Night Empire's figurehead, Father, and they would have questioned my authority to negotiate—"

"So it was your pride that got in the way," Gaheris silkily interrupted. "Perhaps you did not want to lose face in front of the Lightweaver? Or perhaps you were afraid that I would disapprove of the union?"

Alaric remained silent. There was no defense left to him, not when Gaheris was talking in that deceptively gentle manner of his that almost always indicated a taste of pain in the near future. The air in the In-Between grew thinner, dark magic crackling in corners that did not exist in the material realm, strange shapes lurking in the shadows.

"Once again you have let the girl cloud your common sense," the Regent growled. "A revelation of this magnitude— you *know* that you should have informed me right away, and yet you didn't. You hid behind these sariman cages, a flimsy excuse, keeping it secret from me that you are marrying the Lightweaver that you should have killed *months* ago."

"It's better that I didn't succeed in killing her, surely?" Alaric couldn't stop himself from asking. "This treaty would never have been possible without her. The Night Empire would never have been able to stop the Voidfell once it reached our shores."

His father stared at him for a long time, a searching, knowing gaze that left Alaric feeling small, fear and resentment and guilt hollowing out the inside of his chest.

"I am not so certain that you are up to this, boy," Gaheris sneered. "The Nenavar Dominion will draw you in and they will strike at the first sign of weakness. That is their style and Urduja Silim has mastered it. How else do you think she has held on to her throne for so long? There is no doubt in my mind that she is training her granddaughter likewise. The Lightweaver will never return this bizarre infatuation that you have for her, but she will in time learn to wield it against you if you don't nip it in the bud."

"I'm not *infatuated*—" Alaric began to protest, but Gaheris interrupted him with a bitter laugh that echoed off the In-Between's shivering boundaries.

"Shall we call it *obsession,* then?" the Regent demanded. "Shall we call it the fanciful notions of a weakling whom I have been entirely too lenient with? Who is in the end his mother's son?"

Alaric looked down at his feet, humiliated. To hear someone else put it into words made him feel so unbearably stupid—and *angry*—that he'd let Talasyn get too close.

"Don't think that I've forgotten," Gaheris continued, "all those months ago, when she was still a nameless little Sardovian rat, how you put forward the notion that she be allowed to live. You told me that you were curious about the light-and-shadow barrier. But it wasn't *just* curiosity, was it?"

"It was," Alaric tersely insisted. He would never reveal to Gaheris the words that left his lips as he faced Talasyn beneath Lasthaven's shattered skies. *You could come with me. We can study it. Together.* That had been nothing short of treason. "But are you truly *not* curious, Lord Regent? It's a new thing, this merging of magic. There could be other useful applications."

As far as attempts to distract his father from his shortcomings went, this proved to be a success. A familiar old revulsion

307

twisted Gaheris's skeletal features. "I will not allow the Light-weave to taint the Shadowgate any more than is necessary," he spat. "Create the barriers with her until the Voidfell is driven back, but, afterwards, I expect you to lay this part of the alliance to rest. The Lightweave is a plague on the world. On our family. Kesath does not need it to thrive. Is that clear?"

Alaric nodded.

"For your insolence and your abysmal handling of this situation, you will be punished upon your return to Kesath," Gaheris decreed. "For now, we must discuss what is to be done about the Nenavar Dominion and the Sardovians."

"The Sardovians?"

Gaheris lost his temper then, slamming a withered fist on the throne's armrest so suddenly and viciously that it took all of Alaric's control not to flinch. "You imbecile!" In contrast to its previous mildness, his father's voice now roared like thunder, filling the In-Between. "Had you been thinking with your *brain*, you might have seen what was in front of your very eyes! If the Lightweaver truly doesn't know where the Sardovian fleet is hiding, what's left of them will certainly attempt to find her one of these days. They might even be successful. You will have to be ever vigilant. Perhaps even try to extract their location from her if she *does* know it—after the wedding, once she has let her guard down a little."

Alaric frowned. "You mean for me to go through with this?"

"Regardless of the Lachis'ka's identity, the advantages of marrying her still stand," said Gaheris. "Here is how you must deal with the Nenavarene from now on . . ."

The negotiations wrapped up in the early afternoon of the following day. The Kesathese delegation was firm and brusque, the Dominion uncharacteristically acquiescent. It seemed to Talasyn that they had lost more ground on this last day than they'd gained over the past sennight, but Queen Urduja obviously wanted to avoid adding fuel to Alaric's ire. He was in the blackest mood that Talasyn had ever seen, forfeiting all trace of politeness in favor of a sullen menace which made it clear that it would take only one more misstep on the Nenavarene's part for him to rain down the wrath of his lurking fleet on their heads.

Negotiators from both sides took turns signing the contract, the scene acquiring a ceremonial quality as scrawled names blossomed in ink at each stroke of the stylus. Alaric was the second to last to affix his signature, his penmanship an elegant cursive that was a surprise coming from the gauntleted hand that had killed so many and caused so much destruction. He then held the stylus out to Talasyn and she stepped forward on pitifully shaky legs. In line with her newfound resolve to stop acting like a petulant martyr, she offered him a courteous nod. One that he did not return, his expression stony.

Talasyn willed herself to not be mortified, hastily reaching for the stylus. As she did so, her bare fingers brushed against the leather of Alaric's gauntlet and he *recoiled*, jerking his hand back as if he'd accidentally touched something disgusting.

She seethed, her pride taking another hit. Last night he'd called her beautiful and now he was acting as though her mere presence was a personal affront.

She tried to keep a steady hand as she signed the contract. Everyone in the room was watching her, their gazes inscrutable—not even Elagbi would show any emotion at a politically charged moment such as this.

Talasyn set the stylus down on the table. And, just like that, it was over.

Just like that, she was engaged.

"The wedding will be held a sennight after the eclipse," said Urduja. "There will be more meetings over the next few days to discuss the specifics of the ceremony, but for now I think that we can safely say that this one is at an end. I will formally announce the betrothal to the public this afternoon." She turned to Alaric and, with admirable fortitude, politely inquired, "And when does His Majesty plan to take Her Grace to the Light Sever?"

"In four days, Harlikaan," said Alaric. "The sweep should be done by then."

Talasyn fell into a perplexed silence, as did everyone else on the Nenavarene panel. Urduja was quick to recover, though, cocking her head. "The sweep?"

"Yes," said Alaric. "It's one last matter to take care of, so that we may remove all doubts about the legitimacy of this alliance."

Urduja raised an eyebrow. "What doubts could you possibly still harbor, Your Majesty?"

"Doubts about my would-be bride's *other* alliances," was Alaric's terse reply. "With the Zahiya-lachis's permission, Kesath will conduct a sweep of Dominion territory. To make sure that Ideth Vela's forces aren't hiding anywhere."

As the blood froze in Talasyn's veins, the usually taciturn Kai Gitab spoke up. "Does the Night Empire mean to go around barging into houses and ransacking cellars and peeking under beds all throughout the islands?" The rajan's tone was mild yet admonishing, righteous ire flashing in the brown eyes behind his spectacles.

He doesn't know, Talasyn remembered in a panic. Because he was considered one of the opposition, Gitab numbered among the nobles kept in the dark about the deal between Urduja and Vela.

"Not only is that a gross breach of the contract," he continued, "but it is also an insult to the Dragon Queen—"

"The Dragon Queen can speak freely about insults when she turns back the clock and stops one of her subjects from challenging me to a duel during a banquet," Alaric interjected. "At that same banquet, Surakwel Mantes stated in no uncertain terms that he is sympathetic to the Sardovian Allfold. There is no telling how many others think like him in the Dominion court. The Lachis'ka, in particular, is a former Sardovian soldier. I would be remiss in my duty if I were to ignore all of this."

Urduja nodded, her mouth set in a tight line. "Of course. It is vital that you confirm for yourself that Nenavar is not treating with you under false pretenses." The Zahiya-lachis appeared to say this more for Talasyn's benefit, as though she sensed mutiny in the way that her granddaughter was currently glowering. "How exactly do you plan to conduct your search?"

Alaric gestured to Commodore Mathire, who proceeded to elaborate with a smug briskness that grated on Talasyn's nerves. "As we will be searching primarily for stormships and Sardovian airships, we will focus on aerial reconnaissance, sending ground troops only in areas of poor visibility from above. There is no need for us to go through anyone's cellars. With multiple teams sent out, I believe that we can be done in two days, more or less, and take a third day to collate all our reports. The Night Emperor and the Lachis'ka can then head to Belian the morning after."

"To minimize the possibility of collusion, I must also insist that the Lachis'ka stays put here in the palace, where I can keep an eye on her while my fleet is investigating," Alaric added. "On the second afternoon of the search, I will conduct a sweep of my own, on the *Deliverance*, and Her Grace will accompany me."

That's preposterous, Talasyn wanted to snap, with a healthy dose of *I'm not going* anywhere *with you* thrown in for good measure, but Urduja was swift to proclaim, "I trust that you will not object to the presence of Alunsina's guards aboard your ship."

"And *my* presence as well," said Elagbi.

Alaric's jaw clenched. He most likely detested the idea of

311

having more Nenavarene on his stormship than was strictly necessary. "I do not wish to inconvenience you, Prince Elagbi."

"It's not an inconvenience." Elagbi smiled, all teeth. "As a matter of fact, I would cherish the opportunity to spend more time with my future son-in-law."

Alaric blanched, and some small, petty part of Talasyn couldn't help but cheer at his discomfiture.

"Lachis'ka," he rumbled, not quite looking at her, "there will be no training here at the palace. We'll put it on hold until we get to the Belian shrine."

"After you're done terrorizing Nenavar, you mean," Talasyn muttered. Urduja shot her a warning look, which she ignored.

Alaric shrugged. "Call it whatever you like. It is of no consequence to me."

And, with that, the signing of the treaty between the Night Empire and the Nenavar Dominion ended on the sourest of notes.

Logically, she knew that her grandmother had a few tricks up her jeweled sleeve, or else she would never have consented to Kesath's investigation. But logic was no match for fear, and Talasyn spent the rest of the afternoon in a state of barely contained panic. She was jittery by the time evening fell and she was summoned to Urduja's salon under cover of darkness.

Aside from the Zahiya-lachis, there were two other people in the room when Talasyn entered—Niamha Langsoune and Ishan Vaikar. The latter shot Talasyn a mischievous wink.

"As I see it, Kesath will most likely fail to realize that Sigwad exists. It's not visible from the westernmost mainland, and the map of the Dominion that we provided them is an older one, charted before the Storm God's Eye was annexed," Urduja told Talasyn. "Even if they *do* stumble upon the strait, we have a way around that. I don't want you to worry."

Talasyn would have retorted that *that* ship had sailed if her attention hadn't been taken up by what was in the middle of the salon.

A rectangular vivarium constructed from reddish hardwood and crystalline metalglass held one of the brown-furred, palm-sized monkeys that Talasyn had encountered on her first sojourn through the Sedek-We jungle months ago.

The vivarium was connected, via arrays of slender copper wires, to a circle of metalglass jars capped by onion-shaped seals made primarily of nickel and embellished with dials that resembled clockwork gears. Inside each jar was a molten core of sapphire magic speckled with red droplets that dripped and coalesced like mercury.

"What do you know about spectrals, Your Grace?" Ishan asked, gesturing at the creature clinging to a branch.

The little primate blinked at Talasyn with unnervingly large eyes as she replied, "Not much."

"Well, they tend to vanish when they're startled—or as a means to escape from predators. After studying them for years, we have determined that this vanishing is actually a method of planar shift," said Ishan. "In much the same way that you can access the dimension known as the Lightweave, all spectrals possess an inherent genetic trait that allows them to transport themselves to another realm within aetherspace—and back again—at will. We speculate that the dragons utilize a similar mechanism, which could account for their elusiveness despite their size, although of course it is impossible to run our current model of testing on such large beasts—"

Urduja cleared her throat. Pointedly.

Ishan ducked her head, flashing an abashed grin. "I apologize. I get carried away with shop talk." She gestured at the circle of jars and wires. "This is an amplifying configuration. We can make sariman blood pliable for us Enchanters by suspending it in magic from the Rainspring. We have been able to do amazing things with it. For example, we can retain the sariman's inborn trait of affecting its environment within a seven-meter radius while at the same time canceling its ability to suppress an individual's aethermancy. Then, by mixing it with the spectrals' ability to vanish, we can . . . Daya Langsoune, if you please—"

Niamha stepped into the circle. There was a moment wherein she looked the most uncertain that Talasyn had ever seen her, but it passed quickly. Ishan fiddled with the dials on the onion-shaped caps. Once she was satisfied, she stepped away from Niamha and rapped her knuckles gently on the vivarium.

The spectral's reaction was instantaneous. It disappeared before Talasyn could even blink. The copper filaments glowed white-hot and aether flowed between the tank and the amplifying configuration like dozens of thin, glittering streams. A reaction rippled through the molten core of rain magic and sariman blood and it blazed amidst walls of metalglass, and then—

Niamha vanished.

There was no ceremony to it. One second the Daya of Catanduc was there, and the next she was gone.

"We have had great success replicating this effect on an outrigger warship," Ishan said into the stunned silence that filled the Zahiya-lachis's darkened salon. "There is no reason to believe that it won't work on Sardovian vessels, even the stormships." She waved a hand to indicate the vivarium. "The filaments here have also been infused with aether magic extracted from sariman blood. This keeps all those affected by the amplifying configuration invisible, hidden in another plane, until an Enchanter cancels the process."

With that, she wiggled her fingers, and the molten cores of blood and magic within each jar dimmed. The copper wires hummed one last time before stilling. The spectral materialized as soundlessly as it had disappeared, and so did Niamha, looking somewhat startled but otherwise none the worse for wear.

"Utter concealment," Ishan pronounced with all the satisfaction of a job well done. "Completely undetectable."

Urduja took over. "Envoys were sent to Vela's forces several hours ago and they are coordinating as we speak," she told Talasyn. "As long as we position these amplifiers strategically, the shelters and landing grids scattered throughout the isles of Sigwad will be shrouded from sight. From the air, it will look as though the Storm God's Eye is uninhabited. When Kesath flies over this area, they will see nothing but sand and rock and water. If their troops search the dense mangrove forests, there will be nothing there to find. And this is all assuming that they'll even notice that the isles of Sigwad exist. *I'm* certainly not going to tell them."

"Are you all right?" Talasyn asked Niamha.

"I'm quite fine, Your Grace." Niamha brushed off Talasyn's concern. "It didn't hurt at all. It was like being in a strange room with the lights out. I could move around and talk and breathe normally, even though my surroundings were—insubstantial."

"Aetherspace is riddled with dimensions such as these," said Ishan. "Like cells in a honeycomb. Piggybacking on the spectrals' ability takes us to one type of dimension, which is a fairly neutral, sort of *in-between* place, and then there are the dimensions of magical energy like the Lightweave and the Shadowgate. Who knows what else is out there?"

"Let's focus on matters concerning *this* dimension first," said Urduja. "As you can see, Alunsina, it is all taken care of. Once Kesath discovers no trace of Sardovia within Dominion borders, Alaric Ossinast will lower his guard. But the work doesn't end there—you will have to keep on convincing him that you have no idea what has become of your comrades. Every minute of every hour. Carry yourself like you cannot be questioned. Give nothing away."

Talasyn was as awed as she'd been when she saw the dragons for the first time. This kind of technology had so many possible applications. The Night Empire might have invented the storm-ships, but it would take them *years* to catch up to the Dominion's level of advancement.

It was in this moment, in a burst of sharp clarity, that Talasyn truly understood that the Hurricane Wars weren't over. With Nenavar on its side, Sardovia could still take back the Northwest Continent. There *had* to be a way. She would find it. She would figure it out, one day.

Her mind was afire with curiosity. She longed to visit Ahimsa and see for herself what other marvels Ishan and her people were cooking up. But that could wait; she needed to get through Kesath's sweep and whatever else had to follow first.

CHAPTER TWENTY-SIX

One day after another passed without incident, and it spoke volumes about the state of Alaric's life that he was somewhat shocked by that. With Dominion escorts ever on the alert for signs of trouble, Kesathese forces combed through their assigned sections of the archipelago and reported nothing of note save for the occasional dragon sighting.

Mathire had been correct in her estimations; by the second afternoon of the search, the various teams had all but wrapped up their respective routes. All that was left on the agenda was the *Deliverance*'s straight shot across Nenavarene airspace, which at this point was more ceremonial than anything else.

While Mathire finished up traipsing through the jungles with her men, Alaric and Sevraim left for his stormship a few hours ahead of Talasyn and her father. Alaric was eager to leave the cloying walls of the Roof of Heaven. The bulk of the would-have-been invasion force had been sent back to Kesath days ago, and only his and Mathire's fleets remained, and—as his convoy tore away from the Nenavarene coastline, as the hot tropical sun shone on the sight of familiar ironclads proudly bearing the Kesathese chimera hovering above the

Eversea—Alaric breathed easy for what felt like the first time in a long, long while.

The Lachis-dalo were on edge as they disembarked from the skerry that had ferried them from the diplomatic schooner to the *Deliverance*. Talasyn couldn't say that she blamed her guards. While they were technically not in enemy territory owing to the terms of the agreement, the sight of hordes of Kesathese soldiers assembled in the hangar bay for their arrival was still unsettling. In fact, Talasyn herself had spent most of the schooner voyage from Eskaya running through escape scenarios in her head.

Granted, the dress that Jie had wrangled her into wasn't particularly conducive to escape. While the saffron-yellow bodice was so liberally embellished with seed pearls and quartz crystals that it could probably deflect an iron crossbow bolt, it was . . . *staggeringly* low-cut. One sudden move on Talasyn's part would give the Kesathese fleet the type of eyeful that nobody wanted. The skirt was very stiff, too; it hugged her hips and her thighs, flaring out slightly below her knees, gathered here and there into large fan-shaped pleats. If she tried to run, she'd rip a seam.

Talasyn therefore felt rather constrained and unhappy as she stepped into the hangar bay of Alaric's stormship. He headed up the vanguard, with Sevraim behind him.

"So many soldiers, Your Majesty," Prince Elagbi mused as he and Talasyn approached Alaric. "One might think that you don't trust your allies."

Alaric ignored the slight. "Welcome aboard, Your Highness, Your Grace."

He looked at Talasyn, *really* looked at her, for the first time since her arrival, and—

She didn't know what happened, exactly. His gray eyes fell on her face first, then drifted lower. His gauntleted fists clenched at his sides and, for the briefest of moments, a look darted across his pale features that put her rather in mind of someone choking to death on their own tongue. But it was gone as quickly as a flash of lightning, as soon as he drew a swift inhale.

Alaric turned on his heel and marched out of the hangar bay. Talasyn and Elagbi were left with no choice but to follow him, trailed by the Lachis-dalo. Talasyn was puzzled by Alaric's behavior and she made to ask her father about it, but changed her mind. Elagbi, too busy studying his surroundings with awe, had clearly not noticed that anything was amiss. The interior of the *Deliverance* was nothing compared to the floating castle that was the *W'taida*, but the Nenavarene prince had never been on a stormship before, and Talasyn supposed that, for him, every inch of the austere space carried a certain novelty.

Sevraim fell into step beside her. His handsome face was hidden by his obsidian helm, but Talasyn could practically hear the unctuous smile in his voice when he said, "How wonderful to have you onboard, Lachis'ka. It certainly livens up this drab old place."

"I don't doubt that you are alone in such a sentiment," Talasyn said archly.

He waved a dismissive hand in Alaric's direction. "Pay His Cranky Majesty no mind. He's not so bad once you get to know him."

"Sevraim," Alaric warned. "Do not bother Her Grace."

"Is the privilege to bother her reserved only for yourself, Emperor Alaric?" Sevraim quipped, and Talasyn's jaw dropped.

But, instead of smiting the legionnaire where he stood, Alaric merely tossed Talasyn a long-suffering glance over his shoulder as he kept on walking. "My apologies."

Sevraim laughed. The manner in which he teased Alaric reminded Talasyn of how Khaede used to tease her, and there it was again, that abrupt jolt of the chasm of loss at Khaede's absence, at not knowing what had become of her.

It was harder to set aside today than it had ever been, but Talasyn eventually managed—by ruminating on the very odd fact that Alaric could apparently tolerate one of his subordinates talking to him in that manner.

The thrum of aether hearts pulsed through the steel walls, accompanied by the groaning of machinery as the stormship began to move. At Alaric's stern nod, Sevraim left, most likely to take up his position as the *Deliverance* cruised over the archipelago. Alaric led the Nenavarene delegation to the officers' wing, where he stopped and turned to Talasyn and Elagbi.

"Would you care for some refreshment?" he asked.

Talasyn gave a start. "Refreshment?"

"You have been very gracious in adhering to my request that you accompany me outside Eskaya. It would be the height of rudeness to put you up in the lounge without offering the finest vintage that I have on board." The invitation was extended without a semblance of warmth. It was clear that Alaric was going through the motions of social niceties, fully expecting his *guests* to refuse. "I understand if my presence would be intolerable, given the situation. You may feel free to make yourselves comfortable while I'm overseeing the search."

It was impulsive and ill advised, but Talasyn decided to call his bluff. "Some wine would be lovely. And I must insist that you join us, Your Majesty." Petty triumph sparked in her veins as surprise and annoyance flickered over her betrothed's face. "Surely you can delay pressing your nose to the windows and squinting down at the ground for an hour or so."

Alaric glanced at Elagbi as if half hoping that the latter would help him out of the mess that he'd gotten himself into. Instead of courteously declining, however, the Dominion prince was content to follow Talasyn's lead, flashing a brilliant, toothy smile. "Yes, yes!" Elagbi boomed. "Her Grace and I would be most honored to drink with you, Emperor Alaric. Thank you!"

"The honor is mine," Alaric gritted out. "Please follow me."

After the Sardovian Allfold's crushing defeat, the majority of Talasyn's daily routine had been spent in the marble halls and extravagantly furnished rooms of the Roof of Heaven. Thus, the lounge that Alaric showed them to was rather underwhelming, even though the bottom-dweller that Talasyn had once been would have swooned at the luxury of upholstered furniture and windows that spanned the length of the entire wall on one side, displaying a breathtaking panorama of Nenavar's green mountains and sandy beaches sprawled beneath clear blue skies.

With the Lachis-dalo stationed outside, the three royals took their seats—Talasyn and Elagbi on the settee, Alaric in a black leather armchair that appeared too small for him, as Talasyn suspected most standard-sized seating would be. He hunched in on himself and stretched his long legs out further than was strictly decorous. It would have been endearing if he'd been anyone else.

A mousy aide brought in a bottle of wine and three slim flutes carefully balanced on a tray, which he set down on the table. He uncorked the bottle and was about to start pouring, when Alaric stopped him with a crisp "We'll help ourselves, Nordaye."

Giving a deep bow, the aide scurried out of the lounge.

"Ah, cherry wine." Elagbi sounded reluctantly impressed, eyeing the label on the bottle. "Imported from the Diwara Theocracy. This *is* a rare treat, Emperor Alaric. You have good taste."

Alaric blinked, as though the compliment had thrown him off-balance. "Thank you," he said at last, awkwardly. "It is nothing, of course, compared to Nenavar's currant red."

"The Lachis'ka doesn't care overly much for the red. She

finds it too astringent," said Elagbi. "Perhaps the cherry wine will be more to her taste."

And it was, as it turned out. The purplish beverage was earthy and sweet, and Talasyn tried not to let on how much she delighted in each sip. Not even the Dominion with all its wonders had made her any more well disposed toward the bottle, but the cherry wine might as well have been a particularly rich juice.

Alaric, for his part, drank sparingly, more interested in swirling the liquid around in its flute. He was probably waiting for the whole ordeal to be over, counting down the minutes in his head.

"It is good that we have the chance to talk in private, just the three of us," Elagbi ventured after a drawn-out silence. "I thought that I should prepare you both for a certain topic that will doubtless crop up over the coming days as we plan for the wedding. I speak of consummation—"

Talasyn choked on her wine. Alaric's fingers tightened around the stem of his glass so violently that the fine crystal seemed in danger of snapping in half.

"There will be a feast after the ceremony," Elagbi soldiered on. "At some point, the two of you will be expected to abscond to the Lachis'ka's chambers, where you will spend the night in accordance with Nenavarene custom."

"There is no need for that," Alaric said quickly. "I do not expect Her Grace to—" He stopped, clamping his lips together, just the slightest tinge of pink leaching into his pallor.

"Naturally there will be no coercion involved," Elagbi declared in stern tones, giving Alaric such a *forbidding* look that a lesser man would have flinched. "However, the union will not be valid in the eyes of the court until you share your wife's chambers."

"But that is so *unnecessary*!" Talasyn cried. "The Dragon Queen herself knows that this will be a marriage in name alone . . ." Something about her father's grave expression caused her to trail off.

"To be sure, there is no pressure on you as of now," the Nenavarene prince said carefully. "It will be a different story once you have ascended to the Dragon Throne and there is need for a new Lachis'ka, but I believe that is a matter best saved for another time. What the two of you need to discuss *now* is your wedding night and how to handle the issue."

Talasyn wondered if Urduja had put Elagbi up to this: the Zahiya-lachis often employed back-channel negotiations. She would have appreciated *some* warning beforehand; but, then again, it was highly likely that she would have refused to set foot on the *Deliverance* if she had known.

Talasyn snuck a glance at the dark-haired emperor, her mind wandering down a dangerous path that she couldn't keep away from now that the topic had been broached. A flicker of something wild and nervous curled in her abdomen. She took in his massive frame, his thick fingers, his lush mouth. She remembered how she felt whenever their bodies were close together, the warmth and the danger and the butterflies—

No. She was *not* going to think about him in those terms, least of all when *her father* was in the room.

Unfortunately, Elagbi chose that moment to stand up. "I'll leave the two of you to it, then, shall I?"

Alaric started from whatever strange reverie he'd been brooding in for the past few moments. "*To it?*" he repeated, somewhat faintly.

Elagbi scowled. "To *talk*," he stressed, his hard eyes boring into the younger man, "about your situation, in your very much *separate* seats."

Talasyn contemplated pitching herself overboard.

As Gaheris's sole heir, Alaric had devoted his early years to studies and aethermancy training. Then he had spent the last decade fighting a war. There had never been time for women. He'd always considered himself above the bawdy pleasures that people like Sevraim took so much delight in.

Today, however, his very alluring, very infuriating betrothed had the nerve to show up on his ship in *that* dress—that revealing dress which hugged her slender form like molten sunshine, its low neck framing the swell of her cleavage in pearls and quartz—and all Alaric could think about was how her breasts were the perfect size for his hands.

To make matters worse, he'd been trying not to salivate over her while *her father* was in the room, and now the man was taking his leave after telling them to discuss how to handle their wedding night.

Why has my life come to this? Alaric wondered angrily. *I didn't ask for any of it.*

As soon as the door creaked shut behind Prince Elagbi, Alaric leapt to his feet with a frustrated hiss of breath and stalked over to the window, fists clenched at his sides.

"I wouldn't be averse to sharing a room," he heard Talasyn say. "To keep up appearances. It's just for one night."

True enough. He was heading back to the Continent the day after the wedding, and she wouldn't be joining him there until her coronation a fortnight later. After *that,* he had a hard time imagining that they would be seeing each other any more than was strictly necessary.

"I can take the settee," he mumbled. "What is one more inconvenience, after all?"

"You don't have to sound like it's my fault," she admonished.

It is, he almost snapped, only for a potent dose of shame to wash over him, white-hot in its intensity. She was not to blame for the fact that he couldn't control his physical reactions to her.

Alaric stopped glaring a hole into the window and whirled

around to face his betrothed once more. Talasyn sat ramrod-straight, fiddling with the fan-shaped folds of her skirt, sunlight dancing over the ropes of pearls braided through her chestnut hair, enveloping her in radiance. Her neck was bare—the perfect place, he thought bitterly, to press his lips against.

The Lightweaver will never return this bizarre infatuation that you have for her, but she will in time learn to wield it against you if you don't nip it in the bud.

Bile rose in Alaric's throat. Like magic that became a blade, it transmuted into cutting words. "How should I sound, then? Like I'm excited about the consummation?" He flashed her a thin, humorless smile.

"There won't *be* a consummation, you dolt, that's the point!" Talasyn's anger came on like a gust of coastal wind, too sudden, too swift. Her cheeks were quick to stain red, too, underneath the sheer veil of powder. It would seem that he'd struck another nerve in addition to her anger; it took him a beat to identify it as embarrassment. "I wouldn't sleep with you if you were the last man left alive on Lir!"

The barb shouldn't have sunk as deep as it did, slicing into Alaric's skin, to the bone. If he were a stronger man, it wouldn't have. But his father was right and he was a fool. "The feeling is mutual," he hissed. "As far as I'm concerned, this alliance has nothing to recommend it to me, save for securing peace. Else I would have had better options, and none so shrewish."

Talasyn scrambled off the settee and advanced upon him in a flash of yellow silk, invading his space, crowding him up against the window. There was just the slightest flare of gold in her brown irises as her magic roared in its banks, her features twisted with fury and . . . hurt? Why did he think that she looked hurt, that she cared a whit for his opinion of her?

"You didn't mind me all that much when you were calling me beautiful a few nights ago."

Her tone was riddled with contempt, and it was all he could do not to wince. It was all he could do to flatten his spine against the stormship's window, because if he didn't and she leaned in any closer, the inviting swell of her décolletage would very nearly graze his own chest, and he didn't think he could survive that.

"You clean up well," he told her, not as coolly as he would have liked, far more hoarsely than he wanted. But it did the trick and she reeled back as if he'd struck her, and she didn't say anything, and how, he wondered, could everything in him feel so sharp and so empty all at once?

"Isn't it for the best that we're being honest with each other?" Alaric goaded. "This arrangement is complicated enough as it is without us having any *illusions*."

He saw it, the moment that Talasyn hit boiling point, the moment that she lost whatever semblance of caution she was holding on to. He saw it play out all over her face.

"I've *never* had any illusions about you," she growled. "You are *exactly* who I thought you were from the very beginning—a vile, arrogant, cruel, despicable *asshole*. For all your grand talk about securing peace, one day people will have had enough of you, do you hear me? And when they finally denounce you and your despotic goons, I swear to you, I won't think twice before joining them!"

The thread that Alaric had been hanging on to since his and Mantes's duel finally snapped. He was upon Talasyn in a flash, his fingers clamping around her hip almost hard enough to bruise.

"While I share your contempt for this situation in which we find ourselves, do not mistake it as apathy," he hissed. "I hardly expect your disposition to sweeten, but I will be *damned* if I allow my future empress to behave in a manner that reflects poorly on my reign."

"If you *allow*?" Talasyn wrenched free of his viselike grasp, batting his hand away for good measure. "I don't belong to you. I don't belong to *anyone*."

His sardonic gaze flickered over her silk dress and the pearls in her hair. "You are the Lachis'ka, and the Lachis'ka belongs to the Nenavarene. Their fate is entirely in your hands. Should you cross the line, it is they who will suffer for it. Am I making myself clear?"

"I hate you," she spat.

Alaric sneered at her. "See? Already you are acclimatizing so well to married life."

"This isn't a marriage." Talasyn stepped back, widening the distance between them. "It's a farce."

"As opposed to all the other marriages out there, brimming with devotion and contentment?" Alaric frostily countered. "You have been several months at court. You should know better. I neither expect nor want your love or your friendship, but I *will* require your cooperation. And you need *mine* in order to stop the Voidfell. Do you understand?"

She glared daggers at him.

"Good." Alaric inclined his head in a mocking parody of a bow. "I'll show Prince Elagbi back in, and then I must attend to the search that I've been sorely neglecting thus far."

When Alaric joined Sevraim on the metalglass-enclosed bridge of the stormship, the legionnaire took one look at his face and said, "You fought with her again, didn't you?"

"She is the most frustrating—" Alaric cut himself off sharply, then took a deep, centering breath. "It is a lost cause. The advice you previously gave will never be of use. She has made up her mind about me and she will never be able to separate me from the war. So be it. There are more important matters."

Sevraim offered a sympathetic hum. He took off his helm, tucking it under one arm as he leaned against the railing overlooking the busy but well-ordered activity of the *Deliverance*'s crew. "If I may be frank—considering that Nenavar doesn't appear to be deceiving us, as there is neither hide nor hair of the Sardovian Allfold here on their shores—your relations with the Lightweaver might turn out to be *the* most important matter in the future. You need heirs—"

Alaric felt a vein throb at his temple at the sheer rush of stress brought about by the other man's words. "If you value your life, you won't finish that sentence."

"I'll start a new sentence, then," Sevraim said with unabashed cheer. "Judging from the scene I walked into beneath the plumeria trees, I truly believed that you were well on your way to the business of heir-making. I was so proud."

"Do you prefer to die by my magic, or shall I toss you out of my ship?" Alaric blandly inquired.

Sevraim's guffaw tapered off prematurely when the *Deliverance*'s navigator joined them on the bridge, delivering news that they had cleared aerial reconnaissance of two of the seven main islands with nothing untoward to report. After Alaric dismissed the navigator, Sevraim proved himself capable of a rare display of seriousness; for several long minutes, he and Alaric stood side by side, unspeaking, watching the archipelago below them unfold.

"Talasyn was telling the truth, I think," Sevraim ventured. "The Sardovian remnant isn't here. We would have found them by now. They couldn't have escaped at any point between our arrival and this sweep—we would have seen them." He scratched his head. "So where *are* they?"

There was a taut and weighty sensation in the pit of Alaric's stomach as he came to terms with the fact that he had been doing Talasyn a great injustice by treating her so harshly. Upon reflection, most of his anger toward her had stemmed from the possibility that he was allowing his guard to be let down when Kesath's enemies could spring out from behind the sun at any moment.

But the Allfold was nowhere to be found. Talasyn might happily strangle him without a second thought, but she wasn't deceiving him.

"The world is vast," he finally told Sevraim. "We'll keep looking. We'll make it clear that any nation harboring our enemies will be crushed along with them."

CHAPTER TWENTY-SEVEN

The late evening found Talasyn tossing and turning in her bed in the Roof of Heaven, still in a snit.

She *had* to see her comrades. While the enemy was still unaware of Sigwad's existence and had gotten nowhere near the strait, she couldn't shake the feeling that they'd come very close to being found out. Harrowingly close. She was rattled, and it only compounded her doubt that she could see this terrifying long game through to the end. She was making mistakes, as she always did. She couldn't do this alone. She desperately needed to talk to someone. She needed Ideth Vela in this moment, needed the Amirante's resolute, no-nonsense leadership. They hadn't spoken since the Kesathese ships had first been sighted on the horizon.

The residual wrath from her and Alaric's vicious argument on the airship made Talasyn bold enough to take matters into her own hands for once. Kesath had come up short in their search—their guard was down more than ever now. Before she could second-guess herself, she stole out of bed and into her dressing room, changing into breeches and a tunic while mapping a mental exit route. Putting her predilection for gossip to good use, Jie had told Talasyn that Alaric had ordered the

Nenavarene guards away from the guest wing after the altercation with Surakwel Mantes, so it would probably be best to creep along the battlements leading to his chambers and then drop down the palace walls from *his* balcony. Talasyn would just have to be as light on her feet as possible.

Then she could make her way into the city and find one of the seedier dugout proprietors who operated well into the night, who would lend her an airship without asking any questions. She would set course for Sigwad, and if all went well, she'd be back at the palace before early morning to catch up on lost sleep for the rest of the day while Alaric stewed over his reports.

Confident in her plan, she donned a pair of boots and a nondescript brown cloak, cinching her grappling hook around her waist. Excitement nipping at her heels, she hurried out into the orchid garden—

—only to collide with the broad chest of the tall figure standing just beyond her side door.

Talasyn released an outraged squeak, stepping back as quickly as though she'd been burned. Alaric's gray eyes held hers captive in the moonlight, his pale face framed by waves of bed-rumpled black hair. "Where do you think you're going?"

"That's none of your concern," she retorted through clenched teeth and a quickening pulse. She pushed aside her growing panic, forcing herself to remain calm as she searched for plausible excuses.

"On the contrary, Lachis'ka, I am well within my rights to wonder why my betrothed is sneaking out after I specifically ordered that she stay put."

Color flooded her cheeks at the cavalier, offhand way that he referred to her as his betrothed. "Well, why were *you* standing outside my room?" she demanded, buying time.

"I was getting some fresh air." He appeared disgruntled for a moment, as though the Nenavar Dominion was putting him

331

to no small amount of inconvenience. "And you're avoiding my question. How can I be sure that you're not leaving in preparation for an attack?"

"You're ridiculous." She tossed him a look of utter contempt. "Are you my betrothed or my jailer?"

He lifted his shoulders. "You're not exactly providing me with much incentive to see the difference between the two."

Gods, she'd been so stupid, so reckless—but there was a way out of this. There had to be.

Think, think—

Inspiration struck.

Talasyn made a show of releasing an exasperated breath. "Fine. If you *must* know, I'm off to the night market. To get something to eat. I'm hungry and I don't feel like interacting with anyone in the palace. I'll be back before first light."

She fell silent, praying to every Sardovian god she knew and every Nenavarene ancestor she didn't that he would believe her.

"That wasn't so hard now, was it?" Alaric smirked, and, instead of being relieved, Talasyn saw red. Before she could formulate a comeback, he went on to say, "Very well, then. How are we to sneak out?"

She pointed a warning finger at him. "There is no *we*!"

"There is. It's the only way I can confirm that you're telling the truth. Besides, Your Grace"—his smirk widened—"I'm hungry, too."

Shit.

Alaric rappelled down the battlements of the Roof of Heaven with climbing gear that he'd retrieved from his quarters along with a black hooded cloak. Talasyn was a speck dangling beneath him on her own fixed lines. There were certain stretches of the facade that lacked the structure or foliage to shield them from view, but she had timed their descent perfectly; the palace guards were changing shift, and no one noticed them.

It was cause for concern that Talasyn was so good at sneaking around and that Dominion security was so lax, but Alaric couldn't bring himself to care overly much. Not at the moment, anyway. After all the tense negotiations, he relished the physical exertion, the sense of adventure and open space. And he hadn't been lying when he told Talasyn that he was hungry. His stomach complained as he followed her down the limestone bluffs.

"Keep your hood on," she instructed once they had dropped into the city proper. Her own hood was drawn over her face, revealing only her pink lips pursed in annoyance and the stubborn set of her jaw.

He gave in to the temptation to rile her up further. "As you say, dearest," he drawled, watching with some vague, secret glee as that mouth of hers curled into a snarl.

But Talasyn had clearly learned a thing or two from her time at her grandmother's court. "That didn't sound quite as sarcastic as you probably intended it to be," she snapped, shouldering past him. "Keep it up and I might start to think that you actually *like* being my betrothed."

Alaric scowled at her slender back as he trailed after her, grudgingly awarding her a point in his mental tally.

It was his first time walking through a Nenavarene city, and his initial impression was chaos. Despite the late hour, the streets were filled with people setting off firecrackers, drinking at tables set out on the sidewalks, and dancing to the beat of drummers stationed on nearly every block. The curved rooftops were ablaze with paper lanterns. Colorful banners were strung between lampposts and clotheslines, boldly inked with the Dominion's wavelike script.

"They're congratulating the Lachis'ka on her betrothal," Talasyn reluctantly translated for him.

Alaric raised an eyebrow. "*Just* the Lachis'ka?"

"Yes," she confirmed with an air of smug satisfaction. "They don't mention you at all."

Well, he couldn't say that he was surprised. Urduja had done her best to paint the upcoming marriage as a happy event, but people would have seen the Kesathese warships amassed beyond Port Samout. They would have drawn their own conclusions.

The crowd thickened the closer to the night market they got, the masses of exuberant humanity increasing until Alaric was well and truly being jostled on all sides, sweat dripping down his brow in the warm tropical night. Not keen on letting Talasyn give him the slip, should she be so inclined, he grabbed her by the arm. She stiffened but didn't shrug him off, instead guiding him into a maze of brightly lit food stalls, where the air was replete with smoke and various mouthwatering aromas.

His head was spinning. He couldn't remember the last time he'd been in the midst of such a throng when he wasn't cutting his way through them or leading a charge. They shuffled past stalls where there were platters of fresh fish and plump crustaceans on display, as well as fruits that he had never seen before: small round red ones with spikes that made them look like sea urchins; dark purple ones with thick clover-like leaves at the stem; and ones vaguely in the shape of human hearts that, when split open, revealed snowy white flesh speckled with black seeds. Merchants were tossing gelatinous noodles around in deep pots, cooking skewered meat on charcoal embers, frying dumplings and omelets in bubbling oil, and rolling up thin pastry sheets filled with cream ice and crushed peanuts. While they waited, the customers gathered around each stall to chat with one another, the usual singsong tones of the Nenavarene language strained as they all shouted to be heard over the drumbeats and the general roar that came with hundreds of people packed into a jumble of narrow streets.

Alaric received an elbow to the ribs no less than four times.

His foot was trod on twice that number. At least three strangers shouted in his ear while hailing their acquaintances at the next stall or further up the street.

Indignation rose with every passing moment. If these people knew who he was—

But they didn't. That was the thing. He wore neither crown nor wolf's-snarl mask, and his hood hid the gray eyes of House Ossinast. Not that the commonfolk on this isolated archipelago knew anything about House Ossinast to begin with. It felt strange, to be this anonymous, to be treated just like everyone else.

Talasyn, on the other hand, seemed right at home. She led him to a stall that boasted its own collection of small round tables and stools spilling into an alleyway. "Stay here." She indicated a vacant table, speaking almost under her breath. So that no one would overhear her using Sailor's Common, he realized. While the soldiers and Dominion nobles that he'd dealt with thus far were fluent in the trade language, there was no reason for it to be widely spoken throughout these islands.

Alaric sat down, careful to keep his hood drawn low over his features. Talasyn had deliberately chosen a secluded spot, and the people in their immediate vicinity seemed too drunk or too engrossed in their own conversations to notice him, but it was better to be safe than sorry.

She melted into the crowd, leaving him awkwardly sitting there by himself for what felt like ages. Just as he was starting to suspect that she'd abandoned him and this was all part of some nefarious Dominion ploy to get the Night Emperor to wind up dead in a ditch, she returned, gingerly carrying a bamboo tray laden with utensils, wooden bowls of fluffy white rice and some kind of grayish stew, and tankards filled with a mysterious saffron-colored liquid.

"What is this?" Alaric asked once she'd taken the seat across from him.

"Pork with peas and jackfruit. The drink is sugarcane juice," she supplied. "This isn't the best stall, but it's quiet. If you want the *best* pork stew, you have to go a little further up the street, near the drummers."

"You are a fixture, then, I take it?"

"Not as much as I would like to be." She seemed somewhat regretful, and he arched a brow.

"Surely there is nothing stopping you from coming down here whenever the mood strikes."

Talasyn mumbled something about lessons and duties before she dug into her bowl with a barely contained frenzy, chewing and swallowing nonstop while glaring a hole into the table. Alaric almost felt bad that he had forced his presence on her and it was no doubt sullying her enjoyment of the meal.

Eventually, he took his first tentative bite. And then another, and another. Perhaps he was just famished, but the soupy mess in his bowl was delicious, and the cold beverage that he washed it down with was sweet and refreshing.

Since his dining companion wasn't in a particularly chatty mood, he let his attention drift to their surroundings. The table in front of theirs was especially lively, the burly men occupying it loud enough to be obnoxious, their ruddy faces flushed with alcohol. Alaric thought that he caught the word *Kesath* every once in a while.

"What are they saying?" he asked Talasyn, inclining his head toward the group.

"I don't know," she replied. "I'm still learning Nenavarene, and they're talking too fast." She stabbed a chunk of meat with her fork and changed the subject. "You're looking forward to sailing home after the wedding, I'll wager."

She sounded so especially prickly that Alaric gave in once again to the impulse to tease her. "Am I? We won't see each other again until you come to Kesath for your coronation. Perhaps I shall miss you terribly."

Talasyn rolled her eyes, a small quirk blossoming along one corner of her mouth. But then her expression flattened, reminding him of a shield being thrown up, and she ducked her head. "Let me finish my meal in peace," she grunted.

Ever since she sat down to eat, the drunks at the next table had been planning to wage all-out war on the Night Empire. These plans had grown increasingly more outlandish, so much so that changing the subject with Alaric had no longer been enough. She'd had to stop talking to him altogether so that she could focus on keeping a straight face. It was almost worth her real plans for the evening being foiled.

Almost.

"Who does this bastard emperor think he is?" yelled the ringleader. "Waltzing in here, forcing our Lachis'ka to marry him—let's storm the palace, I say! Let's slaughter the Kesathese in their beds!"

Amidst impassioned rumblings of assent, a lone voice strove to get everyone to see reason. "We must trust in Queen Urduja's judgment. She knows what's best for Nenavar, and she'll be furious if we storm her palace."

"Not if it's so we can rescue her granddaughter from the clutches of an outsider!" argued a third man. "Here's what, some of us'll take a bunch of firecrackers and sneak onboard that accursed lightning ship, blow it to smithereens, while the rest of us will lay siege to the Roof of Heaven—"

"And slaughter the Kesathese in their beds!" the group cheered, banging their tankards on the table.

"They'll never know what hit 'em!"

"What's an army to six determined patriots?"

"My hatchet thirsts for the Night Emperor's blood!"

Talasyn fought down a snort, swallowing it along with her mouthful of rice and stew. She diligently avoided meeting Alaric's gaze.

Then one of the men said, "Although—the Lachis'ka is an outsider, too, isn't she? She didn't grow up here, and Lady Hanan, rest her soul, was foreign."

"That doesn't mean that Alunsina isn't ours!" gasped the voice of reason. "She is Elagbi's daughter. She is She Who Will Come After."

"Maybe it *is* for the best that Her Grace will marry the Night Emperor," slurred the drunkest of the lot. "Outsiders deserve each other."

Talasyn pushed her mostly empty bowl away. She no longer felt like laughing and she no longer wished to overhear another word of the men's conversation. She grabbed Alaric by the arm and dragged him out of the alley. "Time to be heading back," she said, in response to his quizzical look.

But they didn't head back right away. Instead, once they left the marketplace, Talasyn took a circuitous route for reasons that weren't entirely clear even to herself. She and Alaric wound up in the side street of a quiet residential neighborhood, where the festive drumbeats rolled only like distant thunder.

Unfortunately, Alaric's sarcastic tones were not as far away. "Is this the part where you stick a knife into my ribs and dispose of my body?"

"You're so paranoid." *And you should be,* she fervently, if silently, conceded.

She realized that she was still holding on to his arm, her fingers digging into an unfathomably *solid* bicep, and she let go at once and widened the distance between them. He'd latched on to her like this earlier and she'd allowed it, not keen on explaining losing him to her grandmother. It had been a matter of practicality. But now she wondered if her touch burned into his skin like his did hers—if he, too, was befuddled by any form of physical contact between them that didn't end in grievous bodily harm.

The memories of the plumeria grove and up against his

wardrobe surged through her in a flash of white heat and phantom sensations. His soft lips all that she could see, his large hands all over her form.

Talasyn fled. That was the simplest way to describe what she did next—aiming her grappling hook at an upper railing on the nearest structure, embarking on the climb once it caught. Below her she heard metal clacking against brickwork and the stretch of rope as Alaric gave chase, but she didn't look back, she didn't stop until she'd scaled all six levels and hauled herself onto the rooftop.

She sat down, balancing precariously on one of the inclines, her legs dangling off the edge. From this vantage point the city was a tangled net of red and yellow lantern-light, glimmering against the dark, beneath the seven moons.

I don't belong here. The thought pierced her in all its bleakness. *I don't belong anywhere.*

Back in Sardovia, she'd grown up waiting for her family to come back. Now that she *had* found her family, it consisted of a grandmother who thought nothing of using her as a bargaining chip and a father who would never side with her over his queen, in a homeland where she was an outsider.

And, as a final insult to injury, she was getting married to someone who hated her—someone whom she would one day betray, for the sake of everyone else.

It was too much. *Everything* was too much. It all weighed down on her like a stone.

Talasyn furiously blinked away the tears that were threatening to spill. Not a moment too soon, as it turned out, because a shadow fell over her and she looked up to see Alaric's sullen features, stark and pale in the moonlight. For such a tall, wide bulwark of a man, he stood on the precarious rooftop ledge with minimal effort, studying her quietly.

When he spoke, it was in a tone that carried a trace of unease. "Is something the matter?"

She wanted to laugh. Where should she start?

"Why didn't you kill me when we first met?" Talasyn burst out, because it was what she'd always wondered, because there was no better time to ask it than here and now, when the moonlight could hold secrets and it was just the two of them above the city, amidst the rooftops, in a sea of weathervanes. "That night on the frozen lake outside Frostplum, before we knew I was the Nenavarene Lachis'ka, before we knew we could merge our magic. I've replayed that battle over and over. You could have easily killed me then. Why didn't you? You even parted the Shadowgate barriers so that I wouldn't run into them. And you shielded me from the falling column and you let me go the day the Heartland fell. Why did you do all of that?"

"Why are *you* bringing it up now?" he countered, looking defensive.

Her temper spiked. She didn't know, either. She had no idea what she'd been hoping to find.

Several flares of light shot up from the streets to the north of the rooftop. They exploded at their zenith in whorls of green and violet and pink and copper, exhaling wisps of potassium smoke as they blossomed against the starry sky. Talasyn stared numbly at the conflagration that was meant to celebrate her betrothal, and she thought about how much she longed to scream. To let all of her fears and frustrations be swept into the light and noise.

She gave a start when Alaric spoke into the stillness that ensued after the fireworks had died down. "I think that I was curious, the night we met," he admitted. His voice cut through the gloom behind her in a low rasp. "I'd never encountered a Lightweaver before. I wanted to see what you were made of."

"And at Lasthaven?"

"I rather felt that it would have been—unceremonious. If you'd died like that."

340

Strangely enough, she understood. Nothing less than a well-earned ending, by his blade or hers, would suffice. It wasn't as disconcerting a realization as it should have been. At the very least, it was something to belong to, something that was just theirs. Even if there was no other way for it to end but in blood and a fallen empire.

She gazed out over joyous, gilded Eskaya. With their fireworks and their feasting, it was so different from what she'd known back then.

"All the cities on the Continent will look like this one day," Alaric said quietly, as though reading her thoughts. He, too, was studying the scene below them, and she thought about the pudding, how he'd finished every last drop, something as simple as soybeans and sugar a revelation. "I will see it done."

"The cities of the Allfold could be well on their way to looking like this, if Kesath hadn't invaded," Talasyn muttered.

He regarded her with disbelief. "You speak so highly of Sardovia."

"It was my home."

"No homeland should allow its people to drink in the troughs with the horses," Alaric said coldly. "The Allfold did not deserve your loyalty, nor anyone else's."

Talasyn stood up and took the couple of steps that would bring her toe to toe with him, walking swiftly and surely over the rooftop tiles, too preoccupied with ridding him of his self-righteousness to worry about falling. And maybe there was a part of her that was scared, too, to let his words sink in too deep.

"If I could go anywhere in the world right now," Talasyn told Alaric, looking up at him with narrowed eyes, her voice low and deadly, "I would take you to the Wildermarch, where we buried everyone who died at Frostplum. I would take you to every battlefield where I saw my comrades fall. I would take you to every village flattened by Kesathese stormships, to every town ransacked by your legionnaires. *That* was where my loyalties lay. That was why I fought for as long as I did."

That's why I'm still fighting. That's why one day I will see Sardovian banners fly over the Continent once more, and I will gaze down on your father's corpse and smile.

Alaric's hands dropped onto her shoulders. It was a gentle pressure, but it went through her heart like a shockwave. He leaned in, so close that their foreheads were almost touching. "I wasn't—I didn't mean—" He took a deep breath. He looked, she thought, very tired. It had been a long day for them, and the ones that would follow promised to be just as grueling.

"My allegiance is to my nation," Alaric finally said, "and I also dislike thinking about what you went through. Surely those two things can both be true at the same time."

"They *can* be, but I'm allowed to call you a hypocrite," Talasyn retorted, even as some tiny corner of her soul reached out with greedy arms to the siren song of someone being angry on her behalf, angry about what she'd suffered. The people in her life who actually gave a damn about her—Vela and Khaede and Elagbi—had been spared the gritty details.

Why had she told Alaric about the troughs, about the knife? In the end, he'd only used it as ammunition against her, provoking her to question the acceptance with which she'd played her part in the war.

His jaw clenched. His hands slid from the tops of her shoulders to curl around her upper arms in a loose grip. "It was for nothing, then. The accord that we found over the last few days, while aethermancing."

"I will still work with you," Talasyn said, hating how she couldn't bring herself to so much as squirm away from his grasp. "But you won't *ever* convince me that the Night Empire saved Sardovia from itself. I told you once that vengeance isn't justice, and I hold to that. Whatever better world you think you'll build, it will *always* be built on blood."

His hands fell to his sides, and every inch of her that he had touched cried out at the loss. Fuming, she made her way back down the building while he followed without another word. She navigated a moonlit path to the limestone bluffs of the Roof of Heaven, and he trailed after her in silence, through city streets that resounded with a merry mood that neither of them could take part in.

CHAPTER TWENTY-EIGHT

In the moment, Talasyn had hoped that setting her anger loose on Alaric might provide some catharsis. But it had only done the opposite. She kept replaying their conversation in her mind, the reckless insults paired with hesitant confessions. She had come far too close to exposing the truths that lay at the center of her heart. Truths that protected not only herself, but the people she cared about. Alaric had a way of getting past her guard, even when she knew that one wrong step could prove fatal. Her determination to speak with Vela only became more urgent.

She hadn't seen Alaric since they returned from the night market, but a steady stream of Kesathese officers had marched in and out of the guest wing well into the afternoon, wearing on Urduja's last nerves. Talasyn knew that she couldn't risk sneaking out via the garden path between her and Alaric's rooms again—but, then, *how*—

She heard voices from around the corner. A man's, light and teasing, mingled with a woman's throaty murmur. Surreptitiously peeking into the corridor that ran perpendicular to the one she was in, Talasyn saw Surakwel Mantes and Niamha Langsoune in the act of bidding farewell to each other. He bowed and she curtsied, and he watched her walk away.

A new idea seized her. As Niamha disappeared around the opposite corner, Talasyn checked to ascertain that no guards were in sight. Then she hurried over to Surakwel.

He smiled when he noticed her approach, but it had a wary edge to it. "Your Grace," he said with another quick bow. "As I understand it, congratulations are in order."

"Spare me." Talasyn had quite had her fill of sarcastic young men.

Surakwel quirked an eyebrow but wisely changed the subject. "I'm off to Viyayin. Queen Urduja has made it clear that I've outstayed my welcome—and that me being Lueve Rasmey's nephew was the only thing that prevented her from chopping me up into tiny pieces and feeding me to the dragons. I suppose that the next time I see you will be at your wedding."

Talasyn knew that all the noble houses had to send a representative, but she'd half expected him to boycott the event on principle. He must have deciphered the bemused look on her face because he went on to explain, "My mother is too ill. I must attend in her stead. I've already sworn to the Zahiya-lachis that I shall do nothing to disrupt the ceremony and I reiterate the same to you. You have my word."

"And how good is your word?" Talasyn carefully asked. "How true is your honor?"

One could hardly be a Dominion aristocrat without the ability to recognize certain cues. Surakwel's walnut-brown gaze assessed her shrewdly from beneath a mess of shaggy hair. "Is there something that you require of me, Lachis'ka?"

"Yes." Talasyn's heart was pounding. "I'm calling in your debt of the self. There are two parts of this payment. First, what I'm about to tell you . . . You can't breathe a word of it to another living soul."

"And the second part?"

"I need you to take me somewhere."

*

345

Surakwel's airship was a small pleasure yacht, customized to accommodate far more void cannons than such vessels usually possessed. The hull was painted a frosted green color, a white serpent emblazoned on the aft end—the insignia of Viyayin's ruling house. It was docked on a grid outside the palace, with the vessels of other guests. Surakwel distracted the guards with meaningless chatter while Talasyn clambered out the window of an adjacent hallway and slipped up the ramp.

Even though she'd sworn Surakwel to secrecy under the terms of the debt of the self, she was all too aware that he was a wild card, reckless and unpredictable. Fortunately, he didn't seem to be hell-bent on rallying the Sardovian remnant into an all-out attack on the Kesathese fleet, but he *was* excited. He'd quite lost his aristocratic poise earlier in the hallway, hissing, "*The Sardovian Allfold is here?*" with his eyes almost bugging out of his head. Talasyn had slapped him on the arm, warning him that he wasn't allowed to tell anyone that he knew. She doubted that Urduja would appreciate her making an ally out of this man.

"This is a nice ship," Talasyn observed once he'd joined her and the yacht had launched into the air. She made herself comfortable in the open well on deck where the cockpit was located, leaning back against a frame of glossy wood. "What's she called?"

Surakwel hesitated, one gauntleted hand hovering over the controls. "*Serenity*," he replied at last, in an uncharacteristically soft voice.

"Oh," was all that Talasyn could manage. Niamha's name translated to *the serene one*. Talasyn had been aware that Surakwel and the daya were close, but . . .

The young lord gave every impression of not wanting to talk about it, so Talasyn fell silent. The late-night breeze tossed strands of her hair wildly about as she and Surakwel sailed beneath the stars.

"What exactly is the Allfold's plan, Your Grace?" Surakwel asked. "I doubt that it entails hiding forever in the Storm God's Eye."

"All information will be dispensed on a need-to-know basis," Talasyn said crisply. The truth was that she herself had only a vague idea of what was going on in Vela's head. From previous visits, she'd surmised that her comrades had spent the last few months repairing their damaged vessels, gathering intelligence over the aetherwave, and learning how to survive in this foreign land.

The *Serenity* was fast despite its squadron's worth of armaments, and they reached the strait in a little under five hours, when a voyage from Eskaya would normally have taken an airship of similar size almost six. Miles and miles off the coast of Lidagat, westernmost of the Dominion's seven main islands, the ocean's flat expanse was disrupted by two long rows of gargantuan, sheer-sloped basalt pillars. Legend had it that these were formed by the collision when the broken body of some nameless ancient god of storms came crashing down from the heavens during a great war among the members of his pantheon, his blood mingling with that of other slain deities to create the Eversea. Between the pillars was the strip of water that one had to traverse for another half-hour before reaching the isles of Sigwad, which were said to be his right eye.

Luck was on Talasyn and her eager companion's side; there was no sign of the Tempest Sever that frequently blew through the strait. *The storm god's restless spirit is taking the night off,* she thought wryly. Back on the Continent—in Sardovia, in Kesath—the Severs were manifestations of the gods, but here in Nenavar the gods were long dead. There was only the Zahiya-lachis.

From the air, Sigwad was a roughly circular smattering of coral islands. Surakwel landed the yacht at its center, on a tranquil stretch of shoreline that glittered in the copious moon-light.

"Wait here," Talasyn instructed as she disembarked. She didn't want to waste valuable time convincing Ideth Vela that this new Dominion noble could be trusted.

"But—"

"Debt of the self, remember?"

Surakwel sighed. "*Fine.*"

Talasyn shot him her fiercest, haughtiest glare and he lapsed into a grudging silence, glowering at her retreating back when she turned to make for the nearby swamp on foot. If only it were *this* easy to shut Alaric Ossinast up—the ass.

She disappeared into the mangrove trees, forging a radiant blade to illuminate her path. The damp smell of brackish water rushed up her nose as she plodded through the wilderness, over mangrove roots tangled together so densely that they formed forest floor, quivering with a variety of soft amphibious things that slithered and slimed and croaked in the gloom.

"Talasyn?"

The whisper cut through the dark swamp. She nearly hurled her light-spun sword at the treetops, but common sense kicked in at the last second and she squinted at the canopy above her. The round face of a young boy squinted back.

"I'll tell the Amirante that you're on your way." He scampered off, hopping from branch to branch until he disappeared in a rustle of leaves.

Talasyn ventured on, over mud and twisted roots and shallow water. The *Nautilus* and the camp that had sprung up around it were on a natural embankment, while the *Summerwind* and the other airships were docked a short hike away. Talasyn saw the stormship first, the curve of it glistening in the seven-mooned night like the carcass of a whale that had beached itself within the mangroves. Surrounding it was a collection of bamboo huts on stilts.

As soon as she stepped onto the embankment, Vela came striding out to greet her. Sometimes it was a bit of an *event* when Talasyn visited, everyone hungry for news from the capital, but sometimes, like now, it was just her and the Amirante, speaking quietly in the evening gloom.

The first time Talasyn visited this hideout in the mangroves, she'd been shocked by the remnant's collective appearance. Sigwad fell under Niamha's domain and the Sardovians wore clothes provided to them by House Langsoune, all light cotton tunics and brightly colored breeches and striped wraparound skirts. Including Vela, they looked more Nenavarene than Allfold.

The Amirante had been informed of the marriage treaty and the threat of the Voidfell by the Dominion envoys who brought over the spectral configurations as a precautionary measure. She had either gotten all the upset out of her system or was doing a spectacular job of keeping it under control; the gaze that she fixed on Talasyn was remarkably composed.

"Enough is enough, Talasyn. You have to learn how to stand up for yourself. I know that you think that you'll be endangering us by doing so, but you don't *have* to be a witless pawn in the Dragon Queen's games. Believe me, she needs your goodwill as much as you need hers. The Dominion has no qualms about deposing an heirless monarch—in fact, they were on the verge of doing so before you showed up. Without you, she risks losing *everything*. It is time that you *remind* her. Do you think that you can do that?"

"I don't know," Talasyn mumbled. "Everyone's afraid of her, even my father. I'm alone—"

"You aren't alone," said Vela. "You have Ossinast."

Talasyn blinked, uncomprehending. The ambient sounds of the swamp filled the tense space between words and Vela leaned in closer. "Power is a fluid, ever-shifting thing, dictated by alliances. Right now, it seems that Urduja Silim holds all

349

the cards because she is the Zahiya-lachis. *But* . . . once you marry the Night Emperor, what does that make you?"

"The Night Empress," Talasyn whispered.

Vela nodded. "While I can't say that I'm delighted by it, Alaric being your consort buys us time. And it gives you—opportunities."

"To spy on Kesath," Talasyn heard herself saying, despite the odd jitters that coursed through her at Alaric being referred to as her consort. Not only was it easier for her to shift into battle mode now that she was in the company of her commanding officer, but the conversation had also unlocked an epiphany that had been waiting for the right nudge to blossom into wildfire. "To learn their weaknesses. To . . ." She trailed off, hardly daring to give voice to such a thing.

Vela finished the sentence for her. "To find the way to Gaheris."

"We can cut off the serpent's head, like we always planned," Talasyn continued slowly. "Gaheris is the real power behind the Night Empire. We kill him, and it will all come crumbling down. And then we'll figure out what to do with—"

The name caught in her throat.

"The man who will by then be your husband," Vela muttered.

Talasyn swallowed. "A minor detail," she said with rather more confidence than she actually felt.

"We can also learn how they're making their void cannons," Vela added. "Alaric brought only one moth coracle back to Kesath. The magic inside it shouldn't have been enough to power entire ironclads. You have to figure out how they did it, and if there's any way to take those armaments out of the equation."

"All right. I will," Talasyn was quick to say. It was a momentuous undertaking, but she felt better now that there was an actual plan.

Vela rubbed a weary hand over her face. "You're going to be in so much danger. You have to promise us that you'll call for an extraction if things go south."

"I will." Talasyn thought of Surakwel Mantes. "I know someone I can send if I need help—and when I have important information and can't meet you myself."

"You have a difficult road ahead of you," Vela said gravely. "Right now, there seems to be no alternative other than for you to walk it. Do you think that you are strong enough?"

Talasyn lifted her chin. "I have to be."

"Very well. Hurry back to Eskaya before your grandmother realizes that you aren't there."

Talasyn watched the Amirante walk back to her hut. She couldn't deny there was a part of her that wished Vela had shown more indignation on her behalf, but it wasn't Vela's responsibility to coddle her and Talasyn had to do her duty, just as Vela had to do hers. The future was uncertain; it spread before her like the yawning mouth of some dark cave. And she would face it, the way she had faced everything else thus far.

Keep moving forward.

CHAPTER TWENTY-NINE

There was a saying in Kesath, one of the many that Alaric had committed to memory back in his schoolboy days because he'd practiced writing it over and over again in the High Calligraphic script of the imperial court: *If you pluck the unripe balsam-pear, you must eat the bitterness.* It meant reaping the consequences of bad decisions. It meant being careful what one wished for.

It was a saying that flashed across the surface of his mind in a censorious loop as he and Talasyn hiked up the Belian mountain range, bearing heavy packs filled with supplies. The airship that had borne them from Eskaya to Belian had been left behind at Kaptan Rapat's garrison, along with their respective guards—although in Alaric's case it was *guard*, singular, in the form of Sevraim, and that had been the problem. The ruins of the Lightweaver shrine were too overgrown and fragile for any vessel to dock there, and Alaric had refused to be outnumbered by Dominion soldiers in the remote wilderness with no escape route. The Zahiya-lachis hadn't been all too keen on entrusting her granddaughter to two Kesathese Shadowforged, either. As a compromise, only Alaric and Talasyn would set up camp at the shrine and train there and *hopefully* catch the Light Sever discharging, so that she could commune with it.

The end result was this—Alaric alone in the Nenavarene jungle with his wartime enemy and political bride-to-be, who was clearly still irate with him because of the quarrel on board his stormship *and* the one on the rooftop in Eskaya.

In truth, his own anger was dulled by the undeniable confirmation that her former comrades weren't sheltering in Nenavar, but the weather was most assuredly not improving his disposition one bit. Early mornings in Kesath were chilly gray affairs, breath curling through the air in garlands of silver vapor. Here in the Dominion, it was already as hot as a Kesathese noon in summer and infinitely more humid—even more so than the last time Alaric had trekked here, in secret, focused only on stopping the Lightweaver before she could get to the nexus point.

It was funny how life turned out, but he was in no mood to laugh. It was so very *warm*.

And it didn't help matters that Talasyn was wearing a sleeveless tunic and linen breeches that clung to her like a second skin, causing his thoughts to go down dangerous roads. He heartily blamed Sevraim for this, with all that talk of heir-making.

"Are you absolutely certain that we're heading in the right direction?" Alaric had to raise his voice because Talasyn was several feet ahead of him, stomping amidst vines and shrubbery with a pointedness that drove home her low opinion of this little sojourn of theirs.

"Forgotten the way already?" she called back without so much as glancing over her shoulder.

He rolled his eyes even though she couldn't see it. "I took a different route then."

"And how *is* the unconscionable bastard who gave you the map?"

"*Commodore* Darius is enjoying the sweet taste of victory and the privileges of his new rank, I imagine."

Why did he say things like this, things he knew would serve only to antagonize her further? She slowed her pace long enough to glower at him and he thought that he might have an answer in the way her brown eyes flashed in the sunlight, in the way her freckled olive skin was framed against all this jungle green and gold.

With a huff, she turned back to the path and continued stamping ahead, and he trailed after her, trying to derive some satisfaction from having gotten the last word.

Talasyn spent the entire morning wishing for a tree to fall on the Night Emperor.

She was also *unbelievably* exhausted. The trek to the ruins of the Lightweaver shrine would have been grueling even for someone who'd had a good night's sleep, and she'd only managed four hours on her and Surakwel's journey back to the Roof of Heaven. She was lightheaded as she hiked, the world around her taking on a parchment-thin quality.

But a curious thing happened as she and Alaric ventured deeper into the jungle, climbed further up the slope. Perhaps it was the fresh air seeping into her lungs, the smell of earth and nectar and damp leaves, the way that the physical exertion was making her heart race, or the verdant wilderness—whatever the case, Talasyn felt lighter than she had in ages. She hadn't been able to appreciate it properly last night, pressed for time and urgency nipping at her heels as she crossed the mangrove swamps of the Storm God's Eye, but here and now, with entire days stretching ahead, she realized how much she needed to get away from the stifling atmosphere of the Nenavarene court, even if it was just for a little while. Even if it was with Alaric Ossinast. Though she had no faith in her ability to not stab him before it was over.

Talasyn's stomach began growling. "We'll stop for lunch after we clear this pond," she announced to the empty space in front of her. There was a grunt of agreement from behind, and she snickered as she pictured Alaric huffing and puffing in the sweltering tropical climate in his black clothes.

The pond was deep and muddy from recent rains and a narrow plank bridge had been built across it. It was half submerged, but it would do. Talasyn crossed without incident, careful not to slip on the slimy wood.

Alaric wasn't so fortunate. A great splash echoed throughout the jungle stillness and she whirled around to see him disappearing beneath the brown water. She made to hurry back onto the bridge, but stopped when his head popped up again. He was sputtering, his drenched black hair clinging to a face coated in grime.

"Master of the Shadowforged Legion but can't cross a pond!" Talasyn exclaimed.

Alaric scowled, spitting out a mouthful of dirt as he paddled in the direction of the bridge. "Lightweaver but can't make a shield."

His retort barely carried across the water, but it reached her ears well enough. She flashed him a rude gesture, palm up and thumb stretched out and index finger curling inward. He blinked, and it seemed to her that he was more surprised than outright offended.

To Alaric's credit, though, not everyone could be as poised as he was while struggling to extricate themselves from what was more or less liquefied earth. He moved with assurance, almost as though he'd *meant* to fall into the pond. Talasyn watched with one eyebrow raised as he scrambled onto what looked like an overturned tree trunk, with the clear intention of using it as a foothold to hop back to the bridge.

Except that it *wasn't* a tree trunk. The moment Alaric's full weight pressed down on it, it . . . *stirred.*

He careened into the water once again, with another mighty splash, just as the hulking visage of a swamp buffalo broke the surface. It was thrice the size of a full-grown man, red gills fluttering in grooves on the sides of its thick neck. Its tough hide was the color of charcoal and its scarlet eyes, set between enormous sickle-shaped horns, focused on Alaric with a mindless, primal fury.

Not only had its territory been invaded, but it had also been trodden on.

It let out a bellow that shook the treetops, and it charged, through the pond water, as gracefully as a fish. Talasyn spun a radiant spear and flung it with all her strength, but the swamp buffalo wove away from it with shocking swiftness before ducking beneath the arc of Alaric's own shadow-smithed lance.

Talasyn waded into the pond to help—she was *not* about to explain to the host of Kesathese warships waiting beyond the archipelago that she'd let their sovereign get gored to death—but the water had barely reached her ankles when Alaric's hoarse command stopped her in her tracks.

"Stay there."

He summoned the Shadowgate in the form of a crescent blade, which he threw toward the muddy banks. As the blade sailed through the air, its handle sprouted a chain of crackling, inky magic, the other end coiled around his gauntleted fist. The blade sank into the earth behind Talasyn and then the chain's links began folding in on themselves and Alaric was propelled along by the decreasing length. The swamp buffalo gave chase with enraged huffs and snorts, horns lowered, as it stampeded after its prey, all the way to the shallows.

Talasyn prepared to spin another weapon, to engage the creature at close quarters, but once the shadowy blade and its midnight-black chain vanished and Alaric scrambled to his feet, he grabbed her by the wrist, and before she knew it, they were running, the swamp buffalo in hot pursuit. It crashed through the undergrowth, the ground trembling beneath its heavy hooves, every toss of its horned head knocking aside young trees as though they were mere kindling.

This is how I'm going to die, Talasyn thought, blood pounding in her ears, legs pumping frantically, the brown and green of the jungle blurring past the corners of her vision. *In the woods. Killed by the world's angriest cow.*

Alaric had let go of her wrist, but he was keeping pace beside her. He conjured a war axe to hack at the low-hanging branches blocking their path, occasionally transmuting it into a spear to hurl at their pursuer and then replacing it with a new axe. It was a display of concentration, timing, and magical ability that Talasyn had never before witnessed, had never been capable of.

Not to be outdone, she conjured spears of her own and hurled them at the pursuing beast as well, one after the other. Light and shadow sang through the air, side by side. But the swamp buffalo was as agile on land as it was in water, and it made dodging the barrage look like an effortless task.

And just when they had been running so long and so hard that a stitch welled up her side and her thighs were on the verge of collapse and her heart was about to give out—

—the minor earthquake and the awful sounds of the dread beast's charge came to an abrupt halt.

Talasyn dared a glance over her shoulder. In the distance, the swamp buffalo had turned around and was disappearing into the bushes, content to have chased the intruders away. Sheer relief made her knees go weak and she sagged against a tree trunk, chest heaving while sweat pooled on her skin and she sucked in one huge lungful of air after another.

Alaric braced a hand on the tree trunk next to hers. He doubled over, panting as well. Several minutes passed with the two of them wheezing and gasping beneath a canopy of leaves.

Finally—when her breathing evened out; when the faint

black dots swimming before her eyes receded—Talasyn turned to Alaric. He was plastered in mud from head to toe, not only from his unexpected dip in the pond but also from his magic dragging him bodily through its wet banks. His waterlogged hair hung limply around a frowning angular face, where the only pale complexion to be seen was in small streaks and patches. His tailored clothes with their fine fabrics were now more brown than black.

In this moment, the Night Emperor of Kesath resembled some new species of glum creature that had just emerged from a mudhole—which was more or less what had happened.

She burst out laughing.

Seeing her smile up at him for the first time was like taking a crossbow bolt to the chest. Her brown eyes crinkled at the corners and sunlight danced off the curve of her pink lips, casting her freckled cheeks in a warm glow.

The breath that Alaric had only so recently regained caught in his throat. No one had ever looked at him like this, with such joy, and when she started laughing, it was deep and vibrant, a song floating through the chambers of his soul. His ears rang with the melody, the sight of her burned into remembrance.

I would give anything, he thought, *for this not to be the last time. For her to smile at me again, and laugh like the war never happened.*

After a while, it sank in that she was laughing *at* him, and he shot her a withering glare.

This served to set Talasyn off even more. She clutched at rough bark as though for dear life, practically *howling* while Alaric flushed red underneath the mud that caked his skin.

Eventually, her laughter tapered off into mostly silent giggles, interspersed with the occasional snort. "Are you *quite* finished?" he asked through clenched teeth.

"Yes." She straightened up, wiping away tears of mirth with

slim fingers. "It's practically a Nenavarene rite of passage, to almost be murdered by a swamp buffalo." She retrieved the map and the compass from her pockets, checking to see if they were still on the right course.

"First the dragon, then the messenger eagle that looked like it would have no compunction about disemboweling my men, and now this bovine," Alaric grumbled. "At this point, I should just assume that all the animals in the Dominion are out to kill me."

"Not just the animals." But there was no real ire in Talasyn's tone; she said it with the offhandedness of habit. She put away the navigational tools and gestured up ahead. "We were chased in the direction of the ruins, at least. There's a stream nearby where we can have lunch and you can . . ." Her mischievous gaze flickered over him, mouth twitching with the beginnings of a fresh surge of laughter. ". . . wash off."

"If an uncommonly large fish doesn't murder me first," he deadpanned.

She snorted, in a manner that was almost—*companionable*. Something that felt uncomfortably like hope stirred in his chest. Had she gotten past their most recent fights? If this was what it took for her to stop being angry with him, then perhaps being covered in mud wasn't so terrible . . .

Minutes later they reached the stream, a clear ribbon of water that burbled down the mountain slope, bordered by moss-covered rocks. As Alaric gingerly perched on one of the rocks and kicked off his boots, Talasyn very deliberately turned her back to him and began unpacking rations with more meticulousness than such a task required.

Her sudden shyness was at odds with how they'd been trying to kill each other months ago. Still, he was grateful for the privacy and sought more of it by ducking behind a thick wall of tufted reeds growing at the edge of the waterline, where he stripped off his muddy garments.

The coolness of the stream was a refreshing balm after hours spent trekking in the sweltering heat. He scrubbed off every inch of grime, idly listening to the song of water over stone and all the unseen, possibly murderous animals chittering in the treetops. It wasn't anything at all like baths back at the Kesathese Citadel or the Nenavarene Roof of Heaven, with the perfumed steam of heated water wafting from marble tubs, but he found it pleasant, nonetheless.

When Alaric emerged from the stream and rooted around his pack for a change of clothes, he eschewed the long-sleeved, high-collared tunics for just a fitted black undershirt and arm-guards. After a moment's hesitation, he tossed the leather gauntlets back into his pack as well. The weather demanded it.

Talasyn had laid out the rice cakes and salted venison, and she was brewing ginger tea in a kettle powered by a Firewarren-infused aether heart. She looked up at his approach and blinked. Once, twice, her mouth parting slightly. Before he could wonder aloud at her strange behavior, she averted her gaze and pushed the woven bamboo plate full of food toward him without a word.

As they ate, sitting there on the grass, he frantically cast around for a suitable topic of conversation.

"Kaptan Rapat was remarkably unenthused to see me again," he ventured.

"Can you blame him?" She popped a rice cake into her mouth. A whole one. "He was happy to see *me*, though."

"Why wouldn't he be?" He had meant to be sarcastic, but for some reason the image of her golden features lit up with laughter rose to the forefront of his thoughts, and his remark ended on a note that was disturbingly sincere even to his own ears. He compensated by clearing his throat and adding wryly, "You are, after all, the paragon of virtue and good cheer."

"We're both well aware that you leave me in the dust where those two things are concerned," she sniped, cheeks bulging

360

as though she were a chipmunk storing acorns for the winter in the forests back home. Then she swallowed, and he tried to recall if he'd seen her chew the rice cake at all. "I hope your legionnaire behaves himself while he's their guest."

Alaric grimaced. "I left strict orders, but Sevraim and *behave* don't exactly belong in the same sentence."

"I can imagine." Talasyn plucked a strip of salted venison from their shared plate. "Bit bold, isn't he? Chatty the other day, too—although he never said a word during negotiations."

"While I have long since given up on instilling even an ounce of decorum in Sevraim, we are fortunate that he is sometimes aware of when to hold his peace," said Alaric. "He is here strictly as my protection and is content enough to keep to that role, since politics bore him."

"You had no trouble temporarily relieving him of his duties." Talasyn bit into the venison, tearing it in half with a sharp yank of her teeth. "Do you really trust me that much?"

Alaric was so aghast watching her fall upon their rations like a starving animal that it took him a while to realize she'd asked a question. He shrugged. "I trust that you have enough common sense to not do anything foolish."

Her words from the other afternoon came back to him. *One day people will have had enough of you. And when they finally denounce you, I won't think twice before joining them.* She fidgeted, and he could tell that she was remembering, too.

"No, I won't do anything foolish." Talasyn looked so upset at having to make that promise that Alaric nearly laughed. "I say things when I'm mad, but I'll try not to make this more difficult than it already is."

He nodded. "As will I. This is most likely as far as we'll ever get to having any faith in each other, but it's better than nothing."

"Agreed," she said as she chewed.

"For what it's worth," he mumbled, "my behavior on the

Deliverance was unbecoming. I shall endeavor to make certain that it doesn't happen again."

There was a part of Alaric that couldn't believe that he was apologizing to the Lightweaver. His father would have a fit if he found out.

But Gaheris would *never* find out. That was the thing. He was an ocean away. Alaric had never felt as far from his father as he did now, here in this wilderness. There was something strangely liberating in that.

Talasyn coughed, as though she'd choked on her food from sheer surprise. To wash it down, she took a generous swig of ginger tea, peering at him over the rim of the cup in something like contemplation.

"Thank you," she finally said. "I shall also—*endeavor*—to do the same."

And while the Hurricane Wars would always be felt between them, like two shards of a cracked pane of glass separated by the spidery white line of fracture, there at least seemed to be a mutual agreement to not talk about it anymore. At last. Instead, Alaric watched in amazement as Talasyn reached for another rice cake and shoved it into her mouth at the same time as the second half of the venison strip.

By the gods. He was unable to tear his gaze away. She ate like she fought. Relentless and without mercy.

It was only when she smacked her lips together, the pink fullness of them glistening from the ginger tea, that some instinct—some sense of self-preservation—made him decide to abruptly become very interested in the grass, the nearby stream, the moss on the rocks, *anything* that wasn't her.

CHAPTER THIRTY

Red-gold sunset was pouring over the ancient ruins in a molten haze by the time Alaric and Talasyn made it to the mountaintop. The Lightweaver shrine had been a vast, ethereal thing when she'd first seen it, silvered in moonlight; in the fiery glow of a dying day its weathered sandstone facade contrasted starkly against the rolling dark green jungle within which it reclined, solemn and immense, like a forgotten god on a long-lost throne, the faces of its multitude of carved dancing figures peering out from vines and bramble with enigmatic half-smiles wherein lurked the secrets of the past.

Alaric regarded the dancers on the entrance arch with interest. "These are?"

"*Tuani.*" Talasyn summoned the term from one of an endless array of history lessons. "Nature spirits. You'll find reliefs like these in a lot of millennia-old structures. They were worshipped by the ancient Nenavarene."

"And now the Nenavarene worship your grandmother." Alaric's gray eyes were fixed on the carvings, their flowing manes forever wild in the wind, their sleek limbs forever raised to some long-ago melody. "And, eventually, you."

Talasyn offered a halfhearted shrug. She didn't like thinking about this—about what would come *after*. She was run ragged enough worrying about the present as it was.

"There's not much worshipping involved," she muttered. "Here in Nenavar the Zahiya-lachis is sovereign because she is the vessel of the ancestors who watch over the land from the spirit world. There are no . . . prayers or rituals, or anything. People just have to do whatever she says."

"As the would-be consort of a future Zahiya-lachis, I'll already be expected to do just that, won't I?" He sounded faintly amused. "Husbands defer to their wives here, from what I've gathered."

There was a fluttering in the pit of her stomach. There was a skip to her pulse, a shortness of breath. The way he spoke so casually of their impending marriage, when he looked like he did now—

Logically, Talasyn had always known that Alaric had a body hiding somewhere under all the black fabric and leather armor. She had even been taken aback by the sheer size of it on numerous occasions. It shouldn't have come as *such* a shock.

But he had emerged from behind the tall reeds in an undershirt that bared his sharp collarbones and broad shoulders, that clung to his defined chest. Paired with trousers that were hung low on his lean hips and emphasized the considerable length of his legs, and black armguards hinting at the solid muscle beneath them . . . the effect had been quite dizzying. It still was.

At least his hair had long since dried and he wasn't raking his fingers through it with a casual, smarmy elegance, and she'd stopped feeling as if she was on the brink of combusting. Sort of. Maybe.

"There you go again, talking about being married to me," she scoffed with a bravado that she hoped he wouldn't see through. "You *are* excited."

"Given your proclivity for pointing it out," Alaric countered, "I'd hazard a guess that *you're* excited that I'm excited."

"You," she hissed, "are the most ornery man that I've ever—"

"Been betrothed to?" he suggested helpfully.

"*Will you stop talking about that!*"

"No. Annoying you is in my ornery nature, Lachis'ka." His tone was even. Perfectly calculated, she thought, to rile her.

And it worked.

Glowering, she made her way into the complex. So did he, this time keeping pace with her instead of trailing behind. They both knew the way to the Light Sever, after all.

Talasyn was no stranger to handsome men with excellent physiques. There had been plenty in Sardovia and there were plenty here in the Dominion. But she had never before experienced this . . . *pull* in the company of anyone else. Her eyes kept flickering to Alaric, mapping him out. Her every nerve ending sparked at his nearness.

In truth, it was the same set of reactions she'd had to him ever since they met, but *amplified*, somehow. As though in the peeling off of his layers, some of hers had been removed as well.

It scared her, this epiphany that he wasn't unattractive. Or perhaps *epiphany* wasn't the right term. Perhaps it had been something that she'd always known, deep down, and it had been lying in wait for the right moment to surface and wallop her over the head.

The right moment being Alaric wet from the stream, all tousled sable mane and sun-flushed skin stretched over sculpted muscle, drops of water tangled in his long lashes.

Talasyn's face grew hot, and she was exceedingly grateful for the gloom that shrouded the dusty, crumbled corridors they were traversing. Gods, there seemed to be nothing more humiliating than being attracted to someone who didn't feel the same. Alaric had told her, in such a cruel and biting manner, that she cleaned up well. There was no mistaking his implication; the only times he ever found her tolerable to look at was when her face was painted and she was draped in silk and precious gems. Without these trappings, he obviously had no impetus to view a former wartime enemy as anything other than a cave troll.

A *shrewish* cave troll, at that.

She felt nauseated. Was *this* what attraction normally entailed—suddenly caring if the other person found one pleasing to the eye?

The Dominion court was influencing her in the worst of ways, Talasyn decided. The emphasis that the Nenavarene placed on fashion and cosmetics had cultivated in her a vanity that had been absent for twenty years. She resolved to work on that, on quashing this new and highly frivolous aspect of herself.

The reliefs that lined the shrine's interior walls almost appeared to move in the half-light, their stone eyes following the intruders. Through it all Talasyn's veins hummed with the golden strings of the Lightweave, beckoning to her as it strained against the veils of aetherspace. However, when they reached the courtyard, all was still, the Light Sever dormant.

The tree that Alaric's magic had felled a little over four months ago was still there, gnarled trunk cracked like an egg over the stonework. Alaric and Talasyn stared at it, and then at each other.

"They're called *lelak'lete*—grandfather trees," she said, more out of a desire to avoid any discussion of their shared rancorous past, which would undoubtedly lead to another ferocious argument, than a pressing need to tutor him in the finer points of Nenavarene botany. "They're believed to house the spirits of the dead who weren't given proper burials."

Alaric's silvery gaze wandered to the stone rooftops surrounding the courtyard, chipped and slumped beneath the weight of the grandfather trees that had grown over them

366

in profusions of twisted trunks and gray-green leaves and ropelike aerial roots. "A lot of restless souls around here, then."

Talasyn cocked her head. "Scared?"

"Not of them. The animals will probably get me first."

His delivery was so perfectly wry, so patently long-suffering, that she had to bite back a grin, thrown once again by the rare flash of his subtle humor.

They set up camp, which involved little more than dropping their packs and unfolding bedrolls near the sandstone fountain. Supper was a silent affair and Talasyn's eyes were heavy by the end of it, the shadows of early evening pressing down on her lids, the fatigue that she'd been reining in since morning now let loose, washing over her bones.

She barely managed to stumble to her bedroll, to crawl into it. The last thing she saw before she sank into a deep sleep was Alaric standing by the fountain, head tilted to gaze at the darkening sky above the grandfather trees. At the pale beginnings of the seven moons, and the faint glimmer of the first stars.

"Wake up."

Talasyn's eyes shot open. The sky was a bright powder-blue and copious amounts of sunlight were pouring into the courtyard. She squinted against the glare, perplexed. Hadn't it been evening mere minutes ago?

The fog of sleep cleared. She sat upright, her body groaning in protest, having become happily accustomed to nights ensconced in fluffy pillows and silk sheets atop an eiderdown mattress. There was no one to blame but herself for getting soft, but it made her feel better to scowl at the man who had roused her, anyway.

Alaric's expression was impassive as he crouched beside her, his shadow sharp on the ancient stone floor. "We have to get started. I let you sleep in a bit because you seemed tired, but we can't afford to waste any more time."

"So thoughtful." Much to her chagrin, the bite that she'd intended to make apparent in her tone was swallowed up by a gusty yawn.

Breakfast consisted of more rice cakes and some alarmingly potent coffee, brewed from grounds that Rapat's garrison had provided. It smelled faintly like the creamy yellow thornfruit that could clear a room when cut open, but it tasted of smoke and chocolate—and it was so strong that Talasyn's heart was beating faster in her chest after only a few sips.

Alaric was unimpressed. "This stuff could strip paint from an airship hull."

Talasyn secretly agreed with him, but principle dictated that she defend Nenavar's honor. "Does the rustic taste offend your royal sensibilities?" she sniped.

"You're royalty, too," he pointed out. "Or has that slipped your mind?"

She blinked. It *had* slipped her mind, actually. And he was arching one dark brow at her and his sensual lips were curved into a smirk and he was wearing that *stupid* undershirt—

His smirk widened in amusement as the seconds passed. "You look like you want to kill me."

"You look like you enjoy it," she snapped.

His eyes were silver in the sunshine; for a fleeting moment, they held an enigmatic sort of mischief that she would never have believed he had in him, had she not witnessed it before it faded, its glint retreating behind the usual steel and frost.

She leaned forward, some small suspicion taking root. "*Do* you enjoy it?" she demanded bluntly. "Getting a rise out of me, I mean?"

He ducked his head, suddenly very intent on his coffee, peering into its depths as though it held arcane secrets. "It's not that I *enjoy* it, but it's different. My father's—*my* court"—

368

his pale brow furrowed as he painstakingly corrected himself, and he looked so young—"they bow and they scrape. My legionnaires stand on less ceremony, especially Sevraim, as you've doubtless noticed. But they are still aware that I am their master. You, on the other hand, don't fear to truly speak your mind. I find that interesting."

"I thought you liked me better when I was still afraid of you." Talasyn couldn't resist throwing back in his face his declaration from their night as prisoners. Until today, she'd had no idea that she even remembered what he'd said.

"To quote an esteemed philosopher," Alaric told his coffee, "*I say things when I'm mad.*"

There it was again, that grin tugging at her lips, unbidden. And, once again, she fought it back. "Well, the next time you wish to be disrespected, you know where to find me."

The corner of Alaric's mouth twitched, as though he was suppressing a smile of his own.

After breaking their fast, they took turns washing up in a spring that Rapat had told them was located on the shrine's grassy grounds, a few twisting corridors away from the campsite. Talasyn went second and, while she cleaned her teeth with a powder of salt and dried iris petals and crushed mint leaves, she reflected on the disturbing camaraderie that she had fallen into with the Night Emperor.

Was it a by-product of the previous morning's events, an unlikely bond forged by the act of escaping death? Or was it this place, so hauntingly picturesque, so remote that they might as well have been the only two people in the world?

Whatever the case, Talasyn had to admit that it was probably a good thing. She had nearly slipped—nearly lost this long game—when she railed about the Continent rising up and her joining them one day. If she'd already been the Night Empress, her words would have counted as treason. Her temper had endangered both Nenavar and Sardovia, as well as her own life.

She was incredibly fortunate that Alaric didn't seem to be holding her stormy declaration against her *that* much.

When she returned to the courtyard, he was sitting, legs crossed, in the shade of a grandfather tree that had sprouted right up against one wall, its branches pushing at the old stonework. Talasyn joined him with some reluctance, dropping down across from him closer than she would have preferred due to the thick, protruding roots taking up most of the space. He smelled like the calam-lime soap from the garrison.

"We'll focus solely on meditation well into the afternoon," he announced. "The objective is for your breathing, your magic, and your body to be so in tune with one another that molding the Lightweave into whatever you want—in this case, a shield—will be effortless. *Why* are you making that face at me?"

"Sounds tedious," she grumbled.

"When I began aethermancing under my grandfather's tute-lage, I would spend whole sennights doing nothing but meditating," he snootily informed her.

She should have taken umbrage at his tone, but . . . "I didn't know that your grandfather was the one who taught you."

"As I've mentioned before, my abilities manifested at an early age." Alaric traced a circle in the dust of ages with his forefinger, without even seeming to realize that he was doing it. "He was very proud of me. He made the time to oversee my training, until . . ."

He never finished the sentence, but Talasyn could guess. *Until his obsession with the stormships grew,* or *Until the war began.* It all amounted to the same thing, didn't it?

She only knew King Ozalus as the one who'd started it all. Who had been possessed by a dream of lightning and destruction that culminated in the shadows of the stormships falling over the Continent. She had certainly never before pictured him as anyone's grandfather, tutoring a solemn dark-haired boy in the ways of magic.

How unsettling, that evil could have a human face. She thought back to what had been, by Alaric's standards, an explosion of rage when they argued over the true instigator of the Cataclysm. She understood it better now. How unsettling, that an evil man could have had people who cared for him so.

It wasn't long before Alaric emerged from his private reverie and began the day's training. They went through the stationary breathing meditations first, and then he taught her more of the moving forms—this time keeping a careful distance, not once arranging her body with his hands the way he'd tried to in the plumeria grove. She wondered if this was a conscious decision on his part, but caught herself. If it *was* a conscious decision, it had been made so he could avoid the awkwardness that had occurred then, when she walked back into him. She was the only one whose heart had taken a long time to stop racing in her dressing room afterward, because she hadn't ever known touch like that before.

The sun was high overhead by the time Talasyn learned all the meditations by rote. Alaric went from instructor and observer to fellow aethermancer, executing the various forms by her side. Despite his solidly muscled frame, he was light on his feet, flexible, executing each step with panther-like grace. He set the pace and she kept up, the two of them traveling in parallel lines across the length of the courtyard, amidst all those old and crooked trees. Legs sweeping back and forward. Arms slashing and pushing and rising to the heavens; wrists like paper cranes soaring and then gliding back to earth. Air flowing through the lungs, urged on by the contractions of chest and stomach, by the twisting of hips and the billowing of the spine.

And Talasyn's magic flowed along with it. For the first time, she could sense every single pathway taken by the aether in her veins. For the first time, she could see her fingertips and her heart and the hidden facets of her soul as nexus points, bound into a constellation by the Lightweave's golden thread.

For the first time, she felt connected to the man beside her in a way that went beyond begrudging tolerance or those surprising little moments of softening, of opening up. She and Alaric moved together, seamless and in fluid tandem, as though they were each other's mirrors, as though they were waves in an ocean called forever, their shadows lengthening on the stone.

Such a blissful state of affairs ended too soon, however.

By sunset, Talasyn was frustrated beyond belief.

She *still* hadn't managed to spin a single shield. In principle, it was the same as forging a weapon—and yet here she was, perched on a section of the fallen grandfather tree's twisted trunk, once again attempting to visualize something that she couldn't replicate. She'd been at it since late afternoon and the results were minimal at best.

Alaric was probably as mystified as she was, but he was far more patient than Vela had ever been, and he tirelessly approached the problem from different angles. In truth, thanks to the meditations, she could *feel* the magic within her slowly being coaxed toward the desired effect. She just couldn't bring it to the surface.

The trunk creaked beneath an added weight. Talasyn cracked one eye open; Alaric had sat down in front of her, mirroring her pose. He gestured for her to continue with an imperiousness that made her bristle, but she begrudgingly complied, retreating into the darkness behind shut lids once more.

"You told me that the first weapon you ever spun was a knife, like the one you stole to protect yourself," he said, and she nodded. "Aside from blades, a shield can protect you, too," he continued. "Build it in your mind, as you did with that first knife. Inch by inch. Carve the hardwood into the shape of a teardrop. Paint over it with resin. Soften the grip with leather. Reinforce the surface with metal. Polish it until it gleams bright in the sun, or the starlight."

His tone was low and deliberate. It sank into her bloodstream, all honey and wine and oak. She had to fight the urge to open her eyes in a frantic attempt to quell the goosebumps that prickled the back of her neck, that danced down her spine.

Talasyn imagined making a shield. A material one, from hickory and cowhide and iron, using Alaric's words as her guide. This time she was also thinking about that first knife, how she'd called it forth at the outskirts of a military encampment in the Sardovian Heartland, with Vela looking on. She had been so desperate to prove herself back then. Desperate to earn her keep. This was the same thing, wasn't it? She needed to master this new skill to prove to the Dominion that she was worth the risk of concealing the Sardovians. She needed to save both the Sardovians and the Nenavarene from the amethyst night, from the jaws of the World-Eater.

And she was almost *there*. Her magic was straining to reach its goal, pushing up through doubts and old habits and learning curves the way a green sprout pushed up through the earth.

When she opened her eyes, a translucent blob of light magic that *could* be a shield if one squinted was shimmering in the grasp of her fingers, growing more and more solid as Talasyn beheld it with wonder.

Alaric was leaning slightly forward, wearing an expression she'd never seen on him before. He looked—*pleased*. Boyish, almost, some of the sternness lifting from his perpetually sullen features. Once again, as she had that day in the Roof of Heaven's atrium, she wondered what it would be like if he actually smiled.

And, with that break in her concentration, the shield winked out of existence. Leaving her with her fingers clutching empty air.

Talasyn's disappointment at the short-lived nature of her competence was similarly fleeting. What quickly took its place was exhilaration of the purest form. It felt as though she had taken the momentous first step on a path that had once been impossible to find. The ability to make a shield was inside her, she just needed to push a little bit more; there was hope like sunbeams at the end of a long darkness. Hope that the world as she knew it would not be devoured.

"I did it," she breathed out, but then caught herself. "I mean, I *almost*—"

"No. You did it." Alaric's voice was soft and raspy. His gray eyes were warm in the fading daylight. "You're doing very well, Talasyn."

And the moment was golden between them, a victory to be shared in this place of stone and wood and spirits, and her magic was blazing high in her heart and the look on his face was open and unguarded, and this was the first good thing to happen in such a long time—

She surged forward, almost tipping over on her precarious perch, and she looped her arms around his neck in a rush of gratitude, of triumph.

His swift intake of breath cut through her giddiness. It may as well have been the sound of cannon fire, for all that it induced her careening return to reality with the most terrible of jolts. Mortified, her whole face hot, she untangled herself from him.

Or she tried to, at least.

Alaric pressed a hand to the small of her back, sending her crashing into him, keeping her against him. His bare palm was a burning sensation, not in the least bit dulled by the thin material of her tunic. His chin came to rest on the spot where her neck curved into her shoulder, the ends of his hair tickling her cheek.

Talasyn blinked at the trees on the rooftop, dark against the dimming sky. It was a revelation, to be held like this, to have someone else's warmth so near, surrounding her. It was hunger, the thing that made her tighten her arms around his neck until there was no more space between them, skin to skin, the urgency with which he had latched on to her echoing everything that her soul had cried out for all these years.

She relaxed into his embrace, breathing him in, the scent of sandalwood water and calam-lime soap and sun-flushed skin. His hand roved over the base of her spine in a slow caress, and she knew that she would feel him there long after he'd pulled away.

But she didn't want him to pull away. She wanted *more*. Her right hand dropped to the collar of his undershirt and slid lower still, until her fingers traced the solid musculature of his exposed bicep. A shudder tore through his broad frame and he compulsively palmed her thigh with his free hand, so warm and big. All of him was so warm and big.

A stifled little half-sigh of sudden need escaped her lips, unbidden. He hummed, low and soothing, and they continued to touch, to hold, as the last of the sun sank below the horizon.

CHAPTER THIRTY-ONE

He could barely remember his mother holding him, and his father certainly never had. He possessed no frame of reference for the feeling of someone in his arms, and someone's arms around him. He had never expected that it would be as though the cold inside him had begun to thaw, everywhere he and Talasyn touched, dragging him headlong into the gladness of summer.

He didn't know—would probably never know—what it was, exactly, that caused them to return to themselves, a stark awareness creeping in along with the indigo of dusk.

Perhaps it was the ache in their backs and their still-crossed legs due to the awkward angle of the embrace. Perhaps it was the tree trunk they were sitting on shifting dangerously. Perhaps it was even the drowsy hoot of a roosting bird from some unseen perch in the jungle canopy around them.

Whatever the case, Alaric and Talasyn slowly extricated themselves from each other. It went beyond the novelty of experiencing something for the first time—even though the moment had passed, he could still feel her waist encased in the curve of his arm, could still feel her arms around his neck and the imprints of her fingers on his bicep. She wouldn't meet his gaze while *he* couldn't seem to stop staring at her. Tucking a loose strand of chestnut hair behind her ear, she licked her lips nervously, and he really wished that she hadn't, his gaze lingering on her pink tongue as it ran over the swell of her bottom lip.

"You, um . . ." She trailed off. Licked her lips *again*, because she'd been put on this earth to torture him. "You're a good instructor," she said hoarsely, her brown eyes trained on the craggy patterns in the tree trunk's rough bark. "You've been very patient. So—thank you."

Alaric wasn't prepared for this, for her shy, faltering praise. Warmth flooded his cheeks and crept all the way up to the tips of his ears. He was grateful that the sun had set, grateful that it would be difficult for her to see how she'd reduced him to a blushing moron with a handful of kind words.

He mustered a grunt of acknowledgement and they clambered down from the tree. He kept a wide berth from her as they prepared their supper and ate in stifling silence.

By the time they bedded down, the awkwardness had worn off a little. To be more precise, Talasyn had stopped jumping out of her skin whenever Alaric moved or even so much as glanced her way. Enough time had passed since the hug to make clear that he had no intention of discussing it, which suited her just fine.

She couldn't stop *thinking* about it, though, which was why she was currently sprawled flat on her bedroll and glaring at the night sky as though it had caused offense.

A shame, really: as far as night skies went, this one was resplendent. A circle of moons, ranging from full to crescent to gibbous, lay embedded in a field of stars that rained down their light in glimmering pulses, so densely clustered that to look at them was almost to fall forever into all that lovely silver and black. She traced constellations that she'd grown up with and ascribed to them the names that she'd only learned months ago. The group of stars that formed what Sardovia called Leng's Hourglass was known here in Nenavar as the Plow, its appearance signaling the start of planting season. Then there were the Allfold's Six Sisters, reborn here in the Dominion as the far-less-poetic Flies, hovering over the celestial carcass of the Horned Pig.

At the periphery of her vision, the lump that was Alaric on his bedroll stirred.

They turned to each other at the same time, eyes locking in the gloom, over an arm's length span of stone tiles.

"Tell me about Bakun," he said. "The World-Eater."

"Don't we have an early start tomorrow?"

"I can't sleep."

"Because you're talking." Still, Talasyn couldn't sleep either, so she launched into the story. Taking refuge in it, in fact, in the hope that a conversation would fully restore the equilibrium that her ill-advised hug had upset. "Back when the world was new and had eight moons, Bakun was the first dragon to tear through aetherspace and make his home on Lir. He laired somewhere on these islands, eventually falling in love with the first Zahiya-lachis, whose name was Iyaram. Dragons live hundreds of years longer than humans do, so Iyaram eventually passed from old age. The grief in Bakun's heart turned into anger, which then turned into a hatred of this world for giving him his first taste of sorrow, for making him the only one of his kind ever to mourn. He swallowed one of the moons and would have eaten the rest, had Iyaram's people not waged a great war against him and driven him back to aetherspace."

Talasyn paused for breath. Alaric was listening intently, moonlight-tinted gaze fixed on her. For a moment, she was reminded of the orphanage in Hornbill's Head, the other children exchanging stories on thin pallets while waiting for sleep to claim them. She had always just listened as stone and straw dug into her back. She'd never had a story of her own to share.

"Even now, that great battle is fought in the heavens time and time again," Talasyn continued. "Whenever there's a lunar eclipse, the Nenavarene say that it's Bakun returning to Lir and trying to devour another one of the moons, until he is defeated by the spirits of the ancestors who fought in that first war."

"And I suppose that once every thousand years he almost wins," said Alaric. "Hence, the Moonless Dark."

"The Night of the World-Eater," she agreed.

"It's interesting how the same phenomenon is explained by different stories from one land to the next," he remarked. "I like the Continent's eclipse myth better, I think."

"What, the sun god forgetting to feed his pet lion so it swallows the moons?" She snorted. "Why do you like *that* better?"

His reply was quiet and solemn. "Because it's not about the loss of someone who was greatly loved."

The breath caught in her throat. It formed a tangle of things she had no idea how to express in words, confronted as she was by the mask of his features straining to contain a soft pensiveness. His mother—he was talking about his mother. In the faint tremble of his bottom lip, in the loss that shaded the spun silver of his eyes, she thought she saw something she recognized.

"Who would have ever thought," Talasyn blurted out on a shaky exhale, "that you and I would end up here? Betrothed and working together?"

Alaric nearly smiled. "Certainly not me."

"Sorry you missed out on your *better options* on my account."

She had meant it in jest. Truly, she had. But the act of bringing up the snide remark that he'd made on his stormship somehow excavated the same wound to her pride—to her feelings?—that she thought she'd moved past, and her tone was more bitter than good-natured.

He went tense. She was seized by the urge to burrow into her bedroll, absolutely mortified.

But she couldn't look away from him. And it wasn't long before he spoke.

"I was angry when I said that. There were no better options; there weren't any options at all. I had no plans to marry anyone. Until you." Alaric's pale brow knitted as he measured out his words with care. "And even though ours will be a marriage in name alone, there will still be no other options for me after we pledge our troth. You will have no cause to feel dishonored. I swear it by your gods and mine."

Talasyn hadn't known that Kesath used the same oath as Sardovia, and that Alaric could sound so wrenchingly sincere that it sent an odd thrill down her spine. She opened her mouth to tell him that there was no need to make such a promise, but then the image of him turning his vague almost-smiles on some other woman flashed through her mind and something in her chest cracked open.

"Yes," she said instead. "We must behave ourselves. Keep up appearances, I mean. It's not like the Dominion nobles need any *more* reason to run you through."

"How unfair, considering that the Kesathese High Command is *ecstatic* that I'm marrying you," he drawled.

Talasyn laughed. Alaric's features softened. And, as they lay there in their separate bedrolls underneath a crown of stars, she found herself wondering what it would be like to close the distance between them once more. She wondered this with a curious yearning that, for a moonlit moment, went as deep as the Eversea.

In the middle of the night, Alaric was jolted out of slumber by a tugging at the edges of his mind. The stars overhead began to blur as the Shadowgate cast its inky nets around him, hauling him into aetherspace.

Gaheris was calling.

In hindsight, it should have been expected, but Alaric had been so focused on his betrothed—on her training—that this felt almost like an intrusion. As though some bubble had been pierced by a dose of cold reality.

Alaric looked over at Talasyn. She was an unmoving, curled-up lump on her bedroll, snoring lightly. He couldn't walk the In-Between now. What if she woke up and he was gone or, worse, she caught him vanishing and reappearing like one of her blades?

It was a security concern. Gaheris would understand. Perhaps.

Alaric skirted out of his father's grasp. He blocked him off and fell back into an uneasy sleep, suspecting that he would pay for this a thousand times over.

The second morning of aethermancing at the Lightweaver shrine saw Talasyn produce three more vaguely shield-shaped blobs of light, in addition to two accidental blast-marks on a very old, very historically significant wall. The exhilaration that she had felt yesterday had completely dissipated. What if blobs were *all* that she would ever be capable of?

At around noon, with the temperature and humidity soaring as the sun approached its zenith, she conducted her meditation exercises beneath the shade of a grandfather tree while Alaric went off to do some exploring.

At least one of us is having fun, she grumbled to herself. He'd been all but glued to the carvings on the entrance arch and he was always studying the ones in the courtyard. She was beginning to suspect that her betrothed was possessed of a rather bookish nature.

But she really shouldn't be thinking about him when she was supposed to be working on her aethermancy.

Talasyn created several more pallid incarnations of a shield, each one petering out after mere seconds without ever solidifying. She was missing a final piece of the puzzle, the piece that would give her magic shape.

Alaric returned just as her latest attempt vanished. "Still no luck?" he asked, looming over her.

"What do you think?" She scowled at him, the effect quite ruined when the breeze sent a strand of hair tumbling down her forehead and past her jaw, and she scrunched up her nose and blew it out of her face.

He smirked, leaning down and chucking her under the chin. It happened so fast that she would have believed it to be a figment of her imagination, if not for the way that her skin burned where his bare fingers had brushed against in a fleeting ghost of a touch.

"Cheer up," he said, unfolding himself to his full height once more. "I have an idea."

He held a hand out to her. She stared at it, confused. A faint pink flush seeped onto the tops of his cheeks and his hand dropped back to his side. It was only then that she realized he'd been aiming to help her up.

Talasyn felt her own face growing warm as she scrambled to her feet. "Where are we going?"

"I found an amphitheater." Alaric didn't look at her as he went over to his pack and rummaged through it for his gauntlets. "Let's spar."

The amphitheater was a perfect circle sunk into a stretch of overgrown wild grass, its sloping walls composed of sandstone steps and hundreds of carved seats. The floor at the bottom was covered in deep gouges, the remnants of Lightweaver duels past.

Amidst the marks of old battles, they faced each other from across a distance. Talasyn seemed a little tentative, a little uncertain, fidgeting with the brown leather gloves and arm wraps that she'd donned for this session.

"I haven't sparred in months," she went on to explain. "Not since—that day."

The day Sardovia fell.

She didn't say it out loud. She didn't need to. The unspoken weight of it darkened the air, another dose of reality piercing Alaric's sun-drenched bubble just as much as his father's summons had.

"Then it is all the more imperative that we do this," he said, before the atmosphere could get *too* tense and accusing. "Sharpening old skills might allow you to tap into new ones. We've already tried everything else."

Talasyn blew out a breath. She rolled her graceful neck and stretched her slender arms, a spark of that old familiar annoyance with him lurking behind freckled features that were making a valiant attempt to remain neutral.

It's for the best, Alaric thought. She could channel those emotions into their duel, maybe even successfully shield because of it. This was all working out according to plan.

What Alaric hadn't planned on was Talasyn shucking off her tunic, revealing her breastband and the upper half of those *infernal* tight breeches. His gaze flickered over the hard plane of her bare midriff and the slight flare of her hips and all that lustrous olive skin, slicked with the beginnings of sweat in the merciless sunlight.

He was well aware that she only meant to move more freely in the tropical heat.

But there was a part of him that couldn't help but think that she was tormenting him on purpose.

He opened the Shadowgate, shaping it into a curved sword in one gauntleted hand, a shield in the other. She spun her usual two daggers with a glare that *dared* him to say something about it.

"You're free to do whatever you wish, but at least try to transmute that"—he gestured at the blade in her left hand—"into a shield when you can. And keep it up. Now, since it *has* been a while, shall I go easy on you, Your Grace?"

He'd added that last part for no reason other than to make her mad, and he would have felt vaguely ashamed of himself if she hadn't risen to his challenge, sweeping her right foot back, arcing one dagger over her head and lifting the other in front of her, one side crackling toward him with lethal promise.

"Have at it, old man," she spat.

He fought back a grin.

They lunged at the same time, Alaric swinging his sword to meet Talasyn's dagger as she brought it down in an overhead strike. She turned on her left heel and he sprang away just in time to avoid her right leg smashing into his ribs, countering with a thrust that she blocked with her other dagger.

"Bit rusty," he quipped, meeting her gaze through the sheen of light and shadow.

"Yes, you are," she loftily agreed without missing a beat. She used their blade-lock as leverage to launch away and then assaulted him with a barrage of strikes so quick and ferocious that he was soon left with no other option but to shove her from him with a shapeless blast of shadow magic.

She skidded backwards several feet.

"You could have fended that off with a shield," he smugly informed her.

"Noted," she said through clenched teeth, before charging at him once more.

For Alaric, it was a beautiful, terrible thing, he and Talasyn dancing around each other and meeting in the middle, again and again and again, fiery little charges of static exploding between them every time their bodies brushed. His veins were alight with a wild exhilaration that he saw mirrored on her face beneath the brilliant sun of afternoon. They anticipated each other's every move and they pushed each other to the limit, the ancient amphitheater reverberating with the roar of magic, the raw power that came bursting in from aetherspace.

Now he understood why she fought as she did—after the life she'd had. In his mind's eye she was a child, scrappy and defiant, stealing out the door with a kitchen knife under her threadbare coat that offered poor protection from the howling ice-winds of the Great Steppe. Here and now, amidst the ruins, she was a war goddess, moving to the beat of a primal hymn.

You're just like me, Alaric thought, uncertain whether the revelation soothed or unsettled him. *We're both hungry.*

We both want to prove ourselves.

Talasyn felt happy.

No—*happy* couldn't even *begin* to describe it. This was *ecstasy*, pure and unbridled, light screaming against shadow, her body falling into all the old forms as she was pitted against another aethermancer after so, *so* long.

At some point down the line, she and Alaric had abandoned chasing each other all over the amphitheater. Now they were fighting in close quarters, loath to separate, the combined heat from their magic within millimeters of singeing her skin. His gray eyes blazed silver and his smirk was wicked; he was taking a twisted delight in this, just as she was. She knew that she should at least *attempt* to shield, but what if it faltered again and the shadows hurt her? And besides, there was some yawning abyss in her soul that insisted she could overpower him if she just moved a little faster, struck a little harder—

But there was such a thing as striking *too* hard.

Her dagger slammed into his shield and he stepped away faster than she expected. She'd put all of her strength into the blow and so she stumbled, one of her two blades disappearing at the loss in concentration. Alaric had stretched out his blade arm just behind her in preparation for his next attack, and she ended up turning into the crook of his elbow.

Talasyn's waist was suddenly encased in the steely curve of Alaric's arm, her side pressed up against his hard chest, her dagger humming at his neck, his sword almost cradling her chin. The two of them were flushed and panting. His skin was hot and sweat-damp against hers. *This is what it's like to burn,* she thought, listening to the growl of the Shadowgate, the high hum of the Lightweave, the skittering rhythm of Alaric's ragged breath above her ear.

"You've been fighting your whole life," he rasped in a low, unsteady voice that sounded not quite like his own and also, somehow, like the truest version of him. "Your instinct is to strike first, before anyone can hurt you. But sometimes it's the blow that molds us." The words were traced in vibrations of air that fanned against her temple as his sword inched up, narrowing the distance between its serrated shadowy edge and the line of her jaw. "Taking it. Letting it ring against our defenses, until we are assured in the knowledge that, when it's over, we will still be standing."

Her toes curled. She shifted her dagger closer to his throat, the motion echoed by her hip sliding against his groin. The shield in his left hand disappeared—why, after all that talk of defenses?—and then he was touching her, the leather of his gauntlet splayed out on her stomach, his thumb grazing the edge of her breastband.

What if he removed his gauntlets?

How would his bare fingers feel, spanning her like this?

Talasyn couldn't think clearly. The thrill of combat had morphed into something infinitely more dangerous. She was so *aware* of Alaric, of how his frame engulfed hers, of how tense his sinews were next to her own.

He exhaled. She turned her head to peer up at him, and the sight stopped her heart.

The look on his face was winter storm and wolf song.

"Your move, Lachis'ka," he murmured, his silver eyes flickering to her mouth.

"You first, Your Majesty," she whispered, without knowing *why* she was whispering or even why she'd whispered *that*, and in the end—

In the end, it didn't matter. They moved at the same time, her dagger sliding against the flat of his sword, sending up a spray of static and aether sparks. He leaned down and she surged up and their lips met, in the glow of light and darkness, over the keening of their crossed blades.

CHAPTER THIRTY-TWO

Alaric had never kissed anyone before and he *certainly* hadn't planned on kissing Talasyn. There was an entire host of reasons not to.

But all logic, any reservations that he might have had—they vanished into the aether the moment that he slanted his mouth over hers. The shadow-sword in his hand was extinguished at the same time as her golden dagger, and she turned fully into his arms and he tugged her close.

He might not have planned on it, but he had wanted it. So badly. He could admit it to himself now, now that her skin was heated and slick against his, now that she was returning his kiss with a clumsy, untutored desperation that mirrored his own.

The sun bore down upon them. It burned against his lids, long after he had closed his eyes. In obeisance to some age-old impulse, his tongue lapped at the seam of her lips and they parted for him in a gasp, allowing him to slide further into her mouth.

This, to him, was a continuation of their duel. It felt the same—angry and frenetic, blood roaring in his ears, passion blotting out all else. Talasyn tasted like iris petals and ginger tea. She was molten light in his hands, all slender planes and soft angles, her fingers tangling in his hair.

I never knew, Alaric thought, kissing her harder, holding her tighter. *I never knew that it could feel like this.*

It was not a sweet kiss. Talasyn would have been foolish to deem Alaric Ossinast capable of sweetness, but she'd heard that first kisses were supposed to be sweet. *This* was violent, almost brutal. His lips were as soft as they looked, but they were relentless. Furious. And she couldn't help but give as good as she got, just as she'd done her whole life.

It was sloppy at first, their teeth clacking together, leading her to suspect that he probably also hadn't done much of this before, if at all. But eventually they fell into a rhythm, they let instinct be their guide. After all, this was just another kind of war. His tongue tangled with hers and he nibbled at her bottom lip and a pair of hands so much larger than her own were wandering down her torso, fumbling and exploring.

Take off your gauntlets, she wanted to command, because she needed more of this skin-to-skin feeling, she needed *everything,* but words were impossible when his eager mouth was swallowing every sound she made. And perhaps there *was* something to be said for the leather, the roughness of it on her spine, on the jut of her hips. Another layer of sensation adding to the wicked onslaught. There was a dark thrill building up inside her; there was a dampness between her legs. His hand slid down her backside and cupped her there and she *moaned* against his lips; in response, he kissed her so deeply that she could no longer tell where she ended and where he began, and her heart was unfurling in her chest, opening itself up to the high dive, the free fall—

A sound like rolling thunder broke the stillness of the mountaintop.

She wrenched her mouth from his. At first, Talasyn believed

that it was her pulse she was hearing, pounding in her ears as Alaric held her captive in his arms. But then she saw the splinters of gold reflected in the bright steel of his irises, and they both turned their heads in the direction of the cacophony.

From their campsite—from the courtyard—a pillar of molten radiance the color of the sun shot up to the azure heavens, gilding the treetops and the weathered stone. Filling the air with its raw hum for miles upon miles around.

The Light Sever was discharging.

Talasyn pulled away from him in an instant, and Alaric reeled at the sudden loss of her, his body impulsively bowing forward to find her again. But she was gone, racing back to the campsite, her eyes only on the soaring column of light. Alaric followed her on shaking legs that felt barely attached to his body. He felt as if he were floating—and *not* in a good way. He was disoriented from how quickly his blood had flowed south.

When they stepped into the courtyard, the whole place was ablaze, the pillar of golden magic at its center so bright that it hurt to look at, so tall that it disappeared into the clouds. However, its width at the base was precisely contained within the fountain, bright fumes spilling like water from the stone jaws of the dragonhead spouts.

The fountain's structure was completely undamaged by the magic. It was nothing short of an architectural feat. The ancient Lightweavers of Nenavar had to have painstakingly mapped out every inch of where aetherspace tore into the material world, crafting the stone around it. They were the same people who had covered this shrine in intricate reliefs, lovingly telling the stories of their land in joyful detail.

It was difficult to believe that they were the same breed of aethermancer who had killed Alaric's grandfather and nearly destroyed Kesath.

Alaric pushed these thoughts that bordered on treason to the back of his mind, but that only allowed more space to recall Talasyn's body, how she had fit against him like a missing piece.

He stopped a few paces behind her as she approached the Light Sever slowly, so slowly, as though she were in a trance. If it was anything at all like a Shadow Sever, the magic would be tugging at her and her heart would be lifting like that of a mariner spying the gleaming shores of home.

But, only a breath away from the radiant pillar, she stopped. She looked back at him, her chestnut hair blowing in an unnatural breeze. She seemed unsure, almost frightened.

Her lips were still swollen from his kisses.

"It's all right," he said thickly over the roar of the Lightweave. How strange it was, to be sought out for reassurance. How new it was, to be looked at as anything other than a conqueror. "Just walk into it. You'll know what to do once you get there."

Talasyn nodded, holding Alaric's gaze for a few moments before turning back to the Light Sever. But *his* gaze remained fixed on her until she vanished from sight, her slight figure swallowed up by magic.

To enter a Light Sever was to dive headfirst into an ocean of sunshine.

And it was—*wonderful.*

Talasyn was submerged in light. It warmed every inch of her skin and flowed into her veins. It bathed her soul in radiant splendor.

And yet it was also a rush to the head, magnified. It was her aethermancy in its purest form, the rapture that swirled through her so intense that she was almost terrified of it. Of how much her heart could hold.

But fear was a fleeting, paltry thing in this place. She felt as if she could do anything. She *could* do anything.

She *understood.*

From afar, the nexus point had looked like a solid column

of light, threaded through with aetherspace's silver fumes. Now that she was right in the thick of it, Talasyn saw that it was composed of thousands, *millions*, of fine golden strands. She touched them and they sang like harp strings. She coaxed them in any direction that she wished, all of it shifting and shining and dancing in luminous tapestries everywhere she turned.

And from each string, a memory unspooled.

Alaric had once predicted that the heart of a nexus point could tether an aethermancer more strongly to the past, and he had been right. Moments long forgotten, things she had *wanted* to forget— they were so much more solid now. They came flooding back to her with sharp clarity; they came to life in whorls of aether's thread. Scenes from her childhood, no longer diluted by time. A lullaby in what she knew beyond a shadow of a doubt was her mother's voice, clear and pure. Hunger pangs in her belly and her fingertips made of ice in the winter. Her boots hitting the ground after her first aerial battle, quickly followed by a splash of vomit, and Khaede patting her back in wordless reassurance. The first time Sol ever spoke to her, marking their beginning as amiable moons in Khaede's orbit—and the ending of that story, his body unmoving on the airship deck.

And then she saw Alaric. Not the man she had left waiting in the courtyard, but the skeletal figure with the snarling wolf's mask and the clawed gauntlets that she'd fought at Lasthaven. The Shadowgate swirled around him, etched in distant lightning, the air cold with the oncoming rains. His crackling blade was tinted crimson in the glow of the eclipse, as red as the blood of everyone who'd died.

"It's over," the apparition said, the words drawn up from the deep well of the past, his voice so strangely soft. At the time, she had puzzled over that tone, unused to anything but lethal calculation from the Kesathese prince. Now she knew him better.

It's over. He had been imploring her to surrender as the Allfold's last bastion fell to the hurricanes.

But he had been wrong. It wasn't over, yet. Not for Sardovia. Not for Nenavar. Not for her.

Show me, she thought. *Teach me how to not strike first. I want to learn to take the blow. I want to protect everything I hold dear. I won't let the Shadow fall.*

Be it World-Eater or Night Empire.

And the Lightweave hummed and raged. It did as she commanded.

Light magic is evil, Alaric's father had told him when he was a boy. *It is the weapon of our enemies. It burns and it blinds. This is why we destroyed the Light Severs on the Continent; they fueled those who sought to steal our stormship technology and bend us to their will. The Lightweave cannot be gentled or appeased. It won't be content until it has cast its harsh glare over everything.*

Alaric had always believed that, and he could still see it here and now on Belian in the way that the Light Sever seared his skin and eyes even from across a distance. It was too sharp, too unforgiving. Nothing at all like the soft coolness of the Shadowgate.

He reviled this form of magic—he *should* revile it—but—

—when the Light Sever finally began collapsing in on itself, folding down from the heavens and back into the earth—

—when the girl in the middle of the fountain turned to him with golden eyes and golden veins running throughout her olive skin, the strands of chestnut hair escaping her braid suffused with light as well—

—when she held up her hand and conjured a solid, blazing shield, not teardrop-shaped like the ones of the Continent but long and rectangular and forked with prongs atop and at its base, like those the Nenavarene wielded—

393

—he could only think that she was beautiful. Every part of her was beautiful.

When Talasyn returned to the world of the overgrown stone courtyard on Belian, the high hum of the Lightweave was still pounding in her ears.

Alaric stood where she'd left him. The molten glow of her light-spun shield flickered over his silhouette, memory and reality juxtaposed like spots behind her eyes. His Shadowforged armor, his weapon, his father's stormships, everything that had been lost.

She dropped her arm and the shield dispelled. The rush of the Light Sever went quiet, and the afterimages vanished.

Alaric became solid again. He was watching her closely, beads of sweat from the Sever's heat glinting on his pale brow. This wasn't the deadly specter from Lasthaven. Yet, she could only stare at him in dawning horror.

He was a few paces away, waiting for her to make the first move. He looked as if he wanted to ask her what had happened—but she couldn't explain all that she had seen. Those memories belonged to her alone. And even more, they had reminded her of the horrible misstep she had just made.

What had she done?

There was no rational explanation for that kiss. None of it could be forgiven. She would have to return to Eskaya burdened by the knowledge that she'd had the Night Emperor's tongue in her mouth. The next time she faced the Sardovian remnant, it would be with the memory of the Night Emperor's hand on her ass.

And she'd liked it.

Gods, what had possessed her, what was possessing her, why had it turned out this way?

"I . . ." Talasyn scrambled for something to say to make him stop looking at her like that. "I made a shield."

Alaric nodded, the corner of his mouth ticking downward. Almost as though he'd wanted her to say something else. "You did."

"I'll try to make one again."

So she spent the rest of the afternoon coaxing the Lightweave into shields of various shapes and sizes. For the sheer joy of doing it, of finally being able to do it, yes—but also for the more than reasonable excuse it provided to not acknowledge Alaric's presence.

For his part, he kept well to the other side of the courtyard, as far from her as possible. She thought she could feel his gaze burning against her back, but whenever she darted a glance his way, he was carefully occupied with something else. She surmised he was doing his best to ignore her existence as well. She even surreptitiously caught him trying to clear their campsite of fallen leaves with a stick. Eventually he gave up and left, vanishing into one of the shrine's many half-collapsed corridors with some excuse about exploring the ruins further.

Once the sky had darkened, Talasyn crawled into her bedroll, hoping to fall asleep before Alaric returned. Her mind was a torrent of conflicting emotions, and her magic thrummed, restless in her veins, as she tossed and turned beneath a diamantine panorama of moons and stars.

As she lay there, a tantalizing possibility broke through the mire of her confusion and her guilt. If she went on communing with the Light Sever, would she be able to go even further back? Would she be able to access more memories of her mother, beyond the scent of berries and the echo of a lullaby? Would Hanan Ivralis spring to life in her mind? Would it be enough?

She was still wide awake when the sound of Alaric's footsteps padded into the courtyard. She squeezed her eyes shut, pretending to be fast asleep, listening to the rustle of fabric as he slipped into his own bedroll.

Then his deep, mildly admonishing tone sliced through the silence. "I can *hear* you thinking over there."

She rolled onto her side so that she could glare at him, only to jolt when she found him already facing her. His gray eyes gleamed starkly against his pale face in the moonlight.

Another memory washed over her, far more recent. The amphitheater. His teeth nipping at her bottom lip. Each caress of his hands.

The smart thing to do now was to stop looking at him, because looking at him and the way he was too big for his bedroll did nothing to ease her racing thoughts. Instead, Talasyn continued staring into Alaric's eyes, over stone and night, until he asked, "What is it?"

He sounded defensive, as though he already knew what was on her mind.

Willing herself not to blush, she blurted out the first safe topic that she could conceive of. "Do you really think that we can stop the Voidfell?"

"Yes," he said without hesitation. "You know how to weave a shield and we have a few months to prepare. It will be all right. Otherwise, we're all dead."

"How inspirational, truly," she sniped.

"I try."

A fraught quiet seeped in once more, and she turned back onto her side, peering up into the silver-black night. The minutes stretched on, and just when Talasyn thought that sleep had claimed him, Alaric spoke again. "I remember being lonely."

She went still. "What?"

"You asked me, back when we began aethermancing at the royal palace, what I remember from my childhood. That is what I remember. Loneliness." She craned her neck toward him again and he flashed her a rueful half-smile. "I am my father's only child, and he demanded that I apply myself to my studies and my training. I was the Night Emperor's heir, and so my

396

companions could not truly be friends. Even Sevraim knows where the lines are drawn." He paused, weighing his next words. And when they finally came, they sounded as though they were being drawn up from the deep well of an old heartache. "My mother was kind but unhappy. I think that she found it difficult to look at me and see what was tying her to her marriage."

Any illusions Talasyn had about Alaric's pampered childhood were being dashed. Now she understood why he'd spoken with such unbridled contempt for marriage that day on his stormship. And, gods, despite everything, despite knowing what a terrible thing she'd done when she kissed him, she was powerless in the face of his vulnerability; she was greedy for more. She didn't think that she could bear it if he turned cold now.

"Why are you telling me this?" she heard herself ask.

He shrugged. "It's only fair. You trusted me with that glimpse of you growing up, the knife . . . My experiences pale in comparison to yours, but they're what I have. So I'll trust you with them as well."

A piercing bittersweetness twinged through her. She thought about the night of the duel without bounds, how alone he'd looked as he faced down Surakwel in front of the entire Nenavarene court. She attempted to gather herself, to focus on keeping her priorities straight, but it was all starlight and confession; it was as though a hand were reaching out to hold hers across all the wasteland years.

"I was lonely, too." She was too afraid to add *I still am.* "I was on my own on the streets. I kept waiting for my family to come back, but they never did. Even when I joined the Sardovian regiments, I still waited. It's probably not something that you ever truly grow out of."

"Do you remember your mother?" His tone was wistful in the dark.

"Not really," she said, but the sound of Hanan's voice inside the Sever rushed back into her ears. She wasn't ready to part with that secret yet, but it felt wrong to dismiss what little else she had. "I know what she looked like because of aethergraphs and formal portraits. When I think about her hard enough, I can smell wild berries. That's mostly it. Although . . ." She blinked hurriedly, before a sudden rush of tears could wet her eyes. "The day I first set foot on Nenavarene soil, I had a—I'm not sure if it was a vision or a memory, or a waking dream, but there was someone telling me that we would find each other again. Maybe that was her, or maybe that never happened and I made it all up."

"It was her," Alaric said, with such gentle firmness, such surety that it couldn't be otherwise, that it was as though a sun were rising in Talasyn's heart. She wanted to stay forever in this tranquil night. She wanted to keep on talking to him about anything and everything, about their magic, about what they'd lost, about the stars and gods and shores they shared—

But she couldn't talk to him about *everything*.

If Alaric ever found out that Talasyn's mother had played an instrumental role in sending Nenavarene warships to the Continent nineteen years ago, to help the same aethermancers who had killed his grandfather—and once the Sardovian remnant made their move and he learned that Nenavar had been sheltering them in the Storm God's Eye—that would be the death blow to any budding intimacy that Talasyn forged with him.

Here she was, letting her guard down with Alaric, *panting after him*, while her Sardovian comrades hunkered down on Sigwad. While the Continent suffered under his empire's cruelty.

Wasn't that what the Lightweave had been telling her, when it showed her that image from Lasthaven? He was the enemy. And he might have lost his mother and his grandfather, but *she* had lost people, too.

Because of Kesath. Because of him.

Enough now. The inside of her chest grew tight. *No more.*

You can't have impossible things.

"In the regiments, I made one friend. Her name was Khaede. She was the one who told me that the Voidfell could be seen from the Sardovian Coast," said Talasyn. "She didn't connect it to the sevenfold eclipse, and I doubt she believed that the amethyst light on the horizon was anything more than an old wives' tale until I came back from Nenavar with news of void magic. But we *did* make plans, years ago, for the Moonless Dark. If there was no battle, if we were stationed in the same place, we'd camp outdoors, in the woods or on a hill somewhere, and we'd stay up until the moons shone again."

Talasyn spoke with the clarity of memory that the Sever had granted her. That day had long been buried by the endless horror and violence of the Hurricane Wars, but it was now solid and vibrant in her recollections—the crowded and noisy mess hall, Khaede speaking with her mouth full, alight with rare excitement as she talked about the night no moons would rise after the going down of the sun. About how she and Talasyn would experience this once-in-several-generations occurrence together. That plan had later changed to include Sol, months after he and Khaede had shot down a wolf coracle and he sailed past a jessamine tree, plucking one of the blossoms and handing it to her as their ships passed each other while their fallen enemy spiraled toward the waiting valley below.

"We won't be able to do that now, of course," Talasyn continued in what was barely above a whisper. "After the battle of Lasthaven, I never saw Khaede again. She was the only friend I ever made, and now I don't even know if she's alive, if the baby she was carrying is all right. Probably not." The words hitched in her throat. It was the first time that she'd ever given voice to this fear. "Your soldiers killed so many of us, after all."

A heavy silence fell. It dragged on for a long time, the charged stillness following a peal of thunder frozen into eternity. A sharp ache sank its hooked barbs into Talasyn's being as she realized that, the night Surakwel smuggled her out of the palace and into the Storm God's eye, she hadn't even thought to ask Vela if the aetherwave had picked up any sign of Khaede.

At some point, without her even being fully aware of it, she had already given up her friend for lost.

That was what the war had done. It had turned people into statistics. It had taken away hope and turned it into something to be buried until there were only bones.

"Talasyn." Her name was low and stricken on Alaric's tongue. "I—"

Time moved again.

"No." A rush of unshed tears pricked at her eyes, but she refused to let them spill. She would never cry before him; she owed Khaede and everyone who had died that much. How could she have forgotten, even just for brief moments over the last few days, that Alaric was the face of Sardovia's downfall? How did the memories of Khaede and Sol and Blademaster Kasdar not burn with her every breath? "Let's just not talk at all."

He sat up, narrowing his eyes at her. They weren't filled with the cold, quiet kind of anger that she'd come to associate with him and only him. There was a wild glint in them, a recklessness. "What about what happened in the amphitheater? Don't you think we should talk about *that*?"

"There's no need to discuss it," Talasyn said stiffly. "It was an aberration."

"An aberration that you enjoyed, if I recall."

"I rather think that *you* were enjoying it more!" Incensed, she rolled over onto her other side so that she wouldn't have to be plagued by the sight of him. Still, his piercing scrutiny raked pinpricks along the back of her neck. "Daya Langsoune once told me that hate is another kind of passion. I was carried away by the duel. I got my wires crossed. That's all."

"It was the same for me as well," Alaric spat without hesitation, and, *oh*, how it hurt. Her chest rang with the blow. It was nothing more than an agreement with what she'd said, but she knew that there was one striking difference.

He was telling the truth. He didn't even find her passing tolerable when she wasn't dressed up.

Of the two of them, she was the only one who short-circuited every time the other drew breath. Or flashed a rare half-smile.

"Why did Daya Langsoune tell you that?" Alaric suddenly asked, his tone brimming with suspicion.

"She was teasing me," Talasyn muttered. "About you."

There was an elegant scoff from the silver-lit gloom behind her. It showed just how little he thought of that, and the ache inside her only heightened.

I am a traitor. Talasyn furtively, furiously scrubbed the welling tears from her eyes, before they could spill down her face and over the lips that still twinged with the memory of how Alaric's had felt against them. *Hanging is too good for me.*

The too-bright sun of a Nenavarene morning pounded against his face, and Alaric woke up the same way he'd fallen asleep—bewildered, furious, and regretful.

Last night, he had allowed himself to get caught up in the moment, to fall under the sway of the false sense of closeness brought about by being alone with Talasyn amidst these isolated ruins. He had been lured into complacency by her lovely face, her sharp wit, her fire. By that searing kiss, and the scent of mangoes and promise jasmines. He hadn't been thinking with his *brain*, as his father would have said. And thus he had lowered his guard, confessing harrowing truths to her that he had never told anyone else.

What had it all been for? What had been the point, if she couldn't forget the past? If she saved it all up to confront him with it when he was at his most vulnerable?

Alaric was distantly aware that this line of thinking was nothing short of reprehensible in light of what Talasyn had gone through. He even understood, on some level, that he was hiding behind this smallness so that he wouldn't have to confront the crushing guilt that she had brought out in him by giving the Hurricane Wars a human name. But he went ahead and thought these things anyway, because rulers of victorious nations did *not* grovel for forgiveness after the fact—and from former enemies whose side had been equally ruthless during a ten-year conflict, to boot.

He feared, though, that he would end up doing just that, or something similarly foolish, although few things could beat confiding to her about his parents and expressing sentiments that he had never voiced to another living soul—*after* he had kissed her until he was senseless. Alaric was genuinely worried as to what other acts of idiocy he would commit if he stayed any longer on this mountain, alone with his betrothed and her accursed freckles. Although surely there was nothing more idiotic than being attracted to someone who would, as he'd told Sevraim, never be able to separate him from the Hurricane Wars.

Thus, it was with some relief that Alaric watched Talasyn stash away her bedroll, the kettle, and all the camping supplies after their painfully silent breakfast and realized that she was packing up for good.

"We're leaving?"

She jerked her head in a brusque nod. "We got what we came for. I see no reason to spend another day here."

He ignored the flickering bloom of an ache that dug through him, as sharp as talons. "As you wish."

CHAPTER THIRTY-THREE

There was a freshly drawn tub waiting in Talasyn's bathroom at the Roof of Heaven. Jie—who had been quite aghast at the prospect of the Lachis'ka gallivanting about in the woods—had even sprinkled yellow custard-apple petals all over the surface of the water, and they gave off a sweet perfume in addition to the scented oils and herbal soaps.

Talasyn soaked in the marble tub until her skin pruned, brooding in a way that would have put Alaric to shame. They'd exchanged few words on the hike to the garrison, and fewer still on the airship voyage back to Eskaya. At least he had then promptly departed for his stormship with the excuse of having urgent matters to work on and she wouldn't have to see him again until the eclipse, when they were to create the barrier so that the Dominion Enchanters could study it.

That gave her some time to firmly anchor him in her mind as someone around whom she couldn't let her guard down. To forget everything that had happened between them on Belian.

I'm sorry, she told Khaede. The Khaede who lived in her head, who might be dead now, for all that Talasyn knew.

There was no response—she was too overwrought even to

dream up what kind of response her friend would give—and there in the safety of the perfumed water she finally let a few tears fall.

With Commodore Mathire attending to business on her flagship, Alaric and Sevraim comprised the entirety of the Kesathese contingent who, on the night of the eclipse, strode out into the same atrium that had been the site of a failed barrier demonstration—and would soon hopefully be the site of a successful one—to find that the Dominion's Enchanters had been hard at work on . . . *something*.

Ishan Vaikar cheerfully explained the mechanics of the amplifying configuration to him as she and her people arranged the wires and shifted the metalglass jars to form a perfect circle big enough for two people to step into.

Sevraim went to take a closer look; then he returned to Alaric's side with a shrug. "It's probably *not* a murder device, but I say that we let them try it out on your lovely wife-to-be first—"

"Try *what* out on me?"

Sevraim snapped to attention and Alaric went rigid. Talasyn had snuck up on them, as quiet as a cat. Jaw clenched, Alaric turned to look at her for the first time since they had returned from the Belian range.

The wild soldier with the unkempt braid and the mud-spattered breeches had been banished. In her place, trailed by her taciturn guards, stood the Nenavarene Lachis'ka in a crown of hummingbirds and rose mallows wrought from gold.

Alaric cast around for a suitably wry remark, but Talasyn's brown eyes slid away from him to some point over his shoulder. A throb of disappointment sliced through him, nauseating in its ferocity.

Talasyn didn't seem to be all that surprised by the amplifying configuration, but she was probably used to Nenavarene ingenuity by now. She went over to Ishan and they spoke quietly, and, after a while, Alaric joined them.

"Sariman blood, Daya Vaikar?" he queried, glancing at one of the shimmering molten sapphire-and-scarlet cores in the jars. "Do you kill them?"

"Absolutely not!" Ishan looked scandalized by the mere prospect. "The blood is extracted from young and healthy specimens by only the most well trained of handlers. It's against Nenavarene law to kill an aether-touched creature for any purpose other than self-defense."

Alaric found himself thinking about the chimera on Kesath's imperial seal. Once plentiful on the Continent, the beast had been hunted in droves for its leonine fur and the medicinal properties of its antelope hooves and eel scales, as well as the sheer glory of slaying one. The last chimera sighting had been a century ago. It had always seemed like a shame to him, and he wondered if he could introduce a law similar to what Ishan had just described.

Surveying the amplifying configuration one last time, Ishan gave a satisfied nod and gestured for Talasyn and Alaric to step into the circle of jars and filaments.

When a moon was in its eclipse phase, it rose over the Continent already a blood-red or silver-gray orb, and it could take minutes to hours before it reverted to its normal state. Here on the Dominion archipelago, where they were several hours ahead of the Continent, they would bear witness to the whole process from beginning to end. Tonight would be an Eclipse of the First, the largest of the seven, and as she rose to her highest point above the panorama of her ghostly sisters the courtyard shone nearly as white as pristine snow.

Talasyn had never seemed as far away from Alaric as she did now, even though they stood within the circle side by side, almost close enough to touch.

"Shouldn't be long," said Ishan. She had brought six other

Enchanters with her and they stationed themselves several paces away, each one standing parallel to a jar. "Let's wait until the First is partially obscured."

The next few minutes passed in silence, with everyone in the atrium looking up at the full moon. And then, slowly, a wash of inky darkness unfurled over its glistening white surface, and bit by bit it melted into the surrounding night sky. Nibbled at by the sun god's peckish lion, or gradually engulfed by the reptilian jaws of Bakun mourning his lost love.

Perhaps it was all the same, in the end. Stories to tell around the fire and put children to bed the world over. Perhaps more than one thing could be true at the same time, when they were the folktales that made a nation. Perhaps the great lion still snarled down at Alaric even though he was in a land far away from his gods.

"*Now*," said Ishan Vaikar.

In unison, Talasyn and Alaric stretched out their hands in front of them and ripped away the veil of aetherspace. She was his radiant mirror, a shield of light pouring forth from her fingertips while his shadowy creation sparked and hissed in response. Their eyes met and they brought their magic together, and underneath the Eclipse of the First that black-gold sphere bloomed to encase them.

Ishan and the other Enchanters moved in unison as well, arms and wrists flowing like water in arcane patterns. The cores of sariman blood and rain magic within the metalglass jars suddenly flared as bright as tiny suns, the glow filling up their containers and spilling out, running through the wires.

Before Alaric could even blink, the sphere that he and Talasyn had made expanded to cover the whole atrium.

Everything was aether. Everything was light and shadow and rain and blood. Alaric's magic was screaming through the air, carried on weightless, jeweled wings, stronger than he ever thought possible. *Amplified.*

It was the signal that the palace guards on the surrounding battlements and balconies had been instructed to wait for. They took aim with their muskets and they fired down into the atrium in a conflagration of amethyst bolts. Each bolt was ineffectual. Each bolt crashed into the barrier and disappeared.

So this was what it was like when a country hadn't spent the last decade at war. When their Enchanters weren't focused on powering stormships. When metalworkers and glass-smiths weren't kept busy creating and repairing frigates and coracles and weapons.

This was what could be achieved.

This was what the Continent had lost in its nation-states tearing one another apart.

"I know," Talasyn murmured. Alaric couldn't pinpoint the exact moment when he'd turned to look at her, when they'd turned to look at each other. But they were doing so now, and her brown eyes were fiery with magic, with wonder, with regret.

"I didn't say anything," he protested.

"You didn't have to," she told him, under these black-gold nets, under this mottled eclipse. "It's written all over your face."

I could kill him, she thought. *Here and now.*

No one could penetrate the sphere. No one would be able to stop her.

If she managed to catch him by surprise, if she moved fast enough to slip a light-woven dagger between his ribs, she would be able to avenge Khaede and everyone else.

But there was the Night of the World-Eater to consider. There was the long game.

And, yet, that wasn't all that stayed her hand.

Talasyn had cut the Belian sojourn short to stop things from becoming too complicated. Now, looking into Alaric's silver eyes, looking at his moon-kissed face reflecting the molten panels of black and gold that were swirling all around them, she feared that it was already too late.

She saw the Night Emperor. She saw the boy who had shared her loneliness. She saw the Master of the Shadowforged Legion she had battled on the ice and amidst a ruined city through which the stormships raged. She saw the man who had chucked her under the chin, who had so patiently taught her how to make a shield, whose dry remarks had sometimes made her laugh. She saw her first kiss, the first time someone else's hands had touched her and made her burn.

She saw danger, in more ways than one.

Eventually, the barrier vanished. Talasyn wasn't sure whether it was Alaric or an Enchanter or her own self who had lost concentration first. It was just a good thing that the guards on the battlements had already stopped firing.

In any case, Ishan was pleased. "Almost six minutes, Your Grace!" She beamed at Talasyn while Sevraim rushed over to make certain that Alaric was all right. "Of course, on the Night of the World-Eater, the Void Sever will flare for an hour or so, and this entire courtyard is only a *fraction* of its range, but you will have almost five months to practice keeping up your shields and you may rest assured that we in Ahimsa will use this time to devise even bigger and better amplifying configurations."

"If anyone can do it, it's you and your people, Daya Vaikar," Talasyn said sincerely.

Ishan ducked her head in a brief half-bow, which was how the Nenavarene tended to respond to praise. However, her excitement remained palpable. "I look forward to reporting these results to the Zahiya-lachis."

Acting on a hunch, Talasyn searched the surrounding towers. There, in one of the highest windows, illuminated by a rectangle of warm lamplight, she caught a crowned silhouette in the act of moving away. "Something tells me," she said wryly, "that Her Starlit Majesty might already have an idea."

CHAPTER THIRTY-FOUR

The days flew by, everyone focused on the upcoming wedding. The remainder of the planning passed without incident, save for a minor wrinkle when the subject of the consummation night cropped up. Talasyn felt that she and Alaric would have handled it a lot worse if Prince Elagbi hadn't warned them in advance that day on the stormship.

Of course, they would have handled it a lot *better* if they hadn't gotten started on the consummation that day in the amphitheater on Belian.

"Our newlyweds will leave the feast first, and His Majesty will allot her sufficient time to prepare before following her to her chambers," Lueve Rasmey was saying.

"Prepare," Talasyn echoed blankly.

"Well, you will need your lady's assistance, Lachis'ka," Niamha Langsoune clarified, "for the fastenings of the wedding gown are difficult to navigate—"

"I get the picture," Talasyn hastened to interrupt, willing herself not to flush scarlet. Alaric looked as though he'd been punched in the gut. "We can move on." She didn't say that they'd already agreed to share her quarters for the night and nothing more. Rajan Gitab was watching intently from behind

409

his spectacles, and Talasyn didn't want to give the opposition cause to question the validity of the marriage alliance.

Fortunately, at this point, Queen Urduja took over. "If His Majesty wishes to transfer any personal effects to Iantas, kindly inform Daya Rasmey, as she is in charge of coordinating with the steward there. We are almost done fixing up the place and it will be ready to move into after the nuptials."

Iantas was Talasyn's dowry, a sprawling castle on a small white-sand island. It had been ceded to Alaric as his permanent Nenavarene residence—and Talasyn's as well, at least until she ascended to the throne and had to hold court at the Roof of Heaven.

"It will be good for Alunsina to have some experience in running a household," Urduja continued. "Her upbringing certainly didn't lend itself to that sort of skill. And she is the youngest Lachis'ka in our recent history to get married."

Alaric worked a muscle in his jaw, and then he gave Urduja a stiff nod. He was taking great pains not to look in Talasyn's direction, and that was fine by her. In fact, if they could just ignore each other until Gaheris was taken care of and the Night Empire fell, that would be *wonderful*.

Like all other major royal ceremonies, the wedding would take place at the Starlight Tower in the heart of Eskaya, and activity in the area increased as it was spruced up and its perimeters were secured. In much the same manner, a veritable army of decorators and cleaners descended upon the grand ballroom of the Roof of Heaven, where the reception would be held, to make sure that no two specks of color clashed and that no single ornament was out of place and that no inch of marble floor went unpolished.

Talasyn spent most of her time attending fittings for her dress when she and Alaric weren't being walked through each step of the ceremony. Although she kept a composed facade in public, it was hard going as each sunrise brought her nearer and nearer to her marriage.

Marriage. Gods. Every once in a while, she pinched herself, hoping to wake up back in a Sardovian barracks room, but no such luck.

The day before the wedding, several Kesathese officers arrived in Eskaya to join Commodore Mathire and Sevraim in acting as witnesses to the ceremony. High up in a tower, Talasyn watched them disembark from their airships, unable to stop her hackles from rising. These people had been her enemies for five years and she instinctively categorized them as such. All it would take were a few well-placed ceramic shells to wipe out most of the Night Empire's High Command. Hell, if Urduja gave her soldiers the order to attack *right now*—

No. It would be for nothing. Gaheris wasn't here, apparently busy ruling in Alaric's absence.

There were other ways to wage war.

Talasyn had to be *patient.*

She continued watching as Alaric strode out to greet his officers. He acknowledged their salutes with a nod and proceeded to talk to them. In their dark, austerely tailored clothing, the Kesathese stuck out like a sore thumb amidst the ornate armor of the palace guards and the glittering outfits of the Dominion nobles.

She would never know if it had been just a matter of horrid timing or if Alaric had felt the weight of her stare in the way that all warriors could tell that they were being observed. Whatever the case, her betrothed suddenly looked up.

Looked right at her.

Talasyn quickly backed away from the window, color flooding her cheeks. *Why did you do that?* she just as quickly chided herself. She should have held her ground—so *what* if he caught her staring? She *lived* here, she could stare at anything she liked . . .

Shoulders squared in resolve, Talasyn darted forward, determined to glare at Alaric until he slunk away with his tail between his legs. However, when she returned to her original spot by the window, the last of the Night Empire delegation was already disappearing into the palace.

Common sense filtered back in. *What am I doing?* she wondered, in both dismay and disbelief at her own actions. She couldn't help but feel that she'd lost yet another round of this strange new battle that she and Alaric Ossinast had found themselves locked into. It didn't bode well for what was to come.

On her way back to her chambers, Talasyn ran into Kai Gitab in the Queenswalk, a long, carpeted hall where the marble walls were lined with enormous oil portraits of every Zahiya-lachis known to history. In comparison to most other locations in the palace, it was shielded from the sun by heavy drapes over the windows, to preserve the delicate art. The only illumination was in the form of the odd fire lamp here and there, adding to the eerie feeling that the beautiful faces in the gilded frames were watching one's every move.

Gitab was standing in front of the portrait of Magwayen Silim, Urduja's mother. He bowed to Talasyn as she approached. "Your Grace."

"Rajan Gitab," Talasyn replied in kind. There were no guards in this hall and she'd given her Lachis-dalo the slip earlier. She was alone with him, alone with a Dominion noble opposed to the alliance with Kesath. She wondered how deep his dissent went, and if he would dare to try anything the way that Surakwel had, but she figured that it couldn't hurt to be polite. "Thank you for all your hard work during the negotiations."

Gitab flashed a cool smile. "The triumph belongs to Daya Rasmey and Daya Langsoune. You and I both know that Her

Starlit Majesty only put me there so that I could report back to my fellow critics that nothing underhanded was in effect."

None of you told me about the Night of the World-Eater. Seemed plenty underhanded to me, Talasyn groused to herself, but it must have shown on her face because Gitab's dark eyes glinted behind his gold-rimmed spectacles as though he knew what she was thinking.

"Still," she persevered, rather valiantly in her opinion, through this patch of small talk that she was starting to suspect might be a field of caltrops in disguise, "it's over now."

"It is," said Gitab. "And thus a new age begins." He returned his gaze to the portrait, Talasyn following his line of sight. The previous Zahiya-lachis stared fiercely down at them, brown-haired and umber-skinned; while Urduja's crown appeared chiseled from ice, Magwayen's crown was a massive, fearsome thing wrought from thorns of iron and dark opals.

"Your great-grandmother was, by all accounts, a strong and capable ruler," Gitab told Talasyn. "Since she knew that the World-Eater would come during her daughter's reign, she spent her later years preparing the realm for it, preparing Queen Urduja for it. If this solution that you and the Night Emperor will employ fails, Nenavar will still make it through Dead Season thanks in no small part to the protocols and counter-measures that Magwayen devised."

"We won't fail," Talasyn assured him.

It will be all right, Alaric had said. *Otherwise, we're all dead.*

She determinedly banished his annoying voice from her head, where it tended to pop up at the most inopportune moments.

"Yes, I suppose that anything is possible with your kind of aethermancy, Lachis'ka. We shall see." If Gitab possessed any of the fear of the Lightweave and the Shadowgate that other Dominion nobles held, he didn't show it. He continued gazing at the portrait of Magwayen while Talasyn debated just walking away, as the conversation seemed to be at an end.

Gitab spoke again, however. "The sun began to set on the Silim dynasty when Queen Urduja birthed a second son, her second and last child. The day she sets sail with the ancestors, Your Grace, a new house will rise. One with your mother's name. Such is the way of our people."

Talasyn was brought up short. This was the first time she'd heard any noble at court mention Hanan Ivralis. Her mother was a taboo subject, along with the would-be usurper Prince Sintan. Mindful not to step on Urduja's toes, Talasyn only indulged her curiosity when she was alone with her father, and even then she never dug too deep, not wanting to cause Elagbi pain.

But her newly regained memory of Hanan singing a lullaby caused some rebellion to trickle in.

"Does it bother you?" she asked Gitab, hungry to know how he viewed Hanan, the woman whose actions had nearly toppled the Dragon Throne. "That it's an outsider's name?"

"I bear the late Lady Hanan no ill will and I am loyal to whom the ancestors bless," Gitab said solemnly. "Your grandmother and I have our differences, to be sure, but my duty will always be to what's best for Nenavar. And if there is a chance that Nenavar can be spared from Dead Season, then of course we must take it. But, after . . ." He lowered his voice. "You can count on me for *after,* Lachis'ka. I trust that we both have no wish to let the Shadow fall."

There was something of Surakwel Mantes in Gitab's face just then. The rajan was twice Surakwel's age and infinitely more softly spoken, but there were the embers of that same fire. A love of country. A firm belief in what was right.

He has earned a name for himself as incorruptible and devoted to his ideals, Elagbi had said. *With him on the panel, no one can accuse the Zahiya-lachis of selling out Nenavar.*

414

Talasyn warmed slightly toward Gitab. She couldn't trust him just yet, but it wasn't a bad idea to start paving the way for her own alliances within the Dominion court.

"I'll keep this in mind, my lord," she told him. He nodded, and she took her leave, walking down the hallway of portraits as he remained where he was, gazing up at the Queen of Thorns.

CHAPTER THIRTY-FIVE

The day of the royal wedding dawned bright and clear. Since the ceremony would be taking place at sunset, the guests started arriving shortly after the noon gongs struck. The skies above the Nenavar Dominion's capital city swelled with all manner of luxurious airships that sported iridescent, multi-colored sails in addition to the insignias of noble families from every corner of the archipelago.

These vessels were directed to the many docks strewn throughout Eskaya, their passengers ferried by a fleet of white-and-gold skiffs to the Starlight Tower: a building made almost entirely of emerald-green metalglass that jutted out like a thorny scepter from the rest of the skyline. As each guest disembarked, bedecked in furs and feathers and jewels and silks, they were escorted through the sparkling doorway and served refreshments while waiting for the ceremony to begin.

At least, that was what the bride assumed was currently happening. As for herself, *she* was in her chambers at the Roof of Heaven, trying not to puke.

"*I can't do this!*" Talasyn all but yelled at Jie.

To her credit, the lady-in-waiting didn't so much as flinch as she performed the delicate task of affixing tiny specks of

The Hurricane Wars

diamonds to the tips of Talasyn's eyelashes. They weren't even her *real* lashes. She hadn't even known that artificial ones existed until her arrival at court. They were unnaturally long and thick and she couldn't *see*.

"You're getting the wedding jitters, Lachis'ka, it's completely normal," Jie reassured her. "Why, my older brother climbed out the window the morning of his nuptials. When Mother's guards apprehended him, he babbled some nonsense about embracing his true calling as a pirate— Your Grace, with all due respect, *no*," she said firmly when she noticed that Talasyn was eyeing her bedroom window in desperation.

"Is Ossinast still here?" Talasyn asked. "Maybe I can talk to him and we can turn to a life of piracy instead."

Jie grinned. "If elopement is more Her Grace's style—"

"What?" Bile rose up Talasyn's throat. "*No.* I didn't mean it like *that*."

Apparently sensing that Talasyn wasn't in the mood for jokes, Jie adopted a more somber expression. "His Majesty has already left for the Starlight Tower. It's bad luck for the groom to see the bride before the wedding."

Considering that this whole affair is cursed from the start, that won't make much difference, Talasyn thought darkly.

She was a mess of nerves and nausea by the time Jie finished pinning the tiara and veil. Talasyn rose to her feet, uncomfortable and overheated in her heavy dress. Jie stepped back in order to appreciate the full picture and broke out into a wide smile.

"Oh, Lachis'ka, you look positively *dazzling*," Jie gushed. "His Majesty is a lucky man."

Talasyn refused to dignify *that* with a response, and she fidgeted under Jie's rapt scrutiny. It was, however, *nothing* compared to Prince Elagbi's reaction. He was waiting for her in the solar and, as soon as he saw her, tears flooded his eyes.

417

"My child" was all that Elagbi could manage to say at first, the words choked with emotion, and Talasyn could only stand there and feel awkward and *strange* as he fished out a linen kerchief from the pocket of his formal blue tunic and dabbed at his cheeks. "Forgive me," he said. "It's just that—so much time was stolen from us, wasn't it? I never got to see you grow up. And now here you are, as beautiful as your mother was when I married her. If only she could see you now. And if only—if only this was a wedding that you wanted. With someone that you cared for."

Talasyn was helpless in the face of all this love. In the face of what had been found and what had been taken away. She didn't know what to do with any of it.

So she just smiled tentatively at her father, and she let him take her by the arm and escort her out of the palace. Into the schooner that would bring them to her wedding.

Too many aethergraphs, Alaric grumbled to himself as he waited for the ceremony to begin. He was in a secluded alcove adjacent to the vast hall in the Starlight Tower where it would take place. He'd furtively poked his head out earlier to take the measure of the crowd, and behind the rows of guests was gathered a horde of correspondents with their aethermanced devices, bright-hot Firewarren-infused bulbs flashing with wild abandon.

When Gaheris swept through the Continent, the newssheets had been one of the first things to go in each nation that he conquered. *Their sole function is instilling fear and panic among the masses,* the former Night Emperor liked to say. *They don't understand what we're trying to do. What we're trying to build.*

It seemed that Queen Urduja did not share this perspective. Of course, given the Dominion's isolationism, whatever *their* newssheets wrote about the wedding would probably not trickle out to the rest of Lir. But the Night Empire would issue bulletins that were inevitably going to find their way to the trade ports. Their ambassadors would bear the news. It might even reach Sancia Ossinast, wherever she was. Assuming that she was still alive.

Alaric knew that he shouldn't be thinking about that woman. She had left in the middle of the night. She was a traitor to Kesath. But it was hard to stop once he got started. Memories poured in, alive in the fiery light streaming in through the metalglass walls.

In Valisa, she had said to him once, her expression wistful, the way it always had been whenever she spoke of her parents' homeland, *when you wished to propose to the one you love, you'd take them somewhere with a lovely view, some place that has meaning. You'd hold their hands in yours and look upon their face, and you would tell them, "The stars guide me home to your heart."*

Is that how you asked Father to marry you? Alaric had wanted to know, young as he was back then, small and ignorant of so many things.

Sancia's eyes had hardened. *No, little dove. He was the one who asked and there was no talk of stars or hearts. It was a true Kesathese proposal in every sense.*

The door to the alcove swung open and Commodore Mathire peered in, jolting Alaric back to the present.

"Your Majesty, your bride is here." She then vanished with the air of someone ticking off yet another arduous task in a long mental checklist.

Once Alaric was alone again, he took a deep breath. Even as he did so, he castigated himself for the sudden onslaught of nerves racking his system. He was Master of the Shadowforged Legion and the Night Emperor of Kesath; he had stormed countless battlefields and made entire kingdoms bend to his will. A marriage ceremony was nothing in comparison.

There was no putting it off any longer. He stepped out of the alcove and into the Hall of Ceremonies.

Located beneath the Starlight Tower's belfry, the chamber's glass walls provided not just a sprawling panorama of the city below but also copious amounts of natural light. More minimalist in design than the ornate interiors of the Roof of Heaven, the hall nevertheless sported a breathtaking ceiling strewn with stained-glass panels that scattered hues of cobalt, rose quartz, jacinth, and lilac across the floor and over the hundreds of people occupying the pews. These people all fell into a decorous yet tense silence at Alaric's entrance. Stone-faced, he ignored them and strode over to the raised platform housing the altar that was the hall's focal point.

Perched atop columns fashioned from pure alabaster, the altar had been carved in the likeness of a dragon, crouched low with predatory intent, tail pointed to the ceiling, wings tucked into its sides, and the curve of its neck twisted forward so that it stared down the length of the hall with blazing sapphire eyes, a bronze censer dangling on a long chain from jaws stretched open in an eternal roar. Streaming down behind it were ceiling-mounted banners with insignias—the silver chimera of the Night Empire against a field of black, the gold dragon of the Nenavar Dominion rising starkly from silk that was as blue as a summer sky.

Alaric took his place at the base of the platform. The officiant was already standing at the top of the steps in front of the altar, draped in rich scarlet robes.

Willing himself not to fidget, Alaric maintained a blank expression as he surveyed the crowd. His officers, smartly turned out in their dress uniforms, occupied the first few rows along with Urduja, Elagbi, and the Nenavarene aristocrats who were highly positioned in court. Everyone looked positively *grim*.

"I've seen happier faces at funerals," Alaric heard the officiant remark to the two initiates who were assisting her, and he fervently—if silently—agreed.

The music started, courtesy of the orchestra in the choir loft. First, a brassy gong was struck three times from up high. Then came the xylophones and reed pipes, soon joined by plucked strings to form a stirring melody punctuated by soft drumbeats. The main doors slid open. Talasyn walked in.

And, for several long moments, Alaric ceased to breathe.

He was dreaming. He had to be.

There was no way that *she* was real.

The Dominion had spared no expense on their Lachis'ka's wedding gown. Spun from lustrous lotus silk the color of magnolia petals, the gold-trimmed bodice was a snug-fitting affair with a scalloped neckline, stiff butterfly sleeves, and a fitted waist melting into a dramatic full skirt that probably qualified as a feat of architecture. It was layer upon layer of chiffon and organza lavishly embellished with diamonds set amidst constellations of gold and silver thread, the back half sloping into a train that glided whisper-soft over floors made of glass. Talasyn's chestnut hair had been gathered into loose curls and pinned atop her head, adorned with a gold-and-diamond tiara from which streamed a veil made of the finest gossamer, shot through with more diamonds and more silver thread to create the illusion of a starry sky. Clutching a bouquet of snow-white peonies that caught the rain of colors from the stained-glass ceiling, she floated down the aisle toward Alaric on the bright, airy strains of the arched harp. She was utterly exquisite in the fiery light of day's end, heartbreakingly lovely in white, silver, and gold.

And she was going to be his *wife*.

Alaric paid no attention to the appreciative murmurs rippling through the crowd. He no longer noticed the ceiling or the altar or the view of the skyline. All he saw was Talasyn.

CHAPTER THIRTY-SIX

As Talasyn embarked on her long, slow walk down the aisle, the awful possibility that she would stumble echoed through her mind. Once she started thinking it, she couldn't stop. It filled her head until she was sure that each next step would be the last. She'd fall flat on her ass and everyone would laugh . . .

Alaric probably wouldn't laugh at her, but only because he was too joyless to laugh at much of anything. As she walked toward him, with his impassive face and his cold gray eyes, she couldn't shake the sensation that she was marching toward her downfall.

The memory of Darius at Khaede and Sol's wedding, wryly asking her if she thought she would be next, couldn't have picked a worse time to surface. Once it did, Talasyn's steady pace faltered as *she* was seized by the urge to laugh. Or to scream. Or to turn around and run for it, run as far as her shoes and her dress would take her—which wouldn't be very far at all.

By some miracle, though, she managed to make it to Alaric's side without incident. Her nape prickling with the weight of hundreds of gazes, she numbly handed the bouquet to Jie, who took it and gracefully melted back into the crowd, and then she looked up at the man that she was about to marry.

Alaric was dressed in a high-collared, long-sleeved black tunic, embroidered with silver curlicues along the cuffs, as well as black trousers and black boots. As if to offset the relative plainness of his attire, he wore a livery collar of obsidian gems, from the back of which hung a brocaded cape of platinum and midnight. His hair was . . . perfect, as usual, all lush and artfully tousled dark waves, topped with a circlet inset with black enamel and wine-red rubies. From afar he looked too tall and forbidding, but up close his pale face was not as harsh as it could have been, and those eyes that had seemed so cold were warmed somewhat by the emerald-tinted light of sunset.

Holding each other's gazes as the music played on, Talasyn and Alaric moved at the same time. He executed a courtly bow while she sank into a curtsy as far as her billowing skirts would permit. This part of the ceremony had been a source of contention between the two negotiation panels; in Nenavarene culture, the groom had to bow to the bride, but the Night Emperor bowed to no one and the Lachis'ka curtseyed only to the Dragon Queen. Daya Rasmey had solved the issue by suggesting that both actions be conducted simultaneously as a sign of mutual respect, so that the couple could proceed to the altar as equals.

Once they'd righted themselves, Alaric held his arm out to Talasyn. She tucked her hand into the crook of his elbow and together they ascended the platform's steps. A sigh rose from the crowd—Talasyn knew that at that moment her train and veil were spilling down the glass staircase like a river of white and gold, an aesthetic effect that had been carefully calculated by a battalion of dressmakers.

Due to the fact that she was navigating a series of slippery steps, Talasyn held on to Alaric tighter than she would have liked. He seemed to instinctively understand what she needed, slowing his pace and keeping his arm steady to support her. She glanced at him, and his sharp profile contained a trace of haughty amusement.

"Oh, *you* try climbing the stairs in these infernal shoes and this kind of skirt," she snapped under her breath.

"I'd rather take my chances with the shoes," he murmured. "Your dress is so loaded down with diamonds that I'm surprised that the floor hasn't cracked yet."

"Shut up."

Once they reached the top of the platform and stood before the altar and the officiant, they signed the two contracts that the initiates brought forward. They were beautifully embossed documents stating that, on this day, Alunsina Ivralis of the Nenavar Dominion was marrying Alaric Ossinast of Kesath.

After raising the parchments to the light to ascertain that the ink had dried, the officiant carefully rolled each one up. She gave one to an initiate and placed the second one inside the censer hanging from the dragon's crystalline jaws. Smoke spewed forth, the acrid smell of burning parchment soon engulfed by the perfume of incense as news of the union was carried to the great warships of the ancestors that sailed paradise, the Sky Above the Sky—or so the Nenavarene believed. Talasyn was absolutely certain that, if the afterlife *did* exist, the ancestors of House Silim would be rolling over in their graves right about now.

She and Alaric turned to face each other, their hands reaching out across the space between them to, with some hesitation, clasp their fingers together. He wasn't wearing his usual gauntlets and her eyes widened at the brush of skin on skin. It was as though a static charge rushed into her veins at every point of contact. Her pulse began to race.

And yet there was also something about his touch that was soothing. Like a cool drop of water sliding down her parched tongue. Talasyn had been running on anger her whole life, be it the inferno or the fumes. The burning was what her magic was built around, was at times all she knew.

But *this* was . . . anchoring. The Lightweave that often surged so restlessly through her veins was now crooning, reaching for its opposite, its dark mirror that lurked beneath Alaric's own skin. The cradle of his hands hinted at somewhere quiet and safe beneath the storm of her hammering heartbeat. It offered a dream of peace.

It—

It wasn't *real*.

Alaric's lips were pressed into a sullen line. He was entirely unaffected, and this went a long way toward spurring Talasyn to gain control over her odd reaction to the feeling of his bare fingers laced through hers.

The officiant produced a red silk cord and looped it around the couple's wrists, to signify that fate had bound them together. The music came to a stop and the scarlet-robed woman lifted her arms to the stained-glass ceiling, intoning in a solemn voice that echoed through the room, "We are gathered here today to celebrate the union between two realms, which in itself signifies the dawn of a glorious new age for the Nenavar Dominion. With the blessing of Her Starlit Majesty Urduja Silim, She Who Hung the Earth Upon the Waters, these two souls now pledge their troth . . ."

Perhaps Talasyn would have been more interested in the officiant's words if she'd actually *wanted* to get married. Perhaps then this farce of a ceremony would hold some meaning. As it was, though, her attention drifted during the speech, distracted by the weight of hundreds of gazes and Alaric's hands holding hers—so strangely gentle, for some reason, as though she were some fragile thing. She had never expected gentleness from this dour, hulking specter of a man. She had never expected to deem him not unattractive.

And she *definitely* had never expected to find herself concentrating solely on him as the officiant droned on. He made her forget the crowd. He *centered* her, in this beautiful, treacherous place, where he was the only one who had known her in the time before, where *he* was the only thing she could honestly say that she knew. They might have been thrust into new roles, but there was still a war's worth of memories between them.

Talasyn remembered the clash of blades in the moonlight, in the ruins, under burning skies. She remembered moving with pure instinct, light against shadow, and how alive she had felt every time she and Alaric fought, the aether singing between them. His fingers tightened reflexively around hers, and for a moment she thought that she could *see* those memories in his eyes, flashing silver in the setting sun.

The officiant gestured over their joined hands. "These are the hands that will love you for all the years to come and comfort you in times of sorrow," she told them. "These are the hands that will work alongside yours to build an empire. These are the hands that will hold your children and help you carry the world. These are the hands that will always reach for yours."

The blessing shook Alaric to the core. These hands of his could never do any of the things that the officiant had mentioned, not when they were so irrevocably stained in blood. He would never be able to fulfill any of the promises that he was making to Talasyn, because his parents' relationship was his only blueprint for what made a marriage, and it had ended in betrayal, in flight.

It was ridiculous—it defied all logic—that the ceremony was affecting him in this manner. It was all for show. But there was a part of him that wished . . .

He should never have eschewed formal gloves. His father had drilled into his head that they were his armor, that they insulated him from the distractions of the physical realm. But Daya Rasmey had sternly advised him that wearing them would be disrespectful to the significance of the wrist-binding rite, and so he'd gone without. As a consequence, he couldn't marshal his defenses when Talasyn's fingers were intertwined with his. A warmth like sunlight flooded into him at every point of contact, seeping into all the icy places where the Shadowgate had taken root. It sated the buried hunger for touch that he thought he had overcome long ago.

He couldn't get enough. He never wanted to let go.

It was all going so, so wrong.

Alaric sped through his vows while trying not to make it too obvious that he was in a rush to finish saying them. He told himself not to meet Talasyn's eyes, but it was impossible to look away. He was trapped within sunset and stained glass, holding the hands of his bride and gazing upon her face as he recited words that he wished he could mean. If only it had been any other life.

And then it was her turn.

"I t-take . . ." Talasyn faltered, trailing off, and closed her eyes briefly before trying again. "I bring you the whole of my heart at the rising of the moon and the setting of the stars."

Alaric wished that she'd kept her eyes closed. Her gaze crackled with intense energy, and it made the words that emerged from her lips all the fiercer, somehow, all the more poignant, even if she was merely echoing what he'd said to her scant moments ago.

"Fire of my blood, sun of my soul, I would raise my armies in your defense and I would stand by your side though the Eversea itself be against us."

A dull pain stabbed through his chest. They were just words, and not even original words at that, but no one had ever before told him that he didn't have to fight alone.

"I pledge to love you wholly and completely," Talasyn

continued, her brow slightly furrowed in concentration, "without restraint, in times of good fortune and in times of trial, in light and in darkness, and in life and beyond, in the Sky Above the Sky where my ancestors sail, where we shall meet and remember, and where I will marry you again."

The officiant removed the red cord and the initiates stepped forward once more, this time with the rings. Talasyn slipped Alaric's wedding band onto his finger, then stood there with a tremulously beating heart as he did the same to her. There was one last hurdle to overcome, and she wasn't sure if she could bring herself to do it.

"I now pronounce you bonded for life," said the officiant. "Lachis'ka, you may kiss your consort."

I can't, Talasyn thought, panic setting in. But she *had* to. There was simply no getting around the kiss. It had since time immemorial been the gesture that concluded the marriage rites.

Talasyn inched closer to Alaric, who for a split second looked as if he wanted nothing more than to run away. She was grateful for her heels for the first time since putting them on, because the added height meant that she wouldn't have to tiptoe. However, it was still a bit of a ways up. Why did he have to be so *tall*? She screwed her eyes shut, and—

It was supposed to be a quick peck lasting no longer than a fraction of a second, with none of the mess of complications that the kiss at the Lightweaver shrine had brought in. She'd had it all planned out. But his lips were warm against hers, and as soft as she remembered. She hadn't counted on the pleasant spark, on the skipping in her soul, on the way her magic shifted inside her like a wild thing pricking up its ears with interest.

And she hadn't counted on Alaric circling an arm around her waist and returning the kiss.

Her head spun. When she could no longer hold her position

and shifted her full weight back onto solid ground, he was the one who leaned down, his mouth chasing hers, his arm keeping her firmly to him. Her hand slid up his chest, feeling his heart beneath her fingertips, how it echoed hers in its wild fluttering.

It lasted too long. Or—it ended too soon. Talasyn didn't know. Her sense of self-preservation kicked in and she broke away first, her entire being teetering on the edge of a cliff. Alaric blinked down at her, his plush lips just the slightest bit parted.

Her ears were ringing, and it took her an embarrassing amount of time to figure out that it was due to *actual* gongs. The ones threaded throughout the Starlight Tower were being struck, sending their brassy musical notes all across Eskaya. The orchestra was playing again. The guests in the pews were standing up to properly herald the wedding exit. The sun was about to dip below the horizon.

Talasyn and Alaric stared at each other in the shadow of the dragon altar. They were married.

CHAPTER THIRTY-SEVEN

Talasyn's giggling lady-in-waiting had detached the silk train before leaving the newlyweds alone in the schooner's private compartment. Even without twelve feet of material dragging behind it, though, the skirt was still a massive, ballooning tent of a thing that made it necessary for Talasyn to occupy three seats in the small cabin. Alaric sat across from her, too tall and broad for the cramped space, his long legs all tangled up in the diamond-studded layers of fine silk streaming off her dress.

He couldn't help but look at her in such close quarters. Even though he tried to restrain himself, his gaze kept flickering back to her face as she looked out the window while the schooner glided over the rooftops of Eskaya. She shone in the gathering twilight, the tips of her lashes spiked with fragments of tiny diamonds that glittered against her smooth, dewy complexion. As beautiful as she was, Alaric missed the freckles that he knew for a fact were underneath those paints and powders, naturally dusted across the bridge of her nose and the tops of her cheeks.

His eyes drifted to her lips. He shouldn't have returned her kiss, but it had been instinct to chase after her mouth, to hold her tight against him. It had felt . . . as though everything else had been blocked out for that brief moment in time and he was free-falling and Talasyn was the only thing anchoring him.

Compared to their kiss in the amphitheater, the one at the altar had been relatively chaste. There was no good reason for it to have affected him so much. For it to be affecting him still.

Alaric looked somewhere else, desperate for a distraction. Unfortunately, he made the mistake of dropping his gaze from Talasyn's lips, past her chin, past the column of her throat, all the way down to the swell of her breasts, enticingly molded by the white-and-gold bodice.

May the gods help me. Alaric resisted the urge to put his head in his hands in a fit of despair. *I'm attracted to my wife.*

"What are you doing?" Talasyn suddenly asked.

She'd *caught* him. She'd caught him *ogling* her chest.

He averted his gaze to the cityscape beyond the window. "What do you mean?" he asked, his tone as bored as he could make it.

"I know I look silly in this getup, but it couldn't be helped. Just be glad that I talked the dressmaker out of a *twenty*-foot train."

Alaric turned back to Talasyn, surprised at the extent to which she'd misinterpreted his actions. Her posture was one of stiff, injured pride, but she was nervously toying with the embroidered star pattern on her gossamer veil. *You don't look silly,* he wanted to tell her.

"Stop doing that," he said instead, reaching out to grab her wrist before she could inflict any serious damage on the bead-work. She shifted her hand in his loose grip and somehow her palm scraped along his and their fingers intertwined on her lap, amidst the diamonds and the shining thread, amidst all those elegant, swirling constellations. It was as natural as reflex, as hungry as second nature. It was a moment that carried as much fluid gravity as the time he felt eyes on him and looked up to find her.

Let go, Alaric's common sense screamed at him.

But he didn't. His fingertips traced the edges of the bony curvature of Talasyn's knuckles. His thumb moved in a haphazard circle, skimming the mound of her palm. Her hand was not an aristocrat's hand—there were calluses on fingers that were thin yet strong. It was all fascinating to him, the texture of her skin, the ridges of uncharted territory. All the while he was staring into her eyes, mesmerized by how, in this light, on this near-night, splinters of gold flecked her dark irises.

The schooner tilted into an upward trajectory, signaling their approach on the Roof of Heaven. It was only then that the spell broke and Alaric released Talasyn's hand. He regretted doing so and, all at once, was relieved to have mustered the will to do so.

Entering the grand ballroom on Alaric's arm, Talasyn saw that it had been transformed into a wonderland of sunset colors, as if the sky that had graced her wedding had been used to gild the reception venue. A dozen enormous bronze chandeliers hung from the ceiling, bearing Nenavar's and Kesath's banners and thousands of candles. The round tables were bedecked in purple cloth, burgundy napkins, ruby-encrusted vermeil flatware, and floral arrangements of cream and dusky pink. On the dais at the end of the ballroom was another table decorated in much the same manner, rectangular in shape and set for two and perfectly positioned so that everyone would have a good view of it.

All the better to be gawked at, Talasyn thought sourly, but the truth was that the guests didn't even wait until she and Alaric were seated to do *that.* All music and conversation ceased and people stood up and every gaze swiveled to them as soon as they appeared in the doorway.

A little old man draped in the royal livery sidled over to Talasyn's side. She didn't notice him until he announced her and Alaric's entrance—in a booming voice that bounced off the rafters and nearly made her jump.

"Her Grace Alunsina Ivralis, Lachis'ka of the Nenavar Dominion, and her consort, His Majesty Alaric Ossinast of the Night Empire! Long may they reign!"

The last part struck Talasyn as odd. She didn't reign over anything. She wasn't the Zahiya-lachis yet—

No, she realized, a chill shooting down her spine, *but I am the Night Empress.*

Or she would be very soon. After her coronation at the Citadel.

There was movement all throughout the ballroom. The lords and ladies of Nenavar were sinking into bows and curtsies and the Kesathese officers were saluting. The music started up again as the imperial couple walked into the ballroom, crossing the dance floor to reach Urduja and Elagbi's table. Talasyn was about to execute a curtsy of her own to the Dragon Queen, out of habit, but Elagbi caught her eye, stopping her with a slight shake of his head. The Night Empress was outranked only by her husband.

"Emperor Alaric," Urduja drawled. "Welcome to the family."

"Thank you, Harlikaan." Alaric's tone was courteous but the muscles of his arm tensed in Talasyn's grasp, through the silk of his sleeve. "The honor is mine."

Elagbi stuck out his hand, which Alaric—after some hesitation—shook with his free one. "Take care of my daughter," said the Dominion prince, fixing the younger man with a level stare.

"I will," Alaric replied in a voice that was slightly strained at the edges.

Elagbi turned to Talasyn and kissed her on the forehead. It was such a tender gesture that a lump formed in her throat, but it was over much too soon and then she had to face Urduja, who merely offered her a brisk nod.

"It was a beautiful wedding, Empress." Whatever Urduja might have thought of the power shift, her painted features were an imperturbable mask, concealing her thoughts entirely.

Elagbi let out a soft chuckle. Three pairs of eyes turned to him, quizzical. "I was merely thinking," he explained, "that this is a most unexpected outcome." He placed an affectionate hand on Talasyn's arm. "When I revealed that you were my daughter at the Belian garrison—had anyone told me back then that you'd one day marry the man you were taken prisoner with, I'd have thought them quite mad!"

Talasyn cringed. Leave it to her carefree father to make things even more awkward. Urduja looked thunderous, clearly unimpressed by her son's attempt at small talk. And Alaric—

Alaric frowned, as though something had just occurred to him and it wasn't adding up.

But he would have had scarce opportunity to dig deeper if he'd wanted to. Now that the exchange of greetings was over and done with, there remained one more custom standing between the wedding party and dinner. Alaric escorted Talasyn onto the middle of the dance floor as the string orchestra launched into a slower melody and the lights were dimmed.

"They *have* taught you how to waltz, yes?" he murmured in her ear.

"A fine time to ask!" she snapped.

The line of his mouth relaxed. "Just checking."

Facing each other in the center of the ballroom, beneath the twinkling lights of a bronze chandelier as big as a skerry, they assumed the closed position—his right hand on the small of her back, her left hand curled on the jut of his shoulder, their other hands clasped together at chest height. They fell into motions that Talasyn had started learning months ago. She'd needed dance lessons because balls were part and parcel of court life, but she would never in a million years have been prepared for her first official dance being the literal *first dance* at her own wedding.

It did not go as smoothly as she'd hoped.

"Talasyn." Alaric sounded annoyed. "You're supposed to let me lead."

"What are you talking about?" she demanded. "*I'm* the one who leads."

"No—" He broke off. Understanding dawned on his face. "Very well. Apparently, they do things differently here in the Nenavar Dominion."

As their dance progressed, she could tell that he was making a concentrated effort to adapt. However, old forms were hard to break. "You're still not letting me lead," she said through gritted teeth. It was less a dance and more a tug-of-war.

Alaric scowled but obediently readjusted his stance, forcing himself to turn pliable in her hands. That was the moment when everything changed.

The music washed over them, airy strains of an arched harp, lightly skipping lutes, a silvery floor zither, the bowed swansong of spiked fiddles. Their audience faded away as they fell into the graceful, sweeping melody. He held her as close to him as her wide skirts would permit, his eyes charcoal-dark in the candlelight. Her dress caught the radiance of the chandeliers and the illusion was such that its swirling panels of gold were reflected on his face.

After their duels, after going through all those forms of breath and magic, they knew the rhythm of each other's body too well to pretend otherwise. They swayed and they glided and she led him into a twirl, feeling the heat of his tall, strong frame even after she spun away, entranced by it every time she came back to him. They moved together like water and moonlight.

*

Alaric felt like a menagerie animal as he sat at the head table with Talasyn while the Nenavarene court scrutinized them. He picked at each dish brought out by a never-ending parade of smartly dressed attendants and took sparing sips from each vintage that was poured to complement the various courses.

Beside him, Talasyn was faring no better, unenthusiastically prodding at her spiced lamb with a bejeweled fork. There was a rustle of silk as she tried to cross her legs and failed, thanks no doubt to the voluminous inner layers of her skirt. She huffed, irritated, and resorted to taking out her frustrations on the lamb on her plate, hacking at it with a viciousness ill-suited to their elegant surroundings.

"That thing's dead enough, surely," Alaric drawled.

Talasyn's eyes remained glued to her plate. She'd been avoiding his gaze ever since the end of their dance, and he could hardly blame her. *Something* had passed between them, some smoldering charge. But with the entire court looking on, there was no space to examine it further.

Alaric's knee started bouncing under the table—a mannerism that he rarely indulged in, but he was bored and uncomfortable and this night couldn't end soon enough. He didn't realize that he was jostling Talasyn's leg until he felt a light slap on his knee and he glanced down to see her hand still poised above it, her wedding band sparkling on her ring finger.

"Did you just *spank* me?" he asked, incredulous.

"Either stay still or sit further away," she told her plate.

Alaric was not, by nature, a petty man. He was also keenly aware that he was six years older than his bride and it would behoove him to act in a manner befitting not only an emperor but also the mature one in this fraught new relationship. However, one glance at Talasyn's ferocious little scowl, her profile scrunched up in annoyance, was all that it took for him to spread his legs wider, encroaching into her space.

She turned to him with a glare, clutching her fork as if she was about to stab him with it. He gave her his frostiest smirk, all trace of discomfort forgotten. Now *this* felt like home.

But something that Elagbi had said earlier was weighing on his mind. Deciding that now was as good a time as any to bring it up, he leaned in closer to his new bride—even if it *did* bring him into worrying proximity to her pointy fork.

"Earlier, Prince Elagbi reminded me that you learned the truth of your origins when we were taken prisoner at the Belian range. You were aware that you were his daughter all throughout the last month of the Hurricane Wars. That's the reason you fled to Nenavar. You knew you'd be welcome here. But why go back to the Continent at all?" Alaric's tone grew softer in his puzzlement as, in stark contrast, tension rippled through Talasyn, pulling every muscle tight.

She glared at him. "The Amirante said that she needed me to concentrate on the war, and I agreed."

"You told me that you'd been lonely all your life," Alaric said with a frown, "waiting to be reunited with your family. And then you *were*, but you left, and you returned to a war that was already as good as lost by that point. I understand that you must have felt beholden to debrief Ideth Vela, but you didn't even think to ask her if you could sail back to Nenavar?"

"I had a duty," she replied, sounding confused as to what his point was. "Of course I had to see it through until the end."

Before he could argue, Niamha Langsoune approached the head table, all sophisticated grace and pleasant smile and copper robes. "Your Grace, Your Majesty," she said in a low voice, "it's time to make your exit."

Unseen by anyone else, Talasyn's fingers suddenly dug into Alaric's thigh beneath the table. They were to leave the Grand Ballroom and retire to her chambers for their wedding night. Granted, it had already been agreed that they wouldn't actually do *anything*, but still . . .

As if on cue, Urduja rose to her feet, effectively putting a stop to all conversation. "Honored guests," she said, holding a glass of wine in her hand, "I thank you for celebrating this historic night with us. Through this union, we have engendered a new age of peace and prosperity for the Nenavar Dominion and the Night Empire. Please join me in a toast to the newly-weds as they embark on the next chapter of their lives together."

Talasyn thought that she was holding up pretty well, all things considered. She had managed to leave the feast with poise, had even offered Alaric a stiff but polite nod before they were escorted to their respective suites for a change of clothes. Away from the hubbub, finally out of sight of prying eyes, with her hair down and her torturous shoes and false lashes removed at long last, she was feeling more optimistic about getting through the rest of the evening with no added stress. But all that changed when Jie marched out of the dressing room, bearing Talasyn's *change of clothes*.

"I am *not* wearing that."

"But, Lachis'ka, it's tradition—" Jie started to plead, but Talasyn cut her off.

"Look at that thing!" She gestured in dismay at the—well, it was hardly even a dress. It was hardly even a *scarf*, by her standards. True, it had long sleeves and it trailed past her ankles, but that didn't matter when it was made of material so sheer that she could *see through it*, with only stylized appliqués strategically positioned to cover her . . . her *bits*. "Who in their right mind would . . ." She faltered, at a complete and utter loss for words.

"It's lingerie, Your Grace," Jie hastened to explain.

"I don't care what it's called," Talasyn savagely declared. "I'm not putting it on."

Jie appeared disconcerted. Talasyn raised an eyebrow, daring the girl to argue with her.

The standoff was interrupted by the sound of chimes. Alaric had arrived outside her solar.

"Lachis'ka, the Night Emperor is here," Jie implored. "There's no more time."

Talasyn should have put up more of a fight. But Jie wouldn't understand, because, as far as she was concerned, what would follow was a legitimate consummation. Talasyn didn't need gossip contradicting that spreading through the court.

"Fine," she sighed, her shoulders sagging in defeat.

Jie worked quickly to extricate Talasyn from the wedding dress, arrange her hair into a simple braid, and spritz perfume on her pulse points. The chimes sounded again just as the flimsy excuse for a nightdress was being slipped over Talasyn's head.

Jie winked. "Someone's impatient."

Talasyn groaned inwardly. *Give me strength.*

At last, Jie curtseyed and stole out of the room, dimming the lamps as she went. Talasyn was left alone in a kneeling position in the middle of the canopy bed, absolutely mortified but trying not to let on, her heart pounding as she waited to receive her husband.

CHAPTER THIRTY-EIGHT

The door of the Lachis'ka's solar creaked open, revealing the grinning face of Talasyn's lady-in-waiting. Yes, the damnable teenager was *actually* grinning, the effect not dissimilar to a prettily dressed shark.

"Her Grace is ready for you, Your Majesty," Jie saucily told him before taking her leave in a flurry of rustling skirts and unabashed snickering.

Alaric breathed out an irritated sigh at the girl's antics. She was Dominion nobility—*female* nobility, at that—and thus she wasn't particularly inclined to act deferential in his presence.

He slowly made his way to Talasyn's closed bedroom door, part of him still unwilling to believe that this was nothing more than an outlandish fever-dream. He knocked to be polite, and then walked in.

Like her solar, her chambers were disconcertingly feminine, all done up in soft orange and pale pink and rosy peach, starry tapestries hung on the walls and iridescent silk panels draped over the canopy bed. It didn't strike him as the kind of decor that Talasyn would have chosen for herself; she would prefer bolder colors, perhaps, and furnishings that could be treated with less care.

The curtains had been drawn against the brilliant seven-mooned evening, but the shadows were edged in gold by perfumed candles on the nightstand, providing Alaric with enough light to see the figure on the mattress. His breath hitched as all thought, all wondering, fled from his mind.

Talasyn was clad in a nightdress sewn from the sheerest, flimsiest mesh fabric that Alaric had ever seen. Every inch of the long-sleeved bodice clung to her slim torso, accentuating her narrow waist and the slight flare of her hips, and, gods, it was as if she was wearing *nothing*, her olive skin clearly visible through the transparent material, obscured only in certain places by an intricate patchwork of embroidered lace. Hibiscus blossoms dripping from leafy vines curled along her wrists and her ribcage and down her thighs; herons were stitched in mid-flight over her chest and the spurs of her hips, as if in some valiant last-ditch attempt at modesty. Her face had been scrubbed clean and her chestnut hair was gathered into a loose braid draped over one shoulder, trailing past her right breast. She was kneeling on the bed, her hands clasped together in her lap. She looked like a summer's eve and like an offering all at once. She looked . . .

. . . very, *very* grumpy.

"Do *not*," she snarled, "say *anything*." Her cheeks were flushed with embarrassment but it only added to the gorgeous sight so appealingly arranged before him.

"I wasn't going to," Alaric forced out through gritted teeth. He cautiously stepped further into the room and her gaze flickered over his white linen shirt, the sleeves rolled up to his elbows, and his loose black trousers. He wondered what kind of man she saw, suddenly self-conscious of his features. The nose that was too prominent, the mouth that was too wide, the graceless asymmetry of cheekbones and chin and jaw.

Desperate to do something, *anything*, that didn't involve

gawking at her, he glanced around her chambers in a futile
search for somewhere to sleep. There was a chaise longue, but
it would barely accommodate three-quarters of his height and
half his width. *The floor it is, then,* he thought with resignation. "Shall I just grab some extra bedding?"

"What?" Talasyn asked.

Alaric turned to her. She was staring at him, and he experienced a moment of déjà vu—the night of the banquet, the
altercation in his room, her hands on his chest, how she'd
forgotten his question.

And then he remembered his father sneering, *The Lightweaver
will never return this bizarre infatuation that you have for her.*

"Extra bedding," Alaric repeated tersely.

"Oh," Talasyn said. "No, there are no extras; you're not
sleeping on the floor. Someone will come in the morning to
wake us. They'll talk if you aren't in bed with me. We can
share for the night. It's no trouble."

I beg to differ, he almost snapped, but at that precise moment
she moved, unfolding herself from her kneeling pose and
scooting over to one side of the mattress, leaning back against
the ornately carved headboard. He was treated to the stretch
of her long, long legs, with their toned calves and their dainty
ankles, and any protests that he might have had vanished into
the aether.

Feeling very far away from his body, Alaric joined Talasyn
on the bed, mimicking her position. His shoulder bumped
against hers with a rush of heat and static and he quickly
widened the space between them, the eiderdown mattress
bobbing at the shift in weight.

At first, this new position seemed more tenable because her
distracting face wasn't in his line of sight. Much to his chagrin,
he soon realized that he had an *unparalleled* view down her
legs. They were slender and they went on for miles beneath
the scattered lace dustings of leaves and hibiscus blossoms.

He wondered what those legs would look like when fully bared. How they would feel wrapped around his waist.

"No more talking." Talasyn extinguished the candles and lay down, drawing the covers up to her chin, hiding those incredible legs from view, much to his—relief? Or was it disappointment? "I have lessons tomorrow, once you've gone back to Kesath. I need to sleep."

Fine by me, Alaric thought. He stretched out on the mattress beside her, careful to maintain distance between their bodies.

It took what felt like an eternity of staring up at the tapestries hung over the bed for him to admit that drifting off was impossible.

"What sort of lessons?" he heard himself ask.

"I *said* no more talking."

"You *also* said that you needed to sleep. Unless you possess the previously unheard-of ability to carry on a normal conversation while you're sleeping—"

Talasyn sat up. Alaric supposed that it was battle instinct, more than anything, that made him do the same. If he had remained supine it would have been far too easy for her to reach over and stab him in the throat.

But then she tugged at the sheer bodice of her nightdress, in an obvious attempt to get its delicate appliqués to lend more modesty, and he was seized by a wave of the same sympathy that she had been steadily unearthing in him ever since they met, much to his alarm.

"If you're uncomfortable wearing"—he waved vaguely at the barely-there silk that hugged her form while trying to keep his gaze chastely on her face as much as possible—"things like that, why not tell your lady-in-waiting?"

"Jie is very sweet," Talasyn said slowly, "but she's also very chatty and she has certain fixed notions of what married life is like. If I were to do anything that ran contrary to those notions, even the blacksmith's washerwoman three cities over would have heard about it by tomorrow afternoon. Sometimes it's just easier to take the path of least resistance."

I wish that you could take it with me, just the once, Alaric thought. Out loud, he continued, "With all due respect to her giggly young ladyship, she has *no* idea what our married life is like."

"Not even the tiniest bit," Talasyn agreed. "Anyway, this is hardly the most onerous of the things I have done for the sake of everyone else."

She unleashed that last bit pointedly enough that her meaning—their marriage—was clear.

"Are your lessons as the Lachis'ka *onerous*?" he asked, quirking an eyebrow at her. "Or is it just telling me about them that you find so dreadful a task?"

"If you really *must* know, my lessons concern politics," she snapped. The belligerence in her expression deepened. "The Zahiya-lachis's brand of politics, anyway."

"You disagree with Queen Urduja's methods? They're efficient." Some of his residual annoyance leaked into his next words. "You have certainly been content to go along with whatever she commands thus far."

Talasyn twisted the section of duvet on her lap between her fingers, as though imagining it was his neck. "And what are you implying by that?"

"You know *exactly* what I'm implying," Alaric bit out, and it was as though some dam had broken, the thread of tension strung through him since the Belian amphitheater finally stretched taut enough to snap. *Come on, darling,* some darkly wicked, impulsive part of him thought, *one last fight before I leave you.* "You wear dresses you hate, you don't commune with your magic's nexus point because Her Starlit Majesty forbids it, you behave according to her specifications, you let this court keep secrets from you, you stay in this palace like a songbird in a gilded cage. Even before that, you ignored your yearning to be with your family because it was what Ideth Vela asked. Do you know, Lachis'ka," he concluded with a sneer at her rapidly paling face, "it occurs to me that you're the sort of person who *needs* to be told what to do. You're too afraid to do anything for yourself."

Her brown eyes flashed. She bared her teeth at him in the moonlight. "You *dare* say these things to me," she snarled, "when you've lived your whole life under your father's thumb? Studying and training to be the perfect heir, swallowing all the lies he and your grandfather spouted about the true cause of the Cataclysm—"

"They aren't lies," Alaric hissed. "It's *Sardovia* that lied to you—"

"Oh, I'm sure! If Gaheris says so, then it *must* be true." She lifted her chin. "Did you even decide to treat with Nenavar for a marriage alliance by yourself, or did you have to ask his permission? Shall I send him a token of my gratitude?"

Alaric stiffened as the barb hit home. He made to turn away from Talasyn, perhaps to even scramble out of the bed, but her hand clamped around his bare wrist and he was frozen in place.

"You wouldn't let me sleep, so let's talk," she growled. "Let's talk about how you castigate me for doing what my family tells me to do when *I* have never participated in the invasion of entire nation-states at their behest!"

His temper spiked, but he tried his best to keep his tone calm. "I do not expect you to understand my father's vision—"

"Gaheris's *vision*," she mocked. "You accused me of parroting my grandmother's words, the night of the duel without bounds, but you're just as bad, if not even worse! You're a parrot *and* a puppet on a string *and* a dog on a leash—"

Alaric's self-control slipped. He inched his face closer to

hers. "I'm not the only one who married the enemy at the behest of a superior, Lachis'ka."

She surged closer to him as well, a vicious triumph blazing in her eyes. "So you admit that Gaheris *is* your superior. What are you, then? Night Emperor in name alone?"

Alaric couldn't believe that he'd let such a sentiment slip. He had always prided himself on his ability to play word games with the best of them, but Talasyn rendered his mind blank whenever she wasn't driving him out of it entirely.

In this moment, it was the way that their faces were a heartbeat apart. It was her accursed nightdress. It was the burning of her fingertips around his wrist.

"We're done discussing this," he said curtly.

She bristled. "You are my consort. You don't get to order me around."

"You are *my* empress," he shot back. "You answer to *me*."

"As long as we are in the Nenavar Dominion, where husbands obey their wives, it's *my* word that's your law! How sad for you, to have *two* masters."

"Lachis'ka." Blinding fury guided him further over her side of the bed. The tip of his nose grazed hers. "Shut up."

"*Or what?*" the insufferable woman shouted, right in his face. "What will you do, *Your Majesty?*"

Alaric lunged forward, without having any idea as to what would happen when he got there. He moved with instinct, with the dark rage of the Shadowforged set free at long last. In the mood that he was in, he thought that he just might go for Talasyn's jugular—

—but, instead, he kissed her.

Although Talasyn had known that there would be consequences to letting her temper get the better of her yet again, she had let it happen, because it felt good to have a justifiable target for all of her anxious fury. She had wanted Alaric to be the flint that she struck against; she would have said anything to make it so. She had gladly tempted fate, come what may.

Yes, she had known what she was doing.

She just hadn't been prepared for the consequences to be— *this*.

His lips on hers. Again.

It was nothing like the chaste peck that she'd given him at the altar or the swift yet gentle way in which he had reciprocated. This was the Belian ruins once more, blistering, all-consuming. She was still clinging to his wrist for some reason, but her free hand whipped up to slap him—

Only for her palm to meet the side of his face without any real vehemence, her fingers curling at his clean-shaven jaw. His own hand curved at her neck, his thumb pressing into her clavicle as he licked at the seam of her lips, just like before. And, just like before, she opened her mouth to him, and a low, primal sound rumbled in his throat as he hungrily pushed forward.

Talasyn felt as though she was burning up, her heart a wild thing, and she was falling, she was melting back onto eider-down and silk sheets. Alaric followed her, their lips still connected, his enormous frame pinning her to the mattress as she looped her arms around his neck.

Some tiny corner of her brain was busily trying to figure out how an incendiary argument could have ended with him shoving his tongue down her throat, but all attempt at rationality soon vanished amidst the clamor of sensations as he palmed her right breast. As the hard length of him ground against her stomach. All while he kissed her as though he were channeling every last bit of frustration left over from the Hurricane Wars.

She whimpered into his mouth when his hand glided over her breast in a rough caress. Her nipple peaked under his touch through silk and lace, and he muttered an unintelligible oath against her lips. His voice was so gravelly that it added to the growing warmth between her legs.

So this is what it feels like, she thought in a daze.

To have someone roll her nipple between his fingers, teasing, caressing, unspooling delight all the way down to her core. To have someone ply her with open-mouthed kisses, fierce and relentless, the hard length in his trousers rocking against her belly.

But this wasn't *just* someone. This was Alaric, her husband, her enemy, her dark mirror, and the Lightweave in her veins soared in triumph, recognizing him for what he was, calling out to his shadows, and everything was golden, was eclipse, was forever, was theirs alone.

More. She raked her nails down his back. *Touch me everywhere, let me know how it feels, let me have this, I want, I need—*

Alaric broke the kiss, dragging his lips from her mouth to the slope of her neck. Talasyn's eyes fluttered open—when had she closed them?—and her spine arched as he sucked and nipped at the column of her throat, his hips rolling against hers. He was so long and broad. He covered her utterly, and maybe she could belong to this, if nothing else. His teeth scraped at a particularly sensitive spot on her neck and she shivered, her fingers tracing the shell of his ear. Her frenzied gaze slid to the Dominion insignia woven into the silk canopy—the coiled dragon rearing up, claws out, wings outstretched, ruby eyes gleaming, surrounded by a field of stars and moons.

The sight jolted her back to reality. Made her aware of the world again.

She couldn't do this.

They couldn't do this.

It would only end in ruin.

"Wait," she gasped out.

He immediately stopped what he was doing, raising his head to peer down at her, cradling the side of her face in one large palm, the pad of his thumb rubbing along her cheekbone as he waited, as she'd asked him to. His eyes were liquid silver in the muddle of moonbeams and stardust, seeing her for what she was, seeing her as what he'd turned her into, this disheveled, undone mess of a girl.

She meant to tell him that they had to stop. Truly, she meant to. But she couldn't bring herself to say the words. She felt feverish and unsatisfied, the heat at the apex of her thighs pulsing with an unbearable ache, an emptiness. Her hand rose up to clutch at his shirtfront.

"Alaric," she whispered.

He went tense at the sound of his name. His eyes darkened. And then, with a growl, he fell upon her.

Or maybe she pulled him in. She had no idea who'd moved first. She knew only that the winter of her soul burst into springtime flowers the moment that he captured her lips in another shattering kiss. A kiss that seemed to beg the same things that her entire being was crying out for.

Don't think.

Just feel this.

There's only us.

Leaving her panting for breath, just as he was, he switched to her neck again, nibbling and sucking almost hard enough to bruise, inhaling the amber-and-rose perfume called dragon's blood that had been dabbed on her pulse point. He mumbled *"Tala"* into her skin over and over, the vibrations rippling through her in tremors like tiny earthquakes, and a bittersweet tear dripped from the corner of her eye because *talliyezarin* was a weed on the Great Steppe but *tala* was the Nenavarene word for star, and there was no way that he could have known that, but she could pretend. She wrapped one leg around his lean hip and his kisses to her throat turned feverish and he rucked her gossamer skirt up her thighs and suddenly—

Suddenly his hand was between her legs, touching her through her underthings.

"Gods above." Alaric pressed a fierce, smoldering kiss to her lips. "You're soaked, beautiful girl," he groaned into her mouth. "My wet little wife."

Talasyn wasn't embarrassed by the dampness that she knew he could feel, although she probably should have been. What she *was* embarrassed by was the flush of pleasure that warmed her all over at his endearment. She sank her teeth into his plush bottom lip, taking advantage of his surprise to flip him over. He let out a soft grunt as his head hit the pillow, gazing up at her with silver-rimmed pupils blown wide.

"If you ever"—she straddled him fully, biting back a whimper of shuddery delight as she ground down on his hardness—"call me that again—"

"Isn't it the truth?" His hands wrapped around her waist, holding her in place as he *thrust.* Just once, but it was enough for a hoarse shout to roll off her tongue at the abrupt, unexpected friction against her core that had her eyes fluttering shut. And then *he* was rolling her over, she was spread flat on the bed once more, held down by him, by his mouth on hers and his knee between her thighs. "Aren't you beautiful?" he broke the kiss long enough to ask, before swallowing her protest with his lips. "Aren't you so small in my arms?" As if to emphasize his point, he ran a hand down her body until the mound of his palm was past her navel, showing her how he could span her midsection like this, the tips of his fingers grazing the undersides of her breasts. "Aren't you wet?" he asked huskily, that same hand sliding lower still, back to where she needed to be touched so badly that it was painful. "Aren't you my wife?" he rasped in her ear.

"Bastard." She contemplated kneeing him in the groin, but

450

somehow her legs spread wider, granting his wandering touches more access. Her right hand slipped under his shirt, tracing the chiseled musculature of his abdomen. "You only think I'm beautiful when I'm all done up. You said so yourself."

Alaric winced against her skin. She felt his shoulders tense, then fall with something like surrender. "I lied," he said, and it was another wall—so laboriously constructed—being demolished. He sprinkled kisses on her brow, her cheeks, and the tip of her nose. Feather-light kisses, filled with a tender reverence that made her soul sing. "You're always beautiful. Even when you want to string my guts up like paper lanterns."

He kissed her on the mouth again and she let him, and she kissed him back, her free hand tangling in his hair as her hips canted toward his wrist, searching for more friction. "Move your fingers," she grumped, digging her nails into his scalp.

He nuzzled at the tip of her nose. "I knew that you would be bossy." He sighed in contentment, and in the dark it felt as though he was smiling against her lips, but before she could be certain, he complied with her curt instructions and slowly glided his fingertips over the increasingly dampening silk that covered her.

Talasyn would have wept with relief that the pressure building up within her was finally being taken care of, if she hadn't moaned first. Encouraged by the sound, Alaric strewed hot kisses along the line of her jaw, matching the rhythm of his mouth with that of his fingers rubbing silk into wet skin. Her body strained into his as she instinctively hungered for more closeness, her head thrown back, her throat exposed to his greedy mouth.

The evidence of his desire rocked against her hip. And there was quite a *lot* of evidence from the feel of it, hot and heavy in his trousers. Wicked curiosity blazed through her and she reached down, working him loose, wrapping her fist around him.

He made a strangled little noise in the back of his throat, as if he were dying. He buried his face in the pillow by her head, panting roughly against her cheek as his hand crept beneath the band of her undergarments, the tips of his fingers gliding along her wetness.

It was a touch that rippled throughout her entire being. She rose and curled like the tide, melting against him, melting all over him. She bit into the round of his shoulder to stifle her whines, completely taken aback by how exquisite it felt to be touched down there by someone else. He chuckled, raspy and deep, and a burst of annoyance caused her to pull back slightly so that she could glare at him even as she tightened her grip on his cock. "That sounded entirely too smug for someone so hard, *husband*."

His eyes flashed silver in the moonlight and he crushed his lips to hers again. "I'm not being smug," he muttered into her mouth. "I will give you anything you ask, as long as you never stop touching me. As long as you come for me."

And slowly, ever so slowly, he pushed one finger inside her.

Talasyn cried out—from pain or from pleasure, she could no longer tell. The lines were blurred. The wires were crossed. She rode Alaric's hand, mindlessly chasing the feeling, her own fist working around him, matching the pace that he set. He was smooth and thick in the circle of her palm, as solid as a rock, growing harder still as his kisses to her face and neck turned half-crazed.

She was almost there. She didn't know what would happen, what it would mean if she came undone like this with him. What would happen after. "Alaric, I'm—" she tried to say and broke off, not recognizing the needy, breathless stranger who spoke in her voice.

But he seemed to understand. "I've got you," he promised hoarsely. His free hand tucked a loose strand of her hair behind her ear. "Let go, Tala. I'm here."

She was distantly aware of herself, muffling a sob into his neck, twisting against the sheets, straining closer, closer, until there was no more space between their bodies and it was *everything*, it was a reprieve from loneliness, it was delight upon delight, Sky Above the Sky.

And she careened into it, and off the edge. The night disintegrated into shards of white heat. She fell into release with a ragged moan, her toes curling at the long, glorious spasms that consumed her in rolling waves.

Alaric kissed her through it all, swallowing her drawn-out sighs, rocking his finger gently inside her until it became too much and she squirmed, and he pulled back his hand.

But that was the only part of him that she would allow to leave her. The hard length of him twitched eagerly in her half-limp palm and, with some effort, mustered through the delicious, lazy, slow fog that had enveloped her, she pumped her wrist in experimental strokes. His breathing shallowed and he thrust into her fist haphazardly and then, with a groan, he was coming, too, she could feel it, warm and wet on her palm, dripping down her fingers in her dazed afterglow.

He collapsed on top of her. Alaric—always so stiff, so inscrutable, so carefully controlled—went slack above her, his mouth moving against her collarbone, torn between prayers and kisses. She couldn't understand what he was mumbling into her skin and she didn't care—there were no words for this. His dark hair was tickling her chin, so she raised her other hand to stroke it flat, her fingers curling into the softness of it, holding him against her as they both caught their breath.

Talasyn came back to herself with all the languidness of a feather wafting to the ground. She blinked to clear the haze from her eyes, staring up at the ceiling. Her gaze fixed on the tapestries above the bed, the sewn stars and the glimmering moons, the dragon of Nenavar . . .

Nenavar. Sardovia. Kesath.

It all came crashing down on her again, all at once.

What were they doing?

She was going to get everyone killed.

Large arms reached around her waist, trying to bring her closer, but she stiffened at his embrace. The embrace of the Night Emperor.

Talasyn drew her hand back from Alaric's hair to push at the wide slab of his shoulder. "Get off of me."

He lifted his mouth from her clavicle. At first, he didn't seem to understand. He squinted at her as though searching for answers, his brow creasing in bewilderment—*hurt*, almost. She remained still beneath him, turning her head to the side so she wouldn't have to meet his eyes.

Then the common sense that had overtaken her must have returned to him, too. He rolled off her in an instant, scrambling as far from her as was possible without actually falling off the bed.

She couldn't deny that something in her broke when he moved away.

Talasyn dove under the covers, pulling them up over her chin. She dared another glance at Alaric, his chest heaving, his lips wet and swollen, his black hair sticking up at odd angles from where she'd run her fingers through. An embarrassed flush colored his moon-kissed complexion as he reached down to rearrange his trousers. He looked as upset as she felt. The perfect pleasure of only a few moments ago had faded, leaving in its wake only a jumble of horrible thoughts, scattered and disjointed.

The man she had just done—*that*—with loathed her, and she was supposed to loathe him in turn. He was an unwilling political ally whom she would someday betray. He was her enemy. He was a monster.

And yet, her fingers were still sticky with his spend.

"You're leaving tomorrow," she said. And, in the act of

speaking, she burst whatever bubble they'd been trapped in for the past month. She ripped away all the illusions they'd labored under; she knew that the moment she saw the resignation creep over his face.

But it was a miracle how steady her voice was, how it didn't falter in the slightest. Talasyn supposed that she could be grateful for small mercies. "We shouldn't have done this," she told him.

He opened his mouth, dark irises flashing silver. Would he argue with her? Did she want him to?

But he seemed to think better of it. He gave a short nod.

She stole out of bed, heading to her bathroom so she could clean up. "I changed my mind," she announced. "You're sleeping on the floor."

Without waiting for his response, she slammed the bathroom door shut behind her. Closing it between them, a shield from further mistakes.

CHAPTER THIRTY-NINE

A pillow slammed into Alaric's face in the early morning, unceremoniously rousing him from slumber.

His eyes flew open with a start. He grabbed the offending pillow and tossed it back where it came from, to his hellcat of a new bride. It landed in Talasyn's lap, and he belatedly registered that she was sitting up in bed and looking at him in panic while a series of knocks sounded lightly on the door.

Every muscle in his body groaned in protest as he scrambled to his feet. He had enough presence of mind to return the cushions that he'd liberated from the chaise longue to their proper place, but he couldn't help scowling at Talasyn as he joined her on the bed.

I can't believe you made me sleep on the floor, he thought darkly. It wasn't that he hadn't gotten what he deserved for taking liberties with her, but he'd had a rough night's sleep and he wasn't inclined to be charitable.

She ignored him, calling out something in Nenavarene to whoever had come knocking. The door creaked open and Jie entered, clearly trying to fight back a saucy leer at the sight of the imperial couple side by side on the canopy bed.

456

"If it pleases His Majesty," Jie said, "the Lachis'ka has to get ready for breakfast now."

As Jie ushered Talasyn into the bathroom, Alaric took great care to avoid looking either of them in the eye. Right before the door closed behind them, though, Jie erupted into rapid, excited chatter. There was no mistaking what *that* tone implied, even if he couldn't parse the language, and regret and disbelief were sharp and heavy in the pit of his stomach as it all came rushing back to him. What he had done last night. With the Lightweaver. With the girl he'd met in battle whom he was now *married* to.

Why had she let him touch her? Why had she returned his kisses and touched him back?

She had called him Alaric. It was the first time he had ever heard his name in the shape of her voice. It had added to the blood pounding in his ears, to the fire in his soul. The memory of it now sent a pang through his chest.

He stared at his hand, holding it up to the early-morning light. The small shards of diamantine gemstones embedded into the wedding band on his ring finger sparkled.

This hand had been between his wife's legs last night. The middle finger of this hand had been *inside* her.

She had fallen apart around him, and that fluttering of her inner walls as she clamped down had been the best thing he'd ever felt—perhaps even better than when he had come all over her lithe hand.

It haunted him: the sound of her soft cries, and the unexpected gentleness with which she'd stroked his hair as he lay slumped atop her, his world irrevocably changed.

But he was sailing home today, home to the nation that had caused her so much suffering. She wouldn't be joining him for another fortnight. By that time, it would be too late to get those moments back.

Wasn't that for the best, though?

*

Not long after Talasyn had finished dressing, an attendant knocked on the door with a summons from the Zahiya-lachis. Talasyn wondered what fault of hers had been unearthed by her grandmother this time, and then it struck her what a sad reaction *that* was to your own family wanting to speak with you.

Had she shared such a grievance with Urduja, the older woman would have scoffed. The Zahiya-lachis of the Nenavar Dominion had little patience for sentiment, and that was never more apparent as when she received Talasyn in her salon minutes later.

"Seeing as no corpses were discovered in your chambers this morning, I trust that you and the Night Emperor had an amicable night together."

By some miracle, Talasyn was able to hold her grandmother's gaze in a calm manner from across the table, even as her fingers twisted nervously into the fabric of her skirt. "It went fine."

"I dearly hope that such a blissful state of affairs won't prove to be the exception to the rule." Urduja paused as though reconsidering her statement, then inclined her head in a thoughtful nod. "Well, up until the endgame, anyway."

Talasyn's heart dropped into her stomach. It wasn't as though she'd forgotten . . .

No. That wasn't true. There were moments on Belian when she *had* forgotten, however briefly. And last night she had *definitely* forgotten long enough to come. She'd let Alaric drive all logic from her mind.

"Things will only get more difficult from here, I'm afraid," Urduja continued. "I will have my people meet with Vela and ask her what she plans to do. The Sardovian remnant cannot hide in Nenavar forever. It would be untenable. We need the alliance with Kesath up until the Night of the World-Eater. Afterwards, though, either the Allfold moves to reclaim the Northwest Continent within a year, or . . ." She paused again, drawing a measured breath.

"Or *what*?" Talasyn pressed. A horrible suspicion began to dawn in her mind, and it blossomed on her tongue. "Or they'll need to find somewhere else to go?"

"We'll discuss that, should it come to it," Urduja said firmly. "But there *is* a limit to the amount of time that I can buy your friends, Alunsina."

Talasyn began to shake with anger—and fear. "You told us that we could shelter here for as long as we needed to. You *promised*. We made a *deal*." A horrifying thought occurred to her and she fired it off like a new arrow from her quiver. "But now the Dominion has a deal with Kesath, too, as well as a mutual defense treaty. So, when the Amirante finally makes her move, whose side will you be on, *Harlikaan*?"

Talasyn spat out the title as though it were an insult, but her grandmother didn't even flinch. Urduja's face betrayed nothing.

"You must learn when to keep your own counsel, Alunsina," the Zahiya-lachis said after a while. "Never let the enemy know what you're thinking. For our purposes, I *am* your enemy right now, am I not? You may continue to deem me as such. I can't stop you. But I *can* tell you this: I account for everything and so I am caught unprepared by nothing, and I will never apologize for that. No treaty between nations is binding forever, especially once the other signatory is dust. Do I believe that such a fate will befall the Night Empire, that Vela's fleet can defeat the Kesathese? Not at the moment, no—and that is why I, as I have said, am buying time." Urduja lowered her voice even further. "Nenavarene shipwrights have completed the repairs on the Sardovian airships. These shipwrights will now work with our Enchanters to optimize the carracks and the frigates, as well as the two stormships that made it to Nenavar. The Allfold's remaining vessels will be outfitted with as much magic as possible while Vela makes her plans. And, in the meantime, the Sardovians have food and shelter. These are things that I willingly grant. These are things that would normally be too much to ask of any queen, least of all one who took no part in the Hurricane Wars."

Talasyn was silent. She had no comebacks. It felt as though her grandmother had spun a web of words from which there was no escape.

With the unerring instinct of a spider sensing that its trapped prey could struggle no more, Urduja pounced. "All that is required of you, Lachis'ka, is to hold up *your* end of the deal. Keep your head down and be a dutiful heir and don't be distracted by the Night Emperor's pretty face. You can't personally contact the Sardovians anymore, it's too risky. You will stay here in Eskaya and diligently attend to your lessons and your public appearances—"

The more that Urduja spoke, the more it became apparent that this was what she had been leading up to all along. This whole conversation had just been another way to make sure that her granddaughter remained firmly under her control, and the resentment that Talasyn had been harboring all these months hit its zenith, magnified by her guilt that she *had* in fact gotten distracted by the Night Emperor's pretty face. She'd accused Alaric of being his father's dog, but he had been right about her, too. She was being manipulated as well, and she kept going along with it because she had no choice.

What Vela had said amidst the mangroves came back to her in this moment.

You aren't alone.

She had Alaric, if only in the sense that she was married to him. And *because* she was married to him, that gave her more influence than she'd ever had in the Dominion court.

It was something like an epiphany, what dawned on Talasyn just then, and she squared her shoulders and held her head high.

You're too afraid to do anything for yourself, Alaric had sneered last night.

It was time to prove him wrong.

"I'm not just the Lachis'ka," Talasyn reminded her grand-mother. "Soon I will also be crowned the Night Empress. Because of me, Nenavar is going to have more power than it's ever known. We will become a major player on the world stage. I'm your one chance for this to happen under your reign, and I'm *also* the only chance you have to make sure that your reign remains stable at all. You have no more female heirs, Harlikaan, and no more Lightweavers to help stop the Voidfell. It's just me." Talasyn's words were weighty and delib-erate over a fast-racing heartbeat. "And you need me just as much as I need you."

She watched Urduja like a hawk, searching for the slightest crack in that icy facade. The stern, thin line of the Dragon Queen's lips twitched, and it felt like a victory, but Talasyn couldn't be certain of that until—

"What do you want?" Urduja asked, as cold as the Eversea in winter.

It took every ounce of Talasyn's self-control to refrain from collapsing in sheer relief. It wasn't over yet. She had to see this through.

"I agree that it's too dangerous for me to keep going to the Storm God's Eye. So I won't. But . . ." And here she laid down her terms, feeling rather out of her body, that this moment was hardly real, as though she was listening to someone else speak, buoyed by nerves and adrenaline. "I want to be able to go everywhere else in Nenavar. I want to learn more about the technology that's coming out of Ahimsa. And I want unfettered access to the Belian nexus point." Urduja's dark eyes flashed but Talasyn stubbornly persisted. "I'll attend every lesson on politics and etiquette that you throw at me. I'll work hard. But in return I want freedom. I want to continue honing my aethermancy; I *will* need the Lightweave for what's to come. The Shadowforged are unpredictable, and I'm no use to you if I'm dead."

And I will learn more about my mother, Talasyn vowed fiercely, silently. She had let her fear of the many ways that the Zahiya-lachis could destroy the Sardovian remnant keep her from delving into the events that had led to Hanan helping send Nenavarene warships to the Northwest Continent, but no more. She would acquire new memories from the Light Sever and she would start asking questions, just as she had with Kai Gitab. She had power now.

She waited for Urduja's response with bated breath. Even now, there was some small part of her that wished for a semblance of warmth from this domineering woman. That wished for Urduja to assure her that she was her granddaughter, first and foremost.

Instead, the Dragon Queen merely nodded. "Very well." Her expression was as impassive as the tone of her voice. "So be it."

It was a small victory. Talasyn left the salon with a strange mix of triumph, vindication, and the unsettling feeling that she had just thrown her hat into the ring of a game that she could barely understand.

Alaric remained in a black mood all throughout breakfast, a mood that only worsened every time he failed to stop himself from glancing over at the girl beside him. His new *empress.* Her hair had still been braided when she'd so unceremoniously woken him up, but now it hung loose past her shoulders, framing her face in neat curls. She was so beautiful. And he couldn't get out of Nenavar fast enough.

Talasyn's obvious discomfort in wearing lingerie had led Alaric to deduce that she was no seductress, despite what his father claimed about the slyness of the women in the Dominion court. But now he wasn't so sure. She'd left him reeling.

Perhaps she *had* been seducing him to bend him to her will.

Even as that thought filtered into his head, Alaric's instincts warned him that it was spoken in Gaheris's voice. Last night had felt honest and raw. It had to have been real.

But since when had his father ever been wrong? Who was Alaric, with all his shortcomings, with all the traits inherited from a weak and long-vanished mother, to contest the man who had brought Kesath back from the brink of destruction?

When the last of the dishes had been cleared, Alaric bade his painfully polite farewells to a frosty-looking Urduja and an only slightly less frosty-looking Elagbi, and Talasyn reluctantly walked with him out the front doors of the palace, Jie and Sevraim and the Lachis-dalo trailing behind. The shallop that would take him back to the *Deliverance* gleamed in the morning sun, and at first it was only Alaric and Talasyn who moved toward it.

He turned back to their companions, puzzled. They had all stopped walking, maintaining a courteous distance with expectant looks on their faces.

"They're giving us privacy," Talasyn explained with a long-suffering demeanor. "To say our goodbyes."

Alaric's gaze strayed to the upper levels of the white palace. A host of servants were huddled at the windows, their noses pressed to the glass, avidly watching.

"You should probably shed a few tears and beg me not to leave, Lachis'ka," Alaric wryly remarked. "Else the blacksmith's washerwoman three cities over will be disappointed."

A smirk fought its way across Talasyn's painted lips, but she was quick to suppress it. "Listen, about last night—"

"I know," he interrupted, alarmed and trying not to show it, which translated into a churlishness that must have surprised her, because she jerked her head back. "There is no need to spare my feelings." He cursed inwardly as he heard himself make a conscious effort to gentle his tone. He was a fool. She

463

had twisted him into knots. "I am well aware that you hold no affection for me, and I'm not so green as to believe that all acts of that nature have to mean something. Our emotions were simply running high and there was no other outlet."

She cocked her head, as though considering. Then she repeated the words from the Belian ruins. "*Hate is another kind of passion.*"

"Two sides of the same coin," Alaric confirmed, even as his heart twinged in a manner that he was in absolutely no hurry to examine. "We were fighting and we got carried away. No further discussion is required. I realize, like you must also, that we can't allow it to happen again."

Talasyn's gaze dropped to her feet. An awkward silence ensued.

Finally, she nodded.

Alaric decided that it was well past time to cut this encounter short. "Your coronation as the Night Empress is in a fortnight. I will see you in Kesath then, my lady." He couldn't resist needling her with the reminder that she was now *his* lady, that they were bound by law.

Talasyn glowered at him. "I shall wait on tenterhooks for our happy reunion, my lord," she all but snapped, her voice dripping with sarcasm, and she once again looked so much like a disgruntled kitten that he nearly smiled.

He turned to go, but then stopped. There was something about the way Talasyn looked, prickly and endearing all at once. He wouldn't see her for a while. He couldn't bear to leave things like this.

"Talasyn." Alaric whirled back to face her. "I will inquire regarding your friend Khaede's whereabouts at the Citadel." Her eyes widened in panic and he almost flinched, hastening to add, "If she is being—detained there, I will arrange for the two of you to meet when you come to Kesath."

It was clumsy, it was fumbling, it was a reminder that her

former comrades were being held in his prisons. It was, in short, the worst possible thing he could have said in this moment, and Alaric wholeheartedly prepared for Talasyn to punch him, knowing full well that he deserved it.

But she didn't punch him. Instead, she exhaled as though she were letting something go. "Thank you," she said—a bit stiffly, but there was a wrenchingly sincere note to it. Her expression was wary but tinged with hope. "If she *is* there, I'd like . . ." She faltered. He watched her hope turn into hesitation, then harden into resolve. "I should like to bring her back with me to Nenavar."

The very blood in Alaric's veins went still. He couldn't permit that. He couldn't free a Sardovian soldier, a prisoner of war. He—

His mind was already racing with ways to accomplish it. He could pass it off as an act of conciliation. A grand gesture to herald the new age of peace. A wedding gift.

He swallowed. "I'll see what I can do."

It was a simple enough statement, but it tinged the air with a hint of treason. It looped them both into the barest bones of some kind of furtive plan. As if they were conspirators now.

Still, when Talasyn's features lit up with a small but genuine smile, dimples peeking out at the corners, Alaric felt that it was somehow worth it.

A flickering burst of amethyst to the far south drew their attention. The Voidfell had activated, causing a conflagration of the shivering magic to sear across the horizon in whorls of violet smoke. It looked—*angry,* and Alaric found himself thinking of a frieze of carvings that he'd studied at the Lightweaver shrine on Belian. Warriors in bark-woven breech-cloths with feathered bands around their heads, winding along one of the walls leading to the campsite, riding elephants and swamp buffaloes, brandishing swords and spears as they charged at a serpentine leviathan with a crater-pocked moon in its jaws.

An eternal battle fought in the spirit world of the Nenavarene ancestors, to stop Bakun before he could destroy all life.

A battle that Alaric and Talasyn would have to fight themselves a little over four months from now.

As he watched the Voidfell now, noting how intensely it flared even from across such a distance, it seemed impossible that the odds would be in their favor. But they had to try—and, if Alaric knew anything about the scrappy soldier girl who was now his wife, she would try.

She was pale and tense, her shoulders squared as she warily regarded the amethyst glow. Her lovely smile had faded and he was all of a sudden incensed by what had caused it to vanish from her face.

Right. He had to leave *now*, before he promised to fight the Voidfell with his bare fists for her.

Alaric turned on his heel and strode swiftly up his airship's ramp. He didn't look back. It took everything in him to not look back. The flare of the Void Sever screeched one last time and then it was gone, with no sign to mark that it had ever been there at all, save for the echoes of sound that lingered in the air like a dragon's roar.

Talasyn returned to Jie and her guards as the shallop prepared to sail, Alaric a solemn, black-clad figure on the deck. Aether hearts glowed a rich emerald and the vessel was lifted into the air on the crackling currents of wind magic, peeling away from the Roof of Heaven, away from the limestone bluffs.

Like the guards, Jie seemed somewhat apprehensive at the Void Sever's fleeting discharge. Not apprehensive enough, however, to refrain from teasing; whatever she saw on Talasyn's face made her ask, with an impudent twinkle in her eyes, "Are you missing His Majesty already, Lachis'ka?"

"Don't be ridiculous," Talasyn scoffed. Over the next several days she had to resume aethermancy training all by herself, navigate what was certain to be a treacherous new order of things now that she had worked up the guts to challenge Urduja, and mentally brace for her return to the Northwest Continent. There were so many things that she needed to do, and missing Alaric Ossinast was *not* on the agenda.

But he had promised to try to find Khaede for her. If he was successful, if Khaede was in Kesath, then Talasyn would move heaven and earth to bring her to Nenavar. If Alaric went back on his word or was unable to keep it, she'd break Khaede out and smuggle her away from the Citadel herself—right under Gaheris's nose, if need be.

Talasyn stood on the front steps of the palace longer than she ought to have. Her mind was afire with schemes and plans, that was true, but as she watched Alaric sail away, her lips were also burning with the memory of his feverish kisses.

We can't allow it to happen again, he'd said.

But what if I want *it to happen again?*

The thought broke past her defenses, rising to the surface with a mutinous ease. She forced it back down, burying it, her heart heavy in her chest, her eyes fixed on his airship as it became a mere speck on the still horizon, until it disappeared into the deep blue of a cloudless sky.

CHAPTER FORTY

Alaric was summoned to his father's private hall at the Citadel within an hour of the *Deliverance* making landfall in Kesath.

He strode into the vast, high-ceilinged chamber that was cloaked in perpetual darkness and it was jarring to him, this abrupt shift from the bright islands of Nenavar. Talasyn would dislike the Citadel, most probably. This place would drown out her light. He would have to make her comfortable in any way that he could, perhaps determine which chambers got the most sun and assign them to her.

Focus, he admonished himself. He couldn't think of Talasyn while in an audience with his father. He needed to come up with a passable excuse as to his recent transgression—when he hadn't answered Gaheris's call to the In-Between at the Belian campsite.

However, the withered figure on the obsidian throne in the middle of the hall had no interest in taking him to task just yet. "Welcome home, my boy." Gaheris's eyes flashed silver in the dark. "Marriage looks good on you. Why, you're glowing."

The dryly affectionate humor was a trace of the old Gaheris, the one who had been king and not Night Emperor. Try as he might, Alaric couldn't help but cling to it, to these bits and pieces of the father that he remembered.

Alaric belatedly realized that something was *off*. It took a searching gaze cast around the hall for him to figure it out. The raw shadow magic that Gaheris loved to drape his surroundings in was not as solid today, and Alaric traced the dilution to a far corner that remained untouched by the Shadowgate and was instead bathed in natural daylight from a high window.

The corner was occupied by a table on which sat a tall, vaguely rectangular object, covered in midnight-black cloth.

"A gift from Commodore Mathire," Gaheris said with a pleased little grin. "Go on, take a peek."

Puzzled, Alaric walked toward the mysterious object, followed by his father's watchful gaze. After he had taken only a few steps, sounds began to emerge from under the black cloth, one lilting chirp after another, eerily familiar. Alaric frowned and quickened his pace. Several more steps and then—

He felt it.

An absence in his being. A hole where the Shadowgate used to be.

The magic had drained from his veins exactly seven meters away from the object.

Alaric broke into a run while more chirping wafted through the air, increasing in agonized urgency with each second that passed. As soon as he made it to the sunlit corner, he ripped the black cloth away to reveal the table and the ornamental brass birdcage atop it, and the little creature perched inside, with its twisted golden beak and its red-and-yellow tailfeathers. With its unique, awful ability.

The sariman's jeweled eyes stared mournfully at Alaric through the brass bars of the cage. It flapped its wings, its chirps taking on a tone of pure distress, of lament. It was clearly terrified, and so far away from its verdant jungles.

"Fascinating thing, isn't it?" said Gaheris. "I knew that I had to acquire a specimen for myself. How fortunate that Mathire's men were able to capture one during Kesath's sweep of the archipelago."

"Why . . ." Alaric trailed off, unable to look away from the sariman in the cage.

"Because Nenavar shouldn't get to have all the fun," Gaheris replied, the smile still evident in his tone even though Alaric was no longer facing him. "Because Kesathese Enchanters need to catch up to the Dominion's technology and surpass it. And because your wife is a Lightweaver and a former Sardovian, and this is how we will find a way to rid her of her magic, once and for all. We will rule the Continent *and* Nenavar. We will rule it all."

Alaric's fists clenched at his sides. The sariman's wings scrabbled against the bars of the cage in a futile bid for freedom, its plaintive melody filling the hall as it sang for its lost shores.

Acknowledgements

This, my first novel, would never have seen the light of day without all the amazing people that I've been lucky to have in my life.

To my parents, Casten and Joy, and to Jayboy, Ysa, Mama Bem, Mama Di, Mama Budz, Manang Tim, Manang Meg, Kuya Jer, TJ, Greg, Anna, Christina, Matthew, Tito Jeff, Tito Peng, Daddy Pal, Mommy Don, Tito Matt, Tita Pinky, Tita Rose, Tita Nons, Lolo Jo, Lola Nelia, Auntie Emcy, Auntie Bec, Uncle Dodong, Jembok—our incredibly huge family has been my rock all these years.

To Lolo Tatay, who instilled in me a passion for literature from an early age; Lola Nanay, who showed me what it means to be strong and brave; and Lola Tits and Lola Rosit, who cared for us like we were their own. Your stories live on in me, and I hope to continue making you proud until the day we meet again.

To Team Bira: Justin G., Ryan N., Anna, Miggi, Neil, Jake, Micha, Drei, Mik, Justin Q., Lex, Joseph, and Caneel the honorary Ilonggo, for cheering me on as I pursued my dreams and being the best support system that I could ever have asked for.

To Tito Jeremy, Tita Rita, and Phil, for always making me feel welcome, and whose coffee machine fueled my entire first draft!

To Team Kakapo: Tiffy, Mayi, Macy, and Kyra, who were some of the first people to ever read my writing. Going strong since high school, and I'm grateful every day.

To EWW: Alexa, Trese, Mikee, Dana, Therd, Jor-el, Lizette, Aida, Andrew, Faye, and everyone else who was there during those crazy times! Listing all the names and memories would require another novel, but I keep Bacolod close to my heart, and my artistic side would never have been nurtured without you guys.

Acknowledgements

To Team No Tanks (Hiyas, Kat, Kim, Trish, Michael, Gabby, and Francis) and Smells Like Team Spirit (Jet, Dado, Angelo, Jasca, Abramer, and Omar), the best D&D players ever, whose creative solutions kept me on my toes and polished my story-telling skills.

To Angeline Rodriguez, the first person I ever discussed the concept of this story with, for believing that I could do it and for helping me shape this world.

To my fantastic agent Thao Le, who was so patient while I was still unsure about diving into this and who still didn't hesitate to take a chance on me, and my editors Julia Elliott and Natasha Bardon, who guided my sometimes very clumsy steps into the realm of original fiction, as well as the rest of my Voyager UK and US teams—Elizabeth Vaziri, Binti Kasilingam, Robyn Watts, Holly Macdonald, Leah Woods, Roisin O'Shea, Sian Richefond, Danielle Bartlett, DJ DeSmyter, Jennifer Hart, Liate Stehlik, David Pomerico, Jennifer Brehl, Richenda Rickard, Charlotte Webb, Jeanie Lee, and Nancy Inglis, who worked harder than anyone to bring this book to life.

To my author friends Katie Shepard, Jenna Levine, Molly X. Chang, Ali Hazelwood, Kirsten Bohling, Elizabeth Davis, Sarah Hawley, Celia Winter, and Victoria Chiu, for virtually holding my hand and for being unbelievably generous with their time, and for all the memes and cat pictures. I am proud to know such brilliant, talented ladies!

To my AO3 readers and fandom friends from all over the globe, who have graced the last several years of my life with the warmest sense of community, who have had my back since day one: I would never have kept writing if it weren't for you guys. I owe it all to you.

And, lastly, to my cat, Darth Pancakes, the fluffiest, most evil boy.

Thank you all for helping me create the perfect storm.

About the Author

Thea Guanzon holds a bachelor of arts in international studies, with a specialization in international politics and peace studies. When she's not writing, she can be found traveling, running a Dungeons & Dragons campaign, or fangirling over villains. She currently resides in Metro Manila, Philippines. *The Hurricane Wars* is her first novel.